HELLO BILLIONAIRE

KELSIE HOSS

Editing by Tricia Harden of Emerald Eyes Editing.

Cover design by Najla Qamber of Najla Qamber Designs.

Have questions? Email kelsie@kelsiehoss.com.

Readers can visit kelsiehoss.com/sensitive to learn about potentially triggering content.

 Created with Vellum

For my boys, who know dandelions are so much more than a weed.

CONTENTS

1

FARRAH

I'm on my way to my seventh job interview this week, and I just realized there's a sucker stuck to my pencil skirt.

Things were going *great*.

And by that, I meant, I needed to take three antacids just to keep my lunch down before I had a complete meltdown. Kind of like the tantrum my five-year-old had this morning because I couldn't find her sparkle dress so she could wear it for the fifteenth day in a row.

I pulled into the parking lot and killed the engine, then licked my thumb to try and get rid of the sugar spot on my black skirt. Now it was wet and shiny, but hopefully the interviewer wouldn't notice.

Getting out my phone, I dialed my best friend Mia's number. After a couple of rings, she answered, and I could hear the echo of the bathroom she always answered my calls from during the workday.

"This was a terrible idea," I said. "I appreciate you getting me the interview, but maybe I should back out. I don't want to embarrass you. I'm not even sure I'm qualified for this. I've had like three part-time interior design jobs in the last ten years, and I'm not even sure—"

"Farrah," Mia whispered, cutting me off. "I wouldn't have recommended you to my boss if I didn't think you could do it. I love you, but I'd kind of like to keep my job."

The sound that came past my lips was somewhere near an anxious laugh.

"You did an amazing job on my parents' new house. It helped their downsizing so much. This is on a different scale, but I know you can do it. You just have to come in and be your fabulous self."

I tried to listen to her words instead of hyperventilating. "Right. Right." I still wasn't convinced.

"Tell me you're here," Mia said. "He hates when people are late."

"I just pulled up," I said. "Wait. He? As in the interviewer?"

"As in my boss."

My jaw dropped. "*Gage Griffen* is interviewing me? Doesn't he have billionaire things to do?"

Mia giggled. "Technically, he's always doing billionaire things. And after the last three bad candidates HR sent through, he decided to handle the process himself."

Gage Griffen. Owner of Griffen Industries. The youngest billionaire in Texas. The *only* self-made billionaire in the country. Mia's demanding boss with expectations higher than the Rocky Mountains. "Okay, now I'm really panicking."

"You'll be great," she said. "And your parents are watching the munchkins, right? You can let go of your worries and just focus in on this."

"Levi's watching them." I cringed. My oldest may have been fourteen, but sometimes I thought his eight-year-old brother was more mature. "Dad had a doctor's appointment and Mom had to cover at their coffee shop, so I was on my own today. But Levi can handle it... I hope."

Mia was quiet for a moment, and we'd been friends long enough for me to know she was not saying what she was thinking. "Farrah, I know you. You can figure out anything for your family," she finally said. "You can do this. Take a few deep breaths and come in. I gotta get back to the desk."

She hung up, leaving me alone in my minivan. I glanced around the car, wishing I felt less like a soccer mom and more like a professional. It would help if the car didn't smell like Levi's sweaty gym bag.

I took a few deep breaths anyway, like Mia suggested, and got out of the car, determined to make the most of this.

Then I heard metal on metal.

My heart sank and I cringed, realizing I'd just door-dinged one of the fancy cars in the parking lot. A Tesla.

"Shit. Shit shit shit," I muttered to myself as I licked my thumb and tried to rub off the streak of white paint. It wasn't budging.

I couldn't afford to fix this kind of car.

But I couldn't leave it either. That wouldn't be right.

I reached into my van, finding a scrap piece of paper from the sketchbook Andrew, my middle child, kept in the car and scribbled down a quick apology with my phone number. Hopefully the owner would just let it go. But judging by the swath of white paint on their otherwise

flawless and perfectly clean black door, I highly
doubted it.

Let it go, I sang to myself quietly, still unable to get that
song out of my head. I needed to be my most poised and
polished self for this meeting. Even if there was still a
sucker stain on my skirt.

My phone rang and I pulled it out of my bag, seeing a
number from the last company where I applied. Tires and
More needed a receptionist, and even though it wasn't
interior design work, it was a paycheck. Something I was
struggling to find, even after a month of job hunting.

"Hi there," I answered with a smile. "This is Farrah."

"Farrah," Mike said, the guy I'd interviewed with.
"Thanks for coming in, but we decided to give the position to someone else."

My heart sank, and I stopped outside of the high-rise
building, blinking quickly. "Do you mind giving me feedback on my interview so I can do better next time?"

He cleared his throat, already sounding uncomfortable. "You did great, kid. Just weren't the right fit."

"Mike, it would really mean a lot. I need to get a job."

Letting out a sigh, he said, "You have a lot on your
plate, Farrah, and we really need someone more focused
on the job. We don't have anyone to sub if you can't
show up."

My voice was small as I said, "Thanks"—and ended
the call.

He said it without saying it. A single mom with three
kids and plenty of responsibilities wasn't exactly the kind
of person who could show up every day without interrup-
tion. And yeah, I could probably sue him for saying it, but
he'd been honest.

I put my phone on do not disturb and slipped it in my purse. The only call that would come through was Levi's number, and he knew not to reach out unless there was an emergency.

The big building loomed in front of me, its mirrored doors seeming to mock the only new clothing I'd bought for myself in quite some time. As a stay-at-home mom, I lived in leggings and T-shirts, but these interviews called for a suit. And it was hard to find one that fit me just right in the plus-size section. I ended up spending way too much on my credit card for this outfit, and I tried not to worry about the sucker spot.

At least my dark curly hair was staying put in the low bun I'd wrestled it into.

A receptionist at the building's front desk gave me a badge and told me to go up to the thirty-fourth floor. I rode the elevator up, looking through the glass wall at the city where I grew up. Part of me was happy to be closer to my parents now that I'd moved back with my kids— Austin had always felt just a little too far away. We were just a little too close, living with them until I could get a job and a place to live.

People came on and off the elevator as I rode up, but eventually the doors opened to a fancy office space. In the back of my mind, I wondered who designed this space and why they weren't working on this new project. There was glittering white tile, walls of windows, stunning art, and a great desk up front where my best friend stood, looking super sophisticated in a tailored black dress.

As I stepped out of the elevator, Mia looked my way, smiling wide. She was so beautiful with her bright smile framed by straight, sandy-blond hair that fell to her shoulders.

"Ms. Elkins?" she said, a coy smile on her lips.

"Yes, Ms. Baird?"

She nodded from behind her desk as I approached, my sensible heels loud against the tile. "Would you like a water or a coffee?"

I shook my head, doubting I could keep even a seltzer water down. "No, thank you."

Giving me an encouraging smile, she said, "Mr. Griffen will be out to get you shortly. You can take a seat."

"No need," a masculine voice said.

I glanced in the direction the voice came from, and it took all my strength to keep standing straight. No amount of Googling could have prepared me for the man walking my way.

Gage Griffen had short hair somewhere between dark blond and light brown. His jaw was strong, like Michelangelo himself carved Gage from stone. He had to be over six feet, but his perfectly fitted black suit made him seem that much more imposing, turning the expansive reception area into a small space that barely contained this giant man.

His dark blue eyes were discerning, piercing, as they landed on me, and he extended his hand, all business. "Gage Griffen, CEO."

He didn't need to introduce himself, but I did. I felt like a nobody in his commanding presence.

"Farrah Elkins, hopeful interior designer," I replied with a nervous laugh.

He didn't smile.

My hand nearly disappeared in his as we shook. I kept

my grip firm, like Dad taught me way back in high school, and made eye contact, even though those blue eyes were doing strange things to my heart rate. I should have asked Mia for an empty cup to throw up in.

"Come with me," he said, turning in the direction he'd come from.

I sent Mia an anxious glance over my shoulder, and she gave me a subtle thumbs-up.

I wish I believed in myself as much as she did. Especially considering I was about to ditch the heels and run out of here.

But then I remembered why I was doing this. I could do anything for my kids. Even interview with a man who intimidated me with only three words.

Gage led me into an office with floor-to-ceiling windows showing the most incredible view. A gorgeous minimalistic desk faced away from the windows, toward a wall of bookshelves packed with every title, leaving no room for decorations or pictures or trinkets.

In fact, there were no photos on his desk, nothing on the walls to show he had a life outside of this office.

Interesting.

Off to the side was a glass table with modern black chairs. He gestured to one of the open chairs, and I took it, saying, "Thank you so much for having me in, Mr. Griffen."

"You came highly recommended," he said, reaching for a manila envelope.

"From Mia." I nodded. "We've known each other almost fifteen years now."

He shook his head as he flipped through the pages in

the file. "From your advising professor at Upton University."

I raised my eyebrows. I had been out of college for over ten years, and even though I kept in touch with Professor Walsh online or with the occasional text message, I hadn't listed her on my resume.

He held the paper away so he could read the text. "In the past three decades of my career, both as an interior designer and as a professor working with some of the brightest scholars in academia, Farrah Elkins has been, by far, my most talented and hardworking student. She understands client needs in a way most people don't. She can turn a space from uninspired to beautiful and functional as quick as a whip." He glanced up from the paper. "Sound like you?"

My mouth opened and closed, stunned at the praise. Stunned by his direct question. "Absolutely," I said, nodding. "I—"

"Sweet Caroline" began playing from my phone, and I closed my eyes. *Please, please no. Not right now.*

He raised his eyebrows.

"I need to take this," I breathed.

Gage nodded, not seeming phased at all. If he wasn't clearly in real estate, I'd believe he'd earned his fortunes playing poker.

I stepped away from the desk and held my phone to my ear, whispering, "Levi, what's wrong?"

Screaming came through the line, his younger siblings clearly fighting with each other.

Over the racket, Levi yelled, "There's only enough peanut butter left for one sandwich, and Cora and Drew are having a fit over it."

"Did someone get stabbed with a butter knife?" I asked, trying not to turn into the momster I felt like becoming in front of my potential boss.

"No," Levi mumbled.

"Fridge didn't suddenly empty of all that food Grandma made?"

"No."

"Then handle it," I hissed, turning off my phone. "Sorry about that, my babysitter—"

"No need," Gage said, cutting me off.

The response took me as much off guard as the man himself. But he waved at the chair as if I should return and began speaking. "The Retreat has completed construction, but we lost our initial interior designer, and we've struggled to find a competent replacement who understands our needs. Your portfolio?"

I'd almost forgotten the leather binder in my bag, but I retrieved it and extended it to him. "I prepared several spreads based on the comps I received from Mi—Ms. Baird."

He waved his hand, silencing me. If I didn't need this job so badly, I'd be more annoyed at his lack of warmth. Was he always this cold? How had Mia dealt with it for three years?

He flipped through the pages, his hands seeming so large on the book. I sat on the edge of my chair, my heart hammering with anticipation. If only his face would give something away, I'd know if he hated it. If I should just leave now and give up completely. Maybe beg Tires and More for another chance.

"This one." He tapped at the second inspiration board I'd laid out. "This is closer to what I wanted. But it needs to be more family friendly, less breakable items."

Family friendly? I could do that. "Do you expect a lot of families to stay at your luxury hotel?" I asked.

He nodded. "There are already plenty of options for luxury business travel. This will be the primary destination for families to travel in style in the Dallas area."

Interesting. This growly bear of a man thinking about the needs of parents and children.

He stood from his desk. "We'll meet at The Retreat tomorrow so I can give you a tour and you can get a feel for the space you'll be working with."

"I have the job?" I stammered, standing across from him. "Just like that?"

For once, a small smile formed on his lips. "Just like that." But the smile was gone almost as soon as it appeared. "As long as you perform, you will keep it." He walked toward his office door. "You'll find our compensation package and benefits to be quite competitive. But as an added bonus, I encourage you to take an extra jar of natural peanut butter from the employee lounge. Wouldn't want any butter knife stabbings."

2

GAGE

The town car rolled to a stop in front of The Retreat, giving me a view of the restored plaster façade. Gutting and rebuilding this crumbling building had been one of the best parts of my job the last year.

While I got out, Fritz, my driver, walked to the other side, opening the door for Mia and Shantel, Griffen Industries' Chief of Staff. I waited on the sidewalk for them, and then we walked together to the front entrance, where a security guard stood by the door. This project was far too important to leave unattended.

I walked to the guard and extended my hand. "Gage Griffen, CEO."

He studied my hand for a moment, seeming surprised by my introduction. "Cliff Wallace. Nice to meet you, sir."

"Likewise." I stepped into the building, past him, still getting over the fact that so many people worked for me that I didn't know. A little under fifteen years ago, I was making my first hire, stressing about providing someone's livelihood. I still stressed about that—only now it was thousands of people depending on me instead of just one.

We walked to the front conference room and went inside. There was a long white desk and a few folding chairs there for now, but I imagined Ms. Elkins would scrap it for the final design.

Shantel opened her briefcase and began sorting paperwork on the table while Mia passed out coffees and set up a small display of baked goods on the table.

We were a few minutes early, so I reached into my pocket for the scrap of paper left under my windshield wiper the day before. I'd worked into the night and hadn't wanted to call the person at such a late hour. Since it was nearly nine now, we should be fine.

Smirking slightly at the cartoon drawing on the back of the sheet, I dialed the number and ringing came through the phone. At the same time, I heard a phone chiming out in the hallway.

My eyebrows rose, and the chiming stopped.

"Hi, this is Farrah," came through the door and then echoed in my phone speaker.

A chuckle nearly escaped my throat, and I could feel Mia and Shantel trying not to stare. "Farrah, this is Gage Griffen."

"I'm on my way right now. I should be a few minutes early..." The door to the conference room opened, and Farrah lowered her phone to her purse. "I'm sorry. Is my watch off?" She tucked a loose strand of dark curly hair behind her ear, her cheeks pink from the February chill.

"You're right on time," I said, taking the paper from the table. "I believe you left this on my car."

I held up the paper, and her eyes glanced from the paper to my face, all the color draining from her cheeks.

"So, I, um," she stammered. "I'll be going then. Sorry to have taken up your time."

She turned toward the door, and my eyebrows furrowed together. "Where are you going?"

"I'm assuming I'm fired, right?" she said, completely dejected. Her face displayed her every emotion so clearly. "Your car must cost more than my yearly salary."

"Irrelevant," I replied.

Her full lips parted, sending a strange feeling straight to my gut.

"What?" she breathed.

"I was just calling to say no worries about the door ding... It's not really fair to have someone worry about it when..." *I'm a billionaire,* I didn't say.

Why was I talking so much? Her nerves must have worn off on me, and I didn't like it one bit. I cleared my throat, nodding toward the table so we could get back to business.

While Shantel led Farrah through the onboarding paperwork, I sipped my coffee and responded to emails on my phone. When they reached the part explaining her compensation, I glanced up to see her reaction.

As she read the number, she covered her mouth with her hand, but quickly removed it, a slight shake to her fingers.

Good.

She was impressed.

I always paid my people well. It made them work harder, be more loyal to the company, and ultimately... I could.

And if they ever chose to leave, they'd know they would never be able to do better anywhere else.

A call came through my cell from my brother, Tyler, and I stepped out of the room to answer it. "Everything okay?" I asked. He and his new wife recently opened a boutique apartment building for seniors, and residents had just begun moving in.

"We're great," Tyler said, excitement making him talk quickly. "Every room is rented as of this morning!"

"That's great!" I said. "Can I take you and Henrietta out for drinks to celebrate?"

"You have time in that busy billionaire schedule for weekday drinks?"

"I never said when. I can have Mia pencil you in my schedule in... eighteen months?"

"Ha ha," Tyler replied. "We have a community get-to-know-you party tonight, but we can do Thursday. Want me to invite Rhett and Liv?"

"As long as Rhett doesn't bring his woman of the week," I muttered. Our youngest brother always had a different girl on his arm, and they weren't all fun to talk to for an hour, possibly more.

"Siblings only, got it."

"I'll have Mia set it up," I said. "Talk to you then."

We hung up, and I went back into the conference room in time to see Shantel packing up her bag and laughing.

"What's so funny?" I asked, going back to my coffee.

Shantel smiled, seeming happier than usual. "Farrah has a good sense of humor. I like her."

I nodded, not cracking a smile myself. The success of Griffen Industries had changed a lot of things. Once you have money, you never know who's being real with you and who's looking to get ahead. Now that I had so much to lose, I needed to be more careful with my words because anything I said could be twisted and put on the news the very next day. But if my employees got along, all the better.

Shantel snapped the clasps on her briefcase and then picked up a croissant from the small pile Mia provided.

Mia gave Farrah a smile. "Want a pastry before Shantel and I get back to the office?"

Reaching for one, Farrah said, "It's better than the crusts of a Nutella strawberry sandwich."

Shantel laughed again. "How old are your kids?"

Love shined in Farrah's eyes as she said, "Fourteen, eight, and five. Two boys and a girl."

"I have one of each," Shantel said. "Twins."

Farrah kissed three fingers and held them up.

I had no idea what strange ritual they were doing, but Shantel did it back, laughing. Farrah already had Mia and Shantel wrapped around her finger. Much better than the last interior designer who had permanent stink eye. I had to let him go because everyone *hated* working with him, including the suppliers who were constantly pushing back delivery dates. He barely managed to complete the pool area in six months.

Mia confirmed my appointments for me and then said goodbye, shooting Farrah a thumbs-up she thought I didn't notice.

I noticed everything. Including the corner of a tag peeking from Farrah's sleeve.

With Shantel and Mia out of the room, it was just

Farrah and me and the crisp sound of her pastry as she chewed it.

"This hotel is fabulous, Mr. Griffen," she said, wiping a crumb from the corner of her full pink lips. "I can't wait to get started."

"Great." I took a sip of my coffee and set it back on the table. "This will be our office for the next three months. Prepare a list of items you'll need to get started —laptop, printer, et cetera, and send it to Mia. She'll handle the arrangements."

"Wait, three months?" she stammered. "What's our timeline?"

"We need to have the rooms designed and set up for the opening in a year, and I've been burned by enough designers to realize I need to take a more hands-on role. At least until you prove your competency."

She coughed like she was choking on pastry and then gulped down her coffee. "Wait, the hotel's opening in a year?"

I glanced at my watch. "Eleven months and fourteen days, actually."

Her eyes bugged out. "With all due respect, that's highly improbable. Most retailers of the caliber this hotel requires request preorders of up to a year or more of lead time. And then there's moving all the items in, staging, working with contractors for paint, wallpaper, window treatments..."

I arched an eyebrow. "I hired you because I thought you could get this done. And with three children at home to provide for on your own, I assumed you would do whatever it took. Was I mistaken?"

Her eyes searched me, shocked, nervous.

We hadn't talked about her children in the interview with me, but I knew.

I knew everything my private investigators could find before hiring anyone to the team.

Farrah Elkins.

Thirty-four years old.

Graduated from Upton University four years after having her first child. Levi Elkins.

Left her husband after multiple counts of infidelity. The divorce was processed by the county a month ago.

The courts awarded her full custody with guaranteed visits for the father every other weekend.

Currently resides with her parents in a three-bedroom, two-bathroom home near Arlington and has for the last month and a half.

She was hungry for a change, and I could feel it in everything about her, from her carefully done curly hair to her returnable black-on-black outfit and sensible heels.

"No, sir," she said, a determined look in her eyes. "You won't regret this."

"I know." I stood from the table and said, "Let's get started."

3

FARRAH

"I'm quitting," I told Mia on my way to pick up Levi from baseball practice. Luckily, my parents had gotten the younger two from school and agreed to watch them until I got off work since Dad's coffee shop closed at two every day.

"What? Why?" Mia asked over her car's speaker. I heard her blinker sound in the background of the call.

"HE WANTS TO HAVE THE JOB DONE IN ELEVEN MONTHS!"

The line was quiet, and my eyes widened.

"You knew, didn't you?" I demanded.

"Well, I—yes, I did. The last two designers royally screwed him over, and it's left him in a tight spot."

"I have three kids who just started at a new school, Levi's doing baseball practice after school, I'm trying to find a house. How am I supposed to do all of that while working on mission impossible?" Her turn signal underscored the panicked beating of my heart.

"Farrah, do you remember when you got pregnant with Levi?"

I nodded, even though she couldn't see me. I'd been nineteen at the time. Caleb and I had only been dating for a few months, and along came a baby. I was barely affording college tuition and my half of the rent while working nearly full-time waiting tables. It had been a lot to manage as a teenager, even before having a child to care for.

Mia said, "No one would have blamed you if you dropped out of college, but you made it work. You found that church nursery to help with childcare at a fraction of the regular rates, you encouraged Caleb to get his insurance license, and even brought Levi to class with you when you had to. You were relentless about getting your degree and providing for yourself and that baby."

"And then I wasted all that effort to be a stay-at-home mom," I said, already knowing I'd never go back and change a thing, even if I could. Staying home and taking care of the kids was the one thing I'd never regret. "Not wasted, just..."

"I know," Mia said gently, her turn signal still flicking.

"My gosh, how long have you been at that turn?" I asked.

Mia muttered, "Shit, forgot to turn it off."

I adjusted my grip on the steering wheel, smiling at my friend.

"The point is, you're going to make it happen, because if anyone can, it's you."

"I wish I believed in myself as much as you do," I said. "But what if I can't do it? What if I fail?"

"Well then you might need to move out of Dallas."

"WHAT?"

There was no humor in her voice as she said, "Everyone knows Gage Griffen. He's not vindictive, but he's honest. If they ask him why he let you go, he'll tell them the truth."

I bit my lip. "You really think I can do this?"

"Absolutely," she said. "And I know he's intimidating at first, but he really is a good guy. He expects the best from people, but he gives his best too."

"Good, because the thought of sitting in the same room with him for three months is freaking me out."

"No need to freak. I'll be in and out too, and you'll be so busy you won't even notice him."

Doubtful, but I said, "Thanks for the support, Mia. I know you went out on a limb to get this job for me. I don't want to disappoint you either."

"Never, but I gotta go. Just pulled up to my parents' place."

"Tell them I said hi," I said.

"I will. Love you."

"Love you too."

We hung up, and even though I still had doubts, I couldn't back down.

This salary was more than generous, and no one was calling me back for another job. In fact, I was getting rejections by email practically every hour because I'd been so dedicated to my job search. Unfortunately someone my age with no job experience wasn't exactly a hot commodity. Even the fast-food chain closest to my kids' school didn't want me in the kitchen.

And the thought of having my own job, my own money that didn't get filtered through Caleb's budgeting system or come through child support... it was pure exhilaration.

In just a few paychecks, I'd have enough to put a down payment on a decent rental, buy myself some shoes that didn't look like they came from an eighties thrift store, maybe even get some extra professional clothes so I didn't have to borrow from my mom or return after a single wear.

I could get Levi that mitt he kept asking for. New art supplies for Andrew so he didn't have to keep using the dime-a-piece spiral notebooks with lined pages. A cute bedroom set for Cora in the new house. She always wanted one of those cute beds that looked like a tiny house. Caleb was too cheap to give it to her, but me? I could cave, this once.

I pulled up outside the practice field at Levi's school, Golden Valley High. He was already walking my way, covered in dirt and sweat, with his gym bag slung over his shoulder. I pressed the button on the trunk, and he threw the stuff in the back before dropping in the front seat and slouching down.

"Rough day?" I asked. He'd been one of the best players on his club team in Austin, but the first few days of practice here had been hard on him, starting out as a freshman player on the bottom of the totem pole.

"Don't want to talk about it," he mumbled, pulling his cap farther over his forehead.

Sometimes it was hard to believe this tall, solid, sullen teen was once my little baby. But I still wanted to kiss away the pain no matter how much he'd grown. "You're just a freshman on the team. It'll take some time to get your bearings."

He gave me a look. He really resembled his dad when he made that scowly face.

"Okay," I said, turning up the radio. On the way to my parents' house, I stopped and picked up a bottle of champagne at the liquor store and then two big pizzas at Slice, the local pizza shop. When I came back into the car with the boxes, Levi perked up. I swear the kid's always hungry.

"We're eating out?" he asked. "How much is that guy paying you?"

I grinned. When I'd seen that number on the page, I realized I was making more than Caleb for the first time in my life.

Back when I told Caleb I was leaving because of his infidelity, he'd said all sorts of horrible things to get me to stay. He'd told me no one would be interested in a plus-size single mom of three. He'd said I would never make enough money to support the kids, even with child support, and that I'd come crawling back. He'd even stooped so low as to say the kids would hate me for making them live in poverty when their dad had such a good job.

He was *wrong*.

"Enough," I said finally, putting the car in gear and driving the few blocks to my parents' house.

"Does that mean I can get my new mitt?"

"Pizza today, a mitt later," I replied with a smile as I parked in my parents' driveway.

Levi carried his bag and the pizzas while I brought my purse and the champagne inside. Dad sat in his recliner, watching the evening news while Mom colored at the table with Cora and Andrew.

"Mommy!" Cora said, dropping her crayons and coming to wrap her arms around me. I hoped she'd never grow out of being this happy to see me.

"Hi, baby!" I said.

Andrew said from the table, "Gramps told me you're working for a zillionaire. Is that true?"

I smiled at my dad, who winked at me. "Close. Who wants pizza?"

Mom stood up, getting the boxes from Levi. "You didn't have to get pizza, Farrah. I could have ordered it."

I held up the champagne. "I wanted to celebrate. The offer was incredible."

Mom grinned, covering her mouth. "That good? Oh my gosh! But does that mean you're moving out? I'd miss my grandbabies if you did."

I chuckled. "Not quite yet. Let me get a few paychecks under my belt first." I went back to the room Cora and I were sharing and changed into lounge clothes. This outfit was still clean enough that I could return it for another one.

When I came back, the coloring books and crayons were already cleared off the table, and the TV muted. We sat around the table, and Mom led us in a short prayer, all of us holding hands.

When we were done, we dug in. Andrew picked the pepperonis off his pizza, giving them to Levi. Cora ate her pizza from the crust backward. It made me smile every time. What a goober.

"How was your first day on the job, kiddo?" Dad asked, running a napkin over his thick gray mustache. Never mind the fact that I was thirty-four. I'd always be kiddo to him.

"It's going to be a lot of work, but I'm excited to get started. I might actually get a little head start after the kids are in bed."

Dad nodded, looking impressed. "Great attitude. Get out there and take it by the horns."

Mom's face was far too expressive. A lot like mine.

"Yes, Mother?" I asked. She hated it when I called her that, and she gave me an annoyed swat.

"Nothing. I just worry about you having so much on your plate."

Me too, I didn't say. But I put my arms around Cora's shoulders, squeezing her and dropping a kiss atop her head. "I'll always have time for my babies."

Levi gave me an annoyed look.

"And my teenagers."

Andrew raised his arms in the air, pinning me with dark brown eyes that said, *what am I? Chopped liver?*

"And my big kids."

He nodded, seeming satisfied, but Cora said, "And princesses."

I giggled. "Always time for my princess."

We finished the pizza, and I went about getting the kids ready for bed. It was nice having Mom around to help supervise the boys working on their homework while I made sure Cora brushed her teeth well and got her tucked in to bed.

She looked so sweet under the covers, even though she'd kick me throughout the night. Sometimes I thought about taking the couch so I'd get a good night's sleep, but Dad always woke up at four in the morning to go open the coffee shop, so that wasn't exactly a great option either.

Andrew was next to go to bed. We read a chapter of his favorite book, *Investigators*, and then I kissed his forehead. He promptly wiped it off and said, "We talked to Dad earlier."

I felt like I'd been hit with a bomb. "What?" I glanced at Levi coming into the room. He wouldn't have had time to call Caleb and let Andrew talk. "When?"

Andrew said, "After school. Grandma called him for me."

"She did," I said, trying not to feel betrayed. Andrew had every right to talk to his dad. "Did you have a good talk?"

Andrew shrugged. "I told him about the art contest at school."

"Good," I replied. "What did he say?"

"He said he'd ask you to send him a picture of my painting."

I nodded. Caleb hardly talked to me at all these days, and he definitely hadn't texted me today. I had this worried feeling in my gut like he was going to let the kids down even more than he already had by breaking up our marriage. He'd already missed his first chance for a weekend visit with them.

Andrew rolled over, tugging his weighted blanket up around his shoulders. "Night, Mom."

"Goodnight," I said. I walked to Levi's side of the room, sitting on the corner of his bed while he got his backpack ready for the next day. "Your phone's on the counter, right?"

"Unfortunately," he muttered.

Ignoring his grumpy teenage tone, I said, "Love you. Goodnight."

"Night," he mumbled.

I tried to ignore that upset feeling in my stomach as I walked to my room and brushed my teeth. Levi was mad —mad about the divorce, mad about moving, about leaving his friends. I just wish he didn't have to throw up so many walls. I was alone too, away from all the mom friends I had in Austin. None of whom checked on me after the divorce. I didn't even have the comfortable house I'd poured all my heart into making a home. But I hoped he'd come around eventually. I wanted my son back.

I finished washing my face and moisturizing and took my laptop to the table so I wouldn't wake up Cora. I opened it up, beginning to sketch out a general plan for the hotel. I would start with the bathrooms. Despite being framed and drywalled, they still needed fixtures, tile, and vanities, and that would take a while to work with the needed contractors.

I was so focused on my work, I almost didn't notice Mom sitting across the table with two steaming mugs of tea. She passed one to me, then held the string extending from her own cup, dipping the teabag in the water. The scent of cinnamon apple hit my nose.

"I talked to Caleb today," she said. "Drew asked me to call him."

I nodded. "He told me."

Mom didn't look up at me as she took a sip. "Drew misses Caleb so much, and Levi seems so angry at you. I wish you'd tell them what Caleb did. You don't deserve to take the fall for his actions. Especially when it comes to the kids."

Here we go. I knew my mom cared for me, but she'd been married to Dad for thirty-eight years. She didn't know what infidelity or divorce felt like. "I know Caleb doesn't deserve my protection, but my kids deserve to love their dad, even if he couldn't love me the right way."

She shook her head, taking a sip of her tea. "Well then, I'll be mad at him enough for all the kids. A marriage, a *family*, is meant to be forever. For better or worse."

I finally met her eyes. They looked so much like my own, but it was her heart I'd really inherited. Mom cared about everything so deeply and could never hide her feelings or her opinions. "I love that you're on my side, Mom, but I'm tired of being mad, of being hurt, so can you just be happy for me? I got an *amazing* job. I'm making more than Caleb is! I finally don't have to lie down next to a man who's been with another woman. Life is..." I couldn't say good. Not yet, but I could say this. "It's better."

Mom lifted a corner of her lips. "I am happy for you."

"Mommy?" came Andrew's wavering voice. His chin wobbled to match. I glanced at my clock—it was only eleven, and the nightmares had already started. At least a couple times a week, he needed me at night to help him get back to sleep.

I squeezed my mom's arm and got up, following Drew to his bedroom for what was sure to be another long night.

4

GAGE

I stopped in the doorway to the conference room, stunned to see Farrah already sitting at her computer desk. Today her curly hair was down, falling past her shoulders in little ringlets. A floral button-up shirt with loose sleeves flowing around her arms.

And the smell in the room... something like coffee and wildflowers.

It reminded me of home.

Which sent this strange mix of sadness and nostalgia spinning in my chest.

I cleared my throat, announcing my presence, and she quickly looked up from her computer, then stood, knocking her desk chair to the ground. I didn't even know that was possible to do. "Oh, hi, good morning, I'm sorry, I'm such a mess."

I stepped in, picking up the chair for her. I was only a foot away, her scent heavy on my senses as I said, "First rule of business. No apologizing. There are no mistakes, only learning opportunities."

"Sorry, you're right—I mean... Thanks?"

I cracked a smile, but only for a second. I went to my side of the table where my laptop was already set up and charging.

"I got you coffee," Farrah said. "I'm not sure what you like, so I got black, then also a cortado and a frappuccino. I like all of them, except for black, so you're free to two out of three."

"That's not your job," I said, confused. Why on earth was she buying coffee for me? I could afford it.

She tilted her head, sending curls over her shoulder. "I like doing nice things for people... unless you're allergic to milk, then I guess the cortado isn't so kind."

"I'll take the cortado," I said, uncomfortable for some reason with her thinking that I had lactose intolerance.

She passed a cup my way, and I spun it in search of the logo. "Barry's?"

"It's my parents' coffee shop. Dad runs it, six to two every day except Sunday."

I took a sip, relishing the hot liquid and its rich flavor. "It's good."

"I think it's the best in Texas," she gushed. "I practically grew up working there."

When I didn't reply, she said, "So I have some ideas for the en suite bathrooms I wanted to run past you."

I raised my eyebrows. "Already?" She'd barely had an hour to work yesterday.

"Couldn't get to sleep," she said, brushing off my question. "Come look?"

I nodded, going to stand behind her. The wildflower scent was there again, and swear, it was more intoxicating than this coffee. Maybe I'd open a Barry's in the hotel.

She had her screen open to a digital mock-up of the bathroom layout. As I scanned it over, she said, "You want it to be relaxing but not look like every other five-star hotel in the area, so we're staying away from all white. We can't do black either, because with kids, every spot will show. I recommend adding some color. A soft green is very soothing, but it will also go with a lot of neutrals as well."

I tracked the design, my eyes landing on the focal piece. A large marble soaking tub. "I like the tub."

"They're great for kids," she said. "I always get disappointed if I'm in a hotel without a bathtub, but this is a massive level up from a basic shower-tub combination."

"Agreed. But marble's a porous material. How does that work?"

"It's actually called cultured marble—they mix limestone and resin, but it looks and feels identical."

"Interesting."

"Gold fixtures will blend well with the green backsplash. And shower tile shaped in half ovals will give the room some character. This gray tile job on the floor will be different enough from other hotels, but also easy to clean."

"Great," I said, unable to find any faults. She seemed to have thought it all through.

She gave some options for flooring, and when we landed on one, she said, "I'll get to making it happen."

"Good." I nodded. I went back to the computer, able to think more clearly without her distractingly good aroma right under my nose.

"It's like talking to my teenager," she said with a small laugh.

I raised my eyebrows. "Excuse me?"

She lowered her voice to mimic mine. "*Good. Agreed. Great.* All I can get out of him is one-word answers."

I hadn't realized I'd been doing it. "My time is at a premium, Ms. Elkins."

"I'm surprised you'd want to office with me then," she replied. "Surely you'd be more efficient in your own space." The little bite under her chipper words made me feel like a predator toying with my prey.

"I'm here because I can't afford for you to mess this up."

"You know that's really not the best way to motivate a person, right?" She leaned forward, and it took all I had to draw my eyes away from her ample cleavage. I *had* to be more professional than this.

She was playing with fire. And so was I. My voice was delicate...dangerous. "Is that so?"

With a confident nod, she said, "If I talked to my five-year-old like that, she'd cry in a corner."

"Good thing you're a thirty-four-year-old woman instead of a five-year-old child." I glanced down to my computer. Conversation over.

She huffed out a little sigh, then got up from her desk.

"Where are you going?" I demanded.

"I need to make a call and don't want to disturb you."

I gestured at the desk. "No need. I'd like to hear how you interact with professional contacts."

Her eyebrows drew together, forming a little line above her nose. The first thought that came into my head was how cute she was.

What a terrible fucking thought.

I was a CEO of a billion-dollar business, which meant

my time, my patience, for these kinds of thoughts, was zero. I put my head down, pretending to focus on my computer as she got out her new company cell phone and made a call.

But when the person answered, she did the strangest thing.

She started talking to them about their day.

Within two minutes of getting on the phone, they were chatting about dinner plans, and Farrah was reciting a recipe for a chicken noodle soup casserole they could put in the fridge and eat throughout the week.

My eyes had to be bulging out of my head. What on earth was happening? And why was she spending so much time not on business?

It took ten full minutes for them to finally circle back around to flooring.

"I really love the natural sand flooring you have for this *massive* project I'm working on, but I'm wondering if you have more options on site?"

She nodded, humming slightly, and I could only imagine if she had a phone cord, she'd be twirling it around her finger. "When could you send a contractor by?"

Her lips pursed, puckering in a way that sent a jolt straight to my stomach.

What the fuck was wrong with me?

And what the fuck was wrong with her? Couldn't they have been done with this conversation by now?

Time was money, and from what I could tell, she had no problem spending it like crazy.

"And their timeline to completion on a twenty-thousand-foot property?"

She let out a sigh. "Come on, Mark, that's so far out," she said, a little pout in her voice. "My boss is such a hard-ass, and he'd never let me get away with that kind of a deadline..." She winked at me, then looked down at the table, nodding. "I know, I get it, I do. I just wanted you to get the commission, especially with your wife due soon. But if I have to go somewhere else, I guess I can. Man, that stinks...." Her lips slowly curled into a smile. "Are you sure?... That would be fantastic. I'll see you here at five."

She hung up and stuck out her hand for a high five.

I stared at it. "What was that?"

"That was me working magic."

"It only took..." I glanced at my watch. "Forty-five minutes."

She shook her head at me, lowering her hand, but that smile still played along her lips. "That forty-five minutes will save you countless headaches later on down the road and months off our timeline. This flooring company is the best in a two-hour radius. They're always booked out at least a year in advance for projects like this, but they're giving us rush treatment without the extra charge."

"Why the hell would they do that?" I asked.

"Because his wife is about to deliver, and I just gave him an amazing recipe, plus the commission will give them a little extra cash while she's at home not working." She shrugged like it was no big deal. But it was a big deal.

People expected me to throw money around because I had it. But with the way she connected so naturally with people, she could be the ace up my sleeve. No matter how much I hated to admit it.

"Five o'clock?" I asked. "I have dinner reservations at six."

"I'll be here," she said. "I can handle it while you're at dinner."

I raised my eyebrows. "The surly teenager and the sensitive five-year-old will be okay?"

She nodded. "But it's anyone's guess with the middle one. He's a wild card." Her smirk caught me off guard.

Pointing at me, she grinned. "Made you smile. Just a little bit."

It took all I had not to roll my eyes. No one joked with me like this except for my siblings. "Get to work, Ms. Elkins. We still have a lot to do and only..." I glanced at my watch. "Six hours left to do it."

"SHE MADE four calls all day, each one longer than the last," I told my siblings and my new sister-in-law at dinner Thursday evening.

The five of us were at an exclusive restaurant on the west side of Dallas, halfway between my office and Cottonwood Falls, the small town where all my family lived. Paparazzi weren't allowed inside this place, and no one who ate here would dream of leaking a photo. Politicians, actors, and famous athletes alike enjoyed having a private meal from time to time. And it was nice to take my siblings here without worrying about the media showcasing them. Even though we were grown, I still felt protective over them.

I was the oldest, then there was Tyler and his wife

Henrietta, Rhett, and our sister Liv. A little under eight years separated the four of us.

After my rant about Farrah and her overly chatty demeanor, Rhett grinned, putting the results of years of braces on full display. "Is she single?"

Liv hit his shoulder, and Tyler groaned. I gave Henrietta, Tyler's wife, an apologetic look. If she wasn't used to Rhett by now, she would be soon.

"She's single," I said, "but she's newly separated. The ink's barely dried on the divorce paperwork."

Rhett's eyes lit up. "So she's single and needing a rebound? You have to get on that."

Liv took a piece of ice out of her cup and threw it at him. He easily caught it, popping it in his mouth.

"What?" he demanded. "You're all alone at that hotel and—"

Even though I knew he was half joking, I shook my head at him. "You're old enough to know business and pleasure don't mix."

Rhett waggled his eyebrows. "So you *have* been thinking about pleasure?"

"I think that's just you," I retorted before taking a sip from my scotch on the rocks. "And besides, even if I liked her and she liked me, I'd rather not be sued for sexual harassment."

Tyler tapped his nose. He'd always been against dating people from work. "Gets messy real fast. Ask Hen."

She nodded, a slight smile on her lips. "We're lucky it ended well for us as a couple, but I know it doesn't always." They'd both lost their jobs over their relationship with each other, and it had caused a huge rift between them before they were able to make things work.

Liv said, "Besides, the power differential is kind of gross. I mean, is she really able to consent if she's worried she'll lose her job if she says no?"

"Bingo," I said. "So can we talk about something else?" That woman had taken up far too many of my thoughts today, and I didn't need her consuming my evening as well.

"Mom and Dad's fortieth anniversary is coming up this year," Liv said, the words like a punch to the gut. "I thought maybe we could throw them a party and then send them on that Alaskan cruise Dad's been wanting to go on?"

Tyler nodded. "We can have the party at the Hen House in the common area."

Hen leaned her cheek against Tyler's shoulder. "That would be a lot of fun. Mrs. Bieker has said how much she misses baking for family gatherings, and I bet she could help out with the food."

Tyler kissed her temple. "So thoughtful, babe."

Her smile warmed the ice in my chest, at least a little. They were so happy together. My brother deserved a love like that.

Rhett said, "You know I can bring the beer."

"Of course you can." Liv rolled her eyes. "As long as you don't break that cashier's heart at the liquor store in the next six months."

Rhett winked at me. "I don't mix business and pleasure."

I shook my head at him and put a few hundred-dollar

bills on the table. "Dinner's on me. I'll cover the price of the cruise. Anonymously."

"Gage..." Liv said softly. "You and Dad can't take this feud to the grave."

I tapped the spot on my bicep, a reminder of what I'd lost and the promise we siblings had made to each other. "He made it very clear he doesn't like me and what I stand for. If that's changed, he could ask to talk."

"Maybe he needs you to make the first step," Liv offered.

I put my wallet back in my pocket. "I don't play losing games."

5

FARRAH

My first several days at work flew by, and when my alarm went off Friday morning, I almost felt sad it was my last day of the week. The disappointment caught me by surprise as I woke up the kids and had Cora join me in the bathroom to get ready.

It made sense that I'd enjoy work. After years of being a stay-at-home mom, it felt amazing to make my own money, to succeed at something outside of packing lunches and keeping house. Even though I missed being around my kids all day and picking up Cora and Andrew from school, I was glad to have this piece of myself back. The professional drive inside me always left me feeling a little unfulfilled in my role at home, no matter how much I loved my kids.

I was halfway through my makeup routine when my phone rang on the bathroom counter. Cora looked up from her spot on the counter next to me where she was brushing her hair and said, "You gonna get that?"

I gave her a look. "Where did all that sass come from?"

She pointed at me and grinned evilly as I picked up the phone. "Hi, this is—"

"This is an automated message from Golden Valley Elementary. School has been cancelled today due to unexpected power outages at the main building. Classes will resume Monday as usual."

"Shit," I muttered.

"Mommy!" Cora hissed, waving her brush at me like it was a big finger saying no, no, no.

"*Shoot.* I meant shoot," I corrected. I bent down to kiss the top of her head full of dark curly hair like mine and then went to find my mom. Dad had already been at Barry's for several hours by now.

I found her in the kitchen with the boys, chastising Levi for being on the phone at the table. "Who could you possibly be texting this early?" she asked.

"Dad," Levi deadpanned.

Mom made an exasperated sound, and I said, "Hey, Mom, Andrew and Cora's school is closed for today."

"It is?" Andrew was way too hopeful.

"Oh no," Mom said, already worrying her hands. "Far, I'm sorry, but one of the baristas called in sick, so I need to go help your dad until the shop closes."

Living with my parents must have brought out my inner teenager because I wanted to stomp and cry and talk about how unfair the world was. I was thankful my parents helped out as much as they did, but working a full-time job with three kids in school, it was only a matter of time before something like this happened. I had only hoped this day would come *after* I proved how indispensable I was to Griffen Industries.

But from my online search of Gage Griffen, I knew he had three siblings. He had to understand unexpected things popped up when you had kids.

I let out a breath. We'd just have to make it work. "Finish eating and grab your art kit," I told Andrew. "You and Cora are coming to work with me."

On the way to the hotel, I called Mia between bouts of trying not to completely panic. The second she answered, I cried, "HELP!"

"What's going on?" Mia asked.

Then Cora said, "Do we get to see you today, Auntie Mia?"

Andrew said, "I can draw you something. Anything you want."

The line was silent for a long moment. "Are you running behind?"

"I wish," I said. "The kids' school is closed for the day, so I have to bring them with me. I have way too much work to call in sick, and I don't think Mr. Grumpy Pants would want me taking a three-day weekend my first week on the job!"

"Can't your mom watch—"

"No, and I already called two of her friends to beg for help. Everyone's busy."

"Shit," Mia said.

"AUNTIE MIA!" Cora scolded.

"Sorry, sorry," Mia said quickly. "Farrah, this is not good."

I bit my lip, glancing over my shoulder at the kids in the back seat. Andrew was coloring a knight in his sketch book, but Cora's eyes were on me. "Doesn't Shantel have kids?"

"She also has a live-in nanny and a stay-at-home husband. I've never seen anyone bring children into the office, and Gage isn't exactly the warm, fatherly kind. I mean, there's a reason we don't have a daycare in the building."

I bit my lip, worry clenching my stomach. "Drew and Cora can be quiet, especially with their tablets going. He'll hardly know they're there."

"I hope so," Mia said, sounding unconvinced. "Hey, Drew, I know what you can draw for me... How about a woman walking off the gang plank into shark-infested waters?"

"Goodbye, Mia," I said.

"Godspeed."

My palms were sweating more than a glass of sweet tea on a hot summer day as we walked into the hotel. Cora pulled her hand from mine and wiped it on her pink sparkly dress. The one I had to wash every night with my dress clothes so she could wear it over and over and over again.

I kept my hands on my children's shoulders as we walked past Cliff, the security guard, into the building. Once we reached the makeshift office, Gage Griffen glanced up from his computer, icy-blue eyes darting from me to my two children. His shoulders stiffened, and I *knew* the worst was coming.

I just hoped he would send my kids into the echoing, empty lobby before he fired me so they didn't have to see me cry.

Before he had a chance to send me packing, I

hurriedly said, "They're not sick, but their school got shut down today, and I have no options for childcare. Trust me, I'd let the neighbor's dog watch them if it wasn't blind." Cora gasped up at me, and I said, "Kidding," then held up my hand like I was whispering to Mr. Griffen. "Not kidding."

If I wasn't mistaken, a hint of a smile shined in his eyes.

"This is not going to be a regular thing, but it's going to have to work for today," I said, feigning confidence. "And trust me, I can do great work while my kids are here. I brought activities to keep them occupied and headphones for the tablets so you won't even hear their TV shows. Right, kids?"

"Right," they echoed, out of sync.

Gage glanced from me to the kids, and I realized I hadn't even introduced them.

"Kids, this is Mr. Griffen. Mr. Griffen, this is Cora and Andrew."

Cora looked up at me, confused. "I thought you told Auntie Mia his name was Mr. Grumpy Pants?"

Ground, if you could swallow me up now, that would be great.

Mr. Griffen leaned forward in his chair, eye level with Cora. "Only my employees call me Mr. Grumpy Pants. You can call me Gage."

I raised my eyebrows. Was my kid really getting to see the sweet side of Mr. Grumpy Pants Griffen? I mean she was cute, but come *on*.

Andrew said, "Can I draw you something, Gage?"

Gage tapped his smooth chin. "Do you know what a windmill looks like?"

Andrew nodded.

"And cows?"

Again, Andrew nodded. He always drew what he saw on our trips between Austin and Dallas, and that, of course, included plenty of farmland.

"Can you draw me a pasture with a windmill and cows around it?" Gage asked. "That would make my day."

Make my day? Who was this man, and what had he done with Mr. Grumpy Pants?

Andrew smiled. "Okay." He looked around at the table. "Is there another chair for me?"

And you know what this man did? He got up from his chair and said, "Take mine."

"You don't have to do that," I said. "We brought a blanket in the bag so they can hang on the floor."

His eyes traveled from Andrew to Cora, now sharing his cushy desk chair that looked so out of place in this room. Even the folding chairs had been removed after that first meeting. Then he met my gaze. "Your children deserve better than the floor, Farrah."

I was speechless. Thoughtless too.

"Excuse me," he said, picking up his phone. "I have a call to make to 'Auntie Mia.'"

I had no idea what was coming as he left the office. For all I knew, he could be calling Mia to have Shantel bring over the paperwork to fire me. If paperwork was required. I'd been out of the workforce forever and had never been fired before. Unless you count that time I got caught making out with my high school boyfriend at the city pool after hours and my boss invited me not to come back the next year.

If I still had a job, I needed to get started on ironing

out the details of the flooring with Griffen Industries'
Finance Department. So I set Cora up with the iPad,
letting her watch one of her favorite shows with unicorn
headphones over her ears. Andrew continued drawing,
lost in his art.

Then I got out my computer and phone, calling
Griffen Industries' finance guy, Benjamin. I kid you not,
the guy works with money with a name like that.

"Hey, Benjamin," I said when he answered, and we
got to work. He trained me over a screen share on how to
submit a purchase order and told me that Mia would be
bringing a company credit card with my name on it that I
could use on smaller purchases. And the "smaller
purchases" he was talking about? Anything under ten
thousand dollars.

The resources at my fingertips were enough to make
me think I was in designer heaven.

I wondered if I'd ever have another chance to design
something so luxurious when this was done.

I'd just gotten off the call with Benjamin when the
door opened. A man in a moving company uniform came
in carrying three beanbag chairs and a pile of folded
blankets. Behind him, another mover brought in three
extra chairs, stacked together. Behind them, Mia had a
massive clear tote full of toys, from Barbie dolls to action
figures. And then Gage Griffen himself came in the room
carrying what looked like a bright red briefcase, an easel
stand, and a massive sketchbook.

My. Jaw. Dropped.

"Presents!" Cora cried, much less stunned than me.

Andrew came around the table, squeezing me around
my middle. "Mom! Your work is the coolest!" He went

back, taking his picture from the table. "Gage! I'm done with your drawing."

"Slow down," I said, "his hands are full."

Gage set his items on the table while the movers and Mia worked around him to set up the comfiest play corner for the kids. He took the sheet from Andrew, his full lips forming a rare smile as he took it in.

God that smile—it was like the sun breaking through the clouds on a stormy day. It transformed his entire presence from intimidating to exhilarating. My breath was shallow and my heart beat faster as I watched the interaction between Gage and my son.

Gage held up the sheet, pointing at Andrew's carefully sketched image. "You drew this?"

Andrew nodded, biting his bottom lip just like I did when I was nervous.

"There's no way." Gage looked at Cora. "You'd tell me if he snuck an adult in here to draw this, right?"

Cora giggled. "He drew it!"

"This is amazing," Gage said, sounding completely genuine. "Mia, can I have the tape, please?"

Within seconds, my friend had a roll of scotch tape in his hand.

"I'm going to hang this up, right where I work, so I can look at it every day. Is that okay?" Gage asked.

Andrew nodded, bouncing up and down with a giddy smile on his face.

My eyes burned with tears as my boss stripped off pieces of tape with his strong hands and hung the paper up on the wall, right by his side of the conference table for everyone to see.

One of the movers said, "Anything else, Ms. Baird?"

Mia scanned the room, already perfectly set up for the kids to be comfortable here. "It looks great, guys. Thanks for your help!"

The movers left, and Mia looked briefly at me before facing Mr. Griffen again. "Lunch is set to arrive at eleven thirty, and the children's art instructor will be here at one."

"Great work, Mia," Mr. Griffen said. "Be sure our coffee bar is stocked for my meeting with Jason Romero."

She nodded. "And then you have a press interview at four."

"Thank you."

Mia sent me a brief, confused smile and then left the room, her straight blond hair swinging behind her.

"Mr. Griffen," I said over the emotion in my throat as my children played with their new toys. "Can I speak with you for a moment? Privately?"

He nodded curtly, his intense mask back in place as if his heart hadn't just grown three sizes.

I walked out of the office and checked once more on the kids before closing the door behind us. The sound of the door closing echoed over the cement floors, and I looked up at Mr. Griffen, trying to understand what had just happened.

"Art instructor?" I asked.

He nodded. "I thought it would be fun for Andrew to have some focused drawing time. And Cora too."

"Fun?" I asked incredulously. "I didn't even know that word was in your vocabulary." God, why was I being such a bitch? "I'm sorry. I'm just a little... surprised is all. That was really kind of you, but you really didn't have to do all that for the kids."

A distant look seemed to cloud his eyes, making them a foggy day instead of crystal skies. "Yes, I did."

"And why is that?" I asked, my voice almost a whisper.

His throat moved with his swallow. "Because, Farrah. You and your children are a package deal."

6

GAGE

When I left The Retreat, Andrew and Cora were in the middle of their paint lesson with Fredricka Aimes, one of the best artists in the area. Farrah thanked me again, giving me a heartfelt smile that did strange things to my stomach.

But I had to get my head in the game for this meeting with Jason Romero. He was running for governor and had caught a lot of heat for outsourcing so much labor in his business. I wasn't sure why he requested to see me, but I'd always take a meeting. Just one, to see if something was worth my time.

I asked Mia for a coffee and went to my office to get a little more work in before Jason arrived.

Working with Farrah and her children had been enlightening and far too distracting. She was so natural with them, firm but loving. She didn't seem annoyed by them, and they seemed to respect her in their own playful way. It added dimension to this woman who was already an enigma to me.

I was so deep in my thoughts, I almost didn't realize when Mia came into my office with a coffee and a middle-aged man.

"Jason Romero," he said, extending his hand.

I gripped it. "Gage Griffen." His shake was solid, but his hands were sweaty. Even though he was in his late forties, his face was nearly clear of wrinkles, as if he'd gotten Botox like my publicist kept encouraging me to do. His skin was lightly tanned, his teeth perfectly white, and his dark brown hair thick and combed to the side. Everything about him said polish. Power. But not the brutish kind—the kind that always showed up when you least expected it.

I tucked that information in the back of my mind as I invited him to sit at my table and then took the coffee from Mia. "I was just having a little afternoon pick-me-up," I said. "Would you like a cappuccino or maybe a tea?"

Jason lifted his chin to Mia. "Why don't you get me a coffee with a splash of cream, doll face?"

Her smile tightened as she said, "Okay."

"Her name is Mia," I corrected as she left to get his coffee. "What can I help you with, Mr. Romero?"

"Call me Jason," he said, leaning on the table with his hands clasped together. I almost watched for a sweat spot to appear on the glass top. He gazed out the floor-to-ceiling windows. "Quite the view. Hard to believe a kid from Cottonwood Falls is sitting up here."

"You'd be surprised by the amount of resourcefulness and work ethic present in my hometown," I replied. "It just takes the desire." I sipped my coffee. "But then again, you know that. West Texas isn't exactly metropolitan."

He nodded. "You and me, we're cut from the same cloth. We both understand what it takes to rise above humble beginnings and create something great."

I didn't exactly consider what I was doing "above" my family farm. Dad worked just as hard or harder than I did to keep it running. Our goals were just different. I wanted to create a business that could support families like the one I grew up in. My dad wanted to support his own family and no one else.

"I was surprised you called a meeting with me," I said, hoping to get to the point. "I'm sure you're busy on the campaign trail with elections coming up next year."

"This was more important," he said. "Everyone in Texas knows Romero Corp. I doubt there's a car on the road here that was made without parts from one of our facilities."

I nodded, having already done my research.

"But a lot of people, a lot of *voters*, are wondering why we outsourced labor in favor of a better bottom line."

Hell, I wondered the same thing. I didn't deal much in manufacturing, but from what I knew, it could be harder to make sure labor conditions were fair when outsourcing.

"So, Romero Corp is announcing a new location in West Texas," he continued. "It will be a smaller plant but should employ a hundred people full-time. The only problem is without a significant infusion of capital, the build won't be complete for another... three years."

"After the election," I said.

He nodded.

He wanted to build a plant to help him win the election, not to help his hometown.

"How long are you planning to keep the plant open?" I asked.

"As long as we can keep it staffed," he said. "It wouldn't be in my... I mean, Romero Corp's best interest to open it up only to shut it down after election. With the deal I'm hoping to cut you, it will take at least ten years to break even."

I chewed over the information and thought about something Will Price, my biggest mentor in life and business, had told me before he passed a few years back. He'd said I was so principled I couldn't see the forest through the trees. Meaning, I got caught up in the details being right that I missed the big picture.

I knew how he'd look at this. He'd say, *The people are getting jobs, Griffen, doesn't matter the motivation. Don't you want to be a part of that?*

Keeping that in mind, I said, "Tell me more."

MIA and I got in the back of a town car with my publicist, Tallie Hyde, to ride to the Headline Building across town, home to one of the biggest news stations in Texas. As soon as I was buckled in, Tallie passed me a sheet of paper with Griffen Industries printed across the top in black and blue letters.

"These are your talking points for the interview," she said as I began scanning the page. "You'll be interviewing with Laney Franklin on her segment, Dallas Daze. Today is all about new businesses coming to Dallas in the coming year. You'll be talking about the hotel and how families will be able to enjoy it next Christmas."

I nodded, memorizing the talking points, although I hardly needed them. I knew this project inside and out.

After a few minutes, Mia passed me her tablet. "This is from finance. They need your sign off on the PO for the new flooring and install. It's scheduled to start next week."

I glanced at the page, my eyes widening at the number. "How did she get them to start so soon without a rush fee?"

Mia smirked. "That's Farrah. She's the best."

"Thank you for that tip on her, by the way," I said. I never would have taken a second glance at her resume with her massive gap in employment, but Mia's glowing review had changed my mind enough to call her in for an interview. When I spoke with her professor, saw her inspiration boards, the desire for the job in her eyes, I knew she would do whatever it took to get this done and do it well.

"Of course." Mia's phone pinged, and she looked down at it, typing back a text. I'd had assistants before, but Mia was by far the best. She and I didn't talk much about our personal lives, but she knew more about me and this company than anyone else.

She knew I didn't take calls from my parents—my mother, really, because Dad would never call.

She knew I had a professional hair stylist come to the office twice a month. A doctor twice a year because I'd rather do bloodwork here than sit in a waiting room. She knew I preferred beef to chicken, that eggs were never to be served cold, and that, unlike my brother Tyler, I took my coffee with plenty of cream.

She knew I stayed in the office until nine most nights.

And that I had no time for a life outside of this business.

And sometimes I worried that she knew too much, especially earlier today when she gave me a knowing smile as she and the movers carried in things for Andrew and Cora.

But that didn't stop me from opening my mouth because she also had knowledge in spades about this woman who intrigued me.

"So, Auntie Mia," I said.

A small smile grew on Mia's lips, and she glanced at me over her clear-framed glasses. "Yes, Mr. Grumpy Pants?"

"I guess I didn't realize you and Ms. Elkins were quite so close."

"We're more than friends. We're like sisters," Mia admitted. "In fact, I'm going to watch her oldest's ball game on Saturday."

"What kind of ball?" I asked, actually intrigued. I kept season tickets to all the professional teams nearby. When I was younger, I played every sport Cottonwood Falls High School had to offer, which admittedly wasn't that many.

"Baseball?" She said it like she wasn't quite sure. "I was told there would be a concession stand."

"Ballpark popcorn is the best. Enjoy," I said as we pulled up to the Headline Building. The car stopped out front, and the driver let Mia out.

Before getting out, I sent a text to my siblings group chat.

Gage: Want to hit some balls at Cottonwood Field this weekend?

Rhett was the first to reply.

Rhett: Only if they're yours.

♥

THE SUN WAS STILL COMING up when I reached the city limits of Cottonwood Falls, having left Dallas at four the next morning to make it here on time. The high school games started at noon, so my siblings and I would get an early start and have some lunch before I headed back home.

I took a sip of coffee as I drove past my old high school. Back then, I'd been a headstrong kid, bent on making the family ranch work for all of us. Now? The closest I got to a cow was if my nutritionist and personal chef included filet mignon on my plate.

My chest tightened like it always did when I got closer to the place I used to call home, but I gritted my teeth and barreled through the feeling. The past needed to stay in the past. We all had different lives now.

The new baseball field appeared in my windshield, just a couple blocks from the high school. I pulled into the gravel lot, seeing Rhett's truck there, dust thicker toward the bottom of the exterior and thinning as it went up.

Exhaust billowed up from his tailpipe, and the taillights shined red through a sheen of dust.

I pulled up next to him and cut my engine, getting out of the car at the same time Rhett exited his truck. Instead of his usual jeans and boots combo, he wore gray sweatpants and a thick black hoodie. In one hand, he held his own travel mug of coffee, his other tucked into his sweatshirt pocket.

"Hey, man," he said, giving me a half hug and patting my back as he grinned. "Glad you had this idea. I haven't played ball in forever."

"It's been too long," I agreed. But that was the cost of running the business I did. I might be the boss, but the company was the one making demands on my time. There wasn't room for much else.

The sound of an engine approached, and we looked over to see Henrietta's red SUV driving our way, Tyler in the driver's seat. She smiled at us and waved through the windshield, her grin contagious.

Just a minute later, Liv pulled up in her truck, dust billowing behind her. She was always running late, especially when she had an early morning wake up. I remembered working cattle with her when we were younger and our parents having to take the blankets off her bed so she'd get up.

After greeting everyone, I got the bag of baseballs, extra mitts, bats out of my trunk, and we were on the field. Liv insisted we warm up, so she, Rhett, and I formed a triangle to throw the ball around while Tyler and Hen passed back and forth with each other.

Rhett called to me, "Are you sure you're ready for this whoopin', old man?"

Liv passed the ball to him. "He just looks old because you've been hanging out with twenty-year-olds."

Rhett threw me the ball. "Do you see the issue, Gage?"

Ignoring him, I rolled the leather sphere in my hands, running my fingers over the seams. "I didn't realize how old I was until my employee brought her kids to the office. Eight and five. I felt like a grandpa crouching down to talk to them and hanging their drawings on the wall."

Liv said, "Grandpa or daddy? Because you're about that age to be thinking about kids."

Rhett folded his arms, putting his glove to his chin like he was deep in thought. "I've been called daddy before."

Liv took off her glove and threw it at him. "Why are you like this?"

Tyler jogged our way, grinning. "I think that's our cue to get started."

As we made a loose formation around the field, I tried not to think too much about what Liv said, mostly because she was right. I was closer to forty than thirty, and although my life wasn't over by any means, I didn't know how I'd ever have time for a relationship. For children. Or if I'd even be any good at it. My business had forced me to make sacrifices, and most of the time, I was content with my decisions. I had to find a way to be satisfied with this one too.

The five of us split the field. Liv at left field, Tyler at right field, Rhett pitching, Henrietta batting, and me at center field.

I knew Hen grew up with brothers, but when Rhett sent her a pitch and the bat cracked on the ball, sending it flying over my head, a grin split my face. Where the hell had that come from?

"That's my wife!" Tyler yelled.

"Baddie!" Liv called.

"I'm backing up next time," I called as I jogged after the ball that had rolled to a stop right before the fence.

Rhett sent her a few more pitches, most of which she hit to the outfield. It felt good to follow the ball with my eyes, snag it with my glove, and throw it in, getting away from thoughts of a potential partnership with Jason Romero and Farrah's wildflower smell. But mostly it was nice to know I had a family still, even if I couldn't go home.

For the next couple hours, we rotated around the field, taking turns in each position. I laughed harder than I had in months when Rhett hit a home run and insisted on sprinting around the bases, only for Tyler to tackle him before he could reach home plate.

We dusted ourselves off, then got in our cars and drove to the main diner in town, Woody's. Just stepping into this place took me back to high school, coming in with my girlfriend, Nicole, on my arm after a big win. Feeling like a god with my friends around, drinking milkshakes and shoveling down fries like our metabolisms would never slow down.

I barely talked to any of those people I used to call best friends. Money made things weird, and time made things awkward. But time seemed to encapsulate in this town.

Barely a few feet into the diner, an older man turned to look at us. "If it isn't those Griffen kids!" I instantly recognized him—Grayson Madigan, the man who owned the ranch nearest ours. We'd practically grown up with his kids, from having mud fights after a rainstorm to getting in trouble after prom. In fact, I still saw his oldest son, Fletcher, regularly as my doctor.

Grayson got up and hugged Liv and Henrietta, clapped each of us boys on the back. "Haven't seen you in a minute, Gage," he said.

I nodded. "Busy with the business. But it's great to see

you again." I meant it. He was one of the few people in this world I'd trust with everything I had. My falling-out with my parents hadn't just stripped me of that relationship. It made coming back to see old friends that much harder. So I mostly skipped it altogether. "How are things on the ranch?"

"Great," he said. "We hired a couple kids from the local FFA as summer interns, and they've kept me on my toes."

"I bet they keep you young too," I teased. Griffen Industries had college interns in most of our departments, from finance to marketing, and I made it a point that they were all paid fairly, even if it took extra time to train and teach them. They brought a liveliness and energy we didn't usually see from people who'd been in the workforce for a while.

"You know it," Grayson said with a smile. "I'll let you all get to your meal. Good to see you kids."

We made it just a couple feet before someone else stopped us to say hello. Four or five greetings later, we reached our booth at the back of the restaurant. Henrietta tucked into Tyler's arm, saying, "Have I mentioned I love this town? It's like everyone here is family."

Tyler nodded in agreement. "There's no place like Cottonwood Falls."

They were right. I just wish I didn't have this ache in the pit of my gut reminding me that living here with a family of my own had once been my dream too.

A waitress named Agatha, who'd been working here since before I was in high school, came and took our orders. She even remembered that I liked vanilla coke. As she walked away, I asked, "How does she remember that?"

Liv smiled. "You're hard to forget."

"Please," I said, looking at the menu. I could order everything listed for the price of one six-ounce steak at the place we'd been last week. I decided on a burger and fries and then waited with my siblings for our food to come out.

For the millionth time, I wished they lived closer so we could do this more often.

At work, I had to be strong, focused, a leader to hundreds of people in the organization.

Here? With them? I could just be myself.

That was until I saw the couple walking into the restaurant.

My parents.

I hadn't seen them since Tyler's wedding a year prior, but it was just as much of a punch to the gut now as it had been then. Dad didn't much like eating out, preferring to cook at home. They'd certainly never come midday on a Saturday, when the restaurant was sure to be crowded. I instantly looked to Liv, knowing she had to be behind this.

Tyler, Rhett, and Hen made a point to look anywhere else, but Liv tilted her head, pleading with her eyes. "Gage, at least try. Please. It's been long enough."

I shook my head, my fists clenching with anger. "That's my decision. Not yours." I'd woken up early on a Saturday, missed a day of work to hang out with my siblings, all to be ambushed by my parents. I got up from the table and walked down the narrow restaurant, aisle between the bar and the booths wishing there was more than one entrance.

Just feet from my parents, my mom said, "Gage, you're looking good today."

"Thank you," I said curtly, then I looked to Dad.

I wished we didn't look so much alike, but there we were, mirror images.

Both six feet, three inches tall. Both with dark blond hair, except where Dad's was mostly gray. We both had strong jaws. Blue eyes. He had a mustache where I was clean-shaven, but if I grew facial hair, we would look that much more alike.

And we were both stubborn as hell.

Both angry.

Hurt. Even after all these years.

"Anything to say, Dad?" I could barely utter the last word.

He looked down at the floor. Weak. Anyone knew in a negotiation, eye contact was an advantage.

Then he glanced back up at me, shook his head slightly.

It was just as forceful, just as painful, as a punch to the face.

"That's what I thought," I said, and then I left the restaurant, my parents, and Cottonwood Falls behind.

7

FARRAH

I was not ready to go into work. Not looking like this.

And that number ringing on my phone just as I was about to head into the building? That only made things worse.

"What the hell do you want, Caleb?" I demanded, pacing several feet away from Cliff, who looked straight ahead, acting like he couldn't hear every word.

"I've missed some calls from you," my ex said.

Bastard. "Stop acting like you don't know what you did. It was Levi's *first* high school game. He needed you there."

"Did he get off the bench?"

I could have throttled him. My heels pounded on the asphalt as I paced angrily. "That's not the point, and you know it," I hissed, my head throbbing. "Your son wanted you there, and you couldn't deign to drive three hours and watch him play on a Saturday afternoon."

"*You're* the one who decided to drag our children away from Austin for some godforsaken reason."

"'Godforsaken reason?' You know *exactly* why I moved here. And that doesn't mean you stop showing up for your kids. You know Andrew told me he heard Levi crying in bed the night of his game?" I'd had a stomachache ever since. "And why the hell were you ignoring my calls all weekend? There could have been something wrong with one of the kids and you never would have known."

"Maybe I didn't feel like having my ex-wife grind my balls for old time's sake."

"God, you're such a loser." I hung up, vindicated that I had gotten away from him and stopped dealing with his utter bullshit. The cheating had only been the final straw.

He hadn't been like this in college. Back when we started dating, Caleb had been romantic. Surprising me with flowers (even if he had picked them from the university flower beds). Sneaking me down deserted bookshelves in the library to steal kisses during study breaks. And even when Levi was young, he'd been a devoted father, taking his turns with the late-night wakeups and getting his license to sell insurance so he could make more money to support us.

But with time and more children, things changed. I stopped wearing my cute lingerie to bed, opting for comfy T-shirts and baggy shorts. He'd left more and more of the housework and childcare to me, since he was the one providing financially. Eventually, we were two people living adjacently in the same home, not two people in love.

Even so, I'd never wanted my children to grow up splitting weekends between their parents. I hadn't been happy with Caleb, per se, but not upset enough to leave. Not until—

"Miss," Cliff said, reminding me he was there. "Are you okay?"

I looked up at the man, embarrassment heating my cheeks. I looked awful, and underneath his thick eyebrows and strawberry-blond mustache, he seemed genuinely concerned.

"I'm okay," I said. "Sorry about that call, by the way."

"Trust me, I've seen worse. Especially when I used to work concerts." He shuddered, making me smile a little bit.

"You'll have to tell me about that sometime. But I should probably get inside. I wanted to show up before Mr. Griffen for a change."

Cliff nodded and held the door open for me. "Have a good day, Miss Farrah."

I smiled, relieved to hear my first name instead of my ex-husband's last. "You too, Cliff."

I walked into the building, thankfully entering an empty conference room. My eyes traveled over the beanbag chairs in the corner, the art easel displaying the painting Andrew and Cora made with the art instructor Mr. Griffen hired.

They had used the tips of their fingers to make a dotted winter forest. My favorite part was the pink owl Cora added in the corner. Gage had gushed over the paintings. He barely knew my kids, yet he'd shown them more care than their own father.

"They really are talented," Gage said behind me, making me jump.

"Oh my gosh." I pressed my hand to my chest, trying to calm my erratically beating heart. "I didn't hear you come in."

For the first time, Gage's stoic expression changed. First shock, and then anger flashed in his eyes, so strong it threatened to incinerate anything in its path.

My heart sped as he crossed the room, taking my face carefully in his hand and turning my chin to see my right cheek. His touch felt like fire on my skin. "Who did this to you?" He scanned the fist-sized bruise, all shades of blue, purple, and even green and yellow. "Was it your ex? Cliff said you had an argument on the phone." His jaw flexed powerfully, and he released my face. "If he so much as laid a finger on you, I swear, I'll—"

I pressed a hand to Gage's chest, broad and muscled under his suit. His pecs heaved with the force of his breaths, his anger. Where was this coming from?

"I'm okay," I said gently. "I got hit by a foul ball at my son's baseball game. Like winning the lottery, but less fun. The ER doctor said I avoided a concussion. I'm just going to look ugly for a few weeks while it heals."

His voice was almost a whisper as he said, "Ugly? You? Those two words don't belong in the same sentence."

My heart stuttered, skipped beats, not understanding this world we'd entered into. Had he said I wasn't ugly? That meant... "Thank...you, Mr. Griffen."

He stepped away, making my hand fall from his chest. "My apologies, Farrah. I crossed a line touching you like that." He shook his head, like he was clearing a haze too. "I'm sorry you were injured, but I'm glad you're okay."

My lips parted, but my brain wouldn't work, confused with the hot and cold and the way my name sounded with his voice still so rough and raw.

He sat down at his computer to work, and my legs carried me to my chair on their own accord as one thought went through my mind...

He'd used my first name.

8

GAGE

I fucked up.

I fucked up big time.

When Cliff told me Farrah had a heated exchange on the phone, my chest got this tight, protective feeling I didn't quite understand. I'd planned to come into the office and ask if she was okay, if she needed me to hire extra security for her off hours, but when I saw that bruise on her face, the size and shape of a fist, I'd lost my fucking mind.

It was like that time this piece of shit assaulted Liv in the parking lot of a restaurant where I was meeting her. This guy had her pressed up against the building, and when I saw them, my mind had gone blank. I'd beat the guy so badly he'd needed a hospital visit. I'd broken ribs.

But I still didn't feel guilty.

No one lays a hand on a woman. Especially not ones I cared about.

Shit.

Even in my head, I was fucking things up. I reminded

myself I didn't care about Farrah. No more than a boss cares about an employee. I tried to tell myself I'd have the same reaction if Mia came to work with a bruised face, but the truth was, I'd never once crossed a line like that with my assistant. Not in the last three years of working together sixty hours a week and sometimes more.

But just a week in with Farrah, and here I was.

An hour passed, two, with Farrah and me not exchanging a word. But I listened to her on the phone with different suppliers, smiling to myself as she spoke with them about installing lighting, bathroom fixtures, delivering massive soaker tubs made of waterproof material that looked exactly like Calcutta marble.

For the rest of the week, I kept my distance, only speaking to her when absolutely necessary and trying not to stare at her bruise as it faded from deep purple to sickly greens and yellows.

I could see the hurt in her eyes when she brought coffee Wednesday morning and I didn't drink it, telling her I already had some. Heard the resignation in her tone when she offered me a stick of gum Thursday that I turned down.

But when she asked if I wanted to get lunch Friday and I declined, her face fell.

"Gage, I—" she began.

I shook my head. "It's Mr. Griffen."

Her eyebrows rose, and a small smile played along her lips. This woman was so confusing.

"Why are you smiling at me?" I'd just rebuked her, for crying out loud.

"You just reminded me of Andrew. Earlier this week, he decided he would only be referred to as 'Flame.'"

A snort escaped me, too soon to repress. "Flame? Any particular reason?"

She lowered her voice, scrunching up the right side of her face. "'Because, it's like, way cooler, bruh.'" She shook her head. "No one ever warns you that when you have boys, you'll go from mama, to mommy, to mom, to... *bruh*."

I chuckled, despite myself. The way she spoke about her children was so infused with love and humor it was hard not to get reeled into her world. "Unfortunately, Mr. Griffen is a little less cool than Flame, but it is more professional." Something I struggled to be when Farrah was around.

She pouted. "But that means..." She sighed and shook her head, making her curls bounce around her chest in the most distracting way. "Never mind."

"What is it?"

She closed her computer and pushed it away, frowning. "It sounds childish."

I raised an eyebrow, keeping eye contact. "Now I have to know."

She practically squirmed in her seat. "It's just..." She let out an annoyed sigh, sounding frustrated with herself. "When you call me Ms. Elkins, all I hear is my ex-husband's name. I know this is a place of work and you're trying to run a tight ship here, but it's like the knife in my back twists every time I remember all I gave up to be Mrs. Farrah Elkins."

That empathetic feeling returned, hitting me straight in the gut. Emotions didn't have a place in business, but with Farrah, it was hard to keep the two separate. Everything she did involved emotions, whether she was talking with the flooring guys or bringing Cliff an extra cup of coffee every morning.

And now, when she looked at me with pain and hope and embarrassment all blending in her deep brown eyes... I couldn't remember how to separate what I felt from what I knew.

My voice was rough as I asked, "Would you prefer Flame?"

She giggled. "Farrah will do."

I let out a sigh, knowing I'd regret this later, but I said, "I am hungry, if the offer still stands."

She nodded, reaching for her purse. "My treat."

The fact that this woman thought she was paying was ridiculous. But I liked her all the more for it. How giving she must be to know I could buy anything I desired but still demand to treat me. And better yet, not take advantage of me.

We walked outside, both clicking our keys at the same time.

"You can't possibly think you're driving," I said.

She raised her eyebrows. "What? Is a minivan not good enough for a billionaire?"

I laughed. "I spent half my childhood in a minivan with all the driving we did to sports games and appointments." Sometimes when Tyler had therapy, I would have to ride along and sit in the car with Liv and Rhett for an hour while he and Mom had sessions. "A ten-year-old Dodge Caravan with light gray fabric interior to be specific," I said. "Showed all the stains."

She laughed, walking to her driver's side door. "Well, this should be a treat. Leather seats. It even has a built-in vacuum."

We got in the car, and she said, "Mia told me about this lunch spot I want to try out." She typed an address into her phone and then hooked it up to a charging cord and dropped it in the cup holder. A map appeared on the dash, giving directions to 214 Brews.

"I know the owner," I said.

She shook her head as she backed out. "Of course you do. Rich people always know people. Isn't that how you get to be rich?"

"Part of it," I admitted.

"Caleb, my ex, he was always 'networking' to help him sell insurance."

"For what company?" I asked casually. If Griffen Industries did any business with them, I'd stop it immediately.

"Green Line Mutual," she said with a shrug. "It's a smaller outfit in Austin."

Noted.

We were silent for a moment, but not the comfortable kind. We hadn't talked all week, and I realized I missed it. Missed her smiles. The emotion she'd draw out of me. She always made me feel slightly out of control, and I seemed to like that feeling more than I should.

"How was the game this weekend? Aside from the stray ball?"

She groaned, glancing at me, then back to the road. "It was awful. Levi didn't get off the bench until the last inning, and then he struck out."

I sucked in a breath through my teeth. "That's rough."

Her hands took turns hanging onto the wheel and moving through the air as she spoke. "And, of course, his dad didn't show. It was one thing to miss a game here and there when Levi saw him at home every night, but now that we live in different towns, it's ten times worse." The knuckles of her hand on the wheel were white with the force of her hold. "Levi was one of the better players on his club team back in Austin, but he was older than the other boys. This is a whole new world, and he really needs all the encouragement he can get while he gets used to those faster hits and pitches."

Wheels turned in my brain, and I made a mental note for later. "I played baseball in high school. I was always big for my age, but I remember it being a huge transition when I joined the high school team. I'm sure he'll get the hang of it... You, on the other hand. We might need to send you to games in bubble wrap."

Her mouth formed a half-amused, half-surprised smile. "Oh really?"

"We can't be losing our interior designer to a foul ball. The floors are looking great, by the way."

The smile on her face lit up the entire vehicle. "Just wait until you see what else I have planned. I found this great place out of central Kansas with the best wall treatments. Our order was big enough that they're sending a team our way in two weeks to apply them. It should be done by the end of the month!"

Pride swelled in my chest at what she'd been able to accomplish in such a short time. But I still worried we'd be delayed in the opening, costing us more money each and every day. "What about the furniture?"

"You let me handle that," she said with a twinkle in her eye.

We parked and went into the restaurant, where

Farrah fawned over everything from the clear glass light fixtures to the rugged brick floors and rich leather booths. I didn't notice the details like she did, but I liked the feel the place gave when we walked in. Not too upscale but nice enough to avoid feeling like a sports bar.

A server took our orders, and Farrah and I sat, her sipping a strawberry lemonade and me with a tea. In our seats facing the windows, the sun came through and shined on Farrah, bringing out the different colors in her hair. It wasn't just brunette, like I'd thought earlier. Now I noticed all the shades of blond, brown, and everything in between.

She tucked a piece of hair behind her ear. "I'm feeling a little bad for unloading all that about my ex earlier."

"Don't feel guilty," I said. "Whatever happened between you two must have been pretty bad."

"I'd say so," Farrah replied, looking down at her glass. "It's hard, you know, because I don't want to talk bad about him to the kids, but they look up to him like he's such a saint, and it hurts every time."

I just didn't understand. In the time I'd known Farrah, she'd only been kind, hardworking, endearing to everyone she met. "How could he have let you go?"

The words were out of my mouth before I could control them, but I couldn't find it in me to regret them. Solving puzzles, finding solutions was what I did best. And some depraved part of me that didn't know how to hold a boundary with this woman hoped maybe this was the key to staying away from her. Maybe this information would give me some kind of red flag to make me stay away—because the obvious fact that she was my employee, newly divorced, with three children just wasn't doing it.

Farrah drew her straw in a slow circle around her glass, making the ice tinkle. "When you have kids, they become your sole focus. Twenty-three hours a day, you think about them, worry about them, clean, cook, and care for them... And then the other hour you're probably asleep or putting off something you should be doing just to take a shower and comb your hair." She let out a small sigh. "Maybe if I had focused more on our marriage, it would have made a difference, but I didn't even know there was a relationship-ending issue between us until I went in for my yearly exam."

My heart squeezed in my chest, terrified she'd tell me she had some incurable disease, something that would take her from me. From her kids. And that he'd left her for it.

But instead, she said, "My gyno said she does an STD test as a precaution for every married woman, and mine came back positive for HPV. I thought it had to be a mix-up with the tests, but when I confronted him about it, he told me everything. The cheating had been happening for years. He'd pick up moms at school events. Sleep with women on business trips. He even slept with his secretary. We had that woman over at our house for dinner multiple times and I never knew." She shook her head, blinking quickly. "I couldn't stay with him after that. Not when the man I thought I knew had been lying to me for *years*, taking time away from his family to sleep with other women, without ever batting an eye."

My grip on my cup was so tight, I thought it might shatter. But the way Farrah talked about herself, the fact that she thought it could have been her fault for not putting in enough effort—it made me just as angry as that jackass who let her go.

This woman was fucking gorgeous. Curves for days. A chest that would overflow even in my large hands. A smile that melted someone as frigid as me.

This guy was a loser.

A fucking joke to think he could do better than the woman in front of me.

Better than his children waiting for him to just show up.

"Look at me, Farrah," I said, my voice as intense as my grip on the drink.

Her brown eyes collided with mine, delicate as the petals of a bluebonnet, raw as the edges of a glacier.

"Don't you ever let a man tell you that you don't deserve his full attention, his loyalty, and his love. Because you do, Farrah. There's not a part of you that deserved what he did."

9

FARRAH

I thought about what Gage said for the rest of the day. We didn't talk much as we worked, but it felt like a lighter kind of silence, not the hard, uncomfortable cold shoulder he'd given me all week.

Toward the end of the day, my phone rang, and I recognized the number from my rental application. "Oh my god," I hissed as I swiped to answer. I could feel Gage's eyes on me as I said, "Hi, this is Farrah."

"Farrah, this is Francesca. I saw your application for the house on Pine Street and loved the note you included. Any chance you're free to tour the place this evening?"

"Absolutely!" I said, doing a happy dance in my chair. Gage had an amused spark in his eyes.

"How does half past six sound?"

"Sounds perfect, see you then!"

When I hung up, Gage said, "I didn't know your voice went that high."

I rolled my eyes at him, standing to get my purse. "I'm

calling Shantel so we can get something about eavesdropping added to the company handbook."

He lifted his hand in a wave. "Good luck. She reports to a hard-ass."

"I don't think he's so bad," I said with a smile and walked out of the hotel floating on cloud nine.

I grabbed Levi from baseball practice, then picked up the younger two kids from my parents' house to go tour a rental home I hoped would be perfect for us. My stomach was still in knots from all that Gage had said earlier, and for the life of me, I couldn't get his blue eyes and his words out of my mind.

Maybe he was just being nice, but it meant a lot to have a man like him say such complimentary words about me. He was good-looking, tall, fit, financially set, and clearly kind enough to lift up a plus-size mom of three.

Add the twisty feeling in my stomach to the tingle of nerves about this rental, and I could barely keep down my lunch.

"Mom," Cora said from the back seat, "is this house close to a park?"

"There's a park just a couple blocks away. We could walk there, or you could ride your scooter!"

Andrew said, "Could I walk backward?"

In the front seat, Levi scoffed. "If you wanted to walk backward into the road, I guess."

I reached over and gave Levi a gentle pinch on the arm. The boys were always getting on each other's case.

Levi brushed my hand away. "I'm fine as long as I get the big room."

"It has four bedrooms," I said. I thought a three bedroom would be okay, but I loved the idea of each of my kids getting their own space in our new home. Especially since I had the means to make it happen.

This house was close to my parents' home, in one of the cheaper suburbs of Dallas, and even though it would be a longer commute for me, it was well within my budget.

"How far is it from school?" Andrew asked.

"Fifteen minutes," I replied. "But there's a bus stop on the corner, so you can ride the bus."

In the rearview mirror, I saw him bring his arm to his side and say, "Yes!"

For whatever reason, he thought buses were the coolest thing—probably because he'd never ridden one before. The kids had gone to a private school back in Austin, meaning I was the one dropping them off and picking them up. And Mom and Dad's house was close enough to their new school for me to bring them myself.

The map on my dash had me turn off the highway, and as we got closer to the neighborhood, I scanned all the houses, the streets. The homes here looked older than in my parents' neighborhood, more spaced out. And even though there weren't sidewalks, the streets were wide and not very busy at all.

A hopeful feeling bloomed in my chest. I could see this neighborhood feeling like home. And it would be a home I'd created, just me and my kids.

From the back seat, Andrew read off the directions, "One minute left!"

Cora bounced her legs against her car seat. "One minute!"

"Yippee," Levi muttered.

My heart sank, and I knew I had to do something to

set the tone before this whole tour went off the rails. I stopped the car alongside the road, even though we weren't there yet, and reached for his hand. Levi was a big kid, getting his dad's height, and his hands were bigger than mine already, even though he was still fourteen.

By some miracle, he looked back at me instead of pulling away.

"Levi, I know this is hard, moving here without your dad. It's hard for me too." I searched his blue eyes, hoping he'd understand. "Can you please keep an open mind?"

"Yeah," Andrew piped up from the back seat. "Give it a chance."

I gave Drew a warning glance over my shoulder before looking back to Levi.

He tilted his gaze down and nodded slightly.

"Thank you," I said, squeezing his hand and then letting go.

We drove the rest of the way to the house with a for-rent sign out front, and my jaw dropped. The front stood out with light brick and a bright yellow front door that made the whole house look like it was smiling at us. There was some landscaping to care for up front, but nothing that we couldn't manage on our own.

We all got out of the car, and pretty soon, another car pulled up. An older woman got out, and I said, "Hi, I'm Farrah. You must be Francesca?"

She smiled at me and my kids. "Yes. We talked on the phone earlier. Can't wait for you to see this place."

"Me neither," I replied, scanning the exterior and the short brown grass up front. I could only imagine what it would look like with a blanket of freshly mown lawn. "It looks lovely."

"Oh, it is," she said, walking alongside us up to the front door. Cora balanced along landscape stones, her arms straight out and her sequined skirt shimmering in the day's last rays of sunshine. Andrew and Levi followed dutifully behind us.

When Francesca opened the door, she said, "Why don't you all take a look around and I'll wait out here."

"Sounds great," I said.

The younger two kids led the way into the house, and Andrew said, "This is *nice*, Mom."

I nodded, unable to speak. When I had looked at the pictures online, I fully expected the place had been staged and edited to look so nice. But the photos hadn't even done it justice.

The front room had dark vinyl flooring and a grand fireplace with ceilings that stretched at least twelve feet high. As we walked farther inside, there was a dining room and then a kitchen with granite countertops and natural wood cabinets.

I half expected Francesca to come inside and tell me I'd been Punk'd. This place was so much nicer than what I anticipated and somehow in my price range. When Caleb and I broke up, I had accepted that I would have to lower my standard of living by quite a bit to make things work, but this didn't feel like a massive step backward. In fact, this was exactly the kind of home I would be proud to live in.

It wasn't as new as the home we had built in Austin and wouldn't be furnished as nicely, but I could picture picking out a comfy couch for us to sit while we watched movies on Friday nights, and I could see us all gathering around a table to have dinners together after work and school. And as we walked back to the bedrooms, I could envision setting them up to each of my children's tastes and styles.

I wouldn't be able to fully furnish it at first, but maybe the fact that this house could always change was part of the allure. It would always be somewhat of a blank canvas.

From one of the bedrooms, Cora yelled, "This is my room!"

Andrew said, "Hey, I wanted this room!"

Because I could hear where their voices were coming from, I laughed. "That's my walk-in closet." I walked around the corner to see him and Cora cozied up in opposite corners of the closet.

Andrew snuggled up on the tan carpet. "It's so cozy."

I laughed, looking from the closet and around the main bedroom. There would be room for a king-sized bed in this space, so Andrew and Cora could sleep with me if they ever got scared at night—without kicking the crap out of my back.

And I would have my own bathroom, one that I wouldn't have to share with Cora or the boys. All of the kids could share the bathroom in the hallway that had double vanities. Perfect for decreasing the amount of fights over sink space in the morning.

"Would this be mine?" Levi called from another room.

I left the main room, joining him in the second biggest room, one with a view of the treed backyard. There was a thoughtful look on his face.

"What do you think?" I asked, leaning in against the doorframe.

He hooked his thumbs in his pockets, shrugging. His lips spread into a smile despite himself. "I'm thinking it's going to be quiet without Drew snoring all night."

I laughed as Andrew yelled, "I HEARD THAT."

We finished walking around the house, and then I had the kids load up in the van while I talked with Francesca. She leaned back against the hood of the car as I approached. "What did you think, hon?" she asked.

"It was amazing. Which kid do I have to give you to move in?"

She tossed her head back, laughing. "I like you. But no kid required. Just a deposit with first month and last month's rent."

My stomach sank as I did the mental math. That would be literally all the money I had after my paycheck came through tomorrow. "Is there any chance we could start the lease at the end of the month?"

The lines around her mouth creased. "I'm sorry, hon, but there's a lot of interest in this place. Actually..." She glanced at the oversized smartwatch on her wrist. "There's another couple coming to look in an hour."

"What would it take to make it ours?" I asked. The thought of this house going to anyone else when it was so clearly made for us made my stomach turn.

Francesca held up two wrinkled fingers. "A signed lease and a check for the deposit with first and last month's rent. As soon as the check clears, you get the keys."

The thought of spending all the money I had to move into a place I couldn't furnish made my heart ache. But I knew I couldn't live with my mom and dad forever. Our stuff was already overflowing their house, and the truth was, no matter how welcoming my parents were, living with them just reminded me of all the ways I'd failed.

I held up a finger to Francesca. "One second."

She nodded, and I turned on the crackling dry grass to walk to my van. Inside, Levi had the music playing from his phone, a rap song with the words moving so fast I couldn't understand.

"Pause it," I said over the beat.

He turned it off, and suddenly the van went quiet. "Guys, I need to know what you think about this place. Is it the one? If it isn't perfect, we can keep looking."

Levi looked at me, then turned back to look at his siblings. Cora nodded quickly. "I love it, Mom."

"Me too," Andrew said.

I looked at Levi, the last holdout. He twisted his lips to the side. "It's not getting better than this, Mom."

And I knew he was right. So I wrote Francesca a check and begged her not to cash it til the next day. With a smile, she agreed.

WHEN WE GOT HOME, the kids immediately told my parents all about the house. Dad gave me a hug and said, "I'm proud of you, kid."

But I noticed there was something else on my mom's mind. I could tell by the way her smile didn't quite reach her eyes. When all the kids were sat down watching a movie and Mom was washing the dishes, I went to join her.

Even though the dishwasher worked, she insisted on hand-washing and then using the dishwasher as a drying rack, saying that the machine didn't clean as well as she could.

I stood beside her, rinsing plates after she sudsed them up and putting them in the dishwasher racks.

After a few dishes, I asked, "Is everything okay? You seemed upset earlier when we told you about the rental."

She pursed her lips together, the day's lipstick almost gone. "I'm not upset, just surprised." She met my eyes for a moment before refocusing on the washing. "I guess I hadn't expected you to find a new place so quickly."

I tilted my head, confused. "What do you mean? We've been here almost two months already."

"Well..." She set down her dish and dried her hands with a rag before facing me, resting her hip on the counter and folding her arms over her chest. "It's been nice having you here."

I raised my eyebrows. "You have to be kidding. I would have been annoyed with us six weeks ago."

She chuckled, then shook her head. "When you lived in Austin, it felt like we hardly ever got to see you because the kids had all those activities on the weekends and then Dad had to run the shop on Saturdays. Having you all here is the first time since the kids were little that I feel like I've really gotten to know them." She wiped at her eyes.

A lump formed in my throat. "We'll only be fifteen minutes away," I said, reaching for her hand. "And trust me, I'm going to take advantage of you for free babysitting."

She laughed. "I'm going to hold you to that."

"I hope you will. Because Caleb hasn't been showing up lately, and the more people the kids have to love them, the better."

Mom nodded and put her arms around me, squeezing me like only a mother could. "Have I mentioned that I'm proud of you?"

I let out a little breath, like my lungs couldn't hold all the emotion I felt. "No, but it means a lot." I pulled back, wiping at the corners of my eyes. From here, I could see the kids sitting in the living room with Dad, focused on the movie and their snacks. "Sometimes I feel like all I'm doing is failing them. But I couldn't stay with Caleb."

Mom reached up, helping me wipe my tears with the pads of her thumbs. "We all make a lot of mistakes as a parent, but there's one thing you can't mess up. Kids need you to show up for them. You've been there for those three every day of their lives. You're an amazing mom, Farrah."

I put my arms around her and held her tight. "Only because I learned from the best."

10

GAGE

After working out Saturday morning, I got in my Tesla and drove to a suburb west of Dallas, my map giving me directions to the one and only Barry's Brews. Even though the building was small and simple, there were cars filling the big parking lot and lined up at the drive thru. From the taste Farrah gave me over the last few weeks, I could see why.

I waited until a car pulled out of a spot, then parked before someone else took the space. Today, I'd dressed in a gray Henley and jeans with a brown Ropers ballcap pulled low over my face, hoping I didn't draw too much attention like I usually did when going out in designer suits.

I didn't give two shits about labels, but a stylist kept me stocked with clothes that would look professional and help me be reputable in the circles I ran in. No matter how much I respected handshake deals and making decisions based on logic instead of emotion, looking powerful was half my success in business meetings and negotiations.

When I walked through the crowded coffee shop door, a blast of warm air greeted me. That and the buzzing of conversation inside contrasted the cold February day. There were a mishmash of chairs around the interior, from worn leather to vintage orange tweed and plastic seats around a motley collection of wooden and metal tables.

Students gathered with their computers and notes spread out. Couples shared drinks around the small electric stove in the corner. And what looked like a Bible study group sat around one of the larger tables, notebooks in front of them as they covered the material.

Before I even tried another drink, I knew half the magic of this place was the feeling you got when you walked in the building.

"Excuse me, young man," said an older lady with a silk scarf wrapped around her silver hair. "Are you in line?"

"Go ahead," I replied, giving her a smile. I heard a table of college girls to my right giggle and had the distinct feeling I had something to do with it.

I may have been in the longest dry spell of my life, but I was not one of those guys who went for younger women. The ones I kept company with had their lives in order and were beyond petty drama. But most importantly, they didn't expect anything long term from me.

When I reached the counter, a barista with a handwritten name tag greeted me. Jenni with a heart over the i had to be a teenager still. "Hi there, what can I get you?"

I glanced over the menu. "I'll have an espresso, a latte, and your house drip coffee."

"Absolutely." She typed on the tablet they used for handling transactions and then turned it to me to pay. "How is your day going so far?"

"Can't complain." I tapped in a custom tip for a thousand dollars. "Is it always this busy?"

She glanced around the seating area. "It's a little slow right now, actually. It'll probably pick up in an hour or two."

I raised my eyebrows. "This is slow?"

She nodded. "Everyone keeps trying to talk Barry into extending his hours, but he says he'd give up a billion dollars and his right ass cheek to have more time with his family." She shrugged. "Seems to be attached to the left one though."

I chuckled. "Good to know."

She looked down at the screen, and her eyes bugged out. "Sir, um, I think you made a mistake."

I glanced at the tablet. "Did I put a hundred instead of a thousand?"

She was white as a sheet, shaking her head.

"It's right. Put it toward something good."

Smiling so big her cheeks had to hurt, she said, "Your coffee will be ready on that side of the counter. Have a *great* day."

I only had to wait a few minutes before all my drinks were ready, and I balanced them in my hands, going to a two-top table and trying each of them.

My business had afforded me coffee from the best beans, the highest paid baristas, in resorts on almost every continent. (Still hadn't made it to Antarctica.) But this

coffee had to rank among the best. Full bodied and flavor-
ful. Not too bitter but not weak either. It was a good cup
of coffee, and I knew my guests at The Retreat would
love it.

Jenni might have said Barry wasn't interested in more
work, but maybe Farrah and I could convince him that
opening another shop, or at least consulting on one, could
be worth his while.

I finished the espresso, half the drip coffee, and
brought the latte with me back to my office. It was quiet
when I arrived, which seemed deafening after sharing a
space with Farrah for this long. Something about her
chatty phone calls had become soothing by some mystery.
So, I put on coffee shop sounds through the speakers and
took advantage of the distraction-free space to get as
much work done as I possibly could.

Even though setting up a temporary base at the hotel
was helping me make sure things were staying on track as
far as the design and setup of the space, it definitely hurt
my efficiency. I had a lot to do. Including firing Green
Line Mutual. As soon as Farrah told me where her ex sold
insurance, I checked with Benjamin in finance and he
said we had several properties insured by them in the
Austin area. We'd soon have a different company
handling that.

I also needed to go over the email Jason sent with an
initial proposal for our partnership. At first glance, the
deal looked amazing. After the initial investment was
made back, I would get thirty percent of the profits for an
additional five years at no cost to me. He also guaranteed
the plant would be open at least as long as it took me to
earn back my investment and the additional five years, so

we were looking at a ten-year guarantee of more than a hundred jobs in that community.

That kind of thing could change a town—bring in better talent for other jobs, more businesses to accommodate the extra people, improved public services because of the extra taxes. The list went on.

Even though Jason wasn't perfect, this was exactly the kind of project Griffen Industries should be involved in.

But then I realized it would just be more work for me. And I had enough on my plate with finishing up The Retreat. I needed to hire a project manager, but for some reason, letting go of this project didn't appeal to me one bit. I tried convincing myself it's because we've gotten off track so many times and not because of the woman I got to work with.

She probably wasn't even thinking of me. She shouldn't be.

I glanced at the clock. She was probably at her son's game right now, work the furthest thing from her mind.

Curiosity got the better of me, and I looked up the school's website. She'd mentioned the team he played for once, and within a few minutes, a livestream of the Golden Valley game played on the flat-screen in my office.

The look of a high school field and amateur announcing took me back to my days playing high school ball. I had an opportunity to play in college, but I'd turned it down to go to technical school and study diesel mechanics to help out with the farm equipment. Back when I thought I'd be running the family ranch instead of a billion-dollar company.

The game played in the background as I worked. But

in the ninth inning, the announcer said, "Up to bat is Levi Elkins, a freshman on the team."

My gaze snapped up to the screen, and I studied Farrah's son walking up to the plate in his gold and black uniform. I'd seen a photo of him when doing my employee background research, but now I realized just how big of a boy he was. Strong but still lanky and growing into his size.

He stepped up to the plate, cheering sounding in the background. I tried to pick out Farrah's cheers, Andrew and Cora's too. I wondered if Farrah's ex had shown up for her son.

I really hoped he had.

"Strike one!" the announcer said. "So far, Levi's batting record is limited, but let's see if he can pick it up on this next pitch."

"Foul ball! Looks like he swung a little late. You know, sometimes it's hard for these younger kids to catch their bearings once they come to play high school ball. Takes time to get used to these fast pitches from seniors who have been training for a few more years. Let's see if he can get a hit off this pitch."

The ball came closer to the plate, and I saw the moment the bat connected with the ball. A crack sounded through the speakers as the ball went flying into the outfield.

"Thataway!" I yelled, clapping my hands. But then the centerfielder caught the hit. Levi hadn't even made it to first base.

"Shit," I muttered, rocking back on my feet. My gut ached for him.

"What are you doing up here?"

I jerked out of my skin, muscles coiling to defend myself. Which was stupid, because it was just my sister. "What the hell are you doing here, Liv? I nearly shit my pants."

She smirked, folding her arms across her chest. "That would have been a sight." She glanced to the TV. "I didn't know the Ropers had a game today... Oh wait." She squinted at the screen, and I fumbled for the remote, hurriedly clicking it off, but not soon enough.

"Were you watching a *high school* baseball game?" she asked.

"No," I lied.

"You're a shitty liar. What were you doing watching a Golden Valley game anyway? We don't have any long-lost cousins there, do we?"

"A friend's kid's playing," I said. It wasn't entirely untrue.

"You don't have any friends."

I grunted. She was right. "A business partner then."

Her jaw dropped open. "It's that single mom you work with, isn't it?"

Why was I blushing like I was a high school kid getting caught making out? I was a grown man. I could watch a kid's baseball game if I wanted. But arguing that with Liv would just open more opportunities for her to ask questions with answers I didn't want to face. "You didn't mention why you came?"

She looked like she wanted to argue, but instead, she plopped down in one of the chairs, setting her purse on my table. "I had to pick up some things in the city, and I wanted to come by and apologize. I'm sorry for springing Mom and Dad on you like that. It wasn't fair of me."

I nodded, surprised by her apology. None of us Griffens were great at saying sorry. "Thanks for saying that, Liv. I know you have this big heart and you just want everyone to get along, but..." I heaved a sigh. "Sometimes people don't have the storybook family they wanted."

My mind drifted to Farrah, learning that her husband had cheated on her, leaving her with three kids. If anyone deserved a good life, it was her and her sunshine heart of gold. If she couldn't get that happily ever after, what hope was there for me? "I'm just a grump anyway," I muttered. "Just a matter of time before people start calling me Scrooge."

"To your face." Liv winked. Then she nodded toward the TV. "But I'm starting to wonder if there's a heart under there after all."

"Don't get your hopes up," I said. Because even if I did like Farrah, it wouldn't matter.

Like I said, not everyone gets a storybook ending—or even has time for one.

Liv had a few more errands to run, but we agreed to meet at my penthouse for supper. Sometimes it was nice to get great takeout and eat it in private without the hustle and bustle of a restaurant and all the hassle that came with the required social graces.

As soon as Liv was safely in the elevator, the door dinging closed, I got out my cell and made a call.

11

FARRAH

"How's your wife doing?" I asked Mark as we did the final walk-through for all the flooring his company had laid in the last month.

I couldn't believe I'd been on the job only six weeks, and this hotel was already coming together in the best possible way. The sandy oak flooring looked incredible with the off-white walls and broad windows letting in the afternoon light.

"Miserable," he said. "She's so big she can barely get up out of a chair. She heard somewhere that eating pineapple can stimulate labor, and I'm pretty sure we've had pineapple in every meal for a week."

I stopped with him in the lobby's grand entrance. "Poor thing. You know my doctor said nipple stimulation is supposed to help."

Mark's cheeks quickly turned red.

"Sorry, that's probably TMI," I chuckled awkwardly.

"No worries." He cleared his throat. "The floors are

guaranteed for ten years under the commercial warranty, but our installation warranty is a year. If you see anything, be sure to call me as soon as you do so we can get it taken care of. After a year, the product is free, but you'll have to cover the cost of labor for any fixes."

I nodded. "It looks great, and I will definitely give your business card to anyone who's looking."

He put his hands together. "Thank you, Farrah. Means a lot."

"Diapers are expensive," I teased. "But the rewards you'll get from watching them grow... that's priceless."

His eyes shined with anticipation as he nodded and told me goodbye.

On the walk to the front door, I thanked my lucky stars that this bruise was faded enough for makeup to cover it. The last few weeks had felt so long, caking on makeup and trying to turn my head so contractors wouldn't see.

When I reached the conference room where Gage was busy working, he glanced up at me, his blue eyes piercing my own. "Flooring look good?"

"It's incredible. It almost looks like a hotel now."

"That's progress. Where are we on everything else?" Gage was all business, had been ever since that strange Friday lunch a few weeks ago. But I had to admit I liked the sound of his voice—it was strong and masculine, commanding. Made me want to hurry up and do exactly as he asked.

"I'm meeting with a local photographer next week," I said, "seeing if we can commission prints to fit the brand. Then I have a meeting with an artist to see if we can get complementary pieces to match."

He nodded. "Just don't make it too touristy."

I raised an eyebrow. Did this man really think he knew more about my job than I did?

"Go on," he said, either oblivious or ignoring my expression.

"The team from Kansas will be here in two weeks and stay in town for a month while they install the wall treatments in each room and behind the front desk. Bedding and all other linens have been ordered and will arrive in two months—all the finest on the market."

Gage said, "Bedding won't matter if we don't have beds."

Man, he seemed testy today. I wanted to ask him what was going on, but already knew he wouldn't answer personal questions anyway.

"All the bedroom furniture is ordered from a company that makes very sturdy, beautiful pieces. They will also assemble it upon arrival. It will be here after the bedding, unfortunately, but it is on the schedule, Mr. Grumpy Pants —I mean, Mr. Griffen."

His lip twitched. "The bathrooms?"

"Plumbers are coming tomorrow to begin installing the vanities, toilets, and shower fixtures. Not all items are here yet, but according to their schedule, everything should get here when they need it to keep going, if that makes sense. It will be like a game of Frogger with the work schedule and shipments. The soaker tubs are coming one piece at a time as they are produced. That's the only part that's iffy."

The clearing of his throat resembled a growl. His eyes were icy as he said, "Iffy?"

I bit my lip, looking down. "They take quite a while to

make in the factory—it's located in France. And an order of a hundred is quite the undertaking, even with the rush fee."

He raised his eyebrows at me. "Rush fee? Is that the first one you've had?"

"Apparently there are only two people immune to my obvious charm," I muttered, still wounded by the grumpy Frenchman on the phone. "Three if you count my ex."

Gage tapped off his finger. "The French, your ex, and..."

"You," I finished with a wry smile. "You are one tough nut to crack, Mr. G., but I will keep working at it."

With an exasperated shake of his head, he said, "We can't delay the opening for a soaker tub."

"We won't. I've already made a deal with the vanity supplier for their soaker tubs. If everything stays on schedule, we may need ten to twenty, and they've agreed to buy back our returns at a reduced price until we get the final product in." He started to speak, but I said, "They're still very nice and won't look out of place in the rooms. They're just not as fancy as the damn French tubs."

He shrugged off his suit jacket, methodically unbuttoning and rolling the sleeves on his white dress shirt. The action was hypnotic, distracting. So much so, I almost missed his next statement.

"You're doing a lot of talking about the bedrooms, but there are other parts of this hotel."

"Oh my god, I forgot the lobby," I deadpanned.

I swear his eye twitched.

I bit back a smile and said, "Many of the pieces are designed to match the bedroom items for a cohesive look.

The front desk and office materials will be brought in after the bedroom furniture has arrived."

For a long moment, he said nothing, until finally... "Seems like you've got everything covered."

I nodded, sinking into my desk chair. "Now if I could just get my own home figured out."

"What do you mean?" he asked, his question just as direct as his gaze.

I undid the clip in my hair and shook my fingers through the curls to relieve the headache that came on every time I thought of our new rental house.

"I got the keys to this place a couple weeks ago, but I can't even move in—and out of my parents' house—because I have no furniture for the kids to sleep on. Caleb would never let me hear the end of it if I had the kids on an air mattress for even a week."

The blond threads of his eyebrows drew together. "Why would they sleep on an air mattress? Don't they have beds?"

"At their dad's house. But those need to be there for when they visit, and I can't exactly take the beds from my parents' house." A spot on my temple ached, and I rubbed it. "I'll figure it out—we've done a lot of thrifting for the other furniture. It's just hard starting over, especially after Caleb kept such a tight leash on the finances for so long."

I'd done that oversharing thing again, but Gage looked at me like it was a nonissue. "Just use the points on your company card."

"What?" I asked. He was saying normal words, but they may as well have been gibberish.

"You've spent hundreds of thousands of dollars so far. If you shop at any big retailers, they should recognize the dollar value of the points. It may not be enough to install a French soaker tub, but it'll keep you and your kids off air mattresses. If not, I'll pay for the beds myself."

"You'd do that?"

He nodded curtly as if my surprise was uncalled for.

Most people talked about billionaires like they were evil mega minds, but when I saw Gage... I studied this man, all decked out in Armani suits, his hair always perfectly trimmed like he had a stylist hiding in the back office. His face so smoothly shaven I wanted to pet his chin. But underneath it all, he was one of the most generous people I'd ever met. He acted like it was no big deal to stock an office for my kids, to pay for furniture to keep them comfortable. For me to use more of his money, beyond the ample salary he was already paying me, to take care of my family.

He may have been two parts bear, but he was at least one part unicorn.

"Is that even legal?" I asked, trying to stem my emotions. "I've never used credit card bonuses before. I kind of thought it was Monopoly money."

"They're very real and handy to use. Everyone who has a company card is entitled to the rewards. As long as you're not charging the business directly and paying any associated taxes, it's completely fine." He got a thoughtful look. "I do have one stipulation though."

There was the catch. "What's that?"

"Make sure you get an easel for Andrew's room. That kid has some talent."

I needed to check the floor to make sure my heart

hadn't puddled there. "I'll tell him you said so."

Gage gave one of his rare smiles, and it practically made my heart stop in my chest. This time he wasn't smiling at my child. He was smiling at *me*.

"Good," he said.

But it was not good. Because my heart was running all over the place with ideas it shouldn't be having. Had I really not learned enough from a failed fifteen-year relationship that I'd go gaga over my boss?

And wasn't I the one judging Caleb and his secretary for hooking up?

I mean, sure, Gage was single, but he was still my boss. And I still needed this job to provide for my family. Even though I worked hard, I knew I wouldn't make this kind of money anywhere else. It was too much to lose. Too much to risk.

And the fact that I was working myself up over imaginary forbidden scenarios with a man who'd yet to express even a hint of romantic interest in me... I needed to get my head checked.

I excused myself from the conference room, saying I needed to measure something in the sweeping lobby entrance, but really, I just needed space for my brain to clear. It was hard in that room where I could smell his cologne. Watch his muscled forearms move under his rolled sleeves. See the track of his blue eyes over his computer screen. Hear the way he commanded the respect of his employees as he managed a company bigger than anything I'd ever known.

Gage left for a meeting about an hour later, and for the rest of the afternoon, I searched for lighting fixtures for the guest rooms and thought about what kind of furniture I might purchase for my first home, thanks to the generosity of Griffen Industries and the man who ran it.

My head felt a little clearer as I drove to pick up Levi from baseball practice. Until a call from my ex came through the car speaker.

"Hello?" I asked, attempting to keep the ice out of my voice. Some days his betrayal hit me harder than others. And right now, he was at the top of my shit list after missing four of Levi's games in a row.

"Tell the kids to get excited—the summer trip in Cabo is on!"

My eyebrows raised, and I had to work extra hard to pay attention to the road. "You're still taking them to Cabo?"

"Of course I am. Why would I change up our family tradition?"

I don't know, maybe because *we're not together anymore?* The thought of my kids spending a week in Mexico without me hurt just as much as the idea of being away from them for the first time in months.

"Are you sure you can handle that?" I asked instead. "Three kids is a lot, and you know Cora has been sleeping in bed with me for the last couple months... She might need a lot from you emotionally."

"They're my kids too, damn it," he snapped, all the joy gone from his voice. His mood swing took me off guard, and I bit my tongue to hold back my venom.

"I know they're your kids too," I said. "I just wish you would act like it when your son plays baseball on the weekends or when Cora and Andrew want to video chat during the work day."

"Look, I know I've been all mixed up, but I'm turning over a new leaf. I mean it."

God, I hoped he was telling the truth. "I'd like that... So Cabo?"

"My travel agent already bought the tickets."

I nodded slowly. "You're not going to cancel at the last minute? It would break their hearts."

"I need this vacation too," he said, wear showing in his tone.

"Okay, I'll let them know."

I wouldn't let them know. Not until I knew for damn sure he was actually going. Fourteen years of parenting had taught me that much at least.

With only a couple minutes left until I arrived at the practice fields, I took a few deep breaths to calm down and braced myself for Levi to be in a bad mood. Being the new guy in school and on the team wasn't easy, especially moving into town in January when your parents divorced. So I tried not to take it personally.

But when I pulled up to the parking lot by the practice field, Levi jogged my way, a grin on his face, his gym bag bouncing against his side. He pulled the door open and said, "Mom, you're never going to believe who was at practice today!"

"Who?" I asked.

"The coach for the Dallas Ropers and the shortstop!"

My jaw dropped. "That's your position!"

He nodded eagerly. "I guess they're starting some kind of outreach program at our high school and working with us to improve. My batting's already way better, and it's just been one day."

I was so happy I could cry. "That's amazing, Levi. I'm

so happy for you. I can't believe they decided to start it at Golden Valley and not somewhere closer to the stadium."

Levi shrugged. "They said they knew someone here."

12

GAGE

Mia and I sat in my office going over notes from the week and the schedule for next week. We'd done this every Friday for the three years that she'd worked with me—her idea—and it had quickly become a ritual that helped us stay productive and manage my schedule better.

She looked at her laptop, reading over her notes. "Dr. Fletcher is coming next week for your annual checkup. Your stylist will also be going through your wardrobe to remove out-of-season items and replenish anything that has been worn out. Do you have any requests?"

"Yeah, I need some new cowboy boots."

Mia raised her eyebrows. "Boots?" She knew I'd grown up on a ranch, but I think it still threw her since she'd never seen me in that arena.

"The Griffen sibling trail ride is coming up at the end of the summer. Want to be prepared."

Scribbling sounds filled the air as she jotted down that note.

"Your nutritionist is going to take your weight and lab

results and adjust the meal plan as needed. If you have any requests for certain meals, be sure to send them my way."

"Will do," I replied, taking a sip of the whiskey on my desk. Usually I didn't work and drink, but Friday afternoons called for it. Especially since it had taken all my self-control to stay strictly professional with Farrah when my mind—and other body parts—were begging me to take things further.

"You have a press conference next week to announce your partnership with Jason Romero on the West Texas factory build."

I poured myself another glass and topped off Mia's. I hated talking to the press, but it was a necessary evil.

"Our C-suite meeting is next week as well, and looking ahead, the quarterly board meeting is next month."

The liquid burned on the way down, and I nodded. "Got it."

She took a sip of her drink and said, "Anything else for me?"

"Can you share your calendar with me again? It's harder to coordinate while we're in different locations, and I don't want to interrupt you while you're busy if I can help it."

"Very thoughtful," she replied, tapping on her track pad. "Shared."

An email pinged on my open laptop, and I clicked through to make sure I had access. The screen appeared, her calendar mostly mirroring mine with a few differences. My eyes immediately flicked to the line showing the current time.

"You need to get ready for drinks and dancing with... Farrah," I said, my throat closing on her name.

"Can't wear a pantsuit to the bar." She grinned, lifting her glass. "Thanks for pregaming with me, boss man."

I rolled my eyes at her. "Don't call me that."

Standing, she said, "Okay, Mr. Grumpy Pants. I'll see you bright and early Monday morning."

"See you then," I replied, settling in to play a little catch-up while the office was quiet.

But my mind kept drifting back to Mia's calendar. The location for her meetup with Farrah was a bar I used to go to downtown when I was in college. It was rowdy, with a massive dance floor and a reputation for being a place to meet casual hookups.

I fucking hated the idea of Farrah going there and the guys that were sure to have their eyes, and maybe even their hands, all over her.

But that was none of my business. I was her boss, and what she did outside of business hours was none of my concern.

Except I couldn't convince my racing thoughts of that. So I picked up my phone and called the only single guy I knew who would be up for a dumbass idea like the one going through my mind.

"What's up?" he answered.

"Hey, do you want to go out tonight?"

I could hear Rhett's smile in his voice. "Thought you'd never ask."

I KNEW I'd made a mistake as soon as we got off the phone. And the feeling didn't go away. Not when I finished up my work at the office. Not when I drove back to my place to get dressed. And certainly not when Rhett showed up at my condo, the belt buckle from his last bull riding win glinting at his waist. But I still couldn't talk myself out of going to the bar.

He came inside, rubbing his hands together. "Should we head out, or do you have some of that fancy liquor here so we can pregame?"

I walked to my kitchen with a view of downtown Dallas. I could almost see into my office from here. Unlike at my office, I allowed myself a minute to enjoy the view I worked so hard for. It was no country meadow with black cattle dotting the hillside, but it was mine.

I opened a modern cabinet door, revealing my collection of high-end scotch, whiskey, tequila, and rum. "Pick your poison."

"You know I like whiskey," he said, leaning up against the bar-height counter. The pearl snaps of his shirt glinted against the spotless countertop.

I pulled out the whiskey decanter and poured a couple shots in glass tumblers for each of us. Rhett and I both took a sip, and as the liquid heated my throat, I said, "You know, I haven't been out to a dance hall in..." I shook my head. I couldn't remember. "Since Tyler got the job with Crenshaw?" We hadn't even gone out drinking for his bachelor party.

"Ten years and counting." Rhett took another sip, then swirled the amber liquid around his glass. "We can go out to eat, if you're too afraid."

I put the bottle back and pinned him with a look. "I am not afraid."

Another drink. "Coulda fooled me."

Shaking my head, I said, "Maybe I'm realizing it's just really fucking stupid to chase down an employee at a bar."

Rhett's eyebrows flew up his forehead. "Wait, what? I'm not here for a guys' night out?"

I glared at him. "Don't be a smart-ass."

He was definitely smirking like one. "So it's the mom, right? Liv told me she caught you watching her son's game on TV. I have to say, the whole digital creeping thing... not your best look."

Yeah, I was definitely regretting this. And we hadn't even left the house.

"Creeping on her at a bar would be worse," I said. "Talk me out of it."

Rhett drained the rest of his glass. "She doesn't own the bar. Who's to say you didn't just decide to go out like the single, thirty-six-year-old man you are? Hell, maybe I begged you to go out with me. You know I don't do well alone." He put his hands on my shoulders, steering me toward the private elevator door. "And of course I would want to go out with you and your fancy car service to drive me home. They don't have Uber out in the sticks. You're keeping me safe, after all."

We stepped onto the elevator, and I shook my head, wishing I'd had a lot more whiskey. "I'm going to regret this, aren't I?"

"The parts you can remember."

13

FARRAH

I crossed the parking lot in the only outfit I had that was remotely appropriate for drinks and dancing, but I still felt more like a dumpy mom of three than a woman about to hit the town with friends.

Even when I went out with the other moms from school in Austin, we didn't go to places like this, ones with packed parking lots and girls walking in with less clothing than one should ever wear on a cold March night.

But here I was in the only pair of skinny jeans I owned—and even these were more like leggings than denim with the amount of stretch required to fit my curvy frame. I paired them with a bright red V-neck shirt that hugged the girls then flared down past my hips.

The black booties I wore were old but trusty, and my hair was doing whatever it pleased with my curls down and free. A few spritzes of perfume made me feel more human.

One of the first things I'd spent money on after the divorce was a new perfume just for me. Caleb always bought me the same kind year after year, and I realized it hadn't been because he liked the scent—it was because he could buy multiple and if he came home smelling like another woman's perfume, it would match my own.

It was an act of rebellion to get something solely for myself. I decided if I ever dated, married again, I wouldn't let a man control things like my scent or hair color. He would have to like me for me and let me make my own decisions, whether it be about my appearance or my bank account.

At the front door, the bouncer didn't even bother checking my ID. That felt *great*. I couldn't believe there was a time in my twenties I was annoyed by suspicious servers or liquor store clerks.

Inside the bar, music echoed off the walls and pounded in my ears, drowning out some of my doubtful thoughts as I looked around for Mia. There was a massive wooden dance floor where couples twirled and spun to country music. Around the edges of the room, people mingled and drank, and then farther back, there was an area with pool tables and booths.

That's where I found Mia, sipping a screwdriver, her drink of choice for whatever reason. Orange juice just gave me heartburn ever since I had kids. But across from her, I spotted a sweating glass with what looked like my favorite—a margarita on the rocks. Salt on the rim.

"Hey, girl!" I said, relieved to see someone familiar.

She got up from the booth, giving me a hug. "Hot, hot, hot, Farrah!"

"You look amazing too!" I gushed, loving the way she filled out her jeans tucked into pointed-toe cowboy boots with worn light brown leather. She had on an off-the-shoulder black top that contrasted her light skin and blond hair perfectly. "How have you kept the men away?"

"Just told them I was waiting on a sexy mama." She winked at me, then sat, angling her mouth over her straw for a sip. "Gosh, it's so good to be out with you again."

I nodded like I agreed. Mostly, I felt awkward, even though I loved hanging out with Mia. "Everyone here looks younger than me," I muttered.

"You're thirty-four, not fifty," she said. "Besides, if you're old, I'm old. And I'm not old."

I shook my head at her. "Having kids makes you old. I feel like these bags under my eyes have been here for years."

"You know you could try Botox," she said. "I have a great girl who could fit you in."

Shaking my head, I replied, "Something about putting poison under my skin doesn't feel right. Besides, I have you to help me feel young."

She grinned as she tucked straight blond hair behind her ear. "So how are you liking working with Gage? I feel like we've been so busy we've hardly talked."

I bit my lip, worried whatever I said would give away just how much I liked working with him. "He's... intense."

Mia nodded.

"But fair."

She nodded again.

"I know I've heard you tell me about him, but I just didn't realize how much it all was until I met him myself."

"He's like that. But he really is the best boss I've ever had. He's even let me take on more and more—it's like I'm not just an assistant; I'm learning to grow in the company when the time comes."

"That's amazing. I always knew you'd be running the world someday." Looking down at my drink and trying to act casual, I said, "Has there ever been anything... more between you two?"

Mia laughed like I'd told her the best joke of the century. "Good one."

My eyebrows drew together. She had to know this man was sex on a stick. "Why is that so funny?"

She adjusted her bra strap before replying. "Okay, I'll admit, I had a little work crush on him at first, but Gage is very professional. He didn't even let me call him by his first name until I'd been working there for a year. And you know how I'm putting in fifty, sixty-hour weeks? He's *always* working after I leave, working when I arrive. Business is his life, and even though his discipline is admirable, a guy being chained to his desk is not sexy. I'd never want to be that woman he showers with gifts and never sees."

A painful, embarrassing twinge hit my heart. Mia was on point with all her logic. And shouldn't I know better? I'd just divorced a cheater who couldn't be dragged away from his work. Why was I fantasizing about someone who would never have time for me, much less my children? And why was I getting so far ahead of myself as to include my children in my romantic daydreams?

"Plus," Mia said, "the whole boss, secretary thing? So cliché. That's for losers like Caleb, not me and Gage."

I laughed, trying to get this heavy feeling out of my chest. I hated focusing on the hard things—I just wanted to smile and appreciate the good parts about life. "Speaking of cliché, I'm a single mom of three who hasn't had a night out in forever. Thank you for inviting me."

"Of course." She grinned. "I thought it would be good for you to dance, maybe get your flirt on with someone who sees you for what you are."

"And what is that?" I asked. Because looking around this club, I hardly expected any man to notice me at all. Most of the women were at least ten years younger than me and way cuter.

"Trust me. Men love a mature woman with curves. We know what we want out of life, we're experienced in bed, and we have plenty to keep their hands full." She winked to my blush. "We're the total package. And besides, do you really want Caleb to be the last man who made you come?"

Damn it, she was right. I needed to get out there, to erase Caleb from my body if nothing else. I downed the rest of my margarita, the sour, sweet liquid tingling on my tongue, and then followed Mia out of the booth, toward the dance floor.

Caleb and I went dancing once or twice in college, but it had never been our thing. Or rather, his thing. He didn't like dancing, so we found other ways to spend time. But I did miss being spun around a dance floor by a man who knew how to lead.

As we wound through the crowded space, I swore I saw Gage near the bar, but as soon as I did a double take, he was gone. Crazy, I told myself, considering Gage would never go to a place like this. He probably went to exclusive clubs that took status and money to even get past the velvet rope, much less through the doors.

A guy who looked ten years younger than Mia and me came and said to Mia, "You're the prettiest thing I've seen in here all night." He had strawberry-blond hair under his ball cap and freckles on his tanned cheeks. Standing several inches taller than both of us, he was nearing six feet and filled out his jeans like nobody's business. I just couldn't help but think he could only be ten years older than Levi. If that.

Mia got a flirty smile on her face, the kind guys always went gaga for, even back in college. "Me?" She put her hand over her chest, his eyes following.

He nodded, holding out his hand. "I'd like to show you off on the dance floor. Make all my friends jealous."

Mia glanced to me, a pout on her lips. "I'd love to, but I'm here with my friend and I don't want to leave her all alone over here. Maybe if one of your friends..."

She barely had the words out of her mouth before the kid had one of his friends coming over. This guy was stockier and a little shorter, but he had a nice enough smile. I absentmindedly wondered how much his parents had spent on braces.

"Can I have this dance?" he asked me. At least his voice wasn't cracking with puberty.

Even though everything in me was thinking how weird this was, I nodded, because Mia was right. I needed to get back out there, stop acting like a woman in mourning. Caleb had moved on before our marriage was even over.

The guy in front of me took my hand, his just slightly larger than mine, and led me to the dance floor. He draped one arm over my shoulder and took my other hand. "Dance often?" he asked.

"Not at all. In fact, it's a good thing you're wearing boots."

With a chuckle, he said, "That's okay, 'slong as you know how to follow directions."

There was heat to his words, and all I could do was laugh awkwardly.

He mistook my laughter for encouragement and pressed his body a little closer to mine. Moved his hand a little lower down my hip.

Man, I did not envy single girls these days.

And then I remembered I was one of them.

Single, at thirty-four years old with three kids. Some of my friends from high school had just started having babies.

"What's your name, darlin'?" he asked, eyes traveling from mine to my lips.

"I'm Farrah, and I have three kids," I blurted.

He froze, and I nearly toppled over. But then he stepped back and raised his hands. "I'm not looking for anything complicated, lady." He turned and walked away, leaving me in the middle of the dance floor, couples spinning around me.

My cheeks quickly heated as shame filled my gut. I knew I was awkward, but I wasn't even worth sticking it out for one dance?

Then I remembered I wasn't worth staying faithful to.

Not to Caleb. Not to this kid who, according to Mia, should think I'm the full package.

Tears pricked at my eyes, and I willed my feet to move, to get me out of there and take me home.

Then I heard a familiar voice say, "May I have this dance?"

14

GAGE

Rhett had to hold me back when that fucking kid put his hands on Farrah, slid his fingers down her back like he was trying to touch the perfect swell of her ass without her noticing.

But my vision went red when he left her standing there in the middle of the dance floor, looking completely lost and alone. I had half a mind to teach that loser a painful lesson on how to treat a woman, especially one as golden as Farrah.

Instead, my feet carried me to her, knowing I would do whatever it took to take the devastated look off her face.

"May I have this dance?" I asked, praying to God she said yes.

Her brown eyes widened, and her perfect lips parted, covered in this shade of plum lipstick that made me think thoughts I should not be having about an employee.

"M-Mr. Griffen?" she asked, her voice barely audible over the twangy music playing through the speakers.

"Tonight, you can call me Gage," I said, taking her hand and spinning her to the music. Her brunette curls flew around her face, catching all the colors from the DJ's lights, and when she fell into my arms, her eyes were bright, her cheeks flushed.

The song changed, and while the dancers around us shuffled to find new partners, I led her in a two-step. I was a little rusty, but my muscle memory took over well enough. Her soft body molded against mine, making it hard to keep my mind on the steps, on her eyes, looking up at me.

"I still can't believe you're here," she said, a hint of wonder in her voice.

"I can't believe I am either," I admitted.

Her eyes were full of questions, so I spun her, giving her a view of the spot where I left Rhett. "See that guy over there? Brown hair, hazel eyes, kinda looks like he's in on a fun secret?"

I watched her brown eyes track the people over my shoulder and then steady. "I see him." Her face fell. "Is that your boyfr—"

"Brother," I finished. Although she had seemed disappointed for a moment... "I haven't been out in forever, and he's practically a professional party boy."

Her laugh warmed the solid hunk of ice in my chest that had formed watching her dance with that childish asshole. "I haven't been out dancing since the last time Mia dragged me out. Maybe four years ago when I came to visit for my thirtieth birthday?"

"That long?" I still didn't understand why the hell her husband hadn't taken her out and shown her off every goddamned night. Farrah was clearly the most eye-catching woman here. She had curves for days and wore this stunning red shirt that drew the eye. Pair that with her contagious smile and... the woman was a knockout.

"Caleb wasn't much for dancing." She frowned. I hated that name on her tongue just as much as I despised her frown. Farrah's lips were made for smiling, and I shouldn't think of what else. "But you seem to be a natural, Gage," she said. "Where did you learn to dance like this?"

My first name sounded so fucking good when she said it. "Lots of practice," I replied, spinning her away from me and then behind my back and to my chest again.

She giggled as I pulled her back to my chest. "Definitely a natural. And are those cowboy boots I see on your feet? I thought you only owned fancy Italian leather shoes."

"There's a lot I don't show in the office," I admitted. *Like how much I want to test the softness of your pillowy lips. Or that I wonder how much of your breasts would spill over my hands.*

I knew the whiskey and the dance floor had helped my thoughts to go astray, but I've been so fucking careful in the office. It was like all these thoughts were a raging river against the crumbling dam of my self-control.

"Thank you, by the way," she said, smiling up at me, and I worried she was about to think I was only dancing with her to make her feel better. Instead, she added, "Levi was over the moon about the head coach of the Ropers and their shortstop coming to his practice."

I gazed over her shoulder, fighting to keep my face even. "Prove it was me." I hadn't done it for recognition, but the way she was smiling at me... next time I'd ask Coach Henson to bring the whole damn team.

"You have at least five books in your office of the team's history." Her fingers softly grazed the back of my neck. "And the team randomly decides to use their free time at a fairly privileged suburban high school?"

I stayed silent.

"It really did mean a lot to Levi and me."

I looked into her eyes, wide and innocent. Like she genuinely believed I was a good guy instead of a demanding boss. How could she live with her heart so open, expecting the best of people? After everything she'd been through? "Levi has a lot of potential. I'd hate to see it go to waste."

"I know! I keep telling him that, but... Wait. How do you know he has potential?" She studied me. "You've never seen him play. He could be awful for all you know."

I steeled myself, knowing I didn't want to lie to her. "I got curious and watched the live stream of the game Saturday. Coach is a dumbass to keep him on the bench so much."

"Exactly!" Farrah agreed emphatically. "How's he supposed to get better in the games without practice? It's not the same as after school drills."

I nodded. "You know, I could..." I shook my head. It wasn't my place.

"What?" she asked.

I let out a breath, knowing I was dancing on the line I should be avoiding. "I could practice with him on a week-end, if your ex isn't helping him out."

She blinked quickly as the music slowed to a close. "Wow, Gage that's..."

Mia came up to us, her blond hair looking windswept, despite being indoors. "Gage, I didn't expect to see you here! Did I forget something at work?" There was something behind her tone. Maybe skepticism.

Which was warranted because her calendar was the only reason I was here. But then I remembered who came with me and said, "My brother wanted to go out. Can we get you two a drink?"

Farrah and Mia exchanged glances before Mia got a salty grin. "Okay, but you're buying, boss man."

I snorted. As if I'd consider letting them pay. "Come sit."

Within fifteen minutes, Rhett and Mia had the four of us doing a round of tequila shots and then they were on the dance floor, leaving Farrah and me at the table, buzzing, and completely alone.

This was a recipe for disaster. A mess even Shantel's expertise in human resources couldn't clean up.

Farrah looked up at me, her cheeks flushed from the alcohol, the heat. "I don't drink that often and, um... I think I'm drunk."

I laughed, the expression coming so easily with her. "You've had a margarita and two tequila shots and you're drunk?"

"Hey, I—" Her lips parted, and then she sent me a steely smile. "You've been watching me, haven't you?"

"Me? I—"

She put her hand on my arm, sending heat jolting all over my skin. "Don't lie to me. That's what my ex always did, and I know you're better than that."

Her words, blurred and made more honest by the liquor, did strange things to my chest, my stomach.

So instead of lying, I stayed silent, telling the truth by omission.

She sat back, distractingly folding her arms over her chest. "You're hard to work with, you know that?"

"I know I require a lot from my people."

She shook her head slightly, reaching for her purse. "That's not why." She slipped the strap over her shoulder and then tilted her head with a small smile. "I'll see you Monday, Mr. Griffen."

15

FARRAH

I woke up the next morning with a text from Mia.

Mia: Did you have a good time last night?

My stomach filled with a flurry of butterfly wings. Or maybe it was a hornet's nest spinning around in there. Because dancing with Gage had made ignoring my crush that much more difficult, even with the excellent points Mia brought up against being attracted to him.

Farrah: I did. It was weird seeing Gage there, right?

Mia: I know. I thought that man lived at the office.

Farrah: LOL me too.

Mia: He's a good dancer. I'll have to make him spin me around at the next charity gala we go to for work.

Farrah: Definitely. What's on deck this weekend?

Mia: Taking Mom and Dad grocery shopping, and then meal prepping with them for the week. You?

Farrah: Levi's game, moving to the new place, it'll be busy.

Mia: Are you sure I can't help?

Farrah: I think it would get too crowded with my parents being there. Come by when we're all set up though, okay?

Mia: I'll bring the wine. :)

Farrah: One of the many reasons we're friends.

I put my phone aside, closing my eyes and going over the night before. I could have sworn there was more to Gage's stare than that of a boss and employee. But maybe I was so desperate from being abandoned in the middle of the dance floor that I'd imagined it.

Either way, we could *not* pursue a relationship. Not with him as my boss and me as his newly divorced employee with three children to think of. So, I threw myself into the busyness of the weekend to distract myself from the yearning building in the pit of my stomach.

I took Levi to his game, dealt with Caleb not showing up—again—and then prepared us to move out of my parents' house.

The for-rent sign had been removed from our new home, and a stack of boxes sat on the front porch—deliveries from online stores bringing new furniture, beds in a box, sheets, curtains, all the fixings of a home, thanks to the generosity of one Gage Griffen.

But these people in the van with me? They would make this home complete regardless of the furnishings inside. For how difficult the divorce and moving had been, starting a new life, a new job as a single mom... I couldn't imagine doing it without these precious humans at my side.

My parents parked beside me in the driveway and we all got out, checking out the place. I handed Andrew my key ring, with the key to the house separated. "Do you want to unlock the door for the first time we stay here all night?"

He nodded excitedly, taking the keys and running to the front door as Levi trailed behind. My dad came beside me, putting his arm around my shoulders, and Mom held Cora's hand as we walked to the front door after Andrew.

"Looks like you have a lot of stuff ready," Dad said, gesturing to all the boxes from my orders.

"We'll be busy for sure," I agreed, thankful they offered to help me put together furniture and get us all set up. Between thrifting trips over the last couple weeks and the orders I made with credit card points, we had just about everything we would need.

Andrew unlocked the door, and we stepped inside. Mom gushed over the granite countertops, and Dad pointed out loose doorknobs and a slanted cabinet door he wanted to fix.

We all came together in the empty living room, and I took it in, knowing this home was a blank page, a new beginning.

Levi pushed up the sleeves of his long-sleeve T-shirt. "Can I set up the TV and Xbox?"

"It's not a home without videogames, is it?" I teased. "You can as long as you build the TV stand too."

With a determined look, he walked to the front door to get the packages he needed off the porch.

Andrew said, "Can I hang up the art I made?"

"Let me get you the tacky." I had a little container of sticky tacky in my purse so we wouldn't leave tons of holes in the walls. Once I handed the case to Andrew, he was off with his stack of drawings to paper our house.

Once upon a time, I might have tried to make the house more aesthetic, but it was important for Andrew to make his mark. To feel like he had a real hand in making this home ours.

Mom said, "Cora Bug, why don't you help me in the kitchen. I'll let you use the scissors on the shelf liner."

Cora clapped her hands together, a little too excitedly. "Can I cut it like a heart?"

Mom chuckled. "We'll see." She patted Cora's back as they walked toward the kitchen, Mom carrying a tub of cleaning supplies.

Then it was just Dad, Levi, and me in the living room. "Where should we start?" Dad asked.

For the next several hours, we whipped through putting bedroom furniture together. It reminded me of working with him in the coffee shop, moving in tandem. He used to have me in charge of cleaning the shop, wiping down all the tables and chairs in between the rush of customers. We'd get to the store early and handle shipments, even get the place ready to open together. I almost forgot how much I liked being on his team.

If I thought about it, Gage was a lot like Dad. My dad was bubblier and more conversational, but he had high standards too and worked harder than anyone else. He expected his employees to be the best, just like Gage.

We started with Cora's bed, a beautiful floor-level twin-size frame that came up, resembling a house. I'd splurged a little on a floral wreath I wrapped around the frame. Mom had washed the sheets for me the day before, so we started airing out the mattress, leaving the pink folded sheets and blankets on top.

Dad pointed at Andrew's art on the wall. "Kid's got some talent."

I stared at the drawing, my eyes stinging. He'd colored in her favorite colors—pink and purple—PRINCESS CORA'S ROOM with a crown atop her name. "He's so thoughtful."

Dad put his arm around me and tilted his head against mine. "I know it's been a rough few months, but I'm so proud of you, kid. Look what you've done with your back against the wall."

I wiped at my eyes. "My back's never against the wall with you and Mom on my side."

He smiled, wiping at his eyes too. "Let's get your bed set up. You'll need somewhere to sleep tonight too."

MY BODY ACHED when I went into work on Monday from the strain of the weekend, but the nerves flitting around my stomach were so much more distracting than sore muscles.

Seeing Gage at the bar, hearing the truths he admitted to me... I shut down that train of thought. Even if he wasn't my boss. Even if I wasn't newly divorced... Gage would still be a busy billionaire CEO. And I'd been burned by love before. I wouldn't settle, not again. Especially not when I knew I could make it on my own.

If I ever got married again, it would be to a man who would put me first. And when he asked me to marry him, it wouldn't be because I was pregnant or out of a feeling of obligation—it would be for love.

I brought two cortados into the office, giving one to

Gage as a friendly gesture. We'd left things kind of weird Friday night, and I didn't want work to be awkward.

His blue eyes darted over me, like he was trying to guess how I'd react after our interaction Friday night. It hit me that I was beginning to sense the moods of this unreadable man, and a strange, pleased feeling warmed my chest.

The ball was in my court now, so I simply smiled and passed him a coffee. "Did you have a nice weekend?"

He nodded. "Rhett stayed over, and we grabbed some things Tyler and Hen needed from the city."

"Tyler and Hen?" I asked. The names sounded familiar. "Do they work for you?"

He chuckled. "Tyler would never. He's my brother, and Henrietta is his wife. They just renovated a schoolhouse and turned it into senior apartments in my hometown."

"Cottonwood Falls, right?"

His dark blond eyebrow quirked. "How did you know that?"

My cheeks flushed. "A friend told me."

"Which friend?"

"Google," I mumbled.

His lips twitched. "You Googled me?"

"Why does it sound dirty when you say it?" I giggled, and he even chuckled. I loved how easily I could make this bear of a man laugh now.

"I had to look up the man I'd be working with," I said finally.

He leaned forward, his elbows resting on the desk, and I found myself leaning closer as well. His voice was a low hum as he asked, "What did you find out?"

I tapped the pad of my pointer finger, loving making him wait. "I found out you don't have an Online Encyclopedia page."

"I made them take it down." I waited for him to laugh, but he didn't.

"Wait, what?"

He shrugged, his large shoulders moving under his perfectly tailored suit jacket. "I didn't like my family's information being on one of the most highly trafficked pages of the internet. It might surprise you, but there are people out there who don't like me."

"They don't like you? No way," I teased.

He rewarded me with an exasperated smile.

I bit my lip. "Gage Griffen, thirty-six years old. Born December twelfth. Star baseball player in high school but didn't play in college despite being recruited by multiple Division 1 universities. Attended technical college to study diesel mechanics, then went to a four-year university and majored in economics with a minor in entrepreneurship. Interned with a Big Four accounting firm, then worked with a well-known realtor in the Dallas area before getting his own real estate license and growing his own business from nothing like no one has ever seen before."

As I spoke, his expression grew serious, curious.

"But that didn't cover any of the things I came to know when working for you," I continued.

His hands stilled on his coffee cup, strong, big, belying the gentle nature he had underneath the exterior.

"I learned you're fair, kind, generous, thoughtful... principled."

As if the spell had broken, he pulled back, sitting up straight. "I believe you have a meeting."

The whiplash of his change in mood left me confused. "What? I..."

As if on cue, a knock sounded on the door. Cliff entered the room with Pascale Wilson, the best photographer in Dallas.

Next to Cliff's very practical appearance and demeanor, Pascale looked that much more artistic. He had chin-length, dark brown hair that almost covered his wide, honey-brown eyes. His wide lips toyed the line between full and thin, and a short mustache covered his top lip. He wore an oversized navy-blue sweater with jeans rolled at the hems and worn leather ankle boots.

Cool was the only word I could think of for him, and I couldn't wait to get started on this project.

"Pascale, it's so nice to meet you. I'm Farrah." I shook his hand, noticing the tattoos at his knuckles that inked their way up his arm, under the sleeves of his sweater.

"Likewise," he replied. His free hand adjusted the distressed leather messenger bag over his shoulder.

"I thought I could walk you around the hotel and then show you my design plans so you can get a feel for the sort of imagery that might enhance a project like this."

"Let's do it," he said.

Cliff waved goodbye and walked back to the front of the hotel to resume his post. Feeling Gage's eyes on my back, I led Pascale out of the conference room and through the spacious lobby, detailing my plans for the furniture, from the warm, sturdy furnishings to the modern check-in desk and dining area.

Then we walked down the hallway toward the elevator. "I'll show you my favorite room."

"Looking forward to it," he replied, his voice low and soothing.

We rode up the elevator, his cologne something woodsy, but not quite pine, reminding me of winter and Christmas tree shopping. At the tenth floor, we got out, walking down the hallway with beautiful hardwood floors. We'd paid extra for underlayment that would muffle all noise underfoot so we wouldn't have to install carpet, and aesthetically, it was more than worth it.

"We're adding textured art pieces on the walls to absorb some sound," I said, "but other than that, your photos will be the star of the show." We reached the end of the hallway with a window overlooking the pool below and then the city sprawling around us. Since the room key system hadn't been activated yet, I opened the door and stepped into the suite.

With the floors and trim installed, the space was full of promise. I walked to the bedroom, separated by a sliding door. "There will be a king bed against this wall with a textured, taupe-colored wall treatment. I'm thinking we could do an abstract painting over the bed, then photos on each side as well as on this wall."

We stepped into the living area, where the fold-out sofa would be. "There's going to be a sixty-inch flat screen on this wall, but there's room over here for maybe a trio of photographs, and then something over the entry table here would round out the suites. There are six suites on each level, and then the rest are double and single rooms."

He began reaching into his bag, but I said, "And don't worry, I have all this written down, along with dimensions we'll need."

Lowering the leather flap, he said, "You're very organized, Farrah."

My cheeks heated at the compliment. I wasn't very used to them. "Thank you."

We walked through a single and double room, and then we went back downstairs, taking the second conference room so we wouldn't interrupt Gage's work. My computer was already there waiting for me, and I offered Pascale a chair while I opened my laptop to my design software and walked him through the pieces that would be coming in.

His eyes were alight with a million thoughts, and he said, "You have incredible taste. I honestly thought this hotel might be stuffy."

I laughed. "I will take that as a huge compliment. Your work is so cool. I'm curious what type of looks you think might go with a place like this. I'd like for it to have meaning without being the cheesy 'pictures of Dallas' type photos."

He leaned his elbows on the table, his chin in his hands. "Is there a feel you're hoping the guests will experience?"

"Savor," I said instantly. "Vacations with family can be so rare, and you're usually rushing around, making sure everyone's okay, knowing you've forgotten something, but you're not sure what. I'm hoping everything about this space will encourage people to savor their moments, because as a mom of three, I know they're gone all too soon."

"Your husband and children are so lucky to have you," he said, making my cheeks heat.

"My ex-husband and teenager might disagree with

you, but there's still hope for the younger two," I joked. "So what do you think? Is that concept doable with the photos or is it too abstract?"

He scrubbed his hand over his chin. "This might seem a little crazy, but I have an idea."

16

GAGE

When Farrah and Pascale walked into the office, the first thing I noticed was that his eyes lingered on her a little too long.

The second? He was standing far too close to her.

I didn't like it one fucking bit.

I curled my hands in my lap underneath the table, trying to chill the fuck out because I was thinking like some hormone crazed frat bro, not the founder and CEO of a billion-dollar company. So I took a breath and focused on Farrah. She had a bright smile playing along her full lips and excitement danced in her eyes as she said, "We have a great idea for photos, but it's a little unique, so I wanted to run it by you first."

Pascale and Farrah exchanged an eager glance. And I knew I had it bad when I got jealous of a simple look.

"No need," I said. *Just get this guy out of my office,* I didn't say.

"Really?" Farrah asked. "You don't even want to give it the Gage Griffen stamp of approval?"

"I hired you because you're the expert, and I trust your taste implicitly."

"But you always wanted to see the inspiration boards..." she said, seeming confused.

"Why are you arguing with me?" My voice was clipped. "Do you want me, someone with limited artistic experience, to micromanage the photography process?"

She shook her head, making her curls move over her shoulder. I wish I could push them back, reveal more of the olive skin at her neck. "But it does involve you."

But I simply shook my head, locking eyes with her. "I trust you."

Those beautiful brown orbs of hers practically gleamed, even under fluorescent lights. She smiled, clapping her hands happily together, and turned to Pascale. "You can pencil us in! We'll see you and your team May thirtieth at two o'clock." Pascale waved goodbye and left the conference room, and it felt suddenly smaller with only Farrah and me inside.

"Mr. Griffen, should Pascale speak with you or your stylist about your wardrobe? Or should we work with his preferred stylist?"

My eyebrows raised. "My wardrobe?"

She nodded. "For the photo shoot."

"You're taking pictures of me?"

"Actually... Pascale's taking pictures of us."

For the next hour, she explained the concept of the photo shoot, along with a preliminary shot list. She and Pascale had the idea to photograph fun and special moments a family might experience during their stay. From ordering multiple plates of room service to kicking off their shoes when they first got to the room.

She had volunteered her children and parents for the shoot. The only thing missing was a man.

"Are you sure we shouldn't hire a model?" I asked. "We could find someone better looking than me and far more experienced."

Farrah's lips twitched like she was holding something back. "Pascale doesn't work with models. Only with 'real' people. I almost couldn't convince him that it was okay to have you in the shoot."

"Why not?" I argued, already defensive for some reason. "I'm a 'real' person."

Her laugh made something in my stomach stir. "You don't have to use finger quotes around 'real' person. I know you're real; you're just not really with me."

I let out a heavy sigh. "Eight hours a day, I'm with you. That should be enough." Words I needed to take to heart.

"According to Pascale, it'll do. So I hope you don't mind sacrificing one of your Sundays, but I really think the final product will be worth it."

Spending a Sunday with Farrah, at work, should have felt like a sacrifice to my limited free time, but it didn't. In fact, how much I looked forward to it scared the shit out of me. And I didn't get scared. Not when I was a kid facing a thousand-pound animal, not as an adult making life-altering business decisions. But Farrah changed everything.

So I simply said, "Have Mia put it on my calendar, and I'll be there."

As if she worried I'd back out, she got out her phone and called Mia immediately. "Hey, girl, hey! So I need you to block off Gage's calendar for May thirtieth for a photo shoot at The Retreat..." My lips twitched as I listened to Farrah describe the shoot and Mia's obvious surprise at my involvement. "Okay, I'll see you for lunch tomorrow!"

I raised my eyebrows. "You and Mia are having lunch tomorrow?"

Farrah nodded, sitting across the table from me. "And our moms. Should be a good time."

"Your moms? Why?"

Seeming confused by the question, she said, "Because we like spending time together?"

I let out a sound between a chuckle and a grunt, focusing back on my computer. I needed to go over these meeting minutes from accounting and make sure I had a comprehensive brief prepared for the next C-suite meeting.

Just a few taps on my keyboard later, and I could feel Farrah staring at me.

I glanced up, looking into her half-suspicious, half-incredulous gaze. "Yes?"

"What was that sound for?" she asked, arms folded over her voluptuous chest.

Don't be a pervert.

"Nothing," I replied lightly.

She waited for my answer, and I let out a sigh. "I just find people who get along with their parents an anomaly on par with... Sasquatch. Kids who aren't sticky. A holiday party without discussion of politics."

Her eyes widened. "So basically, you're telling me, a mom of three, that all of my children will hate me one day, so I should just give up now?"

"Don't be absurd. You have three—odds are one will

need money from time to time." I got the distinct feeling I was lucky to be sitting across the table because she would have wacked me by now.

"But believing in that is like hoping for Sasquatch, right?" she said.

I tapped my nose, looking back down at my screen.

But then my computer shut, and I glared back up at the curly-haired culprit. "What was that for?"

"Don't take your mommy issues out on me, Griffen."

I smirked at her annoyed look, which only made her more annoyed.

She shook her head. "You were with your brother Friday... Do neither of you talk to your parents?"

"Rhett does. I prefer to keep my distance." There was a dull ache in my chest, the one that had been there since I was twenty years old and hearing my dad say the harshest words he'd ever used on me.

"Why's that?" she asked.

I glanced up into her questioning brown eyes, and even though I thought she was genuinely curious and wouldn't use it against me, I kept it vague. "My parents and I didn't see eye to eye."

"What do you mean?" she asked. "I feel like you're speaking in riddles."

I let out a breath, wishing I had some bourbon to ease the knot forming in the back of my neck. I rubbed it out, saying, "My parents have a small ranch outside of Cottonwood Falls, but it wasn't big enough to support multiple families, even though all of us kids would have loved to work on it when we grew up. When I went to college, I worked for a property manager who gave me lots of ideas on how to grow a business, but my dad didn't like them. He thought I was 'money hungry' and heading down the wrong path. So I told him he was playing small and hurting his family. There may have been a few more words exchanged. We haven't talked since then, except for Tyler's wedding."

Farrah's lips parted, about to speak, but I held up my hand.

"Before you tell me it's a petty argument, that's not even what I'm upset about anymore."

"Oh," she said gently. "Really?"

It actually felt good to get it off my chest to someone outside of my family. "It's the fact that the man who raised me, my hero, the one I always looked up to... He was supposed to see the best in me but thought so poorly of me to say those things, and even still, he loves his pride more than he loves me. More than a decade with no apology because I wanted our ranch to be a true family operation." I felt exposed, laying it all out there for Farrah to see. I expected her to tell me I was being childish, to let it go, but instead, she reached across the table, laying her hand over mine.

My skin heated under hers, and I stared at the connection, the way her skin looked against mine, light olive to my red undertones.

When I met her eyes, she tilted her head. "He should have reached out, Gage." She bit her lip. "The thought of spending a week without my kids during their summer break is killing me. I can't imagine a decade of no contact."

I turned my hand, holding hers in my palm—I'd only allow myself a moment. A little bit of this comfort she gave so freely. "That's because you're a good mom." I cleared the emotion from my throat. "Your kids are lucky to have you."

"Thank you." Her smile faltered before she withdrew her hand from mine, and suddenly, the heat from her touch was replaced with a chill. "I'll let you get back to work. Sorry for interrupting."

I pinned her with a stare, because she didn't need to apologize. No, I was the one blurring this line.

17

FARRAH

Meeting up with Mia, her mom, Joanne, and my mom felt like going back to my happy place. Even though Mia and I both grew up in Dallas, we only met our freshman year of college, and over the years, we'd all become family. Mom and Joanne even met up sometimes without us, even though Joanne was quite a bit older.

After catching up, it only took a few minutes for Mia to tell them about my disastrous night. My cheeks quickly flushed as Mom and Joanne, gave me sympathetic looks.

Joanne reached out, patting my arm across the table. "He didn't know what he was missing out on."

"I'm pretty sure he did, which is why he chose to miss out," I muttered, shaking my head. "I feel like I should walk around with a big sign on my forehead that says divorced single mom, not looking for anything serious."

Joanne chuckled, but Mia said, "You know, you can do that on most dating apps now. They let you spell out if you have kids, if you want more, even if you're looking for a casual hookup or something more serious. Could be worth trying out."

Mom nodded excitedly. "That could be a great way to get out there and meet new people."

"I don't know about dating sites," I admitted. "Something feels gross about a guy being able to turn me down without even knowing me."

My mom nodded sympathetically. "I'm glad online dating wasn't around in my day. So much pressure."

Mia shrugged. "It can be fun."

I teased, "It could also be the start to, like, every murder documentary. 'Single woman went out with attractive but secretly psychopathic man.'"

Mom and Joanne laughed with me, but Mia barely cracked a smile.

"Look at all these people here," she said, gesturing around us. "Your next Prince Charming could be sitting in this very restaurant, but you'll never know if you don't put yourself out there."

"True," Joanne agreed. "I was almost forty when I met Mia's dad, and I thought I'd never settle down."

"Maybe I should just be alone," I said, lying to myself because my mind had been running wild with thoughts about Gage. "The last guy just took me for granted and broke my heart. Why would I want to go through that again?"

Mom reached across the table, holding my hand. "You're so young still, Farrah. You got pregnant young, got married young, and you and I both know, both knew, Caleb wasn't *the one*. If Levi never would have come along..."

I shook my head because I couldn't let myself go

there. "I never want to blame my children for being in a bad marriage. I loved Levi and wanted him to have a family unit." And even with my mind going crazy about a romantic future with Gage, a man I could never be with, I had to be practical. "Besides, you always hear these horror stories about single moms dating. About these guys who prey on mothers with young children. I would never forgive myself if..."

Joanne frowned at me, her wrinkles deepening. Even though she was eighty and Mia was almost thirty-six, they looked so much alike with that frown and their pale-colored hair. "You'd never let that happen, Farrah."

My mom and Mia nodded in agreement.

"And these other moms did?" I asked. "And how can you start a relationship with a man when you're seeing him as a potential threat?"

Mom set her drink down, tucking a stray curl behind her ear. "Don't you do the same with babysitters, though? You get them background checked, you interview them, you check their references. You spend time with them and your child to make sure you don't sense any red flags. Seems like you could do the same with a man."

Mia got a wicked grin. "I would happily call references for you."

I rolled my eyes at both of them. "Why are you so desperate to get me dating again anyway? Can't we enjoy the single girl life together?" I asked Mia.

She tossed her blond hair over her shoulder. "Of course we can. As long as you're actually enjoying it. Do you really want your whole life to be work and kids?"

Mom nodded. "You've only had us watch the kids overnight one time since you've been back. You need to take more time to yourself. Let Dad and me help with the kids."

"Hear, hear," Mia agreed.

I bit my lip. "I don't want them to feel like I'm pawning them off. Caleb just started watching Levi's games online, not even in person... and I'm terrified he'll back out of the Cabo trip."

Mom said, "Caleb took so much of your past. Don't let him take your future too."

"I'll think about it," I finally said so we could change subjects. Mia, Joanne, and Mom started talking about a speaker Mia had organized to come to her parents' senior center over the weekend, and my focus drifted to dating.

Or rather, the act that accompanied dating. And the man I'd like to do it with.

Hey, a girl could dream.

FOR THE NEXT FEW WEEKS, I was so focused on work and kids that there wasn't time for much else. I had to finish lining up details for the rooms to be ready, and in the meantime, I had to fully furnish two suites and part of the lobby for the photo shoot.

Since everything was coming in on different timelines, it meant I had to search for some of the items individually. I spent lots of my workdays scouring estates sales, auctions, and thrift or antique stores for decorative items.

It would be a big part of marketing for the hotel as well, telling people that many of the items were sourced secondhand to reduce waste.

I missed seeing Gage sit across from me as often when

I was out shopping, missed watching the expressions he made when a vendor call went over ten minutes. But being away from him made me enjoy the time I did get with him that much more.

I swore, his jawline got more chiseled every day. His cologne smelled better each time I set foot in the room. And that smile he reserved just for me? It turned me to putty every time.

The space from him was good too, because I needed to remember all the reasons I couldn't be with my boss. He was a billionaire bachelor with all the resources and women in the world available to him. A plus-sized single mom of three wasn't exactly the best offer out there. Best not to get my hopes up for something he wouldn't be interested in.

Besides, he would never fit into my world. He worked a lot. And he didn't speak with his parents. I couldn't imagine being with another man who didn't value family the same way I did.

So, I worked myself to the bone and had the bedrooms ready just in time for the photo shoot.

With the bed beautifully made with white sheets and the room lit with found lamps, I sent Gage a text.

Farrah: Come to room 1212.

I bit my lip, glancing around the room and imagining what Gage would think when he first saw it. My favorite part had to be the bathroom. The French company had already sent three bathtubs, and this one was the first to be installed. The tub looked like it had been carved from Calcutta marble and rested on sleek gray tile. Matched with the modern vanity's gold fixtures, and green tiles for the backsplash and shower, it was pure perfection.

I could picture myself in here, soaking in the tub, drinking a glass of wine and reading a book while letting all the stress of the day just roll away.

The opening door sounded, and I turned away from the bathroom to see Gage coming into the room. He had his blazer off, the sleeves of his white shirt rolled to reveal a smattering of light brown hair on his strong forearms. I had an urge to put my finger above his tie knot and pull down, unbutton the top few buttons of his shirt to show his tanned chest.

Maybe I should start an online dating profile, just to get this man off my mind. Remind myself what dating at my age would realistically look like, because this man? He was a fantasy.

Gage's eyebrows lifted as he examined the room, taking in every detail from the four-person table set with place mats, silverware, and ceramic plates to the lounge area with a stylish fold-out couch and a coffee table stacked with large, hardcover photo books about Texas.

I bit my lip, my breath stalling until I heard his thoughts.

"Farrah, it's..." He scrubbed his hand over the light stubble on his cheek. "It's everything I hoped it would be." He crossed the room, taking in the bathroom with an incredulous smile.

My heart skipped happily, my lips tugging into a smile I'd never be able to wipe off my face.

"This is incredible," he said. "And you had these rooms ready in just a few months? How?"

I grinned back at him. "My boss is a hard-ass... but he also believed in me."

His smile lit the entire room. "You deserve to celebrate." He glanced at his watch. "If you have a sitter tonight, you should go out."

"I do have a sitter, luckily. I'm going to stay and put some finishing touches on the other suite, and then we'll be ready for our photo shoot."

"It's still a month away," he said.

I nodded, running my hand over the warm wood of the television stand. "I wanted to have it ready early in case you requested changes."

His finger brushed the underside of my chin, tipping my gaze up to meet his. "Don't change a thing."

I swallowed, his touch short-circuiting my brain. "I won't."

He stepped back as if composing himself and shook his head. "You're incredible, Farrah."

And those words shot straight to my heart, giving me a feeling both terrifying and exciting.

Butterflies.

18

FARRAH

I was on such a high that the second he left the room, I did a happy dance, falling back onto the king-sized bed with a smile on my face.

I'd worked myself crazy trying to make this place everything Gage hoped it would be, and even though the rooms weren't all completed, I felt a sense of satisfaction. A sense of purpose. Like this was all possible, because I'd made it possible.

I'd done it.

I'd left a cheating husband. Provided for three children. Found us a home that we enjoyed immensely. And now?

I needed to celebrate, like Gage said, and I knew just the way.

I kicked off my heels and walked to the bathroom, turning on the bathtub spigot. I slid my fingertips under the stream, feeling the water change temperature. When it heated, I plugged the tub and watched the water pool in the bottom for a moment before going to the minibar stand.

For aesthetic purposes, I'd gotten an expensive bottle of champagne and put it in the ice canister. It wasn't cold, but that didn't matter.

I unwrapped the gold foil over the cork and then pushed with my thumbs until a loud pop sounded and vapor fizzed from the top. Taking one of the champagne flutes, I poured myself a tall glass and took a sip, the sweet, bubbly liquid sliding over my tongue.

Damn, did it feel good to know I'd be taking a bath in a nice bathroom that didn't have any children's toys or dirty underwear littering the floor, drinking a glass of wine, completely undisturbed without the risk of anyone walking in on me or asking me a favor.

Walking back to the bathroom, I used one hand to unzip the side of my black pencil skirt, then I shimmied out of it. I set my glass down on the vanity countertop, then took off my silk shirt, the beige camisole I wore underneath, and the heavy-duty bra I'd had since Andrew was a baby. Then I hooked a thumb through my cotton thong and pulled it down too, doing a spin.

God, it was incredible just to have a moment naked.

Until I caught a glance of myself in the mirror. My breasts and stomach kept moving even after I stopped spinning, jiggling to a halt. The mirror lighting was meant to cast a flattering glow, but the mom bod wasn't the most attractive thing in the world. At least by traditional beauty standards.

Caleb's voice echoed in my mind the night I told him I was leaving. *Good luck finding a guy who wants a fat single mom with three kids.*

I hoped like hell the kids hadn't heard him say that.

He hadn't said anything untrue. I was fat. I knew it, and I wasn't ashamed of it—most of the time. My body brought life into the world, it housed my brain, my heart. It hugged my children and carried me throughout the day and was a sign of *life*. I never talked badly about myself in front of my kids, because there was nothing to feel bad about. Not for me and not for them.

But looking at myself in the mirror, silvery stretchmarks running up the loose skin of my stomach, dimpled thighs pressing together, arms the furthest thing from toned... it was hard not to feel self-conscious. Especially because Caleb cheated on me with thin women. And even though I couldn't find anything online about Gage's love life, I assumed he had model types throwing themselves at him daily.

So, I would stick to my fantasies. And I had plenty to go off of, the way Gage's finger had seared my skin with a simple brush under my chin.

I could only imagine what those capable hands would do to me in the bedroom, the way he would handle me. I wanted to see his blue eyes heat the way they had in the club, just for a moment. And I wanted his straight white teeth to graze my nipples. His breath to land hot on my chest. His tongue to...

I crossed my legs, stunned at how easily the thought of Gage Griffen aroused me.

I should *not* be feeling this way about my boss. But it was only a fantasy. So I retrieved my small bullet vibrator from my purse. (Hey, when you're a mom, you have to take time when you can.) Withdrawing it from the velvet pouch, I took in the sleek pink design and then washed it in the sink with soap and water.

Seeing that the tub was almost full, I took my toy and glass of champagne and stepped in.

The hot water stung my toes and ankles, and I slowly eased myself into the water until I was fully sitting down.

This tub had to be the best design decision I'd ever made. It was wide and deep, allowing me to sink all the way to my neck, fully submerged without my stomach or chest peeking out like it did in the bathtub at home.

I rested my champagne on the bath tray and pressed the button on my vibrator. The whirring sound seemed to echo off all the marble tile, but bringing it under the water muted the noise.

I leaned back against the tub, resting my head on the pillow hanging on the edge. Closing my eyes, I brought the toy to my slit, running it over my folds before swirling it around my sensitive spot and letting out a moan. Fuck, it felt good just to savor this moment.

The image of Gage, inches away from me, came to mind. I imagined how he would tower over me, how he'd slide his fingertips up my thigh, tease me through my underwear before tugging them aside.

He'd smirk when he saw how wet I was, unsurprised by my reaction to him.

"Gage," I breathed. His name came so naturally to my lips.

I sank beneath the surface, holding my breath and closing my eyes. Under the water, it was completely silent, sans the steady beat of my heart and the sound of my vibrator. With all other sensations blocked out, the feel of the vibrations became that much more intense.

I writhed my hips, imagined Gage sliding a thick finger inside me. Two. Stretching me in preparation for his girth.

The thought of his penis had me drawing my head above water and gasping for air.

And that's when I saw Gage Griffen standing in the doorway.

19

GAGE

I came back to the room to look at it again, revel in the work Farrah had done, but I found something else entirely.

Fuck me.

Farrah was a goddamn vision in the water, her cheeks pink, nipples hard and full of color. I imagined what those hard buds would taste like in my mouth. She had a smattering of hair over her pussy, and her brown curly hair flared around her in the tub. This is how she's meant to be—natural and sexy as fuck.

She writhed under the water, and my jaw went slack. As good as she was making herself feel right now, I wanted to make her feel even better. But I couldn't lay a hand on her. Not until we came to an agreement about what it would mean—or rather, wouldn't mean.

The water broke as she came up, water pouring down her face and chest in rivulets, and she gasped my name, moaning.

She was touching herself.

Thinking about me.

My cock went from hard to stony, straining against my slacks, and it was all I could do not to get it out and fuck her like I've been dreaming about ever since she walked into my office for that interview.

Instead, I gripped the door frame, knowing if I didn't hold myself back, I'd do exactly that.

Her eyes widened, full of shock. She scrambled, looking for a towel, but it was all the way on the rack, and I wasn't moving.

"Keep going," I ordered, holding on to the door frame for dear life.

"Bu-but..."

I shook my head, my gaze narrowing in on her. Those lips. "Make yourself feel good. You've earned it."

Her eyes were wide and nervous, shy, darting from me to the towel. But then she slid her hand back down, moving her toy to her sensitive spot. Her gaze drifted away from mine, but I said, "Look at me, Farrah."

Her lips parted and her hips jerked, making water splash against the sides of the tub.

"That's right," I said, my erection clearly visible, but I didn't move to relieve myself. Not with her just starting. "Touch your tits."

She reached up, tweaking a full nipple. Her moan had her eyes rolling back.

"Eyes. On. Me," I ordered. I knew I'd be playing this moment over in my head every night, and I wanted to know I turned her on as much as I could without even lifting a finger.

Her brown eyes collided with mine, her jaw clenched as she spun faster circles around her clit and then rhythmically pinched her other nipple.

"You're so fucking hot," I breathed, clenching the trim harder than ever. "Those full tits, your curves... the way your eyes lock on me as you touch yourself."

She whimpered at my words.

"You've wanted this for a long time," I said. It wasn't a question. Because I knew how fucking bad I've wanted her, and judging by the way she'd said my name earlier, the feeling was mutual. It took everything in me not to pull her from the water and bring her to the bed, wrap my fist around her wet curls and fuck her from behind until she was screaming my name.

"I have," she moaned, her voice guttural.

"You know how badly I've wanted to bury my cock in your tits?" I asked, my voice silky in contrast to the rippling water. "Fuck you until my cum glistens all over your chest. And then have you walk around the office without cleaning it off so everyone knows you're mine?"

She moaned, then cried out, her hips bucking so hard water splashed over the tall sides of the bathtub.

The vibrating sound underwater stopped, but her breathing took longer to slow. "That was... what..."

I bit my lip, allowing myself one last look. "I'll be in the hallway when you're ready to talk."

Using every bit of self-control I had left, I exited the suite, going into the empty hallway. When I was by myself, I reached into my pants, angling my dick down to get it more comfortable because this erection wasn't going away. Not until I took care of it.

But now that I was out of the room, away from her intoxicating body, I dropped my head against the cool white wall. What a fucking idiot I was. I'd come upstairs to look at the room, and I should have left the second I realized it was occupied.

But seeing her like that in the tub had sent my mind haywire. I deserved a medal for keeping my hands off her. But if I had my way, I wouldn't be holding back for long. I'd been trying to quell my thirst for her, like it was even possible. But the only way to truly rid myself of this need was to sate it, and I knew how.

I just hoped she'd agree.

I got out my phone, pulling up the document I needed, and then waited for her. A few minutes later, when Farrah came out of the room, her cheeks were still pink, her wild curls pulled into a wet twist atop her head. She wore her clothes from earlier, but their messy, wet appearance just turned me on more.

"Gage, I am so sorry," she began, but I pressed a finger to her full lips, and she shuddered, closing her eyes.

The feel of her under my finger sent a jolt of desire straight to my dick, so hard it hurt.

"Don't apologize," I said, dropping my hand. "In fact, I should be the one apologizing. The second I saw you, I should have stepped away."

She didn't argue.

"But I... couldn't," I breathed. "If I'm being honest, I've been attracted to you since you walked in for that interview, and holding myself back has been torture."

She folded her arms across her chest, drawing my attention to her beautiful breasts. I wished yet again they were uncovered. That I could feel them. Taste them.

"So what do we do?" she asked, her voice breathy. "Because I've had some not-so-holy thoughts about you. But I can't afford to lose this job."

My jaw clenched. I knew what I was about to ask was crazy, and a woman like Farrah would never agree, but I had to try, because missing a chance to make her feel as good as I wanted her to... I'd regret it my whole damn life.

"We can walk away and pretend this never happened," I said. "I'll resume officing at my main office, giving you the space you need, and we won't have any meetings unless Mia is present."

Her face wore every one of her emotions. She was upset, angry, maybe even a little confused. "Or?"

"Or, you agree to a non-disclosure agreement explicitly stating that this will not affect your work and that we'll keep our arrangement private, and I'll pleasure you exactly the way you deserve."

She caught her bottom lip between her teeth, looking into my eyes.

"The choice is yours," I said, but I couldn't help myself from trying to persuade her. "Look, I'm too busy to give you the kind of relationship you deserve. But you just got divorced, and I'm guessing you haven't found a way to get back out there."

She looked away, confirming my suspicions. My hopes.

Because if I knew of another man touching her, I'd want to throttle him, even though I didn't have the right.

"It's not exclusive and it's not a relationship," I said, "but it's a way to get what we need without making things complicated in our personal lives or at work."

A resolute expression crossed her face, and for a second, I deeply feared that I was going to lose my interior designer and get slapped with a lawsuit, or at least get slapped across the face like I deserved. Maybe both.

Instead, she said, "Where do I sign?"

20

FARRAH

I had completely lost my mind. I knew I had.

But I slid my fingertip across his phone anyway, giving full consent to sexual activities between the two of us, agreeing to keep this relationship between us to myself. The consent to have sex could be revoked at any time, but my silence? That was under Gage's control.

And the freedom of knowing that whatever happened between us was only between us?

It was heady and made me want to do things I'd never done before.

With Caleb, I initiated in the bedroom sometimes and so did he, but over time, sex became more and more infrequent. Even if I dressed up or waxed, it seemed like it was just a method for him to come, not a chance to pleasure me.

But the way Gage looked at me in the bathtub, the way he spoke to me? I knew he was doing exactly what he wanted. And out of all the women he could have... he wanted me.

Whether it was for a night or a year, it didn't matter. Because he was right: a relationship wouldn't work between us. But that didn't stop the desire coursing through my body every time he got near.

So I watched him sign the document himself, and then he said, "There's a copy in your personal email inbox."

We stared at each other for a moment, the realization of what we'd just done, what we were about to do, dawning over us.

"How long do you have your sitter?" he asked.

I glanced at the watch on my wrist. "One second." Tapping at the screen, I called my mom's phone number. After a few rings, she answered, her voice filling the hallway.

"Hi, honey, how's work going?"

Glancing up into Gage's eyes, I said, "Something came up and I'm going to have to work later tonight than I thought... Do you mind keeping the kids overnight?"

"Of course, honey. I'll pack a bag for them and keep them at my house if it's okay."

"That's totally fine," I said. "I'll pick Levi up at ten to bring him to his game."

"Perfect, I'll let the kids say goodnight while I have you on the line," Mom said.

My cheeks heated for some reason. The woman Gage saw in the bathtub and the woman saying goodnight to her children felt like two different people. But then my sweet kids came on the line.

"Mommy, are you working late like Daddy always did?" Cora asked.

In fact, I was working late exactly like Daddy did. But

I wasn't abandoning my family. No, I was no longer abandoning myself and my own desires. So I said, "I hope you have a great night with Grammy, and I'll see you in the morning, okay, sweetie?"

"Okay, but can I bring my hot cocoa bomb with me to Grammy's?"

"Sure thing. Make sure to bring one for the boys too."

"I will," Cora said.

Gage slid his hands over my hips, pulling me closer to him. His hard erection pressed against my front, making it hard to breathe.

"Mommy?" Andrew said.

"Yeah?" I breathed, fighting to keep my voice normal.

"Can I bring my Lite Brite?"

"If Grammy says it's okay."

"Yes!" Andrew said, his voice already growing distant from the phone.

I heard Mom ask Levi if he wanted to say goodnight, but he turned her down. "Well, Levi is being a teenage boy. I'll see you in the morning. Have fun and work hard!"

"I will," I promised. And as soon as the call ended, Gage's mouth covered mine.

His lips dominated my own, and his tongue demanded my attention, warring desperately with mine like we're putting months of sexual tension into this one embrace.

He pressed me up against the wall, our bodies close together, and I pulled at the hem of his shirt, taking it out of his pants and running my hands over the hard planes of his stomach. He moaned and pressed his lips against my cheek, turning my head to get access to my neck, my shoulder, my collarbone.

It all felt so good, my core was already clenching, begging for more than what a pocket-sized vibrator could offer me.

"I want to be closer to you," I said, and he reached over to yank the door open, bringing me inside and kissing me as we walked. As we did a dance between shucking clothes and moving to the bedroom, he kissed me more, lighting my body on fire with every brush of his lips.

I was so caught up in the moment, I didn't realize I was down to my bra and underwear until we stood in front of the bed.

And I nearly panicked.

All the self-doubt from the affair came flooding back. Questions flew through my mind—was I not good enough in bed, was I not attractive enough? Each one hurt more than the last, but I shook it off.

Gage couldn't fake the way he looked at me in the bathtub nor the fire in his eyes now. This man was turned on by *me*—the thick erection straining against his underwear was confirmation enough.

I reached for his underwear, beginning to tug them down, but he stepped back. "You first, Farrah."

The authority in his voice told me it would be useless to argue. So I reached behind my back, unsnapping my bra and freeing my tender breasts. They hung heavy on my chest, and he stepped closer, lifting and kneading them in his large hands before sucking a nipple into his mouth.

That alone had me moaning, but then his tongue

flicked vigorously over the nub, leaving me whimpering, practically begging for more.

He led me back toward the bed until my legs hit the edge, and he lowered me onto the plush surface, kissing down my stomach, nipping my extra flesh along the way, and then he dragged my panties down my legs, leaving me exposed before him.

"You're so fucking beautiful, Farrah," he said.

It was like he hadn't said my name enough, and I loved the way it sounded on his tongue.

I sat up in the bed, reaching for his underwear. CHRISTIAN DIOR J'ADIOR repeated along the waistband, and I pulled them down, revealing the hottest dick I'd ever seen in my life.

It stood thick and straight, veins protruding along the perfectly pink length down to his heavy, manscaped sack.

"Open your mouth," he ordered, but I was already on my way, running my tongue over the broad head of his dick.

He shuddered against my touch, his cock bobbing, and I wrapped my fist around it, barely able to connect my fingers he was so big.

I teased his shaft farther into my mouth, sucking and swirling my tongue around the smooth skin as I worked the base with my hand. The salty flavor of his precum filled my mouth.

"Fuck, Farrah. Your mouth."

His words spurred me on, and I took him deeper, as far as I could until I gagged against his length.

"That sound is so fucking hot."

I pulled him farther in my mouth, pulling gently on his balls.

With Caleb, this was always a chore, and he would take my head, shoving me against his hairy balls. Not Gage.

I was in charge, and though his hands were tangled in my hair, he was telling me what a goddess I was. "You're such a good fucking girl, taking my cock like you were made for it."

I moaned against his dick, and he said, "You like being told you're a good girl? Then be good for me."

He pulled his cock out of my mouth and ordered, "Hands and knees, on the bed."

It took me less than two seconds to get where he wanted me.

"You're fast. But I'm not in a rush."

He drew his hand underneath me and easily found my clit, rubbing it first with his palm and then with his two fingers. With his other hand, he drew his fingers along my slit, then plunged in two digits, just like my fantasy.

"Gage," I moaned, and he twisted his hand, curling his fingers into my G-spot. "Fuuck," I let out.

He danced his fingers inside me in tandem with the pressure on my clit, pushing me closer and closer to the edge. My hips bucked, trying to catch more friction, and he said, "That's it, baby, come for me."

As if his voice were magic, I tipped over the edge into pure fucking bliss, my orgasm shaking my entire body as I cried out his name.

He slid his fingers out of me, and then I heard the tear of foil. He slid the condom over his length, his fingers still glistening with my pleasure.

I lay on my back, legs spread, and he hooked his arms

under my knees, his muscular frame contrasting the soft curves of my legs.

"God, you look so good, spread out for me like this," he moaned, teasing his tip against my sensitive entrance. He took his time, easing himself in inch by inch, giving me time to adjust to his size.

He filled me in a way I'd never been filled, and I rose to meet him, wanting to savor every moment of this experience. Fucking the man I thought was untouchable and knowing this entire time he had been wanting to do the same thing to me.

"You're so beautiful," he said, eyes on mine.

I palmed his cheek, watched the planes of his face, like they were hand carved by the gods. His strong pecs and defined abs flexing with each thrust. "You're hot as hell, Gage Griffen."

He smirked, blue eyes right on mine. "We work well together," he agreed, pumping hard into me, making his heavy sack hit my ass.

The sound of slapping skin, the feel of him driving into me, it was all-consuming. I reached up, clinging to his forearms as he pounded into me over and over again until we were both crying out.

I felt the heat of his load through the condom. And the realization hit me. I'd just had sex with my billionaire boss. Really good sex.

"Fuck," I breathed, rolling over into the comfy pillows and soft bedding. "I feel like I need a cigarette after that."

"I didn't know you smoked," he replied, throwing his condom in the trash and lying next to me.

"I don't." I laughed.

21

GAGE

I'm fucked.

That's what I was thinking as I lay next to Farrah in this king-sized hotel bed.

She got cold and cuddled under the blanket, then smiled up at me and said, "I'm not sure how this works for you, but I like to cuddle afterward."

And how could I say no to those beautiful brown eyes and that tentative smile?

I couldn't. Besides, she'd just given me the best sex of my life. The last thing I wanted to do was leave.

I slid under the thick duvet and lay next to her, feeling her soft skin against mine, aside from the slight prickles of her leg hair.

"I'm sorry," she said. "If I'd known we would be doing this, I would have shaved..."

"How could you have known?" I asked. I hadn't been expecting this any more than she had.

I extended my arm for her, and she rested her head on my shoulder like it was the most natural thing in the world. And in a way, it was. I felt comfortable in a way I'd never been before, but also, electricity hummed through my veins, making me feel more alive than I had in a long time.

Usually, after I slept with a woman, I had a driver take her home and I left the hotel. I never hooked up at my place, and they never stayed the night.

But with Farrah? I was having a hard time even thinking about getting out of bed.

She moved to her side, looking up at me as she ran her hand over my chest. "Is it normally that good for you?"

I chuckled at her question. I knew how to have good sex, but the way this woman had cast her spell over me and made me incapable of walking away? "It's never been like that."

"Me neither," she whispered.

We were silent for a moment, and I scanned her face for a hint of regret. It would have killed me to see it, but I would have known this was a one-time thing. I'd change office spaces immediately, just to make her more comfortable.

But instead, there was only curiosity in her eyes. "I feel like there's so much I don't know about you."

"We haven't worked together that long, and I'm not... open like you."

"Is that a slut joke?"

I snorted, a mix of confusion and laughter in an unattractive sound that would probably have her running for the hills. "No, sunshine, it's not a 'slut joke.'"

"Just checking."

I brushed her slightly damp hair back and kissed her

temple. "You make it seem so easy; you have people laughing and loving you within minutes of meeting you. I have to be more professional. You never know who you can trust when you get to my level. Most people only want what they can get from me."

"Most?"

I nodded. "My siblings. I can trust them. I know because they know all my secrets and they haven't buried me yet."

She giggled. "I'd pay good money to hear those secrets."

"You wouldn't have to pay me. Two minutes with your mouth on my cock and you'd hear them all."

She smiled, lowering herself under the blanket. Laughing, I hauled her back up to my chest where she was lying earlier.

"Tell me about your siblings," she said. "I was an only child, and I always wished I'd had a little brother or sister."

"They're a pain... but I wouldn't trade them for anything." I looked down at her, trying to see what angle she was coming from. Why she wanted to get to know me when most women slept with me for the pride of knowing they bagged a billionaire. But her brown eyes were so wide and trusting I knew I could trust her too.

"I have two brothers and a sister—first Tyler, then Rhett, then Liv. Olivia, really, but no one ever calls her that. Rhett's the one you met at the club, and he's pure trouble. He's a great bull rider, and women love him just about as much as he loves them."

A smile played along her lips, and in the dimming

light coming through the sheer curtains, it was almost magical, this bubble we were in.

"Tyler has always been the responsible one. He takes things so seriously, and he was working his way up to take over a major construction company here in Dallas until..." I let out a sigh, realizing how eerily similar our stories were. Except I could never give up my business, my livelihood, for a woman.

"Until what?" Farrah prompted.

"Until he got married and started senior living apartments."

I kissed her forehead again, soothing myself as much as her.

"And Liv..." I wracked my brain, trying to think of a way to describe her. "She's the woman behind my one and only tattoo."

She raised her eyebrows, curious. "I didn't see it on your ass."

"Ha ha," I said, smiling so naturally around her.

"Where is it?" Farrah asked. "Can I see?"

I lifted my arm that wasn't under her head so she could see the black ink inside my bicep. She ran her fingertip over the design. "A windmill? For the farm you grew up on?"

"Kind of," I said. "It's our sibling tattoo, like a promise that we'll always be there for each other."

"Why a windmill?" she asked.

And despite never admitting this out loud, I found myself telling her. "Because no matter how much a windmill moves, it doesn't go anywhere. And I needed to know that someone would be there for me."

I lowered my arm, waiting for Farrah to tell me I was

weak, needing a tattoo to remind me I had people who truly cared about me in my life. Instead, she reached up and pressed her lips against my jaw. "I can see why you love them so much."

I nodded. "I'd do anything for them." Anything except apologize to my dad for his mistakes.

Her fingers drew circles around my pecs, the relaxed ridges of my abs. "You try so hard to be grumpy, but you're too good of a guy to be that convincing."

A growl passed my lips, and I lifted myself, bracketing her head with my arms as I hovered over her. "You think I'm a good guy?"

I expected her eyes to widen, to look away. Instead, she did something completely infuriating.

She smiled.

"You know what I'm thinking?" she asked.

I shook my head, desperate to know. For how expressive her face was, she confused me so.

"I'm thinking how fun it would be to order takeout and eat everything on the menu off of you."

A defeated grin spread across my face. "I believe that can be arranged."

NO ONE WAS MORE surprised than me when I woke up the next morning with Farrah's head on my shoulder. Her curls tickled my skin as she snored softly, the sound sweet and relaxing. Resting like this, her lips were still smiling slightly, like that permanently good disposition of hers wasn't even affected by sleep.

This melting, full feeling spread throughout my chest

as I looked at her. She would be the end of me, making me both comfortable and uncomfortable to the point of confusion.

Her eyes slowly blinked open, and her lips turned into a lazy smile. "Are you staring at me?"

"Maybe a little bit," I admitted.

She rolled her head closer to me and planted a sleepy kiss on my lips, all ease and grace and happiness that took me completely off guard.

Hooking up with someone wasn't supposed to feel like this. Satisfying? Sure. Enjoyable? Definitely. But... *contented*? That was a new feeling for me.

And even though the night had been fun, full of more sex and laughter than I ever expected, I knew I needed to walk away or I'd never be able to leave. Not just this room, but this woman.

"I should probably go so I can get a workout in," I said.

Her lips twitched at the corners like she was about to frown, but then she smiled and nodded. "I should probably get going too. I need to get ready for Levi's game."

We left the bed, the covers all rippled from the night before, and I walked back into the bathroom, stepping into the glass shower. The water pressure coming from the gold showerhead felt amazing, and part of me wanted to drag Farrah in here and go another round.

But I held back, my feet itching to run away from here and from this feeling that I had.

I just wasn't the kind of guy to catch feelings. I focused on work and family and doing what needed to be done. Not on relationships. Definitely not with one of my employees, and *definitely* not with a recently divorced mom of three.

Part of me hoped she was already gone so I wouldn't get another urge to pull her into the bed with me and beg her to stay the day.

But when I couldn't stall anymore, I got out of the shower, wrapping a towel around my waist. Exiting the bathroom, I found Farrah fully dressed, her purse hooked on her elbow. Her shoulders looked tight, almost bunched around her ears as she said, "So... I'll see you at work on Monday?"

Her worry, the wrongness of it, was enough to make me cross the room to face her. Her eyes drifted from my pecs to my stomach and towel, then back again.

I put my hands on her cheeks, so warm and soft.

Just like I feared, this overwhelming urge to stay filled me, but I needed to do something more. Reassure her. And maybe myself. "This doesn't have to change anything at work. You and I are still on the same team, getting this hotel up and running."

"And after hours?" she asked, her voice a purr.

My stomach clenched, and I drew my thumb along her bottom lip, blood already flowing to my dick despite the night's activities. "After hours... we play."

She lifted her purse to her shoulder, making my hands fall, and a sunrise smile spread on her lips. "I'd like that, Gage."

I loved the sound of my name on her lips, no matter the context. I could feel myself wanting to talk to her, make this conversation last by asking about Levi, if his dad would show or not. And that was when I knew I needed to distance myself and compartmentalize my life like I'd grown accustomed to doing.

So I simply nodded and said, "I'll see you next time."

"I'll see you next time." She lifted her fingers in a little wave and walked out of the room, her hips mocking me as they swayed back and forth.

I was already looking forward to 'next time' way too much.

22

FARRAH

As I walked out of the hotel in the morning, I realized Cliff stood guard by the hotel entrance.

Our eyes connected, and as he looked at me, and then to the parking lot where my van and Gage's Tesla were parked, understanding dawned.

My cheeks were hot, and all I could think to say was *I didn't know you worked Saturdays*.

"Filling in for the weekend crew," he said gruffly. This was just as awkward for him as it was for me.

"Oh, well, um... I'll see you Monday."

He nodded, looking down.

What he must have thought of me. I was so not prepared to be doing the walk of shame today, at my age, at my place of work.

All I wanted to do now was get into my minivan and drive away as I called Mia to tell her everything that had happened.

But then the NDA came to mind, and I realized I couldn't. The biggest, riskiest, most exciting and dangerous thing that I'd ever done, and I couldn't tell a single soul. In some ways, it made hooking up with Gage more exciting, like this little tryst between us was something only we shared. But also, it would be nice to tell Mia and maybe even my mom so they would stop encouraging me to get back out there.

Left to process the experience on my own, every detail played over again in my mind while I drove back to my house. How had my evening gone from taking a simple bath to an entire night of mind-blowingly hot sex with my billionaire boss?

I'd learned so much in the last twelve hours. Like his confidence was definitely merited. That he was a very generous lover but also that he had been attracted to me from the moment we met. A little bout of butterflies danced in my stomach.

Caleb had been wrong about no man wanting me. In my first interview with Gage, I had shared everything about me that Caleb thought other men would be repulsed by. My curves had been on full display. My children called, and I yelled at them. Hell, I even joked awkwardly, and I'm pretty sure my hands had been sweaty.

But he still found me attractive.

So if someone like Gage Griffen, who could have his pick of any woman, found me physically attractive and wanted to hook up, then someone amazing could fall for the entire package and want to build a life with me. Someday. When I was ready to trust again.

For now, I'd enjoy hot, commitment-free sex like nothing I'd ever expected to have in my thirties.

After taking a quick shower and grabbing Levi's gym

bag for his game, I got back in the car and went to my parents' house to pick everyone up.

The van had enough room that all the kids could ride in the back seat, and then Mom and Dad could sit up front and in the middle on the way to the game. As we drove, Andrew told me every single detail from a show that he had watched with my mom the night before. Cora complained that she had to wear a Golden Valley shirt over the top of her sequined dress.

And then Levi asked the question. "Is Dad coming today?"

I glanced in the rearview mirror, seeing my son's eyes looking back at me. He was trying to hide the hope there, but I could sense it.

"Have you called him?" I hedged. It wasn't fair that I always had to be the one to break the news. Even though we both knew it was really Caleb's fault, I was there to handle all the emotions Levi didn't want to admit.

Levi shook his head.

The silence coming from my parents was deafening, all of us screaming inside, *why couldn't Caleb be there for his kids?*

"If he doesn't come, I'm sure he has a good reason," I said, even though we both knew it was a bald-faced lie. There was no reason good enough to miss this many of your son's games, even if you were watching some online. March and April had gone by without him showing up once in person.

We pulled up to the baseball field, the parking lot still pretty sparse since we had to get there a bit early for Levi to warm up. Andrew and Cora went to play on the small playground by the fields, and my parents and I went to the bleachers.

Mom mumbled, "I have half a mind to drive to Austin and drag him up here myself, preferably by the ear."

"Me too," I agreed.

Dad shook his head, half disappointed, half confused. "He didn't seem to be this absent back in Austin."

"He wasn't," I agreed. "But that was when it took ten minutes to drive to the ball field instead of three hours." Caleb would usually do what I asked of him as long as he didn't have to work, but during business hours or times he was "working late"? He was nowhere to be found. Just like right now.

I clenched my jaw and angrily typed out a text to him.

Farrah: I hope you're getting here soon. Your son really wants you at his game.

I looked at my phone for a little bit, and he didn't reply. Of course.

Mom said, "Levi told me last night that he's starting at shortstop today."

My eyebrows rose. "No way! He didn't say anything like that to me. Are you serious?"

She nodded. "He said the coach has been trying out some new things in practice, and with the Ropers helping Levi, he's improved a lot. He even talked about doing some weights at the high school over the summer so he can get in better shape for next season."

My eyes prickled with emotion. At the beginning of the year, it felt like Levi had lost hope, but here he was, having goals, making plans, and a big part of that was thanks to Gage.

I made a mental note to have Levi write a thank you note to him after the game tonight.

The younger two kids played while Levi and his team warmed up, and when the team jogged out to the field, I saw that my mom was right. Levi was there with the rest of the starters. Full of pride and happiness, I jumped to my feet, cheering for my son.

On my right, my dad whistled and Mom clapped her hands together enthusiastically. "Go, Levi!" I yelled.

On my left, I heard a voice echo mine. "Go, Levi!"

I looked over, and for the first time in months, I saw my ex.

Caleb looked exactly like I remembered: tall, thick dark hair perfectly parted and styled. He wore a green T-shirt and dark-washed jeans, probably a pair I'd bought him, seeing as he could never shop for himself.

His green eyes bored into me, and I fought the urge to punch him in the face.

"What are you doing here?" I asked at the same time Cora yelled, "DADDY!"

She ran up two rows of bleacher seats and jumped into his arms.

He chuckled, hugging her back. "It's so good to see you, honey."

As if he couldn't have seen her this whole damn time.

Andrew raced up the bleachers behind her, hugging Caleb too, and Caleb made room for both of them, holding them tight.

Andrew said, "I didn't know you were coming, Dad!"

Of course you didn't know, I barely kept from saying out loud. *He never freaking showed.*

I knew I should have been happy he came, but I was

irate. Three and a half months without so much as a visit or an offer to meet halfway, and here he was, acting like he actually gave a shit.

Mom touched my arm. "Why don't we get something from the concession stand? Caleb, kids, do you want anything?"

"Nachos!" Cora said, settling in her dad's lap.

"Hot dog!" Andrew added, cuddling up next to Caleb on the bleachers, even though it was eighty degrees outside and humid.

"I'm good," Caleb said.

Mom put her hand on my shoulder, guiding me away from the bleachers. When we got out of earshot, she said, "You looked like you were about to murder him, and there were too many witnesses around for me to let that happen... even if I wanted you to."

I gave her a wry smile and then let out a sigh as we walked over the dirt path between bleachers to the concession stand. After getting hit by a foul ball, I made sure to keep a lookout every time I heard a bat make contact. "It's just hard to see him swoop in and be the hero when I'm the one handling everything. You know Cora threw a royal temper tantrum yesterday morning because we were already running late and the braid I put in her hair didn't look *just like Elsa's*? And Andrew's teacher called to tell me that he has no interest in doing his schoolwork. He just doodles. Never mind the fact that Levi barely has two words to rub together these days."

Mom said, "I believe all of that. Especially after all the struggles we had with your hair or talking too much in class. And you too had your teenage moments."

"Hey, I'm pretty sure I still have nightmares about getting my hair done before school."

Her chuckle loosened me up a little. "Kids are smarter than we think, and they know who's there for them at the end of the day."

We reached the snack shack and put in orders for the kids. Just before we were about to pay, I said, "Hey, can we get some Cracker Jacks, too?"

As the high school kid running the booth went to get our snacks, Mom gave me a curious look. "I thought you hated those?"

"I do. I just... know someone who might enjoy them."

Mom's jaw dropped open. "You met someone!" Her light brown eyes danced with excitement. "That's why you had to 'work late' last night, isn't it?"

Could blushing violate an NDA? Because this blush was definitely giving me away.

A knowing smile spread on my mother's lips. "I know, I'm your mom, you don't have to say anything." The kid came back with the snacks, and I held the nachos and Cracker Jacks while Mom took the drinks and popcorn. "I'm happy for you, though, getting back out there. You deserve to have a little fun," she said.

I completely agreed.

When we reached the stands, Dad scooted further from Caleb like he needed us to separate them, his arms folded over his chest. And that was saying something because my dad didn't make enemies.

Cora and Andrew were happy to have their food, and I settled in, leaving the kids between Caleb and me as I asked my dad, "What did I miss?"

Dad opened his mouth to answer, but Caleb said, "Levi missed a grounder."

Of course Caleb would only notice the negative. Dad added, "He caught a pop fly too."

A small smile tilted my lips. "Good."

We cheered for Levi through the first inning, and when he got up to bat, Caleb yelled loudly from the stands.

"GO, LEVI!"

Levi glanced our way on his walk to home plate, and when he saw Caleb there, his jaw fell open. He hid his smile as he walked to the plate, trying to act cool while adjusting his batting glove and then hitting his bat on the ground.

As he squared up for the pitch, I crossed my fingers in my lap. *Please hit it, Levi. Please hit it.*

"You don't need to be superstitious," Caleb said at the same time the ball flew over the plate.

Strike.

"You've got it, Levi!" I yelled, clapping my hands together. "You can do this!"

He squared up again, and I crossed my fingers on both hands this time. Cora did the same.

"Just like your mother," Caleb muttered. It was not a compliment.

Strike.

I glared at him over Cora's head.

Andrew clapped his hands together. "Go, Levi!"

I put my fingers in my mouth, whistling for him, and then crossed my fingers behind my back, hoping he could get this hit. Impressing Caleb mattered so much to him.

The pitcher reared back and sent a curve ball Levi's way. He swung again... and missed.

Strike three.

"I gotta go take a leak," Caleb said, getting up from the stands. When I shot him a look, he said, "What? It's not like I'm missing much."

If my children weren't with me, I would have said a lot of unsavory things to Caleb, but instead, I gritted my teeth together.

Cora patted my arm and said, "Maybe we should cross our toes next time too?"

A small laugh escaped my lips, and I hugged her tightly to my side, trying not to cry. "I think that's a *great* idea."

23

FARRAH

We waited by the stands while Levi went to the locker room to shower and change. Cora and Andrew took turns hanging on to Caleb's hands and flipping backward, giggling as they did.

People were arriving for the game after Levi's, but Levi's coach, Mr. Reynolds, approached us and said, "Hey, are you Levi's cheering section?"

Caleb nearly dropped Andrew in his haste to shake this man's hand. "Caleb Elkins, Levi's father."

Coach shook his hand, saying, "Haven't seen you at the games yet. Glad you could make it to this one!"

I was way too pleased at that comment, no matter how nicely it was delivered. "I'm Farrah, his mom, and these are my parents, Barry and Jenna."

Coach Reynolds pointed at Dad. "I knew you looked familiar. You run that coffee shop over on Maple."

Dad nodded, a shy smile on his face. "That's me."

Despite creating a local, family-run coffee shop that

consistently outsold the major chains, he managed to be one of the humblest people I knew.

"Love your coffee," Coach said.

"Thanks."

Tucking his clipboard under his arm, Coach said, "I just wanted to tell you how great it is to have Levi on the team. I know he's new to town and only a freshman, but he's a real hard worker. I know he gets down on himself when he doesn't perform the way he'd like, but just you tell him to be patient and keep working at it because I see a lot of potential in him, especially after the Ropers guys started working with him."

"Ropers?" Caleb asked. "Like the professional team?"

Coach Reynolds nodded, seeming confused. Caleb's cluelessness was a surprise to me too, since I knew Levi and Caleb talked on the phone at least once a week. "They've been helping out with practices this season," Coach explained.

Caleb said, "Oh, right. I guess I get confused talking about Ropers in Texas." He forced a laugh.

The coach chuckled and said he'd see us at the next game, and Caleb agreed amicably, but the second Coach walked away, he turned on me. "Why don't you tell me about the kids? Huh?"

Sensing the change in mood, my mom said, "Cora, Andrew, why don't we go play at the park while we wait for Levi?"

They easily followed her, but my dad lingered, like he was holding something back. I gave Dad a slight shake of my head, and he blew out a sigh before following Mom and the kids.

"Why didn't I hear about a *professional baseball team* helping at my kid's practice?" Caleb repeated.

"Maybe if you would call the kids more than once a week and actually act like you care, Levi would have told you."

"Are you kidding me? A text was all it would have taken."

Of course he was trying to pin this on me, just like always. "It's not my fault that you're not participating in their lives. You hardly ever answer my calls, and I leave the door open for you to visit every weekend."

"And do what?" he asked. "Stay at a hotel? I can't afford them. Especially with the child support I'm sending your way."

"We both know the child support is far less than the judge would have given," I said. "It just barely covers groceries for them with the way Levi eats. Besides, you always told me that I spent too much money. I'm surprised you're not rolling in cash now that I'm not there."

His jaw clenched, and he looked away from me. "You're the one who took my kids away."

"You're the one who treated our family like it was nothing."

"Not our family," he said. *Just you,* he didn't have to say.

I could feel angry tears building, and I was about to snap back, but then I heard Levi say, "Dad, you came!"

He was still several feet away from us, not close enough to hear our conversation. I looked away, blinking quickly as he gave Caleb a hug.

"Great job, buddy," Caleb said. "Could use a little

work on your batting and grounders, but sounds like the Ropers will help you with that."

Levi's smile fell, and he rubbed the back of his neck. "Yeah, they've been working with me a lot lately. Hope it pays off."

"Well, I want you to tell me all about it," Caleb said, reaching for Levi's gym bag. "I'm gonna take you and your siblings out for something to eat and then we'll hang out at a park or catch a movie or something."

Levi looked overjoyed and surprised at the same time. "Are you for real?"

Caleb glanced at his watch and cringed. "I mean, it will have to be a quick dinner so I'm not driving back too late. Half an hour should be long enough for dinner, right?"

Levi looked at me, frowning. "Can't Dad stay with us?"

I winced at the thought. If I had any money left after renting the house, setting up utilities, and furnishing it, I'd pay for a hotel stay myself.

"Come on, Mom," Levi said. "You and Dad lived together for fifteen years. You can't manage one night?"

There it was. The mom guilt. I promised I'd never be that parent making my kids worry about me and their father being in the same room together. And that started now. "He can sleep on the couch," I said, forcing a smile.

Levi said, "I can sleep on the couch; you can take my bed, Dad. It's really nice." Levi hadn't spoken this many words in the last month. And even though I hated to have Caleb stay in my home, it felt good to have my son back.

But Caleb raised his eyebrows, because he knew his child support wasn't enough to pay for a 'really nice' bed.

He'd meant to starve me out. "Better than the one at home?" Caleb finally asked.

"This is home," I said, then I called Andrew and Cora over because I really just couldn't handle this conversation anymore. Maybe it would be easier one day to be around Caleb and not be so frustrated all the time. But right now, I hated seeing the way he treated the kids like they were his last priority. It was like assaulting an open wound. And I didn't know if I just never realized how terribly he treated me or if it had gotten worse since the divorce or if I had put up with it for so long that it was normal. But right now, I was over his behavior.

Another ball game was starting up as the kids and my parents came over, and I moved Cora's car seat over to Caleb's truck so that they could go out. I loaded them in and told them I loved them. And then I stood by my parents and watched them drive away, my heart aching because this man, who could barely manage to call much less show up in person the last several months, was taking the biggest parts of my heart with him.

Mom put her arm around me, rubbing my shoulder. "Do you want to come over and watch a movie or something? Could be good to take your mind off things."

It was a tempting offer, but I shook my head. "No, I have to do some chores around the house, especially before Caleb shows up and starts judging me."

Dad said, "You know, he could stay at our place if you don't want to be around him. Hell, I'll pay for a hotel myself."

"You've done more than enough, Dad. And the kids would never forgive me," I said. Especially not now that they knew he was staying over.

He nodded. "Call us if you need anything. Anytime."

"I will. I love you, Dad." I gave him and Mom a hug and waved goodbye before getting in my car.

I drove back to the house, and for the rest of the afternoon, I cleaned up all the messes that had piled up over the week. Now the only time laundry and dishes got done was late at night after I was already exhausted and finished helping the kids with their homework or spending time with them. I knew Andrew especially got really lonely at his new school. He had a harder time making friends than the other two.

I ran a few loads of laundry and did the dishes, wiped off the counters and swept the floors, even though I knew I shouldn't care what Caleb thought anymore. I wanted him to see what a good life I had made for myself and the kids without him. I wanted him to walk in this house and see all the nice things we had and know that he had absolutely no part in it.

I ate dinner by myself, and just as headlights appeared through my front window, my phone pinged with a text.

Gage: I saw Levi's team won today. Tell him good game for me.

I bit my lip, smiling at the screen.

Farrah: I will.

The door opened, and Cora came shuffling up, holding up a teddy bear almost bigger than her. It was so heavy she had to pop her hip out and lean back to keep it off the floor. Andrew sulked behind her holding a baseball glove and bat. Behind him, Levi and Caleb walked beside each other, Levi holding the brand-new mitt I'd been saving for.

"Did you guys go shopping?" I asked.

Caleb nodded, and I noted the frown on Andrew's face.

"I didn't know you liked baseball," I said to him.

"I don't," he muttered, walking past me and going to his bedroom.

Confused, I looked at Caleb for an explanation.

He rolled his eyes. "Drew wanted fingernail polish. But I told him he should get something that we could do together."

"And you can't do fingernail polish together?" I asked, feeling Cora and Levi's eyes on me.

"Not if I don't want him to get picked on at school. You already said he's having a hard time making friends."

I fought to keep my voice even, knowing our kids were listening. "If the kids are picking on him for wearing fingernail polish, it's *their* problem, not Andrew's. He should have gotten what he wanted."

He folded his arms over his chest, towering over me where I sat at the dining room table. "Great way to welcome me to your new place. Complain at me for doing something nice for your kid."

"Our kid," I corrected.

"Oh, now he's mine," Caleb muttered, stepping past me to look at the kitchen. "This is a pretty big place. Rent must be sky high."

Levi said, "It's not as big as the house back home, but it's comfortable."

The pain in my chest just increased.

Cora said, "Come see my room, Daddy. I'll put Prince Charlie by the rest of my bears."

"Okay, sweetheart," Caleb said, holding her hand and letting her drag him back to her room.

I followed them, wanting to keep an ear on what he said about the place. He looked around her room silently as she placed the teddy bear by the rest of her stuffed animals. He said, "This is a room fit for a princess."

She spun happily, her skirt flying around her.

"Let me see your room, Levi," he said.

We followed Levi farther down the hall to his room. And once again, Caleb was quiet at first.

Levi said, "Mom got me this really nice dresser and a desk for me to do my homework , but I always end up doing it at the table. Most nights anyway."

Caleb ran his hand over the black desktop. "You found all this at a thrift store, Farrah?"

"No," I replied. And I hated the way his tone implied secondhand furniture was somehow less. Like it was all I could get. "I ordered it online."

Levi chimed in, "It was like better than Christmas when we first moved in. There were a million boxes coming in all the time. I put the TV stand together by myself."

I grinned, loving the pride in his voice and that he said something positive about the move because we really didn't talk all that much and it was hard to gauge how he felt. I wished he would say more to me.

Without complimenting, or even commenting on, Levi's space, Caleb said, "Well, let's see Andrew's room... although he's mad at me. I'm kind of regretting the bat right now." He guffawed.

I didn't find the joke funny at all. Andrew had missed his dad for months, and then Caleb basically dismissed him and his interests. We walked to Andrew's room, his door covered in drawings. A new one was up on the door, portraying a hastily scribbled skull and crossbones with the words KEEP OUT.

My heart ached for him. I knocked on his door and said, "Drew, can we come in?"

"You can," he replied. "Not Dad."

Caleb looked pissed and opened his mouth to say something, but I just held my hand up and said, "Give me some time with him."

I pushed my way inside Andrew's room, noticing that the baseball bat and glove were nowhere to be found. Then I spotted the end of the bat sticking out from under his bed. I let out a soft sigh, and my eyes landed on the framed painting above his bed. The one that Gage had paid for an instructor to make with Andrew.

It hurt my heart that someone who'd known Drew for thirty minutes was more considerate of his interests than the man who gave him life. "Hey," I said gently. "I'm sorry about the fingernail polish."

Andrew held his pillow to his stomach. "It just looks like so much fun when you and Cora do it and make little designs. I thought it could be fun for me to have my own."

I reached out, rubbing his shoulder. "I didn't know that you felt that way. But next time Cora and I do nails, you can join us, okay?"

He nodded. "Thanks, Mom. Did you know that there's a glow-in-the-dark kind of polish?"

"Glow in the dark? That's amazing."

"That's what I thought," he said. "But Dad said fingernail polish was for girls. He said I could do baseball instead." His little lips screwed up, and I could tell he was on the verge of tears. "I told him I hate baseball, but it didn't matter."

"Babe, you don't have to play baseball if you don't want to. And anyone can paint their nails, okay? It's literally just colors. Not a boy thing or a girl thing."

He looked up at me. "I don't have to play Little League this summer, right?"

"Not if you don't want to," I said.

He nodded, looking down at his bed. He'd gone for a bedspread that was designed after one of his favorite video games.

"Drew, Dad isn't perfect, and neither am I. But he's here now, and I know you've missed him."

Andrew nodded, wiping at his eyes. "Dad said he's sleeping on the couch. Does that mean that we can play video games until he goes to sleep?"

"I think that's up to Dad," I said. "I might just spend some time in my room."

"Can't we be together like a family?" he asked.

My heart ached for him. He was just too young to really understand. And to be fair, no eight-year-old should *have to* understand. "We are a family, Drew, but not the same kind that we were before. And that's okay."

His lips trembled slightly, and I pulled him into a hug. After a few minutes, he took a deep breath and said, "I'm going to ask Dad about the video games."

"I think that's a great idea."

He pushed himself off the bed, giving me a playful look. "Maybe our new family can play more video games?"

I chuckled, walking behind him. "Nice try."

We walked to the living room, where Caleb and Levi

were battling each other in a video game while Cora played with one of her dolls on the floor.

"Can I play with you?" Drew asked, sitting by Levi on the couch.

"Sure, buddy," Caleb said. "You can have my controller."

I folded my arms across my chest, hating the sight of Caleb in my place. It felt so wrong for him to be here, taking up space in my fresh start. But I knew it was best for the kids if he had time with them. "I'm gonna go to my room," I said, putting my thumb over my shoulder. "I figured you could put the kids to bed tonight and I will see you all in the morning."

I was about to walk away when he said, "Wait up. I want to talk to you about something."

"What's up?"

"Privately." He stood from the couch.

I didn't want to take him to my bedroom, so we stepped onto the back patio. There wasn't much to the backyard, but we'd strung up some discounted Christmas lights and put a used picnic table out. The setup made it look so magical and happy back here.

"What did you need to talk about?" I asked.

His expression quickly changed from amicable to accusatory. "Griffen Industries canceled all their accounts with Green Line."

I raised my eyebrows. "Okay?"

"I know you had something to do with it."

His anger had no place back here, but neither did my own. "Caleb, I don't know what you want me to do about it. I work in interior design. It's not like I have anything to do with the company's insurance decisions."

Raising his eyebrows, he gestured at the house behind him. "Where did all this stuff come from?"

What the hell did this have to do with insurance? "I told you I bought it online, but I'm not really sure how that's any of your business anymore."

"I know how much things cost, Farrah. The average salary for an interior designer in Dallas couldn't afford all this. You're lucky to be making rent and utilities and getting the kids what they need for school. And I know you're not that great with money."

I was already getting angry, but that last line shoved me over the edge. "The only reason I'm not great with money was because you insisted on controlling it for our entire marriage. And now I know it's because you didn't want me to see all the shit you were buying for your mistresses. The only thing that I had control over was a budget for activities with the kids and groceries. I've had to figure this out on my own, get a job after sacrificing my career to take care of our children and support your career. But I'm figuring it out."

A smug look dawned on his face. "I'm sure you are."

"What the hell does that mean?" I practically growled. I didn't know why it was important to me, but I needed him to know that I'd been thriving without him. "For your information, I got a job, a great job. And I work for a man who believes in me and supports me, and he pays me what I'm worth."

A sneer curved Caleb's upper lip. "I knew it. You're fucking him." He pointed his finger at me. "That's why they fired Green Line and that's how you have all this shit."

White flashed over my eyes. "Get out of my house," I said through clenched teeth.

"You're kicking me out?"

"You do not speak to me like that anymore. This is my home that I pay for with my money from my job. And while I will always give you access to the kids and make sure that you have chances to visit them and talk to them on the phone, staying in *my* house is not a necessity. You are welcome to book a hotel tonight or drive back to your place, but you cannot stay here unless you sincerely apologize and change your behavior."

"You're such a bitch," he spat.

My voice shook with rage, and I barely held back angry tears. "No. I'm just not your doormat anymore. Go tell the kids that you need to go."

He glared at me before walking inside and said, "Kids, your mom asked me to leave. I'll see you later." And then he walked out the front door, leaving me to deal with the fallout as his engine roared in the night.

24

GAGE

After a morning session at the gym, I showered and grabbed one of the blue suits from my closet with a tie Farrah had complimented me on a few weeks back. On the way to The Retreat, I stopped by a coffee shop and got Farrah her favorite drink. It was called a "turtle mocha," and even though I liked my coffee a little sweet, this was practically dessert for breakfast.

My mind flashed back to Friday night, in the early hours of the morning as we sat cross-legged on the bed, breakfast between us. She'd looked so damn cute with one of the hotel robes wrapped around her, a smile on her lips only for me, as she fed me a piece of a chocolate chip pancake.

I hoped we could do that again, and soon.

Parking my car in the lot, I grabbed the coffee before heading to the front door. Cliff lifted his chin in a nod as I walked inside, not quite meeting my eyes. Luckily, I'd had the foresight to make security sign an NDA, requiring them not to share private details about me. But Cliff was a good guy. I trusted him anyway.

When I got to the conference room, I set the coffee in front of Farrah's chair. The place felt so empty and cold without her here, making me wonder how it would feel when I moved back to my regular office. Working alongside her was some of the best fun that I'd had in years.

I liked accomplishing tasks and reaching new goals, but hearing the way she spoke to vendors and listening to her funny stories about her kids... it added a light to my day I wasn't used to.

On top of the incredible sex?

I was screwed.

Because we both knew this relationship couldn't go anywhere. Honestly, I'd hoped banging one out with her would help me get her out of my system, but it was like the more I had of her, the more I wanted.

I thought of her all weekend, both in good and pleasurable ways. But now, sitting in this office waiting for her to come in, I felt like a kid waiting for Santa on Christmas morning. Excited, and as a thirty-six-year-old man, a little bit pathetic.

Her entrance to the room didn't disappoint. She'd worn a short-sleeve, navy-blue dress that hugged her curves and showed her cleavage. As she drew closer, I noticed little white flowers on the dress, and they reminded me of the perfume she wore.

When she saw me, her face broke into a smile that brightened the entire room, and I realized I'd been right to anticipate this. "I got you dessert."

Her eyes lit up. "A turtle mocha? I *so* needed this."

She sat down, taking the cup in both her hands and drinking deeply.

"Rough night?" I asked.

"More like rough weekend," she replied.

"Everything okay?" I asked, searching for another bruise. "You didn't get hit by another ball, did you?"

She chuckled, then she sighed, shaking her head. It took another sip of the turtle mocha to steel herself before she could tell the story. "Caleb decided to show up for one of Levi's games, which was great, until he decided to suggest that the only reason I have nice furniture in my house is because I'm having sex with my boss."

I cringed, sucking in a breath through my teeth. "What the hell is wrong with that guy?"

"He's jealous," she said, shaking her head and swirling her drink around in her cup. "He told me when I left that I'd never be able to make it on my own and that I'd come crawling back. And maybe that's why he hasn't seen the kids, because he thought we'd be back any day. But I think seeing me in my house and doing so well solidified for him that it's really over."

"So what did you do?" I asked. I hoped she'd put him in his place. She deserved to be treated better than that, and her kids needed a better example of a man.

"Oh, this is where it got worse." She set her coffee down, placing her hands on the table, like she wanted to flip it. "I can take Caleb saying crappy things to me, because, well, I've been dealing with it for a while, but *then* he walked in and told the kids that I was making him leave, and you should have seen the look on Levi's face. I'm pretty sure he's going to hate me forever. Cora was crying, asking why Daddy wouldn't come back, and

Andrew threw the baseball glove and bat that Caleb got him in the garbage. So I was dealing with *all* the feelings."

I shook my head. "All I did over the weekend was some extra work and hit the gym."

She had half a smile as she picked her drink back up. "Do you know how lucky you are?"

I gazed at her. She was so beautiful, even frustrated and slouched over her coffee. "You have no idea."

Her eyes met mine, holding my gaze for a moment. "He did say something else..."

My fists clenched under the table. "Something worse?"

She shifted uncomfortably in her seat.

"Farrah," I ordered.

Meeting my eyes again, she said, "He said Griffen Industries dropped Green Line Mutual."

My shoulders squared. He was still an idiot for leaving Farrah, but smarter than I thought to make the connection. "We did."

Her lips parted. "Why? They have the best rates in Texas, maybe in the country... Wouldn't that cost your company a lot of money to switch to another provider?"

Our eyes locked, and I tilted my head, wanting her to see me. The real me. Not just the hard exterior everyone knew. "I might be a businessman, but I'm also a human. I have no desire to work with a company that lets its employees cheat on the job and then keeps them on board."

Her lips parted. "How did you know..."

"I have a PI." And I'd learned way too fucking much about Caleb Elkins and his slimy boss to ever work with Green Line again.

Farrah nodded. Then nodded again. "Wow."

"What?" I asked.

She looked up at me with wide brown eyes that were impossible to turn down. "You did that for me?"

For a woman who was so easy to read, she was gauging me just right. Seeing too much.

Deny. Deny. Deny. "It wasn't for you—it was for the company," I lied. "My conscience, if you can believe I have one."

She smirked. "Gage Griffen did something nice for me. I knew it!" She pointed at me.

I reached across the table, gripping her hand, and suddenly her perfect lips parted, and it felt like all the air had left the room, replaced by a charged tension.

Her throat moved deliciously as she swallowed.

"I can do something else for you too," I said, my voice low. "What would make you feel better?"

She nodded toward her coffee on the table, keeping her hand in mine. "This is a good start."

"A start?" I asked.

Her full lips curled into a smirk. "I'm not sure I'm allowed to do all the other things that would make me feel better."

"Says who?" I asked.

"My boss." She quirked an eyebrow. "He's a real hard-ass sometimes."

"I think, under extenuating circumstances, he might understand."

"Well, in that case..." she said.

I let go of her hand and walked around the table until I was facing her. When I put my hands on her shoulders, sitting her in the chair, she inhaled a quick breath and held it as I pushed the rolling chair until its back stopped against the wall.

I lowered myself to my knees before her, ready to worship her like the queen she was. Her brown eyes were wide in surprise, making me grin up at her. When I was done with her, that asshole's name would be the last thing on her mind.

"You wore a dress for this, didn't you?" I asked before kissing her thigh.

She shifted her hips, her voice breathy as she said, "You like dresses?"

I took off my blazer, dropping it on the desk, and kissed higher up her leg. "Love them on you."

I brushed her hem up higher, seeing a lacy thong underneath. Blood filled my cock, already straining against my pants. She'd dressed up for me.

"Lift your hips," I commanded.

She pressed her feet into the ground, giving me enough room to slide her panties over her curvy hips and thighs, then down her calves. I balled them up and put them in my pocket. "Mine."

"You know those are twenty-dollar underwear, right?" she asked.

"I can buy you a truckload of these if you promise you'll wear them every day."

Her cheeks flushed even more, and I continued kissing her, running my hands up her legs until my thumbs hooked in the crease between her hips and thighs. With her dress out of the way and her knees separated by my shoulders, I could see her beautiful pussy, but this time, there was no hair.

"You shaved," I said, looking up at her.

Her cheeks were bright red as she said, "If I'd known what would happen Friday night, I would have shaved on Thursday."

I sliced my tongue up her slit, making her shiver. "I like you exactly as you are, Farrah. Shaved, waxed, natural, I don't give a shit, as long as it's you."

Her eyebrows rose, and I instantly read her emotions. "You don't believe me," I said, rocking back on my heels.

She bit her lip. "It's just... I know you're probably used to better than..." She let out a sigh and gestured at herself.

Anger flared in my chest, and I backed away from her, rising to my feet and pacing the floor. "Who the fuck made you think there's better than you?"

With this incredulous look on her face, she said, "Maybe that guy who walked away from me in the club? Or my ex, who told me no one would ever want a fat single mom my age."

"Fucking idiots," I growled. I approached her again, putting my hands on the arms of her chair and my face up close to hers. "You are a fucking goddess, Farrah. You have curves and dimples and hair and stretchmarks like an adult woman does, and I've never been more turned on in my life than when I walked in on you in the bath, touching yourself and making yourself feel good. Because you deserve that, Farrah. You deserve to feel good. And you deserve to know that you are everything I stay up at night thinking about."

Her breath hitched in her chest, and before she could argue with me or utter another word, I lowered myself. Kneeling at her throne and bringing her to my lips.

In minutes, I had her screaming my name.

25

FARRAH

Even though it had been two days since our morning tryst in the office, I still could hardly be around Mia without blushing. She knew me better than anyone else, and she knew Gage just as well.

Which was unfortunate, because I was terrible at lying and Gage had a last-minute lunch meeting come up with Jason Romero when we were supposed to meet Pascale to go over the shot list. Mia was the only person Gage trusted enough to decide what he would and wouldn't do in a shoot. Which made me a little jealous, but I needed to focus on my job. The shoot was under a month away, and Pascale said he needed our feedback before securing additional props and wardrobe.

Gage might be able to play it cool in front of Mia, but me? Not a chance. I wore all my emotions like a brightly colored hat, whether I wanted to or not.

A knock sounded on the open door to the conference room Gage and I had been using and Mia came in, giving me a big hug. "I know we technically work together, but I still feel like I never see you," she said.

"I know," I replied. "I was so excited to work with you, but I feel like I spend more time with Gage than anyone else." I instantly fought a smile, because I didn't mind the time I spent with him so much anymore.

"Now you know what it feels like to be me," she said.

God, I hope not. I chuckled awkwardly. But then I had to wonder... Had he made her sign an NDA too? No, I decided. I knew Mia too well for her to be able to lie to me. When I'd asked her directly about a potential crush on Gage, she had been genuinely against the idea.

If she asked me outright, I'd have no choice but to fold. She'd know instantly.

"How's work been going?" I asked, hoping to change the subject. "I just realized that I don't really know a lot of what you do every day."

She laughed. "Pretty much anything Gage asks me to do, I guess. Like I had to schedule a last-minute dinner, make reservations for him and Jason *doll face* Romero. I made travel plans for him last spring when he had to speak at a congressional hearing on real estate monopolization. I'm working with the event planner to prepare for the annual Fourth of July picnic for the company. Lately, I've been taking on a little more—helping him prepare reports for C-suite meetings and learning more of his role."

My eyebrows lifted. "My god, Mia, that sounds like three jobs instead of one."

"It is." She laughed. "I pretty much handle everything, from having his car buffed out after someone doordings it"—she winked at me—"to making his doctor appointments. You know he has someone come to his apartment for that?"

"You're kidding. That's something that rich people do? That sounds amazing." I shuddered. "Last time Cora got an ear infection, I had to sit at urgent care for three hours."

Mia nodded. "You can have anything, if you're willing to pay the price."

I chuckled. "I'd have to be doing a lot more than interior design to afford that. Maybe I should be a stripper? There are people into the whole mom, stretch mark thing, right?"

The words were out of my mouth before I realized *our boss* was into that. I blushed, hard, then choked on my own salvia, going into a major coughing fit.

Mia said, "You're so off. I haven't seen you blushing like this since you started dating Caleb... Maybe when we went to that Magic Mike movie. You talked about Channing Tatum for *weeks* after." Her jaw dropped, and her eyes lit with excitement. "Oh my gosh! You have a crush!"

My cheeks flamed bright red. "I do not."

"Who is it?" Mia asked excitedly. "How did you even meet him? Did you try online dating finall—"

The sound of voices came through the open door. Another knock sounded, and I looked away from Mia to see Cliff standing next to Pascale. "Have a good day," Cliff said to Pascale, then left the three of us alone.

Mia immediately kicked me under the table, and my cheeks got even hotter. "Pascale?" she crooned. "I'm Mia, Mr. Griffin's assistant. Farrah has told me *all* about you."

I didn't think I could get more embarrassed, but I was blushing even harder than before, and a spark of a grin hid in Pascale's dark eyes as he looked between Mia and me. "I'm flattered."

"Pascale, it's great to see you," I said, extending my sweaty hand.

"Likewise." He held on to my hand a second longer than necessary, and I could feel Mia's silent squeal rightly along with the squish of moisture between our palms.

This was *not* the message I wanted to send her. Although, it would be nice to distract her from Gage and me.

I gestured at an open chair for Pascale, across the table from Mia and me, and sat down.

"So, Mia," he said, getting his iPad from his bag. "You're the one who runs the company?"

Mia chuckled. "Pretty much. He may be the head, but I happen to turn the neck."

I laughed. "I always thought Mia would run the world someday."

She smiled at Pascale, saying, "I can't wait to see what you came up with for the photo shoot."

He nodded, swiveling the iPad so we could see it. Then he tapped on the screen with his tattooed fingers, pulling up a presentation that said THE RETREAT.

Pascale took a few minutes explaining the concept of the photo shoot to us. A refresher for me, but a crash course for Mia. When he was done, I saw the smile on her face.

"I love it," she said. "It's going to be perfect for this place."

Pascale asked her, "You know Gage really well... Do you think he'll do okay with this kind of thing?"

"Oh, he's great in front of a camera," she said. "I

think the attention makes him uncomfortable, but he's really photogenic."

Pascale asked, "What about portraying emotions? Do you think he'll be able to do that even if he and Farrah aren't in a relationship? I want it to look authentic in front of the camera."

Mia smirked. "This might be TMI, but he just asked me to buy women's lingerie for a woman he's seeing. I'm sure he can pretend Farrah is whoever this mystery woman is."

I choked again, coughing loudly as the liquid stung my windpipe. Mia patted my back, laughing. "Farrah's a little shy."

Thank God that's what she assumed, because I felt like I was seconds away from getting busted. How many plus-size women could Gage be sleeping with? Because if Mia knew about the lingerie order, she knew what size he requested. Weren't executives and billionaires supposed to be into women with toned bodies and personal trainers who only drank green juice? Whatever the hell that was.

I finally recovered and croaked out, "Pascale, I'd love to see the photos."

With a slight chuckle, he nodded and said, "Let's get started." He swiped his finger over the screen, showing one photo after another. Pictures of toes dangling out of the bathtub or room service trays covering a bed. And I already knew without a doubt that this was exactly the feel Gage wanted. And to be honest, I was so excited that I would get free family pictures while I was at it.

Caleb always thought that group photography was stupid and that the pictures I took on my phone were good enough. But the problem was that I was hardly ever in them. The fact that Pascale would be capturing my children and me in happy moments, even if they were posed, was something I really looked forward to.

"This is incredible," Mia said. "I'm not sure how Gage will feel about putting a towel on his head, but other than that, it's great. He can inconvenience himself for a couple of hours for great art that will last years."

Smiling, Pascale nodded. "I think that's a great idea."

"Although..." Mia said. The look on her face was one she'd only worn when we were in college and trying to get into bars while underage. What was she up to?

"Yeah?" Pascale said.

"Well, you're an artist... And Farrah is an artist."

Where was she going with this?

Mia tapped her chin. "I'm wondering if you two could get together and talk about your shared interest? Could be a great networking opportunity for both of you."

Just as I was about to tell Pascale that he didn't have to "network" with me, he said, "That sounds like a great idea, as long as we can add a little red wine."

Mia nodded enthusiastically. "I can babysit the kids, Farrah. Maybe next Friday after work?"

"I'm actually free that day at seven, and my friend recently opened a wine bar..." Pascale said.

They both looked at me expectantly, and I hoped the smile on my face didn't look too forced. I couldn't turn down this date when it was such a good distraction away from Gage and me. "Sounds great."

Pascale scribbled his personal number on the back of his business card and passed it to me with a wink. "See you soon."

As soon as he left, I turned on Mia. "What the hell was that?"

She grinned smugly. "Only the world's finest wing-woman at work."

"I told you and our moms that I was okay being single."

"But you were so cute when he was on his way. All blushes and giggles. And it's not technically a date; it's a *networking opportunity* that could lead to something more, romantically or professionally."

"Are you calling me a hooker?" I groused.

"No!" she laughed. "This is exactly how Gage does it. He gets contacts, meets with new people. You never know when someone you meet could be your next business partner or connect you with someone really important."

"And Pascale is going to do that?" I asked, still not convinced. "I already have a job."

"If you stay at Griffen Industries after this project, you might be able to pass some more work his way. Or if you are on the hunt for another position, you'll have his contact. He's worked with tons of businesspeople who might need an interior designer."

My stomach nosedived with the realization that I hadn't asked Gage what my career would look like after this project. Would I not have a job anymore? I had just assumed that he would find another place to use me, but Mia was right. I needed a plan for the future.

"Fine, I'll go. But only for work purposes. Nothing more."

Mia smirked. "Whatever you say."

26

GAGE

Around seven on Thursday night, my phone pinged with a text message from Farrah. I looked away from my office computer to my phone resting face up on the desk.

Farrah: I just got a very large, very embarrassing delivery.

My lips spread into a grin.

Gage: Is that so?

Farrah: When you said you could order me a truckload of new underwear, I didn't think you meant a literal truckload.

My smile grew even wider, thinking of Farrah walking out her front door to find the pop-up lingerie store I'd ordered for her. Since I knew intimately the brand and size she wore, I hired a company to set up the back of an unmarked box truck with a store holding all the colors and styles that brand made in her size. They were to drive to her house, knock on the door and let her know they'd wait until she had some time to make her selections.

Gage: Did you see anything you liked?

Farrah: Just about everything. And the purse to carry everything in was a nice touch. Until Andrew snuck into my room and came out with a thong looped over his shoulders like some kind of inappropriate Nacho Libre.

I snickered at the mental image.

Gage: You made me laugh.

Farrah: I'm glad one of us is laughing.

Gage: It's a total boy thing to do. Rhett and Tyler used to put on Mom's water bras and walk around squeezing each other... Actually, now that I think about it, that explains a lot about Rhett's personality.

Farrah: As long as Drew doesn't put this in his memoir, I think we'll be okay.

Gage: But if he does write it, he has to title the chapter COMMANDO.

Farrah: So not funny.

Gage: You're smiling.

Farrah: Maybe a little bit.

I turned away from my desk, facing the window and the glittering view of Dallas at night.

Gage: I'm sorry I was so busy this week. I missed touching you. Tasting you.

Farrah: Your schedule actually let me get some work done. Although I wouldn't mind a repeat of what happened Monday morning.

Gage: What about tomorrow night? Can you get a sitter last minute?

Farrah: I promised the kids we'd watch *Inside Out*.

Gage: Saturday?

Farrah: Caleb's coming to watch Levi's game, and he promised to be on his best behavior, but I think after what happened last week, it wouldn't be a good idea to go out all night with my boss... no matter how much I want to.

God, I wanted to be with her again. Something about

Farrah was so addictive. And not just being with her in bed. When we'd spent the night together last week, it was the most I'd laughed in months. Maybe even years.

Gage: You're killing me.

Farrah: Text me Saturday night after the kids are in bed.

Farrah: But until then...

A picture came through our message thread that I'd never be able to get off my mind. Farrah stood with her back to the camera wearing only a black lacy thong. The dark material contrasted her pale skin, and her curly hair spilled down her back. The way she positioned herself, I could just imagine digging my fingers into her hips and railing into her from behind.

Gage: Have I mentioned how much you turn me on?

Farrah: Maybe once or twice. But it's nice to hear all the same.

If she liked to hear it, I'd tell her. Every damn day, I'd tell her.

Gage: You are the sexiest fucking woman I've ever laid eyes on. Not just because of your body and the things I want to do to it, but because of how you exist in the world.

Three dots appeared on the screen, disappeared, and then appeared again.

Farrah: What do you mean? I'm just... me.

I paced in front of the window, wondering how she could not know? Her essence was exactly the thing that drew me to her. But if I laid all my cards out there, I could be giving her the wrong message. This was a strictly physical relationship, and we both needed to remember that.

So I carefully typed out my words and waited for her to reply.

Gage: Seeing you every morning is like watching the sun rise in the sky. And that ass? Better than the fucking moon.

Farrah: Thank you for the smile. Goodnight, Gage.

Gage: Goodnight, Farrah.

But I scrolled back up to the photo of her perfect ass. This woman kept surprising me.

Knowing I wouldn't get any more work done, I shut down the computer and left my office. The entire building was quiet, save for a nighttime security guard who walked our floor. I made it down to the parking garage and then drove back to my place, taking the elevator all the way to the top floor, where I lived in the penthouse.

Usually, I'd head to the kitchen and make myself supper, but I went to the bedroom instead. That photo of Farrah had been on my mind the entire drive, and I knew I wasn't getting rid of this hard-on until I took care of it.

I went to the shower, propping my phone on the soap holder, open to the photo of Farrah, and turned the water on hot. I slipped out of my clothes and stepped in, letting the pressure berate my skin.

Taking my cock in my hand, I pumped it, staring at Farrah's ass, the sexy way her thong disappeared between perfect, fleshy cheeks.

I'd pull her thong aside and tease her hole, feeling how wet she was for me. God, she turned me on like no other woman ever had. She'd moan, wiggling her hips back, trying to get me to sate the need we both felt.

Instead, I'd wrap my fist through her hair, pulling her back until her chin lifted and the back of her head was against my shoulder.

"Farrah, baby," I'd say, my voice low. "Patience is a virtue."

"I don't want to be patient," I could practically hear her say as the water continued to beat a steady stream against my bare skin.

I pumped faster, my balls tightening, cock growing even harder as hot water flowed down my arm and flew from the motion.

"Me neither then," I'd say, bending her over and pressing into her in one quick motion that made her cry out. She was so tight and wet, warm, squeezing against my girth. It was the best fucking feeling to move inside of her. I'd experienced it several times that weekend, and I fucking *thirsted* for more.

"Do you feel what you do to me?" I growled out loud, staring at her picture. "You make me lose all fucking control."

I wanted to feel her ass slap against my thighs, sense the tightening of her pussy with her pending orgasm, hear the way she cried out when she came.

The thought had thick ropes of cum spurting from my cock and landing on the shower wall.

But the fantasy didn't stop there.

I remembered her telling me she liked to cuddle after sex. Felt the soft tickle of her hair on my shoulder, reveled in the gentle touch of her fingertips over my chest and stomach as she felt my skin. Saw her smile up at me.

And I wished it could happen again.

I was so fucked.

I finished rinsing off and got out of the shower, wrapping a towel around my waist. My fingers itched to text Farrah, let her know how crazy she drove me. But I hooked my phone on the charger atop my dresser and changed into underwear and lounge pants.

Then I went to the kitchen and started making supper for one. At times like this, I really hated that my circle was so small. I had a contact list full of people, full of potential business partners and experts on various matters, but very few people that I could really confide in. And I didn't exactly want to tell my siblings what was going on because I already knew what they would say.

They would just tell me that I was being stupid—that if I met a girl I liked, I should date her and see where it goes.

That wasn't how life worked for me. When you made as much money as I did, when you had as much power as I did, people didn't want you for who you were. They wanted you for what you could do for them. And even though Farrah didn't really seem to be a gold digger, wasn't she only in my circle because we were working together? If we'd met on the street, and she didn't know that I was Gage Griffin, billionaire CEO, would she be interested? I would never know. And truthfully, neither would she.

So instead of calling my siblings to ask for advice I didn't want, I texted them to see if they wanted to catch the Ropers game with me on Saturday to take my mind off Farrah. The team had a home game, and I had a box available. Usually, I used my seats for networking or gave them away to employees as gifts. But this time, I wanted to use them for myself.

Gage: I have a box for the Ropers game on Saturday. Anyone up for coming?

The microwave dinged, and I took my meal to the table, sitting and eating the steak, sweet potatoes, and corn with a beer from the fridge. I was almost through the food when the first text came through.

Tyler: Sorry, I have Mom and Dad coming over for supper that day. You're welcome to join us though.

I ignored the invitation. We both knew that I would not be going.

I got up, taking my plate to the sink and bringing my beer to the couch. I didn't watch much TV, but I used the remote to search *Inside Out*. It was a children's movie, and I pushed play.

Rhett: Sorry, I'm out of town practicing bull riding with a buddy in Texas. I'll catch the next one though.

Liv: Looks like you're stuck with me?

I smiled at the phone.

Gage: The other two are missing out.

27

FARRAH

I'd never sent a photo like that in my life, but something about Gage encouraged me to explore new, exciting places. He made me feel sexy and free. Especially with all my beautiful new underwear now nestled safely in my top drawer. For a split second, I'd worried he wouldn't like it, but his text response made me feel better.

Except I'd underestimated what it would be like to face him knowing he had a photo of me like that on his phone. I thought my face would melt from embarrassment when I went into the office Friday morning.

Before reaching the conference room door, I squared my shoulders and took a deep breath. We were both adults. Surely he'd gotten a nude before.

But when I walked inside, he took the two coffees from my hands and set them on the table before backing me up against the wall. His chest was pressed against mine, his nose against my cheek, as he roughly whispered, "Do you know what you did to me last night?"

My voice came out breathy. "What's that?"

"I fucked my fist in the shower to that picture, wishing you were there."

My stomach swooped with desire. "I'm here now."

Somewhere in the back of my mind, I knew this was unprofessional to the nth degree. I knew we should be focusing on work. That Cliff could bring a contractor back at any moment. But Gage's presence was so over-powering, overwhelming. Everything from his hard body up against mine to the delicate scrape of his chin against my cheek and the subtle scent of his masculine cologne had me forgetting what I *should* be doing and chasing after what I wanted.

"Let me show you what I imagined," he said.

My eyes rolled back for a moment, but soon he had me spinning against the table, my long hair wrapped around his fist. He pulled until my neck arched back and the top of my head rested against his shoulder.

"You drive me crazy, Farrah," he said against my temple.

A whimper passed my lips. "What do you think you do to me?"

He answered by pressing me forward, so I was bent over the table. Jerking roughly, he pulled my skirt over my hips, baring my ass and my new thong to him.

"Fuck," he moaned, lowering down, sliding his hands over my hips before jerking my thong to the side. Then his face pressed against my backside, his tongue drawing up my slit.

I shuddered against him, barely holding myself up on the table as he began his assault on my clit. He nipped, sucked, blew puffs of tantalizing air, making it hard not to scream.

And just when I thought I was going to come, he pulled away from me, leaving me limp. Desperate. "Gage," I begged, my forehead rolling against the table.

"Now you know how I felt last night. So fucking lonely without you," he said, and the sound of a ripping condom wrapper filled the room. "Hang on to that coffee."

I looked up, barely taking hold of the coffee cups before he pressed inside me, stretching and filling me to the hilt. "Gage," I whined.

"Take it like the good girl you are," he commanded. And he thrust into me over and over again until I was mere pieces shuddering around him, until I finally fell completely apart, crying out his name as I came.

He finished inside me, clinging to my hips and pulsing deliciously against my tender parts. Before pulling out, he brushed my hair aside and kissed where my neck met my shoulder.

"That's what I imagined," he muttered. "But this was so much fucking better."

He pulled out and moved my underwear back in place before sliding my skirt down over my hips. I released my grip on the coffee, realizing only a little bit had spilled, and stood up, smelling us in the air.

He tossed the condom and wrapper in the trash can, then turned to me, taking my face in his hands and kissing me so deeply, feelings stirred in my chest. Could he really kiss me like this and feel nothing more than a physical connection? Because my heart was getting all kinds of confused.

If I was being honest, the fact that he had texted me after Levi's game meant a lot. It was like I wasn't just an employee or a random hookup to him. He cared about me *and* my kids, and he hadn't even met Levi yet. But I needed to focus on other things before my thoughts got me in trouble.

"I should get back to work," I said softly. "I have contractors coming by today."

"Of course," he replied, straightening his jacket and tie. "I have a press conference with Jason Romero, so I won't be around the hotel."

My heart sank. I missed spending time with him. But maybe it was good to get some space. "I'll text you tomorrow night."

His lips curled into a delicious grin. "Looking forward to it."

FOR THE NEXT FEW HOURS, I busied myself, helping the people coming to install the rest of the lighting fixtures, but at a certain point, there was only so much I could do. So I went back down to the empty office to check my email, when a news notification came through my phone.

LIVE: GUBERNATORIAL HOPEFUL PARTNERS WITH TEXAS BILLIONAIRE ON MASSIVE FACTORY BUILD

I tapped through the notification and was taken to a news page with live footage of Gage sitting next to a man I'd gotten countless political postcards from already, Jason Romero.

Jason looked like he belonged in a wax museum, so flawless it was almost unsettling. He spoke smoothly into the microphone, saying, "Gage is a true Texan, having grown up in a small town and headquartering Griffen Industries here in this great state. I'm excited at this budding partnership with someone who represents Romero Corp's values—he's hardworking, smart, offers jobs to countless Texans, and is always pushing for progress while maintaining traditional ideals."

Clapping sounded in the background, making it seem like they were at a political rally instead of a press conference.

Gage spoke next, saying, "My goal in building Griffen Industries has always been to support families here in Texas. Opening a Romero Corp plant in West Texas lines up perfectly with that vision. I'm excited to see what this partnership brings."

A reporter came over the recording, asking, "Do you have a date for the groundbreaking?"

Jason Romero shook his head. "We are very much in the planning stages of this process, but you can visit my webpage and join my email list for regular updates."

They cut to a reporter from the news station, the thin, dark-haired woman saying, "Since announcing the partnership with Griffen Industries and this new project, Romero has gone up fifteen points in the polls, placing him narrowly ahead of the other candidate..."

For the first time since meeting him, I felt a little sad for Gage. His world was all a chess match, moving pieces for gain. I hoped he knew I wasn't like that. The only thing I wanted from him was... himself. But in some ways, I knew even that was too much to ask.

28

GAGE

I went to bed Friday night thinking of Farrah and her family watching that kids' movie. It was cute, and I wished it had been around when I was a kid fighting with all the complex feelings of growing up.

She was a good mom, prioritizing her kids, even though I missed the hell out of her.

But luckily, Liv would be in town tomorrow and we could spend the day watching the Ropers game and hanging out. It would be a good distraction from all these thoughts of Farrah swirling around my mind.

THE NEXT MORNING, Liv knocked on my door at ten o'clock. Right on time. I had Levi's game playing on my phone, but I was smart enough to silence it before going to answer the door. She was all decked out in a brown and gold Ropers jersey and holding up her brown foam finger. "Go, team!" she said. Then she frowned at my dark-washed jeans and white T-shirt. "You're changing, right?"

"This is what I usually go in," I said, glancing down at my outfit. "Actually, it's a little more casual. Should I put on a button-down?"

She shook her head at me as if disappointed. "I could have sworn you wore a jersey last time."

"Nope. I think I have a brown shirt somewhere, though... Oh! And I have my hat." I grabbed it from the hat rack in my closet. "There. All decked out."

"If we're going to the baseball game, we're going to do it right." She took my arm and practically dragged me out to my car, drove to the department store closest to my house, and walked me back to the Men's section.

I tried to keep my Ropers ball cap down so no one could see my face, but I still caught a couple people staring.

"Here," she said, holding out a jersey from an endcap. The gold was all gaudy and sparkly and didn't even have the name of a player on the back.

"This shirt is fine," I groused. "I don't need to look like sparkled shit."

"I like it," she insisted. "Buy it."

"Has anyone ever told you that you're bossy?"

"I prefer 'an excellent leader,'" she replied, taking the shirt and me to the register. As soon as I paid, she ripped off the tag and forced me to put it over my head while still in the store.

"I feel like a little kid going back-to-school shopping," I grumbled on the way back to my car. "You remember how we would always take off the tags and wear things out of the store as soon as Mom checked out?"

She giggled. "I still do that sometimes."

"Well, we can't all grow up," I replied with a smirk. She hit my arm, and I pretended to be wounded as we got back in the car.

As I drove toward the stadium, I said, "Distract me from how stupid I look. How is your job going?"

She frowned, making me worry. "I know it might just be in my head, but I feel like the new supervisor is sexist against me. He always asks the other guys to do the harder jobs, and anytime there's an option for paperwork or anything like that, he's passing it off to me."

Her words put a bitter taste in my mouth. "You're probably not imagining it." I'd come across several people like that in my business and was quick to have them shape up or ship out. "You know, you could always come work for me."

She raised her eyebrows. "I didn't know you had an opening."

"I can make one."

Shaking her head, she said, "No. I need to stick this out and see it through. I mean, he's only been the manager for a couple months now. Maybe he's just trying to, like, assert authority or something like that."

"Maybe," I replied, focusing on the road and fighting the twinge of pain in my gut. My whole life I dreamed of having a family business, and when my dad shoved me out of the ranch, I'd kind of hoped that Griffin Industries would eventually be it. But none of my siblings wanted to take what they considered my "charity." We were all too damn proud for our own good.

What they didn't realize was that by working with me, they'd be giving me far more than I could ever give them.

Needing to change the subject, I asked, "Dating anyone?"

She scoffed. "I might be the only woman on the feed-lot, but I'm pretty sure they'd be more interested in the cows."

"Liv," I scolded.

"You know how a lot of the guys are there. They want a cute little wife to come home to at the end of the day with a home cooked meal and an ice-cold beer. They just don't like a woman in power."

I rolled my eyes. "That is one thing I do not miss about farm life. Some of those guys working in agriculture are really great people, but some of them still think they're back in the 1800s."

"Yep," she popped the p.

"No one outside of the feedlot?"

"Rhett would make sure there isn't," she said. All of us were protective of Liv, but Rhett especially so since it was just the two of them in Cottonwood Falls for a long time. Tyler used to travel a lot for work, and I stayed busy in Dallas.

"Surely he approves of someone," I said.

"Well, someone would have to be interested in me first for us to find out," she replied.

"When they are interested, I'll know that they have impeccable taste." I smiled over at her, and she looked up at me with a grateful smile in return.

"Thanks. You know, it's kind of weird. I always thought you would be the first one to get married, but here Tyler is with a wife."

"Nicole was the only one I ever considered marrying," I admitted, but moving away from Cottonwood Falls had sealed our breakup all those years ago. We weren't high school sweet hearts destined for forever.

She nodded. "But there's still time for you to be second in line."

I rolled my eyes at her. "Give up."

With a shrug she said, "At this rate, Rhett's bound to get married one drunken night in Vegas before you or I settle down."

"True." I laughed.

We pulled into the parking lot closest to the stadium, people already walking down the sidewalks to get to the game. I parked and got out, and we walked beside each other, me feeling ridiculous and looking like a walking merch store.

I showed my ID at the VIP entrance, and we got in the elevator, riding to the top with other box seat holders. On the way to our suite, I passed a few people I knew as acquaintances and introduced them to my sister. But then we got to our own private box, and Liv got in one of the cushy armchairs and reclined. "Gosh, having a rich brother does have its perks."

Laughing, I sat beside her. "Wait until the server comes and offers you free drinks."

Her eyes widened. "Oh my gosh, I completely forgot that was a thing!" She grabbed her foam finger and held it up. "Gooo, Gage!"

A knock sounded on the suite door, and I called, "Come in," expecting a server.

Instead, Rex Whistler, manager of the Ropers, walked inside.

Liv's jaw dropped, but I stood, extending my hand. "Great to see you, Rex."

He gave me a lopsided grin, his leathery skin wrinkling with his smile. "Likewise. Can't stay long, but thought I'd check in since I heard you're here."

"Have you met my sister yet?" I said, gesturing toward Liv. "Pretty sure she's your biggest fan."

She got up, taking her foam finger and extending her hand. "It's an honor to meet you, Coach."

He chuckled, shaking her hand. "Likewise." Then he turned to me. "Thought I'd let you know that Levi is making a lot of progress. And our guys are having fun working with the Golden Valley kids. It's been good all around."

"I'm glad to hear that," I said. "I saw he started at shortstop last week."

Rex nodded. "He just needed a few nudges in the right direction. He'll get better as he matures."

"Glad to hear it."

Putting his hat back on, Rex said, "Better get down there for warmup. Talk soon."

"Good luck," I said.

As soon as the door shut behind Rex, Liv stared at me, incredulous.

"What?" I asked.

"Golden Valley?"

I clenched my jaw. I didn't like the tone in her voice.

"You're having the Ropers coach and players work with your coworker's kid."

The accusation in her tone put me on the defensive. "And? It was just to do something nice."

Liv scoffed, looking ridiculous to be so offended dressed up like she was. "You're kidding, right? No guy gets a *professional baseball team* to go play with a high school team for a girl they're not into."

Well, to be fair, Liv didn't know that I was already technically getting with her, but also, "Can't someone just care about kids?" I asked. "It's a nice thing to do, and I can afford to do it."

She shook her head. "You can do it all you want, but even though you're a nice guy, I don't know that you're *that* nice. Surely you have tons of employees who have kids who like baseball. Why this one?"

I lied to my sister, and maybe to myself. "I don't know."

GAGE

As soon as Liv headed back home for Cottonwood Falls, I got in my Tesla and drove toward Farrah's house because I couldn't stand being away from her any longer. When I arrived, I pulled along the curb but out of view of the front window and turned off my headlights. That mixed with the lack of streetlights made me feel a little bit like a stalker, but I wasn't just going to hide out.

I got out my cell phone and sent Farrah a text.

Gage: Kids asleep?

The front window looked dark save for the glow of the TV screen.

Farrah: They're not asleep, but I'm alone in my room. ;)

Gage: You should go outside and look at the moon. You might be able to see it from the south side of your house.

I chewed the inside of my cheek, hoping she'd go out the front door like I suggested instead of looking out her backyard.

A few moments passed, and then the front door opened. Farrah slipped out, her curls pulled into a high ponytail and leggings hugging her legs and ass. She wore a baggy, light gray sweater that almost looked white in the dim lighting.

She wrapped her arms around herself, her face tipping up toward the sky.

My heart jolted with Liv's words. *What is it about her?*

It was this. The moments when she was full of wonder, completely herself, even when she didn't think anyone was watching.

Gage: Check behind you.

A moment later, she reached into her shirt, pulling her phone out of her bra and making me chuckle. As soon as she read the text, she glanced around, and her eyes landed on my black Tesla. With her mouth open in a surprised smile, she walked toward me.

I rolled down my window as she drew close.

Her hands rested on the open window. "What are you doing here?"

"I wanted to see you."

Even in the night, I could see color flood her cheeks.

"Get in?" I said.

Her head turned toward the house and back to me, brown eyes alight with energy. "My kids are in the house!"

"With their dad, right? Surely they won't miss you for a few minutes."

She smirked. "So you're saying it will only take a few minutes?"

"With the way your ass looks in those leggings, you'll be lucky if it doesn't take a few seconds." I reached across the seat, pulling the door handle, and she got in the car, grinning wide.

"I feel like a teenager sneaking out of the house," she said.

"You snuck out when you were younger?" I asked, surprised. "I figured you were the kind that could talk your way into anything."

"You haven't met my parents." Then she smiled. "But you will, at the photo shoot, and then you'll understand."

"I'm looking forward to it," I said, putting the car in reverse and backing away so no one in her house would guess we were driving by. At Farrah's curious look, I said, "I did my fair share of rebelling in high school too."

Farrah reached across the car, putting her hand on my thigh. "Can't wait to see what trouble we get into."

30

FARRAH

I texted Caleb that I was going on a walk to enjoy the beautiful night air. A buzz of excitement spread in my veins as Gage drove away from my house with the headlights off.

This man next to me made me feel alive in the best possible way.

I roved my hand up his thigh, reaching the hard tip of his erection straining against his pants, and lost the breath from my lungs. Sometimes it was hard to believe this cock was mine to enjoy.

"I don't know this area," he said. "Is there a good place to park?"

"Maybe," I replied, "but I have another idea."

"What's that?" he asked, but I was already working my hand to the waistband of his jeans, pulling at the hem of his white T-shirt, reaching for the button.

"Farrah..."

I glanced up, noticing his dark eyes focused on the road. His jaw clenched. I loved the intensity of his stare, especially knowing that he hid a generous heart underneath.

The button came free, and he shifted his hips, letting me slide the zipper down and free his cock from his jeans.

In the light from the dash, I took it in. The length, girth, soft skin and broad tip. "Have I mentioned I love your cock?" I wrapped my fingers around it, pumping slowly.

"The feeling is mutual," he muttered, closing his eyes briefly before focusing back on the road.

I hadn't given road head since I was in high school, and that had been a bucket list item for my boyfriend at the time when I was reckless and thought the world lay at my feet. Now, at thirty-four years old, I felt so much less fearless.

"What are you waiting for, baby?" he asked, curling a hand through my hair.

I sat back, biting my lip, and tears stung my eyes. God, could I please stop crying with my not-boyfriend's cock in my face? It had to be a huge confidence booster for him. "I'm sorry."

Gage pulled alongside the curb on a dark residential street. He zipped his pants back up and reached across the console, brushing my wet cheek with his thumb. "Baby, what's wrong?"

"I'm sorry," I said again. I wiped at my eyes, trying to stop these emotions, these fears, from breaking loose. But being around Caleb today, hearing him mention he was dating someone, it brought all those feelings back from when I first found out I was being cheated on. Sometimes I wished Caleb would have just left me instead of cheating, so I could believe it was just me he had the issue with, not that he had found someone better.

"Don't apologize," he said, wiping my tears. "Just tell me what I can do to fix it."

But the thing was, he couldn't fix it. Because I knew this thing between us would come to an end, and... I didn't want it to. I liked the way I felt when I was around Gage. I liked being sexy and wild and desired.

And I knew it wasn't hot to admit how scared I was, and our time was limited, and I was wasting it with these tears when we could both be making each other feel good. But I couldn't stop myself.

So I lied, keeping it close to the truth. I hadn't given Caleb head since his last birthday more than a year ago.

"I don't even know if I'm good at giving head, and I don't want to embarrass myself in front of you more than I already have." I choked out a half-sob, half-laugh. "Is crying or bad head worse?"

31

GAGE

How was she making me smile even with these tears running down her cheeks? Instead of thinking about it, thinking how much I would miss her when she found a man who could give her more than stolen kisses, I reached across the console, placing my lips against hers, feeling her wet skin against my face.

She whimpered softly, leaning into my kiss, and I put my hand at her neck, twining my fingers through the loose curls in her ponytail. Her mouth moved against mine, searching, and I met each curve of her lips with a push of my own.

Our tongues slowly mingled, feeling out this moment and pushing away the tears, the insecurities, until it was just her and me.

As she broke apart, her breathing ragged, I said, "You are enough, Farrah. Exactly as you are."

A tear slipped down her cheek. "You can't say things like that."

"Why not?"

"Because you'll make me fall for you."

And because it was already too late for me, I kissed her again. Hungrily. All the reasons I'd been holding back fell away as I pulled her onto my lap, and we kissed more passionately, slowly losing the layers between us until I put on a condom and sank my cock into her, moving my hips underneath her weight and spinning my fingers over her clit until she clenched around me and I poured all of myself into her.

After we cleaned up, I dropped her off at her house. And as I drove away, a sinking feeling filled my stomach.

This wasn't just a hook up. Not anymore.

I was going to tell her how I felt. And not in a car on the side of a road. No, I'd do it the way she deserved.

And I hoped like hell she wouldn't turn me away.

32

FARRAH

I played my good mood playlist on the way to drop the kids off at school, singing along to every song.

Levi pretended to cover his ears, but he couldn't hide the smile on his face. This last weekend with Caleb coming to watch the game and then staying the night had gone so much better. He kept his mouth shut about my personal life, actually bought a rock painting kit for Andrew, complimented Levi on his game, and played well with Cora.

And that late-night tryst with Gage? Well, that made things all the better. I couldn't wait to see him today. I was already hoping for another car ride with him, so I could have a second chance at giving him road head. Without the tears this time.

But just as I pulled up to The Retreat, my phone began ringing with a call from Andrew and Cora's school. I pushed the button on the dash, answering, "This is Farrah Elkins."

"Ms. Elkins, this is Nurse Palmer at Golden Valley

Elementary. Andrew had a serious accident on the play-ground this morning, and we're bringing him to the emergency room to have him checked."

If I'd have been holding my phone, I would have dropped it. "Oh my gosh. What happened? Which ER?"

"Golden Valley Memorial," she answered, and I immediately whipped out of the parking lot, driving toward the big hospital closest to my house. "He was playing on the jungle gym and fell, knocking his chin on the bar. He bit through his bottom lip, and we suspect he has a concussion."

My heart felt like ice in my chest. "Is he alert?"

"Yes, but he's exhibiting some of the common signs— dizziness and nausea especially."

"Oh my gosh. I will be at the hospital in twenty minutes."

"I'll let him know."

We hung up, and I pressed my foot to the gas pedal, weaving through traffic to get to my baby quickly. I couldn't imagine what pain he must be in, and I hated that I wasn't there for him right now.

I punched in Gage's number first, and as soon as he answered, I said, "I'm so sorry, but I won't be in the office today. Andrew was hurt on the playground and is going to the emergency room."

"Shit, Farrah, is there anything I can do? Which hospital?"

"I don't think so. He's going to Golden Valley Memo-rial. It's a good one, as far as I know."

"Keep me updated?"

"I will," I said.

As soon as we got off the call, I dialed my mom's

number to let her know what happened. She said she'd meet me at the hospital and keep Dad in the loop while he worked at the coffee shop.

I was almost to the hospital when I realized I hadn't yet called Caleb. Guilt swept through me at the fact that I'd called Gage before him. But then I reminded myself that Gage was my boss. He needed to know when I would and wouldn't be at work. At least that's what I told myself.

Caleb answered after a few rings, and when I filled him in, he offered to drive to Dallas. All past hurts aside, it was good to know that when push came to shove, he'd be there for the kids.

"Let me get a feel for things at the hospital before you head this way, but I think we have it handled here. Plus, you'll see him at the end of the week for Cabo. I'll have him video call you as soon as we can, though, okay?"

"I trust you, Farrah," Caleb said. It was the first nice thing he'd said to me since the split.

"Thank you," I replied. "I'm in the parking lot now. I'll text you as soon as I know anything."

Once I walked into the hospital, the nurse up front directed me to emergency room eight, and it took all I had not to sprint to Andrew. When I reached the room, he was lying back on the bed, blood seeping through the bandage on his lip. A woman I guessed was Nurse Palmer sat next to him.

"Mommy?" Andrew rasped and then winced.

Tears filled my eyes. "Oh, honey, I'm here. I'm here."

I dropped my purse in the chair and sat next to him on the bed, pulling him into my arms.

The woman next to him stood. "Ms. Elkins, I'm Nurse Palmer. The doctor's already been in, and they're planning to stitch his bottom lip. He thinks it will take ten to twelve stitches. The concussion seems mild, but they'll want him to rest for the next couple days."

"Absolutely," I said. "Thank you so much for staying with him."

She smiled at me. "Of course." Then she squeezed Drew's hand and said, "You get to feeling better soon, okay, buddy?"

He nodded, his blue eyes wide.

"Hopefully I'll see you before school lets out, but if not, have a great summer," she said with a smile and left the room.

With just me and Drew there, I said, "I called Grammy and Grandpa. Grammy's on her way, and Dad said he'd come if you wanted him to, but you can just call him if you want."

"Call," Andrew said, limiting his words.

I got out my phone and called Caleb, filling him in on what Nurse Palmer said and letting him know Andrew wouldn't be one for conversation.

"Video call me?" Caleb asked.

"Of course." I pressed the button and soon Caleb appeared on the screen, dressed sharply in a black suit, backdropped by his office. I turned the phone so he could see Drew more than me.

"I'm so sorry you got hurt, bud," Caleb said. "Mommy told me it hurts to talk, so you don't have to say anything. I just want you to know I love you and I'm here if you need anything. If you decide you want me to come, I'll be there in a few hours."

Andrew nodded.

"I love you, honey."

"Love you," he said, cringing afterward.

I faced the phone back at me, and Caleb had an empathetic look in his eyes. "Man, he looks miserable, but he's so strong."

I ran my hand through Andrew's hair. "The toughest."

The door to the room opened, and an older woman in a white coat came in carrying a kit of some sort. "Hi, I'm the nurse working with Andrew here. You must be Mom?"

I nodded. "And we have Dad on the phone."

"Great. I'm going to put some numbing cream on Mr. Andrew here, so he won't feel the stitches at all."

I hoped she was right.

✌

ANDREW, Mom, and I walked out of the hospital a few hours later with instructions to keep the stitches clean and let Andrew rest for the next couple of days. We parted ways so I could get Andrew home and Mom could grab Cora from school.

Seeing my baby get stitched up was hard on my heart, and I was ready to cry myself. I just wanted a sign, something to tell me things were looking up. And then when we got back to my place, I saw it...

A dandelion in the yard.

I bit my lip, smiling at it, and then walked Andrew inside, leading him to his room and helping him get comfortable. I went to the kitchen to make lunch and got out my phone to call Gage.

"Hey, is everything okay with Andrew?" he asked.

"He's doing well. I can't believe how brave he was when they stitched his lip. The doctor says we need to do at least a day with no screens and dim lighting, so I'm trying to figure out what we can do besides just draw. He should be good to go back to school on Thursday, though. Just in time for his last day."

"That's good," he said.

I leaned my hips back against the kitchen counter, breathing a sigh of relief. "I feel like the universe sent me a sign."

"With his injury?" Gage asked.

"No, with a dandelion... I was feeling really sorry for Andrew and sorry for myself when I walked up to the yard and saw one there."

"So what's the sign?" Gage asked. "That your landlord needs to spray the yard?"

"No!" I laughed. "Dandelions have always been a good sign for me."

"What do you mean?"

I moved from the counter, looking in the fridge for the ingredients to make homemade mac 'n' cheese, Andrew's favorite. "When I was a young mom and staying at home with Levi, I was having a hard time. I felt like my whole life was busy and overwhelming, and I worried so much that I was failing as a mother. And one day I was crying to my mom on the phone, then Levi came up to me with a little yellow dandelion. Here he was, this little two-year-old with nothing in the world, and he loved me enough to bring me the only thing he had. He saw it and thought of me. *Me.* And I thought, maybe I'm not so bad at being a mom, because this little boy has a heart as golden as that flower. It was everything."

I smiled at the memory, filling a pot with water to boil. "Eventually, they saw how happy it made me, and every day I would have a bouquet of dandelions by supper time. I'd always set them in my best vase on the table, and they'd be so proud of what they brought me. It made everyone so happy. And it seems like every time I hit my breaking point, one of the kids brings me a dandelion. So to me, dandelions aren't a weed. They're a sign of love. That everything is going to be okay." I shifted my phone to my other ear. "I know that probably sounds silly—"

"It's not silly at all," Gage said. "It's you."

33

GAGE

Farrah came into the office Thursday morning with two cups from Barry's. "Cortado for you," she said, handing me one drink and then a folded piece of paper. "And a thank you card from Andrew. The 3D printing pen was an amazing gift for him. It helped so much since we had to limit screen time."

I rubbed the back of my neck. "It was nothing, really. How's he holding up?"

She sank into her chair across from me, rubbing her temples. "He's back at school today, with strict instructions to stay off that jungle gym. Let's hope he can stay uninjured the last two days of school."

I chuckled. "You're handling it well."

"It's been a hell of a week. All the kids are going on a trip to Cabo with their dad next week, so I had to buy all the kids swimsuits, not to mention do laundry."

"Wait. Your kids are going to be out of town next week?"

She smirked. "That's all you heard out of that, huh?"

"I heard I'm getting you all to myself." My cock was already getting ideas. Part of me wanted to put off telling her how I felt so that I could have the week with her. If things went bad when I confessed my feelings, I knew we wouldn't go back to having this casual relationship anymore.

But I also knew if I didn't tell her, I'd end up blurting it out at the worst possible time. And Farrah didn't deserve that. She deserved romance. Candles. Flowers. The whole nine yards.

"When can I see you outside of work?" I asked. "Friday night?"

Her features fell with disappointment. "I have a... thing Friday night. And I have to bring the kids to Austin on Saturday. I can come over when I get back that night?"

I didn't want to wait, but I nodded. "And pack a bag, because there's no way I'm letting you leave."

Her eyes flamed with a mix of excitement and desire, and it took all I had not to bend her over this desk and give her a preview of what was coming.

"You know," she said, "I've never been to your place before. What if it's just a smelly bachelor pad?" she teased. "Maybe you should stay with me?"

I snorted. "Your house is great, but mine is the furthest thing from a bachelor pad. You'll see."

She chewed her lip, worry in her eyes. She wore all of her emotions like the pages of a book.

"What are you worried about?" I asked, reaching across the table for her hand.

She ran her thumb over mine. "I just don't want to be another girl you hide at your place."

My heart stuttered in my chest. Did that mean she was starting to feel the same way about me? The hope I felt was dangerous. "I've never brought a woman over."

Her eyes widened. "You're kidding."

"No."

"Lying?"

"Not a chance."

"Celibate?" She had a playful smile on her lips.

But I wasn't joking. I leaned forward, making sure she had a clear view of my face, of just how serious I was. "I don't bring women to my home. Ever. We stay at a hotel or her place. You are the first, Farrah. The only." *The last.* I was too close to giving it all away, so I straightened. "I have a lunch meeting I need to prepare for, but I'll certainly be looking forward to Saturday."

She smiled tentatively. "Same here."

BY SOME MIRACLE, I made it through the week without blurting out the way I felt. So when Mia and I met at four on Friday, I poured us both a glass of scotch and passed one to her, lifting my glass.

She eyed me skeptically before clinking her glass to mine. "We haven't toasted since you partnered with Petersons on the condo building in Port Aransas."

"First order of business," I said. "I need you to have a florist deliver two dozen bouquets of yellow dandelions to my place Saturday morning."

"Dandelions... like the weed." Mia seemed unconvinced. "I thought Farrah was the only one who liked those."

If I'd been mid sip, I would have spat it out. Steeling myself, I said, "Out of seven billion people, there's sure to be more than one, right?"

Mia arched her eyebrow. "A truckload of lingerie, and now you're buying weeds in bulk? You must be serious about this girl."

I couldn't help the smile that formed on my lips. I felt young. Light. For the first time in a long time. "Possibly. I think you'll like her."

Mia's eyes practically bugged out of her head. "I've been working with you for three years, and you've never once been this smitten. One-time dates to functions, sure, but an actual girlfriend with over-the-top gifts? Who is this magical unicorn of a woman?"

I chuckled and took a sip of my scotch. "You'll find out if everything goes well Saturday."

Mia shimmied her shoulders excitedly. "Romance must be in the air. Farrah's got a date with Pascale tonight."

I felt like I'd been punched in the gut. The face. The nuts.

"Actually," Mia continued, "I forgot to mention, I'm babysitting for Farrah at six, so I need to be out of here by five thirty."

I downed some scotch, trying to settle the irrational emotions going through my mind. I *knew* that fucker liked Farrah.

And I also knew I told her we would not have a relationship.

So of course a beautiful woman like her would get asked on a date.

And I should let her go, right? Stop being selfish so

she could have a relationship with someone who didn't have a billion-dollar company to run.

But then again, I'd never been the kind to lie down and give up on what I wanted.

And I wanted Farrah to be mine.

Only mine.

34

FARRAH

I finished changing out of my work clothes into a comfortable black cotton dress, adding a necklace and earrings to match. Cora watched me from the stool in the bathroom. "Can I put lipstick on you?"

I chuckled. "Only if I can put some on you."

She smiled big. "Deal."

I reached into my makeup bag, pulling out my favorite shade of plum, and passed it to her. "Be careful though; it can stain."

I held my breath as she brought the lipstick to my mouth, tracing the pattern of my lips. When she was done, she stepped back, squinting at me and admiring her work. "So pretty, Mommy."

I chanced a look in the mirror. She actually hadn't done a bad job. I rubbed my lips together and used my finger to wipe at the corners. Then I took the color and drew it over Cora's mouth.

With it done, I capped the lipstick and made a kissy face at her.

She blew a kiss back. "We're pretty, right, Mama?"

"So pretty," I agreed, picking up my phone to take a picture of the two of us in the mirror.

The doorbell rang, so we finished our impromptu photo shoot and walked together to the living room, where Levi and Andrew were playing video games.

"Thanks for answering the door, guys," I said, and of course they ignored me, completely absorbed in their game.

Cora came with me to the door, and when I swung it open, she jumped into Mia's arms. "Auntie Mia!" she cried.

Mia picked her up, spinning her around. "Cora! Show me the new digs!"

Cora led Mia on a tour of the house, and then Mia asked Cora to go pick out her favorite stuffed animals for a tea party. As Cora ran off, Mia said, "Are you excited for the date?"

I glanced to the boys, glad they hadn't heard, and back to Mia. "It's a *networking event*." I still hadn't talked to the kids about me dating someday. Although my feelings for Gage made me think I might be ready sooner rather than later.

The kids didn't know that their dad cheated on me, so in their eyes, this divorce was confusing. Me dating another man? I worried it would just upset them more.

"Right." Mia winked.

Cora came out of the bedroom, carrying a teddy bear so big she had to lean back to balance its weight.

Mia giggled, taking the bear from her. "You go have fun, Far, and we'll see you when you get home. No curfews."

"I'll be home by ten at the latest," I said.

"Midnight," Mia replied.

I laughed. "You're the best bad influence ever. You can order food—I'll Venmo you for whatever it is. And make sure the boys both get showers in tonight."

"Aye, aye," Mia said, saluting me and making Cora giggle.

"Bye, boys, love you," I said.

Their eyes stayed glued on the screen.

"LOVE YOU!" I said louder.

Levi nodded, but Andrew glanced my way and said, "Love you."

"Never grow up," I replied, giving Cora a big hug and planting an even bigger kiss on her cheek that left a plum lip mark. "Love you, sweet pea."

"Love you, Mommy."

Waving goodbye, I made my way outside. The stark memory of walking out the door and seeing Gage in his Tesla flashed through my mind. He'd looked so sexy in his T-shirt and jeans, peeking at me through the rolled down window.

What I wouldn't give to be spending this evening with him instead of Pascale. But Mia was right—business connections were important. And I still hadn't brought up the future to Gage yet. I knew I should have, but part of me worried talking about anything but the present would blow up this bubble we had. I wasn't ready for that. Not yet.

I got in my car, typing in the address to the wine bar and driving across town with music playing on the radio. Only twenty-four hours, I reminded myself.

Twenty-four hours until I had a whole week to spend

in the arms of Gage Griffen. I'd miss my kids like crazy, but a week with Gage? I tried not to let my heart get carried away, reminding myself that Gage was not mine, no matter how many imaginative liberties I wanted to take with the fact that I was the first woman to see his place.

Since I couldn't parallel park to save my life, it took me a while to find a parking spot, and I was already ten minutes late when I rushed into the dimly lit bar. Smooth jazz came from a small stage up front, and I quickly spotted Pascale.

He looked all dark and broody at the back table with his brown hair falling over his face and his tattooed hands wrapped around a glass tumbler. When he caught sight of me walking in, his lips spread into a sultry smile.

"Sorry I'm late," I said, approaching him. "I couldn't find a place to park."

"No worries," he replied, sitting as I did.

"Do we order at the bar?" I asked.

"A server will be by."

Silence hung between us. *Awkward*. So I said, "How was your day?"

"Better now."

An uneasy feeling swept through me. I really didn't want Pascale getting the wrong idea. "I'm excited to talk more business with you," I said, trying to set the tone. "How did you get into photography?"

That opened the floodgates. He was halfway through telling me a story about his first camera when a server came by. All the wine I drank was out of a box, so I pointed at the cheapest glass on the menu, hoping it would taste okay, and continued asking Pascale about himself.

He'd had an interesting career, starting out as a portrait photographer but eventually making his way to art installations. "Larger corporations have more money to spend on creative, so it made sense to give me the kind of life I want to live."

"And what kind of life is that?" I asked. "What's the dream?"

He quirked his lips. "A glass of wine with a beautiful woman on a Friday night is an amazing start. But I also want a life full of travel, adventure, growth. I've never been the kind to stand still for very long."

The waitress brought my glass of wine, and I sampled it. Not bad.

"You like?" Pascale asked.

I nodded. "It's great."

"And you?" he asked. "What is the dream for the talented Farrah Elkins?"

I smiled slightly. So much of my life had been wrapped up in my children—giving them the quality of life I believed they deserved. Space to explore their interests, but mostly a mom at home who would always have their backs, just like my mom had done for me. I liked working too—creating something beautiful from a blank slate. Because I knew someday all three children would fly the coop, and I'd be alone.

The feeling hit me like a ton of bricks to the chest as I met Pascale's curious gaze. "I want to live a life full of love."

"The best way to receive is to give," he said.

But I wasn't so sure that was true, because I'd given to

Caleb. I'd given more than I could even put into words. The only man who'd given to me so unselfishly was... Gage.

From the moment he met me, he'd given me a job. A pass on door-dinging his car. Credit card points to furnish my new home. An opportunity to excel professionally. Mind-blowing sex. But was that where it ended?

"I have to use the bathroom," I said.

Pascale tipped his head toward a restroom at the back of the bar, and I stood, taking my purse and walking that way.

In the quiet of the stall, I got out my phone and made a call.

35

GAGE

My ringtone played through my AirPods, and I put down the weight bar, glancing at my phone. Farrah's name was on the screen.

It was only... a quarter past seven. And I was an hour into my workout, trying to forget the fact that she was on a date with another man. Ignoring the reality that she could decide to be with someone other than me.

I sat up on the bench and caught my breath before answering the call. "Farrah?"

"Hey," she said gently. Her voice was like the first morning sun on a cold day.

"What's up?" I asked. "Everything okay?"

"I was just... working on an idea for the front entrance, and I wanted to get your take on it."

A smile formed on my lips.

She was calling me on her date.

Me.

"Let's hear it," I said.

She paused. "A coat tree."

"A coat tree?"

"Yeah," she said. "They hold... coats."

My smile only grew wider. "Wouldn't our guests want to bring their coats up to their rooms?"

"Good point," she said. "I knew I needed to run it by you."

The sound of a toilet flushing came through the phone, and I said, "Are you working in your bathroom?"

"Needed some privacy from the kids, you know?"

"Sure," I replied.

"Thanks for talking that over with me," she said.

"Of course. If you have any more ideas... I'm here."

She was quiet for a long moment before she said, "I'll see you tomorrow?"

"See you tomorrow."

36

FARRAH

Mia was disappointed when I came home at nine with only a business card to show for my "date."

But I wasn't. Pascale and I had decent conversation, and he told me he'd connect me to anyone he knew who needed an interior designer. The evening was exactly what it needed to be.

And hearing Gage's voice on the other end of the phone? It was a balm to my soul that I didn't know I needed. And that scared me, because he'd been very clear about what he wanted from me. What if I told him how I felt, and he ended things? What if he didn't end our casual fling, but couldn't commit to the kind of relationship I wanted? Would it be too painful for me to continue?

All the worries and fears swirled through the back of my mind that night and the next morning as I helped the kids get ready for the drive to Austin.

We packed all of their things into the minivan, and on

the way, I tried not to cry at how much I'd miss them while they were gone. I realized that in the last several months, we'd made a home here in Dallas. We had a rhythm, a routine, that worked for us.

And being away from them? It would feel like missing a limb.

Cora, Andrew and I played I Spy and road sign ABC most of the way while Levi sat up front, managing the playlist and texting on his phone.

"Who are you talking to?" I asked, trying to make conversation between games.

"Alyssa," he said, not looking at me.

A girl? *Be cool, Farrah.* "Oh... is she a friend from school?" *I think that was okay?*

"Yeah."

Gosh. I wished I could get more than one-word answers out of him. "How did you meet her?"

"Chemistry."

I let out a small laugh at the irony.

"What's funny?" Levi asked.

There was two words. One more than usual. "Your father and I met in a chemistry lab second semester of freshman year at Upton. He accidentally poured acid on my lab coat, and we had to use the emergency shower in the classroom to make sure I wouldn't get a chemical burn."

"Gross!" Levi said. "You had to shower in front of everyone?"

I laughed. "I was fully clothed. And it turned out fine. We ended up with you."

The tips of his ears turned pink.

From the back seat, Andrew asked, "Was it love at first sight?"

I smiled slightly, realizing that thinking of the past with Caleb already didn't hurt like it used to. "Not quite. I was still mad at your dad for the whole acid thing."

Levi chuckled, and I held on to the moment.

"Maybe Alyssa can come by for movie night when you guys get back?" I suggested.

He shook his head. "I don't want to embarrass her. But if I can take her out to the movie theater..."

"That sounds fun," I said.

He smiled, typing on his phone again.

It struck me that the world was wide open for Levi. His own love stories, heartbreaks, and comebacks were all ahead of him still. And even though I had so much life behind me, I realized... I still had a lot ahead too.

We reached the Austin city limits, and Cora said, "I remember this place."

I laughed. "You should remember it; we lived here almost your whole life."

"It's been a while," she said.

"True."

Memories hit me, one after another as we got closer to the house. Moving into our first home. Caleb getting promoted, working more hours away. Building a bigger, better house. Finding receipts for six bottles of my perfume, two for one, in his pocket. Rationalizing that he was stocking up for birthdays and anniversaries. Weekend trips with limited phone calls to me or the kids. Telling myself it was because he was a dedicated provider. Feeling like we were roommates instead of husband and wife.

And then the proof. A positive HPV test.

Searching through his phone.

Finding a text from his receptionist asking when he was leaving me.

And his reply.

Soon.

Before finally, he admitted the truth.

I parked in the driveway behind a car I didn't recognize and got out of the van.

The kids piled out as well, and I went to the trunk, unloading their suitcases as they ran to the front door.

Caleb came outside, followed by...

My jaw went slack.

"Kids, do you remember Melinda and Adabelle?" he asked them.

I walked toward the spectacle, drawn to it like a bug to a zapper. Caleb had his arm around the waist of a thin blond, and a little girl held on to her hand. I knew he'd been dating someone, but this was the last person I expected.

Melinda was a single mom from the kids' old school, and Adabelle had been Cora's best friend. Now I knew why she hadn't called me after the split.

Cora ran to Adabelle, squealing and wrapping her in a hug. "I missed you!"

Melinda smiled at Andrew and Levi, not making eye contact with me at all. Levi's shoulders were stiff, his jaw tight.

"Levi, you've grown a foot!" Melinda said. "And Andrew, you look like you're sixteen already!"

Andrew groused, "I'm only eight. Birthday August second."

"Kids," Caleb said, "why don't you go inside and play while we get your bags ready?"

Levi glanced at me like he was asking permission. I nodded, letting him know it was okay.

When the door closed behind them, I said, "Melinda, what a surprise. I wasn't expecting to see you."

She smiled awkwardly between me and Caleb. "I'm sorry I didn't reach out after you left..."

Caleb squeezed her shoulder, saying, "I've been meaning to tell you. Melinda and I ran into each other at the grocery store a few months ago and got to talking, and well... Here we are."

He squeezed her even tighter to his side, and she smiled adoringly up at him, and it was all... wrong.

"A few months ago?" I asked, doing the math in my head. That was about the time he started watching Levi's games online. Had Melinda been the one to push him to show up for his kids?

Caleb nodded. "I was going to tell you, but..." His words trailed off.

"Tell me what, exactly?" I asked. "That you were going to surprise the kids with your new girlfriend? That wasn't fair, Caleb. I could have prepared them to meet her."

Caleb rubbed the back of his neck awkwardly. "I didn't want you putting bad feelings in their heads."

The words felt like a slap in the face. "I never told them about you cheating on me, yet you thought I'd turn them against your girlfriend now that we're divorced? You didn't deserve it, but no one's protected you to them like I have."

Color flooded Caleb's cheeks, making them ruddy. "I think the trip could be a good time for everyone to bond."

My jaw fell open. "Wait. The trip? You're going *together?*"

Melinda's eyes were wide and scared. She whispered, "I told you we should have let her know, Caleb."

But he brushed her off, back to his overconfident self. "You already knew and liked Melinda. The kids know her. She's a safe person and an amazing mom. There was no need to get your permission, Farrah. Just like you didn't ask my permission to move into a new place I'd never seen before or, I dunno, sneak off in some guy's Tesla the night I was there."

My eyes pricked with angry, embarrassed tears. "That's not the point."

"Then what is?" he asked.

Overwhelmed, I said, "I have done everything for these kids since we left Austin. *Everything*. It's going to hurt like hell to be away from them this long, and now the trip I'd mentally prepared myself for is some kind of... blended family bonding activity? I feel like I have no idea what's going on with them, and it makes me worry."

Melinda held up her hands like she was trying to soothe a wild horse. "I totally understand, Farrah. I don't want this to be uncomfortable. In fact, I hope we'll eventually be able to co-parent the kids successfully."

"Co-parent?" I asked.

Then I noticed it. The giant rock shining on Melinda's ring finger.

I sat down in the middle of the lawn, unable to stand anymore, and tried to take deep breaths.

"Oh my god!" Melinda came to my side. "Are you okay?"

I waved her off. "Can I have a word with Caleb? Alone?"

Melinda nodded, but Caleb said, "Melinda and me? We're a package deal. And I'm their parent too, damn it. I have partial custody, and I know I was in a bad way after the divorce, but I've stepped up, haven't I? I've started showing up to games, and I've made child support payments on time, every time."

"You have, but that's not all there is to being a parent. You don't get to check out and in when you feel like it because you sign a check."

"I know," Caleb said.

I pushed myself up from the ground, standing on shaky legs. "Those kids are my world, Caleb. And from now on, you need to tell me when things are changing in their lives here. Both of you." I pinned Melinda with a stare. "Do you understand?"

Caleb nodded. So did she.

"I don't like it," I said.

"I know," Caleb replied. "You don't have to."

I walked past him and Melinda into the home Caleb and I used to share. But most of the decorations I'd slaved over were gone, replaced with Melinda's touch. Even the accent walls I'd painted were now covered with a bland greige. It was like he'd completely erased me, erased my voice.

I'd expected to be hurt, but instead, I felt a sense of... relief? Exhaustion? Because Caleb and I were over in every single way that mattered. But these kids? They would always tie us together. They would always be ours. Not just mine.

All the kids were in the living room, and when I reached them, I said, "Adabelle, can you go get your mommy?"

She nodded, running toward the front door.

"Kids, follow me."

We walked to the back room. It used to be a play-room, but now it looked more like a home office. I closed the door behind us and faced all of them. "Look, I didn't know your dad was seeing anyone, and I know it's prob-ably strange to see one of your parents dating, but he decided to invite Melinda on this trip without telling me so I could warn you." I took a deep breath. This week was supposed to be their week with their dad, my week with Gage, but I would give it up, give anything up for these kids. "If you're uncomfortable in any way and decide you don't want to go, you can come home with me. It's your choice."

Cora said, "I want to go! I can't believe Ada and I are going to be sisters!"

I fought to make my smile seem genuine. "Great, honey." I turned to Andrew and Levi.

Levi's jaw worked angrily, but Andrew faced the ground. His little voice wobbled as he said, "I wanted to go boogie boarding."

"You can still go," I said, rubbing his shoulder. "It won't hurt my feelings at all. I want you to have a fun week, however you decide to have it."

Andrew nodded. "I want to go, if Levi wants to go."

All of us looked at Levi, and he said in a rough voice, "Can we talk alone?"

I nodded and said, "You two can wait outside."

Both Andrew and Cora hesitated.

"Three... two..."

Cora groaned and Andrew pouted, but they both walked to the door. When they left, I looked at Levi and said, "I'm here, babe. What's up?"

Levi said, "What the fuck?"

"Language," I said, but honestly, I was thinking the same thing.

"Seriously." He jerked his arm toward the door. "You're here making it work as a single mom, taking care of us, and he's shacking up with some ho from the PTA?"

It was the most words I'd heard from him in months, and it made my heart ache. "She's not a ho."

He shook his head. "I know he was cheating on you."

My eyes widened. I'd worked so hard to keep it from the kids, not wanting them to see their dad as a villain. "How did you find out?"

"I heard Dad on the phone with his secretary one night. He tried to pretend it was a work call, and I believed him, but now..." His voice broke. "How could he do that to you?"

Suddenly, Levi wasn't a teen on the verge of becoming a man. He was my little boy again who thought a plastic sword could protect us from the world's evils. He hadn't known that the people who hurt you most are rarely faceless strangers, but the ones you trust with all your heart.

I pulled him into my arms just like I had when he'd scraped his knee. "People make mistakes," was all I could say. "And we have to decide what we'll tolerate. Cheating was one mistake I couldn't deal with."

He nodded, sniffing as he pulled back. "I'm so mad at him."

"It's okay to be angry," I said.

He nodded, looking toward the ground.

"And I mean it—you don't have to go if you don't want to. It can be a Mom and Levi week, if you want."

Levi shook his head. "Andrew said he won't go if I don't go. And he's gonna be torn up if he can't do that sand art he saw on YouTube."

"It's nice of you to think of him, but I'm sure we can find a lake with a sandy shore near home."

Levi let out a mix between a growl and a groan. "I don't want to miss Cabo because Dad's an idiot."

I snorted out a laugh. "That beach is just calling your name, huh?"

He gave me a sheepish smile that quickly fell. "It's just weird, like how could he move on so fast? And why does he want us to act like we're some big happy family with Melinda and Adabelle when our family went to Cabo *last year*?"

"I know it's hard to understand, but our marriage was over for a long time before the divorce."

"That's not the greatest love story," Levi said.

"It's not." I held him close, wishing he wasn't too tall for me to kiss the top of his head. "The greatest love story of my life will always be you and your siblings."

He looked at me a moment, tears in his eyes, before saying, "I love you, Mom."

My heart melted, and I hugged him tight before letting him go. "You know, I like this Levi. The one who says more than a syllable at a time."

"Don't get used to it," he said, but he was smiling slightly as he did.

✌

SAYING goodbye to the kids knowing Melinda was going on the trip with them instead of me made me want to pull my hair out. And of the three-hour drive back to Dallas, I spent the first hour crying.

Not because Caleb had moved on, but because the reality of divorce settled in even deeper. This was the kids' week with their dad. He was in charge. And even if I gave my opinion, I wasn't really in control. He could bring whoever he wanted on the trip, and I had no say.

The second hour, I called my mom and cried some more.

And the third hour, I tried to calm down enough to see Gage. I just wanted to get this horrible morning off my mind and distract myself with amazing sex with my boss.

In the parking garage of his apartment building, I freshened up my makeup, unable to completely hide how hard this day had been. Then I got out of the car, holding my travel bag, and walked to the elevator. I pressed the call button, ringing PH.

"Hello?" Gage's smooth voice came over the speaker.

It was a balm to my aching heart. "It's Farrah."

"Come up," he replied, and the elevator doors dinged open.

This had to be the fanciest elevator I'd ever set foot in, and that was saying something because The Retreat had some swanky elevators.

But when the numbers climbed all the way to the top and the door slid open, my jaw dropped.

Gage's condo was impressive. But even more stunning?

It was filled with bouquets of bright yellow dandelions.

A sign.

That everything was going to be okay.

37

GAGE

Farrah's hands covered her mouth... and she immediately began sobbing.

I strode across the apartment to her, taking her in my arms. "What's wrong?" Had I messed up somehow? "Did something happen?"

She held on to me, crying into my chest, and I couldn't believe how natural it was to stroke her hair and kiss the top of her head.

"I'm sorry," she cried. "I just had a rough morning. And this... it's all a little overwhelming."

"Sit with me," I said, pulling her toward the sofa. She cuddled in under my arm, resting her cheek on my chest.

"Tell me what happened," I said, brushing back her hair.

She used the heels of her hands to wipe at her eyes, leaving black mascara streaks behind. "It was hard enough dropping the kids off and knowing I'd be without them for a week. But when we got there." Her voice broke. "Caleb surprised us all with his new fiancée and future stepdaughter and said they were all going on the trip together. And it's not that I'm jealous; it's that I had no idea he was even seeing anyone. I didn't even have a chance to warn the kids."

"What the fuck," I uttered, speaking the first thing that came to mind.

"Exactly," she said, gesticulating. "What the fuck? Shouldn't I be notified about something like that before I pull up and see her standing on the front lawn with a rock the size of Rhode Island on her finger?"

"Was it the same woman from... before?" I asked, a protective instinct taking over. "Or was she a total stranger going on vacation with your kids?"

"We used to have playdates together," Farrah said bitterly. "So at least I know she's safe, but still."

I nodded. "I wouldn't be comfortable with that either if I had kids." I pulled her tighter into my hold. "I'm sorry. That was a really shitty thing of your ex to do."

She nodded, sniffling. "And I was so worried about how the week would go for us, since the kids and I have never been apart this long, and wondering if I did the right thing, and then I walked in here and saw this." She gestured at all the flowers. "It was like a sign from the universe that the kids are taken care of, that everything is going to be okay."

I took her hands in mine and hoped like hell the dandelions were a positive sign for me too.

"That was thoughtful of you to get them for me," she said. "I can't believe you even remembered me rambling on about them."

"I remember everything you say," I replied. It might not be the sexiest thing to admit, but it was true. "Farrah, I never considered myself a relationship guy. I thought I would be a brother and an uncle and a business owner and that would be it. But then I met you."

Her breath grew shallow. "What are you saying?"

I shifted so I could hold both her hands against my chest and look her in the eye. "I'm saying I want something real with you, Farrah."

Another tear slid down her cheek, and she slipped a hand from mine to wipe it away. "I thought you said..."

"I know what I said, and I was a dumbass. Ever since you walked through the doors for that interview, I knew there was something about you. I couldn't get you out of my head, and the more I got to know you, I couldn't get you out of my heart. I know you said you weren't looking for a relationship and you still have to raise children with your ex, but I can't go on pretending like this doesn't matter to me, because it does. I want this to be something real. Something more."

Her chest caught with her breath. "I..." A million emotions played across her eyes. "I signed an NDA, Gage."

Reaching into my pocket, I retrieved the release my lawyer worked up yesterday and handed it to her. "You have a copy in your inbox. If we're doing this, it's out loud."

Her eyes darted across the document on my screen, tears slowly building along her lower lashes. "Is this for real?"

I nodded, feeling like I was standing on the edge of a

cliff, rocks tumbling beneath my feet. Would she pull me back, or would she let me fall?

"You're so busy with work," she said.

I nodded. "But I usually only work until eight or nine, and I take most Sundays off."

"And I have kids."

"I've met two of them," I replied, a small smile on my lips. "They're equally as endearing as you are."

She stood up, pacing across my living room, looking beautiful and troubled amongst all the yellow flowers. "And I'm crying half the time we're supposed to be hooking up."

I chuckled. "I think I'm getting used to it."

Fighting a smile, she shook her head at me. "I'm a mom, Gage."

"We've established that."

"But I need you to understand... It means my kids are my life. They come first. And I'm not going to start a relationship, a serious relationship, with someone who isn't all in. Who doesn't understand that my kids and me are a package deal."

I stood, crossing the room and taking her face in my hands. "Farrah, I'm all in, with you and your children. How can I prove it to you?"

"You're saying everything I want..."

"But." My chest felt tight. I felt so close to falling, hitting the bottom.

She looked up at me with big doe eyes. "You're saying everything I want, but... I promised myself that when I dated for real again, I wouldn't settle. Caleb only married me because of Levi. And I don't regret my kids at all, but if I do it again, I promised myself that my man would put me first. He'd spend evenings with me, weekends. He'd encourage me in reaching my goals, support and love my children as if they were his own. He'd have a family that loved me and my kids equally, didn't look down on me for my previous marriage. And if we ever got married, it wouldn't be out of obligation, but because I was the one he wanted by his side forever." She barely paused long enough to take a breath. "And I know it's a lot to think about before we've even gone on a real date, but it's what I need, Gage. And if you can't give that to me long term, just tell me now before I get more invested than I already am."

Her words did strange things to my heart. "You're invested?"

She let out a mix between a laugh and a cry. "Of course I am. How could someone not fall for you, Gage? The real question is... why me?"

"Why you?" I stared at her, incredulous. "Can't you see what you do to me? I'm not the kind of guy who buys flowers and tries to impress a woman. I'm not the kind of guy who shows up at a bar because I'm worried a woman will be interested in someone else. I'm not the kind to do this and beg for you to be with me. But here I am, Farrah. Because it's you. I *liked* my life before I met you. I never dreamed of having a relationship, but you marched in with your coffee and your laughter and your sunshine and you showed me the darkness I was living. And now the thought of living without you is eating me alive."

Her lips parted, and I knew I had to talk fast before she came up with any more doubts about me. "And you want a family behind you? Ever since you've started working with me, my siblings have been begging me to ask you out. If this turns into something real, you have nothing to worry about, because they're already your biggest fans."

"Really?"

I nodded. "And I promise I'm better with kids than you'd think."

She chuckled, coming closer to me and putting her hand on my chest. "I know you have a good heart, but it would have to be serious, really serious, before we integrated our lives that way."

My eyebrows drew together, and I covered her hand with my own. "Look at me, Farrah. I'm as serious about you as I can get without dropping to my knee and putting a ring on your finger." And if that's what it took for her to give me a chance, I'd do it.

She searched my eyes for a moment, and I knew before she spoke the words that I wouldn't like them.

"If you want to take this to the next level with me, involve my children, you need to make amends with your parents, and I need to meet them."

My heart stalled in my chest. "It's been years, Farrah. Too much water has gone under that burning bridge."

Tears spilled down her cheeks. "I promised myself I wouldn't settle, Gage. Don't make me choose. Please," she added in a whisper.

There we were. All our truths, our desires, laid bare. And Farrah was asking me the one thing I wasn't ready to do. Not right now. "I will, but... Will you give me some time?" I asked.

Taking her smiling lips between her teeth, she nodded.

My smile had never been this big. I almost didn't

believe how lucky I was. I bent, taking her lips with mine and kissing her deeply. Excitement mixed with apprehension whirred through my veins. Because even though I'd gotten the girl of my dreams, I had to face my nightmares.

38

FARRAH

Even if nothing came of our relationship, this would stand up as one of the best weekends of my life. Gage and I spent all of Saturday in bed, kissing, hugging, making each other feel good. Talking about our families, our lives. Getting to know each other, every piece of information an exciting discovery.

But on Sunday morning, I learned one of my favorite parts of Gage's apartment: his shower.

There was so much room in here, the water pressure was incredible, and you could even make water and steam come from different directions aside from the rainfall showerhead. Plus, he had fresh eucalyptus hanging from a hook, making the whole place smell like a spa.

If I didn't have a job, kids, a hot man waiting for me —I might never leave.

But eventually I got that hot, sweaty feeling you get after too long in a shower and stepped out into the steamy room, reaching for Gage's terry cloth robe. The man may have kept his decorations sparse, but he did not skimp on luxury items. This thing was softer than a baby kitten.

Smiling to myself, I walked out of the bathroom to his bedroom, trying to decide if it was worth it to change into fresh clothes or if I should just slip under the covers and wait for him to come back from working out and continue what we started earlier this morning.

I heard the elevator ping and then the doors slide open "Did you order takeout?" I called. "Because I am *starving*."

Footsteps sounded over the wood floors, and he came into the room carrying a box wrapped with a ribbon, a sly smile on his lips.

"What is this?" I asked.

Setting the box on the bed, he replied, "Your outfit for tonight."

I raised my eyebrows. "You bought me more lingerie? Okay, now I know I've died and gone to heaven."

With a shake of his head, he said, "We're eating dinner at the Skylight Lounge, and my siblings are coming to meet you."

My jaw dropped, and I wrapped the robe more tightly around me. "I'm meeting your siblings already?"

He reached out, cupping my face with his hand. When he did that, I felt so loved, protected. "When I said I was in, I meant I was all in, and I cannot wait for your biggest fans to meet you."

"My biggest fans?"

"I wasn't exaggerating when I said they've been begging me to date you since you started."

"Why?"

"Maybe because I complained for half an hour about the way you made phone calls," he teased.

My cheeks heated, and I shook my head. "So what is in the box? I'm assuming it's not a teddy."

His chuckle warmed all the corners of my heart. "I assumed you didn't pack any evening gowns, so I thought I would take care of it for you."

"I didn't think to pack an evening gown. But maybe I should have, considering my boyfriend is a billionaire." I tapped my chin. "You know, boyfriend sounds kind of strange for someone like you. So serious and responsible."

He played with the tie around my waist. "You're the responsible one, managing three extra lives. I only have to take care of myself and a business."

"With more than a thousand employees," I pointed out. He acted like he didn't have a million things on his plate.

"Fair," he replied. "So are you going to open the box? Because I'm pretty sure this dress is going to look amazing on you." He tugged harder on the waistband on my robe, and I swatted his hand away.

"It's already four o'clock, so I need to get ready if we're having dinner out. Especially since you're so obsessed with being on time."

He pouted. And I've seen a lot of Gage Griffen, his laughs, his smiles, his frowns. But his pout was absolutely adorable.

I reached for the box, pulling the end of the satin bow, and it slowly slipped apart. Then I lifted the white edges of the lid, seeing a deep red satin gown inside. My jaw dropped. "Gage, it's *beautiful*." I reached in, lifting the bodice. The material was so light, it fluttered to the floor.

"I feel like this is too fancy for me." I stood, holding it to my chest, amazed this dress was mine.

"You could be wearing a crown, and it still wouldn't be fancy enough for you," he replied.

I smiled, shaking my head. "I know we're dating, but you don't have to treat me to expensive gifts. I've never really needed to have the finer things in life." I set the dress down in the box. "Okay, maybe it would be nice to have a machine that dispensed Sonic ice whenever I wanted it, but I'm happy with my life, you know? You don't have to do all this for me."

He gripped a loose fold of my robe and tugged me closer to his chest. He had to tilt his head back so our noses wouldn't touch. "That's one of the things that I liked best about you. I knew you never wanted me for my money."

I smiled up at him. He looked so beautiful this close. "Well, my mom always said if you marry a man for his money, you earn every cent."

He chuckled. "Your mom's a smart woman... I can't wait to meet her."

"She's going to love you."

His blue eyes widened, and for a moment, I caught a glimpse at the vulnerable person underneath his strong exterior. He was nervous. "You think so?"

"I know so." I kissed the tip of his nose. "Now, it's gonna take me some time to get ready and look good enough for this dress, so shoo, or I'll get too distracted."

"Okay," he replied, giving me a last kiss that stretched from seconds into minutes that I wished would last for hours. "But hurry."

I smiled against his lips. "I will."

He left the bedroom, giving me run of his bathroom, which really should have been called a spa. The shower was amazing, but there was also a luxurious soaker tub that could rival the one in the hotel. And dual vanities with so much counterspace my younger two could lie end to end and still have plenty of room leftover.

The thought of my kids made me miss them more than I already did. We talked last night and this morning, but none of them were that great on the phone. I couldn't wait for them to get home so I could hold them in my arms. And even though I was nervous to tell them about Gage, I was excited for them to get to know him because he was one of the most amazing men I knew.

I just hoped he would follow through with his parents because I was already falling hard. And even though I was strong, I didn't always want to be.

While wearing the robe, I did my hair and makeup, then went back to the bedroom, slipping the red dress over my head. The material pooled to the floor, leaving enough space for me to stand in the heels left in the box. I checked the size and realized Gage really must have done his research. They weren't too tall either, but I didn't mind hanging on to his arm all night for balance.

Meeting siblings was a big deal, especially with the way he felt about his brothers and sister. He acted like he wasn't worried about them liking me, but I was. With Caleb, I'd been so naïve, thinking our love would be enough to sustain us even though his parents didn't like me. It just made our relationship that much more uncomfortable as the years went on. He would see them on weekends with the kids, and I'd stay home because I didn't want to hear their snide comments paired with his silence.

I didn't want to do that again, no matter how much love I had for Gage now. Because I knew that these fluttery feelings? They would fade and hopefully give way to a deep respect and companionship that could last.

I reached behind me, trying to pull the zipper up my dress. Realizing I couldn't do it on my own, I left the room, holding up the bodice of my dress so my chest wouldn't spill out. The bedroom door opened so silently, Gage hadn't heard me, and I caught a peek at him in his element.

He sat at the counter in his kitchen, sipping amber liquid from a crystal tumbler, reading a book I *had* to know the title of. It was sexy as hell, seeing him like this.

As if he could feel me watching, he turned his gaze on me, a smile quirking his perfect lips. "Hey, beautiful."

I smiled, tilting my head and making my curls fall over my shoulder. "Can you help zip me up?"

He slid from his chair, and I noticed what he'd changed into. Black slacks and a white shirt, cuffed with silver cufflinks. The way his muscles shifted under the fabric as he walked my way had my mouth watering. Was this real life? Because his body, his soul, it was straight out of a fantasy.

"Are you checking me out?" he asked, his voice husky.

"Do a spin," I ordered.

With a small smile, he turned slowly, and I reached out, slapping his ass.

He practically jumped, and I doubled over laughing. "Did I scare the big bad billionaire?"

"You caught me by surprise," he laughed out, his eyes

lighting with mirth. "No one's spanked my ass since I was eight years old."

"Maybe we should fix that." I winked.

"Turn around," he replied, swirling his finger, still smiling.

I moved my hair over my shoulder so it wouldn't get caught in the zipper, and his knuckles slid over my skin as he slowly lifted the zipper up my back. My breath came more quickly, shallowing, as I imagined him taking the dress off me later tonight.

I could feel his chest pressing against me as he stepped closer and lowered his lips to my ear. "You look sexy as hell in this dress." Then he slapped my ass. And I chased him all the way to the elevator in three-inch heels.

39

GAGE

I was never riding in anything but a limo with Farrah ever again.

Her eyes lit up the instant she saw it waiting for us in the parking garage, and she thanked the driver profusely for opening her door. Inside, she sat down, running her hands over the leather seats, her eyes lit up like a child with full run of a candy store.

"I know I said I don't need fancy things, but I'm in love with this," she said. "Look." She lay out flat on the seat, stretching head to toe with space to spare. "There is *so much room!*" she said, sitting back up.

Her eyes widened as her gaze landed on the wine fridge up front. "And there's booze in here? I thought that was only true in the movies!"

I grinned, reaching for the fridge. I used the bottle opener to pop the cork and poured her a glass of champagne.

She took it with both her hands, swirling the bubbling liquid. "What happens if we hit a speed bump?"

I laughed. Only Farrah would think of that. "Better drink fast."

Taking a careful sip, she said, "You know what I've always wanted to do ever since I saw *Vegas Vacation*?"

"That movie with Chevy Chase?"

She nodded.

"Play the lottery?"

She shook her head.

"Have a love affair with Wayne Newton?"

She giggled.

"Swing like Tarzan over the Hoover Dam?"

"No!" she laughed out. "That part gave me anxiety. No, I've always thought it would be so fun to stand in the moonroof and look at the city lights."

I bit my lips together, holding back a smile, because this woman made me so damn happy. When I sat with her, it didn't matter that I had a hundred unanswered emails in my inbox or that a thousand people were depending on me to keep a roof over their heads.

Here, I could enjoy the moment like I never had before.

I reached for the button that controlled the moonroof and slid it back. All these years riding in limos and town cars, I don't think I'd opened a moonroof once.

Then I tapped on the window separating us from the driver. He scrolled it down, and I said, "Be extra careful for a bit?"

"Yes, sir."

Farrah's feet danced on the floorboard she was so giddy. "No freaking way!"

I nodded. "Someday we'll do this in Vegas, but for now... here's your chance."

She slipped off her heels and got up, crouching as she walked to the middle of the limo. She rose through the moonroof, her chest above the window, but I had the perfect view of her plump ass.

She cheered, happily swinging her hips. Damn, was that dress perfect for her.

"You have to see this!" she called, poking her head back down. "Come on."

The tips of my ears heated. Gage Griffen, CEO, didn't exactly dance in the back of limos. But Gage Griffen, Farrah's man? He'd do whatever put a smile on her face.

So I got up, going to stand beside her, the space just big enough for both of us with our sides pressing together.

The air was warm against my face, but with the limo moving slowly in downtown traffic and the sun slowly setting, it was the perfect temperature. The view of the city was mundane, but with Farrah beside me, her curls blown back from her shoulders, her lips in a giddy grin... it was *magic*.

Farrah smiled up at me. "You look good with the wind blowing through your hair."

"I probably look like a damn golden retriever," I huffed.

A thoughtful look took over her features. "With that pout, you're more of a bulldog."

"Take it back," I said, tickling her side.

She snorted with laughter, making me laugh with her.

"Oh my god, so not sexy," she said, flushing red.

I reached up, tucking a windblown curl behind her ear. Her brown eyes twinkled in the city lights, and even though we were surrounded by traffic, it felt like it was just the two of us here. I bent, kissing her slowly.

Cars began honking around us, and she smiled up at me. "Sounds like they approve."

I smiled. "As long as you do."

"I do," she replied and began lowering herself through the window. "You remember what happened in that movie?"

"*Vegas Vacation?*" I asked, sliding down to join her.

She nodded.

I shook my head as she tucked herself under my arm, resting her head on my shoulder.

"The girl accidentally pressed the button to close the window and nearly suffocated."

"I'd never let that happen to you," I said.

She giggled. "I like how protective you are."

I crossed my ankle with hers. "I take care of what's mine."

With a warm look my way, she bent to put on her heels, but I said, "Let me."

I knelt on the limousine floor, taking one foot in my hand, smiling at the red polish on her toes, and then slipped the black sandal over her foot. The suede was soft under my hand as I reached for the clasp and secured it around her ankle before reaching for the other shoe.

She watched me quietly, a pensive look in her eyes.

"What are you thinking?" I asked, drawing my fingertips up her calf and sitting next to her.

Pressing her palm against my cheek, she said, "I was thinking you're a beautiful man, inside and out."

The moment was tender, raw, more vulnerable than I ever allowed myself to feel.

And that vulnerability scared the hell out of me. Because when you spent your entire adult life building a billion-dollar empire, you had a hell of a lot to lose.

$$\sqrt{2}$$

FARRAH LOOPED her hands through my bent elbow as we walked into the Skylight Building. "Did your siblings ride in limos as well?"

"They're all riding together in Hen's car. She loves that thing."

"And Hen's your sister-in-law, right?"

I nodded, flattered that she'd listened. Usually people just cared what I said when they could make money off it. "She's married to Tyler. Moved here from California last year."

"Wow, that's amazing," she said as we crossed the lobby. "And what kind of car does she have?"

An elevator attendant let us onto the elevator and pressed the button for the Skylight Lounge.

"It's a Jeep Cherokee. Bright red."

"Cute," Farrah said. "I used to think when I wasn't a soccer mom anymore, I'd get a sporty SUV like that, but by the time that happens, I'll probably be a soccer grandma."

I loved the way her eyes lit when she talked about her future.

"I added it up," she continued, "and by the time Cora graduates high school, Levi will be twenty-seven. I'm sure I'll be a grandma before I hit fifty."

"Don't count your chickens," I replied. "My mom thought the same thing, and none of us kids have children yet. Although, I suppose..." I let my words drift off. I wasn't used to dating, but I still knew better than to scare her off.

"What?" she asked, looking up at me.

The elevator climbed several floors as I decided what to say. "When I make amends with my parents, they'll have three grandchildren in a matter of moments."

Moisture shined in her eyes. "Gage..."

The elevator dinged as we reached our floor, and Farrah's jaw fell open. "No freaking way." She let go of me, stepping into the glass enclosure that had several seats and a massive bar. "This is *beautiful*."

"Wait until you see outside," I replied.

A host greeted us, and when I said the name on our reservation, he led us through the glass enclosure to a rooftop restaurant, decked out with candlelit tables covered in white tablecloths and rimmed with twinkle lights. From here, we could see all of Dallas and its suburbs.

Farrah covered her mouth with her hands. "I want to remember this forever."

Looking at her, I knew I would.

"Here you are," the host said. "A server will be with you shortly."

"Thank you," Farrah said, smiling. "Is it okay if we walk around to see the view?"

The host smiled back at her. "Of course."

She walked to the railing, still several feet back from the edge of the roof, and looked out over the city. The breeze blew her curls back over her bare shoulders, giving me the best view in the house.

I never took photos, ever, but I got out my phone and

opened the camera. Just as she glanced back at me, I captured the moment, forever.

"I thought paparazzi weren't allowed," she teased.

I turned the camera toward her. "Look how beautiful you are. I couldn't let it pass."

Farrah opened her mouth to reply, and then her eyes darted over my shoulder. A voice sounded behind me, "Well I'll be damned if it isn't the woman who's got my brother whipped."

I turned on Rhett, just in time to see him mimic the whip movement with his hand and make the sound of a cracking whip. Tyler, Henrietta, and Liv walked behind him, eagerly taking in Farrah. I hoped she didn't feel like an animal in the zoo, even though she'd be in good company with my wild family.

"Farrah, these are my siblings." I wrapped my arm around her waist. "This, is her."

40

FARRAH

My skin shivered with the way he introduced me. Like they'd spoken of me a million times before. And judging by the smiles on his siblings' faces, it had been all good things.

Rhett extended his hand, casting a flirty glance my way. "Nice to meet you outside of the meat market, Ms. Farrah."

I chuckled at him. "Good to see you too."

Henrietta, a beautiful dark-skinned woman, stepped forward. "I'm Henrietta, but you can call me Hen." I shook her hand as well, noticing the ring on her finger. "I love your wedding ring. It's gorgeous."

Her smile was so wide and genuine as she held her hand to her chest. "I'm in love with it—almost as much as the man who gave it to me."

The guy slightly behind her kissed her temple and then extended his hand. "I'm Tyler." Of the three, he looked the most like Gage, except where Gage had dark blond hair, Tyler was brunette. He looked slick in slacks and a button-up shirt, with less of a western flare than what Rhett wore.

A curvy woman beside Rhett smiled and brushed light brown hair behind her ear. "I'm Liv. And I apologize in advance for anything my brothers say. Especially this one." She pointed her thumb toward Rhett, who grabbed her wrist and tried to bite it.

I was already smiling at the banter between them. It was clear how much they all loved each other, and I could already see why Gage cared so much for them.

"It's so nice to meet y'all," I said. "Gage says the best things about you. It makes me wish I had siblings too."

Liv said, "So you're an only child? Living out my life-long dream."

Rhett elbowed her gently, and she winked. "Can we sit down? I could go for a margarita."

"Oh my gosh, same," I said.

Hen grinned at me. "You're going to fit right in."

We walked back to the table, and Gage held a chair out for me, the perfect gentleman. And then I realized Tyler was doing the same for Hen, and Rhett followed suit with Liv. They all had such great manners, I knew I had to meet the woman who raised these men. She'd done something right to have such incredible, welcoming, warm children.

The server came by, a cute twenty-something in black slacks, a vest and a white button down. He took our drink orders, and as soon as he left, Liv said, "Tell us about you, Farrah. And your kids! You have three, right?"

Under the table, Gage reached for my hand. "Farrah's children are so talented. Her oldest is a great baseball player. The middle is an incredibly gifted artist, and I can tell her daughter, the youngest, is going to rule the world someday."

My heart was so full it could burst. "They're my best accomplishment, even though it's been fun designing The Retreat with Gage."

Henrietta said, "So two boys and a girl? I was the only girl, too, except I have three older brothers."

"Do any of them live nearby?" I asked.

She shook her head. "My entire family's back in California. I miss them like crazy, but luckily Gage has been generous enough to give us flight points so we can visit each other as often as we like."

I squeezed Gage's hand. See? Heart of gold.

"What do they think of the Hen House?" I asked. "Gage told me a little about it, but I'd love to see it."

"They love it. Grandma keeps saying we should open one in California. Maybe someday." Hen's smile was wistful. "But you come visit any time. We'd love to give you a tour."

Gage kissed my temple. "We'll make the trip sometime. It's definitely worth seeing in person."

I smiled back at him. "I know Rhett works on a ranch. What do you do again, Liv?"

She frowned, taking a deep pull on her margarita. "I'm the assistant manager at a feedlot outside of Cottonwood Falls, but we'll see how long that lasts. My boss is an asshole, and it doesn't look like he's going anywhere."

Gage gave her a sympathetic look, and I said, "That sucks. Any idea what you'd do instead? Are there other feedlots to work for in that area?"

She shook her head. "It's kind of an old boys' club. I had to work my way up at this one. I'm not really sure what else I'd do. I like working with kids, but all the germs at a daycare..." She shook her head. "Maybe being a nanny would be fun? I don't know. There aren't really a lot of options in a small town."

I nodded emphatically. "The job search is rough, even in a big city."

"So were you always an interior designer?" Liv asked. "Or did you stay home?"

Shaking my head, I said, "I was just a stay-at-home mom until the divorce."

"Just?" Rhett said, shaking his head. "Our mom stayed home with us until we were all in school. It was the best damn thing she could have done for us. You should be proud of yourself."

Gage squeezed my hand like he agreed, and my cheeks flushed. I'd expected this meeting to feel awkward. To be treated with skepticism for being a single mom dating a billionaire. But these people already felt like family.

THE SIX OF us stayed at the Skylight Lounge for hours, talking and getting to know each other, and when I got back in the limo with Gage, I was so overcome with emotion. Could this really be coming true? Could I be getting an incredible man with a family that would welcome my kids and me with loving arms?

We cuddled in the back seat, despite all the extra space, and I looked up at him. "Thank you for that."

He nuzzled his nose against mine. "They loved you."

"I loved them. Rhett is hilarious. And Hen and Liv? I

want them to be my best friends. Of course Tyler was so sweet, the strong, silent type. I think you two are most alike."

He held my hand to his chest and then kissed my knuckles. Maybe there were too many words for him to say out loud, but I felt them all. Tonight was a step forward for us, a big one.

The ride back to his home went quickly, and when we got inside, he had me sit on his bed as he knelt to undo my heels. The action so intimate and sweet, it had tears brimming in my eyes.

When he looked up and saw the moisture, he asked, "What's wrong?"

I wiped away the tears, taking his face in my hands, and kissed him, pulling him back onto the bed until he was over me.

He kissed me back, slowly gliding his tongue along my lips and deepening our embrace.

When we pulled apart, he looked at me, a question in his dark blue eyes.

"I'm in love with you," I said. "I know it's too soon and I should be practical, but tonight... It was perfect. You are perfect. And you don't need to worry about saying it back, but—"

He silenced me with a kiss, and when he pulled back, he said, "I love you too, Farrah. With everything I have."

I pulled him to me again, kissing him deeply, needing to be closer to him than these clothes would allow.

I ran my fingers over the buttons on his shirt, loosening each one. When they were free, he slid the shirt down his muscled arms and took off his pants and underwear, baring himself to me.

Then he had me stand, turn, his fingers leaving a trail of heat down my back as he slid the zipper down and unclipped my strapless bra. I felt the length of his erection against my back and then side as I turned to face him.

He gripped my shoulders, taking me in. "Have I mentioned how beautiful you are?" His palms slid down my arms. "Every inch of you tells a story... The life you created, the fun you've had, your indulgences." He ran his fingers over Cora's C-section scar. "Your pain." His fingers found my jaw, causing our gazes to meet. "Your resilience."

I flattened my hand against his chest, thinking of the story his body told. One of dedication, strength, and focus. But I couldn't help thinking, for him, the best story was his heart that lay under the surface.

As if he could sense my thoughts, he covered my hand with his own, and kissed me. This kiss felt different than all the ones before. Instead of hungry or desperate or savory, this kiss was full of *love*.

He walked me back to the bed, laying me down on his luxurious linens, my head sinking into the surface.

My fingers flowed through the short hair at the back of his head as I held him and kissed him with everything I had. His erection pressed into my hip, and the brimming feeling overflowed my heart, spreading through my body.

"Gage, I need you closer."

He reached toward the night stand for a condom.

"I'm on the pill," I said, not wanting to wait another moment.

"Are you sure?" he asked, his gaze serious.

I kissed him in confirmation, pulling him closer.

He angled his tip at my entrance and rolled his hips over me, filling me to the hilt. I closed my eyes and held on to his shoulders, needing all he had to give.

"Eyes on me," he said, pausing inside me.

I opened my eyes, meeting his blue gaze. What I saw there... amazed me. There was reverence, adoration, vulnerability... *love*.

We were making love. For minutes or hours, it didn't matter. Time existed outside of us and this world of possibilities Gage opened up to me. My past may have hurt, but this man was giving me a future beyond anything I ever imagined.

The realization sent me over the edge. "I'm coming," I gasped, clenching around him.

He rode all my waves and spilled himself inside me as he said my name.

41

GAGE

Usually, in the mornings, I got out of bed to the sound of my alarm, changed into workout clothes, and went to the gym in my building to sweat for an hour. But today, Farrah's soft body molded against my back. Her arm curled around my middle, and her soft breaths landed against my bare shoulder blades.

She was spooning me, and it was the best thing I'd experienced in my life.

This entire weekend had been filled with firsts. Bests.

The first time I told a woman I loved her since my high school sweetheart.

The first time I introduced a girlfriend to my siblings in just as long.

The first time I'd ever made love with my entire heart on the line.

I closed my eyes, savoring her warmth, her touch, the way she made me feel so comfortable even in her sleep.

It was perfect.

Almost perfect.

Aside from the fear pitting itself in my stomach.

Most of what Farrah asked of me was simple enough. I could find a way to be needed less at work, promote someone or three to help with my work. Hell, I could go public, sell a majority of my shares, and be set for life.

It would be hard to let it go, but I could do it.

Making amends with my parents on the other hand?

More than a decade had passed since we'd had a real conversation. Seeing them at Tyler's wedding had felt like a punch to the gut. My dad's hair was nearly all gray. My mom had wrinkles on her face I'd never seen before.

They were getting older, and all that time between the fight and now? It was gone forever.

How much time was too much time to lay down our differences? And did I want to?

What did Dad think of me now, the owner of a billion-dollar company, when he'd called me selfish just for my desire to expand the ranch enough to support a few families? If he'd thought I was greedy then, he must think me the devil incarnate now.

And facing that? Getting confirmation of the thing I feared the most...

It scared me more than I liked to admit.

I tried to run my business in an ethical way, to give my time and money when I could, but he didn't see that. He probably wouldn't care to understand.

And my mom? The woman who raised me and loved me? She chose him. Listened to him speak those words about me and said nothing.

Farrah shifted behind me, and I rolled over, looking into her sleepy eyes, a touch of a smile on her lips. "Good morning, handsome," she mumbled.

I kissed the tip of her nose. "How did you sleep?"

"So well you'll be lucky to get me out of bed in time for work." She closed her eyes, snuggling into my chest.

"I could stay in this bed all day, but we have a meeting with HR at seven."

Her eyes flew open, searching mine. "What? Am I fired?"

I chuckled. "No, we just need to come clean about our relationship before it hits newsstands at eight. Give PR a chance to handle it."

She nodded, then she sat up. "Oh my god, I need to tell Mia."

"Mia?" I asked, then I remembered they were friends before all this. Farrah treated everyone like her best friend. "You can call her while I take a shower?"

She nodded, sitting up with her back against the cushioned headboard.

I leaned in and pressed a kiss to her lips. "It's going to be okay."

With a slight smile, she said, "I can handle a meeting with HR and Mia and the whole world, as long as my kids are okay with you."

"Same here," I replied. I took my phone off the nightstand and walked to the bathroom. With the door closed, I sent Liv a text.

Gage: When should I talk to Mom and Dad?

She didn't reply right away, so I got in the shower, barely hearing Farrah's murmurs over the water pressure. When I finished washing up and got out, there was a message from Liv.

Liv: *shocked emoji*

Liv: Is this Farrah?

Liv: Is this a prank?

Gage: No. It's time.

Liv: It was time ten years ago. What changed?

Gage: Farrah.

Liv: I like her.

Gage: Me too.

I set my phone down and brushed my teeth, then walked out of the bathroom, a towel wrapped around my waist.

Farrah looked up at me, fire in her eyes. "Oh my god, I didn't realize I had that fantasy, but damn, that was hot."

I looked around, confused. "What are you talking about?"

"You in that towel!" She grinned. "Do a spin!"

Laughing, I turned away from her, undoing the towel in front and holding it out to hide my private parts. When I spun to face her, I moved the towel again to keep me modest.

"Damn, Griffen, if you weren't already insanely rich, I'd say you could make a good living giving stripteases."

"Channing Tatum, look out," I said, dropping the towel on the floor and going to my walk-in closet for clothes. "How did it go with Mia?"

"She didn't believe me," Farrah said, frowning.

That was about the last thing I'd expected. "What do you mean?"

"She thought I messed up April Fools' Day again."

"Wait, what?" I asked, peeking my head out of the closet to see her still on the bed. "How can you mess up April Fools' Day? It's always the first of April."

"It's not important. The point is, she was very

surprised and a little doubtful but said she's happy for us."
Farrah shrugged. "And she's pissed you NDA'd me. You
might get an earful about that later."

I chuckled, going back into the closet. "Fair enough."

As I got dressed, I heard her answer another call and
start talking to Cora, Andrew, and Levi on the phone. She
was so sweet as she asked them about their plans for the
day. Made sure Andrew was actually changing his underwear instead of just turning them inside out.

I had to chuckle quietly at that one.

When she told the kids she loved them and said goodbye, I went to her, kissing her cheek. "You're such an
amazing mom."

Her smile was tentative. "Sometimes I worry that I'm
going to end up in their memoir. And not in a good way."

The thought made me laugh. "What are they going to
say? 'My mom smiled at us too much? She tried too hard
to make us happy and provide a good home?'"

Her cheeks flushed. "Well, Levi will definitely
complain about my sunshine playlist and how loudly I
sing along to it. Andrew will say I didn't let him play
enough video games. Oh, and that I forgot pajama day at
school one too many times. And Cora? Well, jury's still
out on her."

"You love them; that's what matters."

She smiled softly, the expression like the delicate
sunlight streaming through the windows. "I should probably get ready, huh?"

I nodded. "I'll make breakfast. Any requests?"

"You cook?"

"Not usually," I admitted. "But for you, I will."

"I love a good skillet—you know, eggs, potatoes,

sausage, toast. And I'd kill for some coffee. Someone kept me up too late last night." She sent me an accusatory glare.

"*Someone* will be making up for that with the best skillet of your life. See you when you're done."

42

FARRAH

The meeting with HR was... awkward.

Especially when Shantel reminded us it was against company policy to fraternize on company grounds.

My cheeks flushed bright red, thinking of all the things we'd already done, during and after work hours at The Retreat. When Shantel saw my reaction, she barely bit back a smile.

"I know you're the owner of the company, Gage, so you technically can't be fired or demoted, but you do set the tone for your employees. If you ignore the rules, the more likely it is that your team may do the same."

Next to me, Gage wasn't the sweet guy with a soft side; he was the commanding CEO I first met. "We understand."

I nodded in agreement, instinctively reaching for his hand. But he shrugged away from my touch, and my cheeks heated again.

This would be strange... It was one thing to have a purely physical relationship and pretend nothing was happening at work. But to have my heart beside me and act as if it meant nothing all day? That would be a challenge for me.

"In fact," Shantel said, "now that we know about your relationship, company policy advises against you two working alone together. Any meeting you have should be attended by a third party or take place with the doors open. And Gage, it's high time you moved back into your office. Farrah is clearly doing a great job at The Retreat, and we have security present, so it isn't unsafe for her to work there on her own."

My stomach sank. Working at The Retreat by myself? Unable to see Gage every day? I thought this meeting was about coming clean, but it felt like it was designed to break us apart. A strong pang filled my chest as I realized how little time we'd get together once he moved back to this building. I had three kids to care for as a full-time mom. I couldn't shuck my responsibilities at home to get extra time with him outside of work.

Of course, I'd sound pathetic to say any of this out loud, especially with Shantel here.

Since we didn't have any more questions, she called in Griffen Industries' head of public relations, explaining that we needed training on how to interact with the media.

She introduced herself as Tallie, giving me a firm handshake. From her charcoal pantsuit to her slicked back red ponytail, I could tell she meant business.

After brief introductions, she gave me a laminated sheet with talking points, saying, "Please go over these as quickly as possible. Paparazzi got shots of you two eating dinner with Gage's family last night, and it's very clear you're romantically involved. With Gage's celebrity status, it's likely you'll be confronted by reporters sooner rather than later. Remember, you can always say, 'No comment.'"

I looked over the list, reading the lines she wanted me to have ready.

GAGE *and I met during work and quickly realized we admired each other.*

OUR RELATIONSHIP IS COMPLETELY *separate from the business, and business always comes first.*

"I can't say this," I said, gesturing to the list. "What would my children think if they heard me saying we come second to his job?"

Tallie tapped her chin. "We should probably bring your kids in for a press briefing as well."

"We won't be bringing my children in for anything," I nearly growled. "They're not a part of this."

"They absolutely are," she said. "It won't be long before reporters have pictures of your entire family on social media or interview your ex about you. Have you checked your social media yet today? You've gained a fifty thousand followers in the last half hour." She looked at Gage. "You really should have consulted me before starting a relationship. Jason Romero's approval rating is already down fourteen points, and he has been blowing up Mia's phone line demanding a meeting with you."

My eyes widened. "It's hurting his campaign for governor? *Why?*"

"According to social media sentiment, it's because they don't trust that your intentions are pure. Divorce is a big no-no for a large number of his supporters. Add on the fact that a broke single mom suddenly gets a high-paying job at Griffen Industries after years off work, and then it comes out she's sleeping with the boss when she's only been divorced a few months?" Tallie shook her head sagely. "It also seems impulsive on Gage's part. Two things people don't want in a company leader?" She held up two fingers. "Impulsivity and gullibility."

My jaw dropped open at her words, angry tears filling my eyes. "How could you say that?"

"She's not saying it's true," Gage explained. "That's just how voters are perceiving it."

She nodded resolutely. "With some reassurances and time, this nightmare will blow over, but until then, we need to play our cards very carefully or we risk Romero pulling out of the deal."

Did she really just call my relationship with Gage, my first relationship post-divorce, a nightmare? "I'm going to need a second," I said, pushing up from the desk.

Gage made to follow me, but Shantel said, "Three people at a time, Gage."

We met eyes across the conference room before I left and stepped into the hallway. Two seconds from crying, I went to Mia's desk and said, "Where's somewhere private I can go that's not the bathroom?"

Worry in her eyes, she said, "Gage's office. Come with me."

We walked from her reception desk through the glass door of Gage's office. As soon as it shut, the room fell silent save for my heavy breaths.

Mia stayed silent as I walked to the wall of windows overlooking the city. When I glanced down, my stomach turned. We were so high off the ground, and I already felt like I was falling.

When I turned back to Mia, she was watching me with concerned brown eyes.

"Tallie said Romero's approval rating dropped fourteen points today alone. Because of me."

Mia nodded. "Voters can be fickle, but it doesn't look great. He's already left me a voice mail saying Gage needs to take a meeting in an hour or it could mean bad things for the project."

I placed my hand over my pounding heart, hoping I could stop the ache. "Is our relationship bad for Gage?"

Mia tilted her head. "There's a difference between bad for business and bad for Gage."

Her words didn't comfort me at all. "Is there? Because outside of his siblings, it seems like this company is his life."

"He's spent a lot of his life building it," she said.

I paced over the floor, the meeting playing over in my mind. "Tallie wants us to tell the press that our relationship comes second to his business."

Mia nodded, seemingly unsurprised.

"How can I say that?" I said, looking back out over the city from Gage's throne. "What if my kids hear me say that and take it to mean we're less important than a job? I don't want another repeat of what happened with Caleb, us four always coming second to work."

Her heels clacked against the floor as she stopped me and put her arm around my shoulders. "I know you do everything with your whole heart, Far, and I love you for it."

Tears stung my eyes. "But?"

"But see it from the outside world's perspective. To you and Gage, this has been building for weeks. Months. But for the rest of us, it's all new. It would be silly to think he'd put his new *girlfriend*, not even a wife, ahead of a business that people count on for jobs, their retirement accounts. Their children's college saving funds... Everything."

I nervously chewed my bottom lip. "I hate it when you make sense," I said, still overwhelmed with all the worry and doubt clouding my vision. This morning, everything had seemed so perfect. But now, outside the walls of his home? I hadn't expected it to feel like this.

Mia said, "You really like him, don't you?"

I nodded, afraid of how much I liked him. How much I loved him.

"The kids don't watch the news, right? I mean, Levi could come across something on social media, but you can explain the situation to him."

I dropped into Gage's desk chair, feeling defeated. "I wasn't going to tell the kids until I was ready for them to meet Gage as my boyfriend."

"And how far out is that?" Mia asked. "Because you have a photo shoot with all of them Sunday after next."

I covered my face with my hands. God, this was such a mess. Would that even be soon enough for Gage to talk to his parents? Would I be going back on my word?

A knock sounded on the office door, and we looked up to see Gage standing on the other side of the glass.

43

GAGE

Farrah and Mia snapped their gazes toward me, and I saw completely different emotions on their faces. Mia looked sympathetic. But Farrah? She seemed torn.

Mia walked to the door and opened it. She was about to walk out, but I said, "Wait, can you stay in here, for appearances?"

She glanced at Farrah, and Farrah nodded. In that moment, I realized just how close they were. Mia may have been my employee, but she was fiercely loyal to Farrah.

Mia took a chair to the corner farthest from us, giving us as much privacy as she could while tapping on her phone.

I met Farrah at the other corner near the wall of windows and lowered my voice. "Are you okay? Tallie can be very direct, and while I like that in my executive team, I know it's a lot to deal with."

She turned her gaze away from the windows and tipped it up to meet my own. "I was on cloud nine this morning, and that meeting knocked me down real fast. And then to hear a major business deal is in jeopardy because of me? I don't want you to give up what you've worked for."

My chest squeezed in fear. I did not want to lose her over this. "Look, it was a hit to see Romero's ratings come down like that, but there's still plenty of time before the election. You don't get to my level by being scared when you see a little dip. It will be fine. I promise."

She nodded, looking down.

I wanted to put my arms around her, comfort her, but I knew I couldn't do that publicly. And to be honest, I didn't know if she wanted me to. She wouldn't meet my gaze anymore, and she had her bottom lip caught between her teeth, chewing it anxiously.

"What else is worrying you?" I asked. I needed us to be okay.

She glanced toward Mia and back to me, finally meeting my eyes. Her irises were dark brown storm clouds filled with worry. "I don't want to play second fiddle to your business for the rest of my life. I understand now, so early in our relationship. But what about a year from now? Five years from now?"

I couldn't help it. I reached up, using the crook of my index finger to lift her chin. "Just because you're not first, doesn't mean you're last."

Emotions warred on her face, so many there fighting for dominance. When her lips parted, I could pin it. Fear.

"I don't want to lose you to the real world, Gage. These past few months have been a fantasy, but there's so much more to consider."

I palmed her cheek with my hand. "Maybe our time

together has felt like a dream to you, but you have to understand me, Farrah." I swiped my thumb over the curve of her cheekbone. "This has been the realest thing I've ever felt."

A soft cooing sound came from the corner, and Farrah and I both glanced toward Mia, remembering she was there.

"Sorry," she said quickly. "Sorry. That was just really sweet.... Go back to pretending I'm not here."

I chuckled softly while Farrah looked up at me, more color in her cheeks than before.

"Are you sure you can do this?" she asked. "Make my kids and me a priority and take care of your business?"

"Believe it or not, I'm more worried about talking to my parents."

She cracked a smile. "Thank you for doing that for me, for us."

"I wouldn't have it any other way." I dropped my hands, stepping back before more people saw us than probably already had. "I'll go back to the conference room to talk with Tallie. She wants us to do a press conference this afternoon and then an interview with a local cable show. But if you don't want to do it, I'll tell her I'll handle it on my own."

Farrah bit her bottom lip again, and it took all I had not to reach up and free it before capturing her mouth with my own. "Do you think it will help your business?" she asked.

I nodded. "Tallie wouldn't be asking us to do it if it wouldn't help."

She took a deep breath. "Okay. I'll do it."

And then her phone began ringing. She drew the

device from her purse, and we both stared at the name on the screen.

Levi.

From across the room, Mia asked, "Who is it?"

Farrah took a deep breath, swiping her phone to answer.

44

LEVI

I was walking down the beach with my stomach full of breakfast and warm sun hitting my skin, but the last thing I felt was happy. Actually? I was pissed.

The last few days with Dad and Melinda had been super awkward. They were all over each other. Dad constantly held her hand or she sat in his lap. And the kissing. God, it was gross seeing my dad make out with this woman.

It felt like a betrayal to Mom, being here and seeing all of that. And supporting this new relationship felt like a betrayal to Melinda, too. Alyssa told me one time at lunch that once someone cheated they usually did it again. Did Melinda know what she was getting into with my dad? How would Adabelle handle another divorce? It was really freaking hard on my siblings and me. My mom too.

Mom seemed lonely, just going to work and coming home and maybe hanging out with Mia sometimes. But when Alyssa sent me the picture from Dallas's main gossip blog with a giant picture of my mom sitting with her boss and his siblings at a romantic restaurant, her hand on his thigh, I felt like everyone had been lying to me all along.

The headline read SINGLE MOM BAGS HER BILLIONAIRE BOSS.

The betrayal of it all made me want to punch something.

How long had this been going on?

I dialed her number, needing to hear the truth, for once.

"Hey, Levi, how's the beach life?" she asked.

She sounded happy. Was it because of *him*? "Mom, are you dating your boss?"

The line went silent for a moment, leaving me alone with the sound of the beach and all the happy people around me. I checked the phone to make sure she hadn't hung up, but seconds just kept ticking past.

Finally, she said, "Yes, I'm dating him. His name is Gage Griffen."

I froze where I stood, the packed beach sand suddenly feeling like sinking sand instead. "When were you going to tell us? When you got engaged and he moved in? Oh wait, he's rich, so you'll probably lug us all to his mega mansion, huh?"

Anger kept spiraling in my chest, flaring out like a wounded animal. I'd been so furious on her behalf that Dad moved on, and here she was dating some rich guy!

"Honey, I hear you're upset and probably even feeling a little betrayed, but I need you to take a deep breath."

Tears pricked at my eyes, but I ran my forearm over them and took a breath. "Now what? Another lie?"

"The truth," she said. "I am dating Gage, and yes, I

have real feelings for him, but I didn't want to introduce you to him until I was sure he was someone who would stick around."

My fists balled at my sides. "So two surprise engagements in a year from my divorced parents? Great."

"There is no engagement," she said. "We are dating, like two single adults are allowed to do. And you will meet him... soon. But only as my boyfriend, nothing else. He won't be moving in with us. We won't be moving out. But he may come over for dinner from time to time or come cheer you on with me at a summer game."

My legs felt shaky as the anger faded into another feeling I didn't want to deal with. *Fear.* My dad had already left us, clearly cared for Melinda and Adabelle more than us. Who would we have left if Mom got all wrapped up in this new guy?

I took a few steps away from the packed wet sand and sat on the softer beach, drawing my legs in. Resting my elbows on my knees, I held the phone to my ear.

"So you're dating," I said, hiding the shake I felt in my chest.

"I am," she replied. "But Levi, you have to know that you and your siblings will always come first. Remember what I said to you at your dad's house?"

My throat got tight.

"*You and your siblings* are the loves of my life," she repeated.

I wiped at my eyes again, trying to rid myself of saltwater that belonged in the sea. "This family vacation is totally fucked."

"Language," she said with a halfhearted chuckle. "But

I know. I didn't want you to find out about Gage this way."

"Were you going to tell me at all?"

"I was, when I knew he was someone worth bringing around."

I blew a soft laugh through my nose. "You sound like a hard-ass. I mean, butt."

"When it comes to my kids, I'm as protective as a mama bear... And speaking of my cubs, are you okay? I know it's a lot of information all at once."

A small grumble filled my throat. "Can you just promise me you won't be making out all the time in front of me? Dad and Melinda are worse than kids my age."

"Ew."

"I know," I replied.

"Gage and I will keep it PG, I promise," she said.

I nodded, feeling wrung out and hung to dry.

"How did you find out about Gage?" she asked.

I shook my head, thinking of the text. Seeing them together had felt like a slap to the face. "Alyssa sent me an article she saw on Dallas Deets."

Mom let out a sigh, and she sounded so much like herself it hurt. I missed her. But I was fourteen. I wasn't supposed to miss my parents. Or admit it, at least.

"You promise you'll always be there for us?" I gritted out. "You won't ship us off to Dad's when you move in with Gage?"

"I promise. A million times I promise."

"Good." I looked over the water, thinking about the days we still had left on this vacation and wishing I could be home again. "You should probably tell the younger two, though. Before Dad sees it and says something stupid."

"Good idea," she said. "Gosh, you're growing up so fast. You'll be grown and gone before I know it."

I shook my head. "I'm not like Dad. You won't get rid of me so easily."

"You have the biggest heart, Levi. And I hope this talking thing keeps happening. I've missed you."

"I missed you too," I admitted, even though I was too old for it. "I'll call you when I'm back at the hotel so you can talk to the younger two. I went for a walk, so it won't be right away."

"Sounds good. Love you, honey."

"Love you too," I mumbled and hung up.

I blew out a shaky breath and lay back on the sand, staring at the cloudless blue sky. Maybe I was still a little worried, but I knew I could trust her. I just hoped she'd chosen a better man this time, one who wouldn't break her heart.

45

GAGE

I felt like Farrah and I were on better footing when she left to The Retreat for her workday. But I still couldn't get her worry and disappointment out of my mind. I didn't want us going public to be the thing that tore us apart. Especially since living in the public eye was such a big part of my life, whether I liked to admit it or not. It came with the territory.

A knock sounded on my glass door, and I glanced up to see Mia standing beside Jason Romero. Despite his smooth, doll-like features and placid smile, I could sense his anger in the set of his shoulders, the tightness of his eyes.

I waved my hand for Mia to bring him in, and she held the door open. He completely ignored her, stepping into my office. "We need to talk, Griffen."

I directed my words toward Mia. "Thank you for bringing him back. I'll have a green tea. Would you like anything, Jason?"

His features slipped for a moment, long enough for me to catch his scowl. "Nothing."

"Very well," I replied, sitting back in a chair at my conference table, giving off the appearance that everything was fine and dandy. "What brings you in today?"

He yanked out the chair opposite and sat down, leaning forward. The act probably intimidated other people, but not me. "You know very well why I'm here. You and the broad you're banging brought down my approval rating fourteen points!" he hissed.

I narrowed my eyes, leaning forward. "Her name is Farrah, and if you refer to her as anything other than her name, we'll have more to talk about than your temper tantrum."

His skin purpled, and a vein bulged from his forehead. His eyelid was probably seconds from twitching. "I don't think you realize that this deal isn't all that profitable for Romero Corp. In fact, you'll fare far better than I will for several years to come. You should take this more seriously."

"What I don't take seriously is the reaction of voters after a big news item. You know just as well as I do that Farrah and I will be old news by next week. Some celebrity will get pregnant or the president will do something stupid, and this blip will be long forgotten."

Jason ground his teeth. "Two points is a blip, Griffen. Fourteen is campaign ending. When we announced the factory, my rating went up three points. *Three*. And the only reason I partnered with you on this project was because you had the cash and a drama-free reputation. I can certainly spend my dollars to help me win the campaign instead of building this plant."

Times like this I wished Mr. Price could sit beside me and see how right I was to hesitate on deals like this. Jason wasn't in this to help those people in his hometown. He was out for number one, and those people would be left in the lurch the second things didn't go his way.

"Look, Jason, Farrah and I have a press conference later today, and I guarantee this will all sort itself. If you don't see a rebound in your numbers in the next month, we can talk again about other solutions that don't include fleecing a hundred people out of a job."

He studied me for a moment. "You really care about those people, don't you?"

I nodded sharply. "And if you're to become governor, I'd hope you care too."

Mia knocked again, holding a clear mug with tea inside.

I waved her into the office, and Jason stood. "One month."

I stood too, and Mia and I watched as he left the office.

Passing me the mug, she muttered, "Ain't he a ray of sunshine."

I shook my head. "Can you get Tallie to come in here? We might need to help his team do some damage control." I couldn't let that community be hurt because Romero cared more about his campaign than his hometown.

46

FARRAH

Gage and I sat at a table in front of a small crowd of reporters. At least a dozen microphones were propped up in front of us, and the flash of cameras was dizzying. But I still knew this was likely to be one of my easier conversations today.

I'd spent the better part of an hour on the phone with my kids this morning, letting them know that I was seeing Gage more seriously and that they would get to know him when I felt like it was time.

I wished I could have had that conversation face to face, but I was starting to realize that dating Gage meant the whole world was in on our relationship. Or at least parts of it.

They all seemed to take it okay. Cora asked if he had any kids she could play with. Andrew wanted more art stuff. But the conversation I had with Levi earlier was the hardest. When the kids got back to Dallas, I wanted to make sure to take him out, just the two of us. I couldn't imagine what it would have been like for both of my parents to split up and then start dating again, all in my freshman year of high school.

Tallie gave Gage the signal to start from where she sat up front, sandwiched between reporters. Nerves swirled in my stomach, thinking about how many people would be watching this on TV. I wished Gage could hold my hand, but here in front of a crowd, he was the intense, intimidating man I'd met on the first day of my job. As soon as he began speaking, the room quieted.

"With the word spreading about mine and Farrah's relationship, we wanted to clear the air and set the record straight." I kept my gaze on him because if I stared at the audience too long, I'd puke. "Before the questions begin, I'll share the major details. Farrah began working for me five months ago. A few months in, it became clear to me that this woman was one I couldn't ignore."

A slight smile touched my lips to match the audience's chuckle.

"We began seeing each other privately, and when we decided it was something to pursue, I introduced her to my family. We plan to continue our relationship, publicly, while working together, being sure to follow the professional guidance laid out by Griffen Industries' Chief of Staff, Shantel Williams." He turned to me. "Anything else?"

I shook my head slightly. "I think that covers it." Nervously, I tucked my curls behind my ear and faced the reporters, trying to remember to breathe.

A reporter with long hair pulled in a ponytail raised his hand, and Gage nodded at him.

"How long have you been divorced, Ms. Elkins?"

"That's public record, and you know it, Liam," Gage

said. "Maybe do a little better research next time, or ask the question you actually want to know."

Liam's cheeks went pink. "Did the relationship begin before or after the divorce?" he asked.

"After," we said at the same time.

An older woman raised her hand next. "What are you doing to protect your assets in case Ms. Elkins has ulterior motives for your relationship?"

"First of all, we're not married, only dating," Gage said. Then he sent me a smile that turned my insides all warm and gooey like a brownie fresh from the oven. "And Ms. Elkins is the most unassuming woman I've ever kept company with. She prefers dandelions to roses. Chooses quality time over gifts. And after she accidently door-dinged my car, she even offered to pay to fix it." He chuckled, and so did the reporters, eating out of the palm of his hand, just like me. "I trust her implicitly."

Under the table, he reached for my hand. Relieved, I squeezed back.

Another man stood up, looking at us through thick glasses. "What do you say to constituents who are concerned Jason Romero's judgement in partnering with you?"

"I may have founded Griffen Industries, but my team has helped make this company what it is. The success of this company does not lie fully in my hands, but in the hands of people who come to work every day at every level."

Admiration swelled in my chest, not only at his command of the room but also at his view of the company. The fact that this press conference was about him and me and he was still finding a way to highlight his employees, it showed true character and humility.

A younger woman toward the back stood. "Ms. Elkins, how do your children feel about you dating a billionaire?"

I smiled at her, wondering if she had kids of her own. "We're still very early in our relationship, and they've yet to meet him as my boyfriend. He has to prove himself first." A small chuckle went through the audience. "But they are very fond of the accommodations Gage made to my office so they would feel more comfortable there."

"What accommodations?" the woman asked.

I glanced at Gage, seeing a soft smile on his face, and he nodded. "Art supplies, a handful of toys, and more comfortable seating for children."

Another woman stood. "What will you tell your little girl about sleeping your way to the top?"

My head jerked back with whiplash from the question, and Gage's jaw clenched. He opened his mouth to speak, but Tallie gave him a pointed look, nodding her head toward me. This was my question to answer.

"I wouldn't have that conversation with my daughter because she's five years old. But I will tell her about hard work and letting her results speak to her competence. Regardless of my relationship with Gage, The Retreat will be a beautifully designed luxury experience for families who need a relaxing stay together."

The woman's face soured.

"Oh," I added, simply for myself, "I might also tell her to support other women instead of looking for ways to tear them down."

The woman who asked the earlier question began

clapping, and soon the entire audience was clapping for me. Gage had a full-blown smile now, one usually reserved for just me. *Good job*, he mouthed.

Leaning forward so his face was closer to the microphone, he said, "I believe that's enough questioning for today. My girlfriend and I have work to do."

The g-word did strange things to my heart, making it flip and somersault while a torrent of butterflies took off in my stomach. Gage had claimed me publicly, and soon, this information would be everywhere.

Gage Griffen was mine. And me? I was his.

47

GAGE

I rolled over in my bed and faced the empty side I already considered Farrah's. Not having her pressed up against my back as I woke made my gut ache in a way I didn't like.

How had I gone every day of my life waking up alone?

How had a week made me need her so damn much?

How did one morning make me miss her beyond belief?

Farrah had picked her kids up from Austin yesterday, which meant she was busy all day catching up with them. Plus doing a mound of sandy laundry, according to her. I offered her the use of my cleaning service, but she quickly declined, saying she found the sound of running laundry to be soothing.

Reaching for my phone, I picked it up and sent her a text.

Gage: I miss you.

Farrah: It's been one day!

Gage: One day too many.

Farrah: I miss you too. Maybe I can ask my parents to watch the kids an evening next week so we can have a date.

The thought of staying apart every day and night aside from the occasional date night was already eating me up inside.

I typed out a text.

Gage: What if I buy a mansion for all of us to stay in? Each of the kids can have their own room. We could get married tomorrow if you want.

Delete. Delete. Delete.

Gage: I could buy the house next door to yours?

That was even worse than the last one. *Delete.*

Farrah: Lot of text bubbles over there.

Gage: I'm meeting with my parents the weekend after the photo shoot. I'm serious about moving forward with you. And I'm hoping someday you'll be okay with me staying over because I gotta be honest. This bed feels really empty without you.

Farrah: My heart.

Farrah: I miss waking up next to you too. Last week was so amazing. Do you know what you're going to say to your parents?

Gage: Maybe you can help me workshop it?

Farrah: Okay, tell me what you have so far.

Gage: *takes a deep breath* I got nothing.

Farrah: LOL just tell them the truth? If you tell them how you feel and it goes nowhere, at least you'll know you tried.

Gage: It's hard to sort it all out. It's sucked building this company without my parents ever saying "I'm proud of you." Which feels pathetic to admit, but it's true.

Farrah: It's not pathetic. It means the world when my parents say they're proud of me.

Gage: Here's the thing, though. It's been more than ten years since the fight. Not once did my dad reach out to me. And I know I didn't reach out to him either, but he's the parent, damn it. Shouldn't he be the one?

Farrah: As a mom, I have to let you know... we're all still human. Sometimes it takes us a while to figure things out.

Gage: I just hope I can. For us.

Farrah: I hope you can too... but for you. You're so strong, but I can see the weight this puts on you. I know your relationship will never be like it was before, but maybe things will feel a little lighter than they did when you weren't talking.

I was stubborn enough to carry this battle to the grave, but making amends was important to Farrah. And if I was being honest with myself, I wanted a relationship with my parents, for me. They weren't getting younger, and neither was I.

How could I go to their funerals someday knowing I'd let pride and anger and hurt keep me from having a relationship with them?

How could I become a part of Farrah's family and not let my parents meet the most amazing woman and children in the world?

Before the fallout, I loved my parents so much I was willing to work in a family business with them. That love hadn't just disappeared. For me at least.

Gage: Thank you for pushing me. A lot of people let me have my way, but you make me better. I need that in my life.

Farrah: I hope you'll do the same for me.

Gage: Can't fix perfect. :)

Farrah: Just wait until you spend more time with me. You'll definitely see my dark side.

Gage: The sun doesn't have a dark side.

Farrah: Maybe. But sometimes I leave clothes in the washer so long they mold. *facepalm emoji* I had to buy Levi a whole new jersey one time because it had these little mildew spots all over the white and it wouldn't wash out.

Gage: I'm sure he forgave you.

Farrah: Oh, and sometimes, I sneak the last ice cream bar while the kids are at school so they can't ask me for it. And then when they see it's gone, I blame one of the kids. *cringe emoji*

Gage: Now you know what it's like to have siblings.

Farrah: One time I even hid my candy bars in an empty frozen peas bag. Every bite tasted like shame.

Gage: You're going to hell for that one.

Farrah: I know I am.

Farrah: Levi has a meeting for his summer baseball league this morning – better get up and get ready for the day before I win the worst mom ever award.

Gage: You're a great mom. And I'll see you later.

Gage: Oh, and can you send his summer game schedule to Mia to put in my calendar? I'd love to go to some games. If that's okay with you and him of course.

Farrah: We'll see how Levi feels about it after meeting you at the shoot next weekend. But thank you for asking. It means a lot.

Gage: Of course. Have a great day, sunshine.

Farrah: You too. <3

I clicked my phone shut, smiling to myself. I could see a life with her, giving her everything she wanted and more, because Farrah didn't want for much.

The only thing standing in the way was my relationship with my parents. And if I was being honest, that fear shook me to the core.

In the last decade, I'd met with presidents, actors, musicians, other world leaders. But it was still my mom and dad who challenged my confidence the most.

48

FARRAH

Having my kids back was like having a part of myself returned. But waking up every day without Gage next to me, without seeing his blue eyes on me first thing and feeling his warm lips against my forehead as he called me beautiful in his scratchy morning voice... I missed that too.

I hated feeling like I had to choose him or my kids, and I wished he would hurry up and make amends with his parents. Because this waiting? It was eating me alive. And I could tell this feud was eating away at him too. If they made amends, they could rebuild their relationship. And if it didn't go well, he'd at least have the closure he'd need to move on.

But I couldn't wallow or forget my standards, because it wasn't just about me. I had three children depending on me. Looking to me for an example of how to love and how to be loved in return.

Luckily, it seemed like they all had a good time in Cabo. Andrew brought back several bottles of sand art that he'd made while he was there. Cora had a new favorite dress. Of course she'd bought it with Melinda, which put a sour, jealous taste in my mouth, but seeing her twirl in the brightly colored, beachy patterned dress made me smile every time.

Raising my kids, watching those bliss-filled moments? It felt like encountering all the best parts of myself. The joy, the wonder, the beauty of life.

That was the one thing I missed about being married to their dad. Every now and then, when we were both home and doing something with the kids, they'd do something cute. And Caleb and I would meet eyes, sharing a smile. Like saying, *can you believe these humans? They are so cool. And maybe a little weird. But also beautiful.*

But there were hard moments too, and plenty of worries. Levi seemed different after the trip. Older. Maybe even a little jaded. Not refreshed or rejuvenated like the other two.

On Wednesday, I asked him if we could go shopping before his baseball practice. His club team practiced later in the evenings because it was getting so darn hot during the day. And since he had a date with Alyssa on Saturday, and I thought it would be nice to get him something new to wear. Especially since my finances had been leaner than usual the last six months.

We dropped Cora and Andrew off with Mom, then stopped by the coffee shop to get drinks. With my latte and his sweet tea in hand, we walked into the mall, heading toward the store where we usually got his clothes.

"Are you excited for your date?" I asked as we flipped through a rack of button-down shirts.

Levi shrugged. Back to his quiet self.

"You haven't talked much since you got back from Cabo. Did everything go okay the last few days you were there?"

Levi picked up a black and gray shirt, folding it over his arm. "Dad got weird after he saw your interview with Gage on the news."

"Weird?" I asked, holding up a blue and black shirt.

He shook his head at the shirt. "I think he was a little jealous. I overheard him and Melinda fighting that night."

My chest got tight. Caleb and I had always tried to save our arguments for after our kids were asleep, and I didn't know how he and Melinda fought. "Were they loud?"

"No. They thought we were all asleep, but the casita had, like, an open-concept thing and I was sleeping in the living room, so I heard them whispering in their room." He picked up a red and brown plaid shirt that I never would have thought to choose for him. "She just didn't know why he was so upset, and he told her you two have history but that he'd never..." His words trailed off and he avoided my gaze, focusing extra hard on the shirts.

"It's okay, Levi," I said. "You're not going to hurt my feelings."

"He said he'd never want to be with you again and that he was only ever with you because of me..." Levi's gaze clouded over.

I'd lied. Because that did hurt. Caleb had written off our entire history and made Levi question himself in one fell swoop. It was a double punch to the gut—once for me and once for my child, who, despite trying to be strong, still looked so hurt.

I crossed the rack, putting my hands on his shoulders.

Luckily the mall was a dead zone this time of day, so we were the only customers, and there weren't any store employees to be seen. "Levi, you may have been a surprise, but you were always wanted." I ducked my head so he'd have to look me in the eyes. "There's not a part of me, not even the nail on my pinky finger or a single gray hair on my head, that regrets you. Do you understand?"

He sniffed, nodding, and looked back at the clothes. "Do you think it's too hot for long sleeves?"

I chuckled slightly. Change in subject. Noted. "Maybe? I think there are some cool T-shirts over there. Or maybe we could get some shorts to go with the long-sleeve shirt and wear it kind of open?"

"Long sleeves and shorts?" he asked, seeming skeptical.

"You wear pants and T-shirts, don't you?"

He still seemed to be mulling over that logic as we walked to another rack of clothes.

Disaster hopefully averted.

That was, until my phone started ringing. Mom's name was on the caller ID, and I answered just in case something was going on with Cora or Drew.

"Hello?"

"Farrah Marie, how could you not tell me you're dating your boss?!" Mom hissed.

"Wh-what?" I managed, my brain short-circuiting. Had I really not told her?

"I have to learn from my five-year-old granddaughter that we're meeting your boyfriend on Sunday. And when I ask her how she found out about this boyfriend, she said you told her and then she WATCHED IT ON THE NEWS."

I held my phone away from my ear, cringing. "Sorry I didn't tell you, Mom. I really wasn't trying to keep it a secret." Not any more at least.

"Good, because I'd hate to think you're ashamed of us. I know your father and I aren't rich, but we worked hard to provide a good life for you."

"I know you did," I said gently. "You and Dad were the best. And I think you're going to adore him, Mom. He's a really great guy."

I could feel Levi listening, even though he was pretending to browse a couple racks away.

"Dad said he'd watch the kids tonight so we can have some girl time," Mom offered. "Let's have margaritas and you can fill me in."

"You know I can't say no," I replied with a smile. "I'll talk to you soon."

Shaking his head, Levi said, "Just when I thought I was going to be the only one dating this year."

I smiled. "This is a first for all of us."

And hopefully, it would lead to even better memories than the ones we already had.

EVEN THOUGH I'D been working at The Retreat without Gage for a week, it was still hard to walk into that conference room and not see him there. He'd even brought Andrew's and Cora's paintings with him, so the walls were bare again.

The place seemed to echo it was so empty, and I was half tempted to pick up the younger two from Mom's house or ask Dad to drop off Levi after his shift at the coffee shop so I could have someone around. But I busied myself, making calls and directing the furniture installers in the building.

Our orders were beginning to come in, and it struck me that I'd never spoken with Gage about what was coming after my job, despite my worries.

I picked up the phone, dialing his number. He answered almost instantly. "Hello?"

"Hey," I said, my voice quiet but still bouncing off the walls.

"How are you?"

"It's quiet here," I answered.

He was silent for a moment. "It's way too quiet here. I never thought I'd get used to constantly hearing you yammer with vendors, but here we are."

I giggled. "I do not *yammer*. I converse."

"Potato, potahto."

I shook my head, smiling to myself. That tight feeling in my chest was already easing up.

"I am getting a lot more work done without the... distractions," he replied, inuendo in his tone.

If I had a phone cord, I'd be twirling it around my finger. "I happen to miss the distractions."

"Is that so?" His voice was husky, and I could tell he was turned on. Getting up, I went to the conference room door, shutting and locking it. Then I moved my computer by the door, playing music just in case.

"What is that?" he asked.

"Mood music," I replied, a wink in my tone. "Are you alone?"

He groaned. "I have glass walls, Farrah."

"Go to the bathroom," I suggested. "Or better yet, do it under your desk. It will be our little secret."

His voice came out a whisper. "Are you touching yourself?"

Dipping my fingers into the waistband of my skirt, I leaned back against the wall where he used to sit. "I am now." I let out a soft moan, feeling so good. We hadn't touched each other in a week, and I missed being with him like I'd miss breathing. "What would you do to me if we were here all alone?"

"First of all, I'd bend you over that table and spank you for distracting me from work." His voice was hoarse.

"That was bad of me, wasn't it?" I'd never been into spanking before, but when Gage slapped my ass during our week together, the mix of pain and pleasure was so delicious I wanted him to do it all over again. I drew my hand up from my clit, teasing my nipples through my bra.

"When that full ass is red with my handprint, I'll get on my knees and kiss each cheek better before running my fingers over your nub."

"God, that feels good," I whimpered, acting out his words with my hand.

"Then I add my tongue, tasting you from behind. You're already so wet because you like being bad sometimes."

My fingers weren't cutting it, so I dug through my purse, getting out my little vibrator and using a baby wipe to clean it. I licked it for moisture and turned it on, getting back to my sensitive spot. "You're so hot when you eat me," I moaned softly. "But I want to taste that big cock of yours and make you feel good."

"You're getting on your knees, aren't you?" he asked, his voice rough.

"I am, and I'm taking your cock from your pants. It's so big, Gage. I'm running my tongue over the tip, and it tastes so good filling up my mouth."

"Fuck, Farrah."

"I can barely fit it, but I take it all the way to the back of my throat until I make that sound you like."

"Shiiit."

"I can taste your precum, you're so turned on."

"I am, baby. Take me faster."

"I'm moving my head over your cock, taking as much as I can."

"You're so good at knowing what I like," he whispered. "But I'm not coming in your mouth."

"No?" I asked, already quivering with how hot it is to be talking to my boss like this on the job. Knowing he probably had people walking outside his office while he fisted his throbbing cock to my voice.

"I'm laying you back over that fucking table, and you're going to take me. All of me."

"God, I'd love that," I moaned, pleasure spreading from my center all the way to my fingers and toes.

"Your ankles fit so perfectly over my shoulders, and I press into your entrance. God, you feel so good and tight, Farrah, and so wet, just for me."

"Only you can get me this way," I breathed, closing my eyes and imagining my powerful and sexy boss towering over me, his dark blue eyes storm clouds as he filled me up in every way. "Only you, Gage."

"Fuck, say my name again."

"Gage Griffen," I moaned, my core tightening.

"Come with me," he said. It was an order. A plea.

And I fell apart at his command, hearing his soft grunts on the other end of the phone as he uttered my name.

We stayed silent for a moment, our quick breaths the only sound.

And then he said, "If HR knew what we just did, I'd be fired."

I laughed. "Maybe you'd get away with a spanking."

49

GAGE

Up until the photo shoot Sunday, Farrah was busier than I'd seen her, which was saying something, considering the breakneck pace at which we needed to get this hotel ready for opening day. It had been hard staying professional. Especially when I found out she was just as good on the phone as she was in person.

I would never see my desk the same way again.

And I had never missed her more.

But the day of the photoshoot, I had to put those sensual feelings aside because I'd be meeting her children and her parents for the first time.

Not as her boss.

But as her boyfriend.

It wasn't something I took lightly, and I knew she didn't either.

On the way to the hotel, I got out my phone and called Liv. She was so good with children, and I needed help making a good first impression.

"Hello, lover boy," she answered on the fourth ring.

"Don't call me that."

She chuckled. "Did you call to grump at me?"

Letting out a sigh, I said, "I'm meeting Farrah's kids today. I mean, I've met Cora and Andrew once, but not as her boyfriend. And I've never met her oldest before. What if..." I didn't finish the words. Because Gage Griffen, CEO, didn't get nervous or doubt himself.

But Gage Griffen, the guy who thought he'd be single forever and was now head over heels for a single mom? Yeah, he was freaking the fuck out.

"What if what?" Liv prompted.

"What if it doesn't go well?"

She stayed quiet for a moment, and I grunted, "The hesitation isn't giving me tons of confidence, Liv."

Chuckling, she said, "You know, after Nicole, I expected you to take a break from dating. But when five years passed, and then ten, I just kind of thought you would stay single forever. I knew you'd make a great uncle, but I never expected you to look at someone the way you looked at Farrah that night."

My chest constricted. I didn't know how I looked at Farrah, but I damn sure knew how I felt about her. "None of it will matter if I can't get along with her kids."

"I know, and I understand that you're worried, but you're a good guy, Gage. It might be awkward at first, but you'll stick around and make it work because that's what you do. Don't forget who you are."

"Thanks for reminding me." I leaned my head against the window for a moment as I drove closer to the hotel. "You know, times like these, I'm really glad Mom disappointed me by having a little sister."

"Only took you twenty-eight years to come around,

but I knew you would eventually," she teased. "I'm actually about to go to a babysitting job, so I'll talk to you later?"

"Sounds good." We hung up, and a few minutes later, I reached the parking lot of The Retreat.

There were more cars than had been there since construction finished, and my chest instantly loosened when I saw Farrah's van. Now there was blue paint on the back window saying GO TITANS! The O in GO was designed like a baseball. That must have been the mascot for Levi's summer team.

The sight brought a slight smile to my lips, and I allowed myself to imagine what life would be like going all in with Farrah *and* her family. I pictured myself as a baseball dad, watching all Levi's games on Saturdays, taking everyone out for dinner afterward to celebrate his hard work.

I imagined sitting with Cora and Andrew in the stands, explaining the game to them while Farrah cheered the loudest of everyone there. I already knew she was that kind of mom—the kind who loved her kids so loudly they never questioned where she stood.

I imagined wrapping my arm around her waist, cheering and kissing her after Levi scored a home run.

And by the time I walked into the building, I was smiling as if my imaginations were real instead of a preemptive fantasy.

A flurry of activity greeted me in the main lobby. The entire main floor was set up for the photoshoot with racks of clothing, bins full of props, and fully assembled lighting equipment, along with a dozen people from Farrah's family and the photographer's employees.

Cora yelled, "MR. GAGE!" and sprinted up to me, slamming into my legs and hugging me tight.

I chuckled, taken off guard. "It's good to see you too, Princess Cora." Already some of my nerves had eased.

Andrew came running next, holding up a piece of paper. "I drew this for you! It's your hotel pool with a dragon in it... Mom said you'd let us go swimming there when it's done."

I ruffled his curls and said, "You can come swimming any time you want. Hopefully without the dragon."

He pumped his arm, saying, "Yes! I knew you weren't *that* grumpy."

Farrah's cheeks already glowed pink as she walked toward me with her parents and her oldest son, Levi. He had her dark hair with natural golden highlights, but his short, messy cut revealed straight hair instead of curls like the other two kids. When they reached me, I realized he was just a few inches shorter than me, nearly six feet tall as a freshman. "You must be Levi," I said, extending my hand.

He shook it, his grip big and clumsy like most teenagers. He still had growing to do, and with his size, I could already see him going places in baseball if that was what he wanted. "Thank you, sir, for getting the Ropers coach to help with practice," he said. "I've already gotten a starting spot on my summer team."

"I'm happy to help," I replied. "And you can call me Gage."

Farrah smiled between the two of us, then said, "Gage, I'd like you to meet my parents, too." The older woman on her other side looked just like her, short and curvy with salt and pepper curls and a contagious smile.

The man wasn't much taller, but he wore a happy expression with kind blue eyes and weather-worn skin. "I'm Barry, and this is my wife, Jenna." His shake was solid, and I realized I instantly liked him.

"It's nice to meet the man who's helped my daughter so much, professionally speaking," he said. "She's always talking about how much she loves her job. I guess now I know why."

A fresh wave of color overtook Farrah's cheeks. "*Dad.*" I could feel the tips of my ears heating too—damn, it had been a long time since that had happened.

Barry chuckled, patting my arm. "Only teasing, son."

A few claps sounded, and Pascale's voice cut through the chatter. "Let's get everyone in hair and makeup."

Cora asked, "Can I sit by you, Mr. Gage?"

"If it's okay with your mom," I answered, glancing up at Farrah.

Her nod was jerky, a little strained, and I wondered what was behind it. But Cora slipped her hand through mine, hanging on mostly to my first two fingers. Her little hand did something strange to my heart, requiring me to clear the unexpected emotion from my throat as we walked to the chairs set up for makeup.

While Farrah, her mom, and Barry sat at the hair stylists' station, Levi, Andrew, Cora and I sat in makeup chairs.

Levi asked no one in particular, "Do I have to wear makeup?"

Andrew got a rotten grin. "Worried *Alyssa* will find out?" He started making kissy sounds, and Levi's cheeks flushed just like his mom's always did.

With a growl, he said, "I'm throwing your glow-in-the-dark fingernail polish away while you sleep."

The color drained from Andrew's face. "You wouldn't dare."

The makeup artist, a younger woman with dark hair and olive skin, said in a British accent, "This makeup is mainly to even out your skin tone and make sure there isn't any extra shine since Pascale uses flash photography."

The boys stopped arguing instantly.

As the makeup artist got started on Levi, Cora flipped her hair over her shoulder, looking at me and whispering loudly, "They always fight like this. You'll get used to it eventually."

I had to chuckle at her explanation. "I had three younger siblings, so I'm pretty used to it already."

Cora said, "I keep trying to talk Mommy into giving me a little sister so we could have two girls and two boys. It's only fair. But she said no." Her little lips stuck out in a pout.

Andrew leaned over the arm of his chair, brown hair falling in his eyes. "You know, Cora, babies are a pain. When you were born, you just cried all the time and poop came out the back of your diaper a *lot*."

After sticking her tongue out at him, Cora faced me again and said, "Mommy told me you grew up on a farm. Can I ride your horses someday?"

An unexpected twinge hit my chest. Hadn't I always dreamed of raising my own family on the ranch? Teaching them all the things I learned growing up? Now I was so far removed from that lifestyle. Maybe if my parents and I made amends...

"That sounds fun, doesn't it?" I asked.

She nodded quickly.

"When I was a kid, we used to ride horses to a creek near our house, then tie them on a tree branch and go swimming in the stream."

"I love swimming!" Andrew said. "Can I come too?"

"That would make me awfully happy," I answered honestly.

When the makeup artist moved on to Andrew, Levi got up from his chair and walked back to his mom and grandparents. I wished I knew what to say to him to get to know him, but maybe that chance would come with time.

While Andrew got his face done, he asked the woman —her name was Mira—all kinds of questions about doing makeup, especially for special effects. It was fascinating, watching the curiosity light his eyes, seeing how he made Mira smile in a way she probably wouldn't if she were just working with adults.

I glanced over my shoulder and caught Farrah looking our way. I gestured at Andrew, mouthing, *he's so* cool.

She tilted her head with a smile I couldn't quite read. I hoped it was good.

50

FARRAH

My heart pounded quickly in my chest.

That thing I missed with Caleb—sharing moments over my kids?

Gage and I just had that moment. And it was like... all that fear I'd been holding on to about my kids not liking him or him not appreciating them... it evaporated.

I knew it would take time for them to form a relationship. Heck, it usually took me a few months after giving birth to fully know and love my babies, and I was their own mom. But still, I could see the future playing out. And now, instead of being afraid that it wouldn't work out, I worried it would work out too well and that, if the day came, saying goodbye to Gage would tear me apart.

Mom bumped my arm, whispering, "Seems like Cora's really taken a shine to him."

Her hair stylist, a man name Pierre, reminded Mom to sit still.

A smile played along my lips as I looked from Mom to Cora. She was using a makeup brush to "help" Mira apply powder to Gage's face. "He's good with them. Which is surprising because he doesn't have any nieces or nephews."

Mom tapped her lips thoughtfully. "Some people have a natural way with children."

"True," I replied. "You were always great with kids. I remember you coming to school events and having a whole crowd around you."

She chuckled. "I always felt like that guy from *Despicable Me* followed by all the Minions."

The visual made me laugh. "You are way more attractive than Gru, Mom."

"Some days..." she laughed.

Pierre finished touching up Mom's curls and then moved on to me. "How do you feel about straightening it today?" he asked me. "It will hold up better in the photo shoot, especially when we have the towel wrapped around your hair."

"That's fine," I replied. I usually wore my hair naturally or in a bun because taking the time to straighten or curl it just wasn't practical with three kids. But now that Cora was getting older and starting to do more on her own, it might be good to play around with new styles.

When we were all done with hair and makeup, Pascale clapped again and yelled loudly, "Let's have the happy couple go up to the large suite first."

Happy couple?

Mom nudged me toward Gage, and I realized Pascale was talking about us. Gage looked over at me, his lips pressing together and a muscle twitching in his jaw. As we walked to the elevator while Pascale and his team gathered props, I whispered, "What's wrong?"

"Your hair." His voice was clipped.

I reached up, touching the smooth strands. "Do you like it?"

His fingers played along the bottom edge of my hair, twisting a lock. "It's pretty; don't get me wrong. It just doesn't look like you."

The elevator doors pinged open, and we stepped in together. Gage punched the button for the top floor, his eyes barely leaving me.

"Isn't it fun to pretend to be someone else sometimes?"

With his heated, almost angry gaze on me, the elevator felt tight, and I already sensed warmth creeping up my neck. He crossed the inches between us and pressed me against the elevator wall, his lips grazing my skin. He nipped and kissed his way down to my shoulder, drawing my blouse to the side so he could access more skin. God, he was already turning me on.

"We don't have enough time," I whispered, my voice breathy.

He moaned against my shoulder, nipping it, and then worked his way back up. "Then don't be so goddamned irresistible."

I gripped on to his shoulders, wishing the elevator would freeze and leave us trapped here long enough to finish what we'd started. It had been a week without physical sex, and I wanted him so badly.

But then the elevator dinged, breaking the spell, and we walked to the suite. Gage adjusted his hard-on on the way, making it just a little less noticeable.

I giggled. "You know, sometimes I'm glad I'm a

woman so I can get turned on without everyone knowing."

His lips curled into a salacious smirk. "Oh, I can tell when you're turned on."

I shook my head at him, pushing through the door and going to the bathroom so I could put my hair back in place before Pascale and his assistants arrived. The mirror instantly showed my flushed cheeks, but then I noticed a spot hiding under the edge of my blouse.

"Gage Griffen!" I hissed, turning to push his shoulder. "You motherfucker."

He smirked. "I suppose I am technically a motherfucker."

I fought back a smile, still angry with him. "I'm serious!"

"What?" he asked, looking half amused and half confused.

I pulled my shirt aside, showing him the mark he'd left on my skin. "You gave me a hickey!"

"And?" He was far too casual about this.

"And I'm a *mother*. I'm thirty-four years old. I'm far too old to be getting love bites!"

Gage took my arms in his hands, drawing me back against the wall like he had in the elevator. Except this time, he didn't kiss me. He traced his nose over mine and then tilted his head so his lips were millimeters from mine.

I wanted him to kiss me so badly.

This was torture.

"You're a mom twenty-four hours a day, Farrah. But these stolen moments, where it's just you and me? You're *mine*."

I was ready to melt into a puddle, but the door to the

suite opened, and I about jumped out of my skin. Gage only straightened his shirt and assumed a stoic look. One day, I would learn how he stayed so calm and collected, but today was not that day.

I walked out of the bathroom, speaking way too perkily. "Pascale! I'm so excited to get started!"

His gaze had cooled a bit from what I'd come to expect of him, but I also knew he had a lot on his plate today.

"Gage, let's start you undressing," Pascale said.

If I'd been drinking coffee, I would have spit it out like some kind of cartoon character. "Pascale, I thought this was going to be a family shoot."

He smirked. "It is. Just your shoes for now." He winked at Gage, who loosened up slightly and laughed.

Gage kicked out of his leather shoes, and then Pascale directed him to sit on the bed. His lighting assistants moved around big flashes, and they took several shots from all different angles. Even though I wasn't a photographer, I could picture the idea coming to life.

The best feeling after a long day of traveling was always kicking off your shoes and stretching out in bed. He was recreating that.

A petite woman with short, jet-black hair came to my side and whispered, "We can start your wardrobe change, Ms. Elkins."

I nodded, following her back to a rack of clothing. "You can call me Farrah."

"Dominique," she said with a smile and then flicked through the hangers of clothes and passed me a terry cloth robe. "This is yours."

I glanced at it. "Is it one size fits all? Because I hate to say it, but that's not always true for people my size."

She smiled. "Pascale has all your clothing sizes. This will be nice and comfy."

"Perfect," I said, taking the robe and walking out so I could change in an empty room.

I stepped into the suite across the hall, gazing around. All the wallpaper and window treatments had been installed. And even with boxes of furniture waiting to be opened and assembled, the space was gorgeous.

I stepped into the bathroom and changed into the robe, which had come with a white cotton underwear set.

Two men had bought me underwear this year. More than double the year before.

The thought brought a smirk to my lips. I didn't mind this change.

Once I had the robe on, I walked back to the suite at the same time Gage stepped out of the bathroom in a robe matching my own.

I had to giggle, because Gage was not a robe guy. He was a walk-around-in-designer-underwear-like-he-stepped-out-of-a-magazine kind of guy. But with him aiming that incredible smile back at me, I thought he could fit more than one label.

He could be the powerful CEO and the kindhearted boyfriend.

The modelesque man and the guy I could laugh with.

And I liked every single version.

51

GAGE

After the photo shoot, we all went to Farrah's place for pizza. I'd only been there once before, and then I'd only been on the outside at night.

In the daytime, the house looked that much more *her*, dandelions in the yard and all.

Cora and Andrew ran ahead, and Levi followed them with his grandparents. Farrah and I walked behind them, and I put my arm around her back, curling my fingers at her waist. "I'm excited to see your place."

Apprehension filled her eyes. "It's nothing fancy."

I reached out, tipping her chin up briefly. "It's *you*. That's what I like, remember?"

She nodded, smiling slightly as we walked slowly over the sidewalk. "The photo shoot was fun today, don't you think?"

"I'm never going to forget you and Cora sitting at that corner table in your robes with towels on your heads, eating chocolate strawberries. It was adorable."

Leaning her head against my shoulder, she said, "It

was the best. Pascale made the whole event so fun for the kids. I was worried they'd get restless."

"They did great," I agreed. "You've done a wonderful job with them, Farrah."

She smiled up at me before reaching the open door. "This is our home."

We stepped into a space that instantly felt like her. I could see her touch now in the pictures hanging of her kids, the way she'd spotlighted Andrew's art, giving it a home on almost every wall.

Her living room couch was large, cozy, perfect for the hours they surely spent together there. But it was simple too. There weren't any overstated pieces or intrusive designs. Perfectly Farrah and her sweet little family.

My condo might have had all the luxuries a person could possess, but being in this space made me feel richer than I ever had before.

The boys sat down to play video games while Cora pulled her grandma along to her room to look for toys. Farrah and her dad sat at the table while Farrah typed on her phone to order pizza, and I joined them.

"I've been enjoying the coffee Farrah brings from Barry's," I told her dad.

He clasped his hands on the table, a slight smile playing on his lips. "I heard you've been by the shop. Now I know why you were so interested," he teased, nodding toward Farrah.

"Dad," she said, setting her phone down. "Wait." She looked at me. "You went to Barry's?"

I nodded. "We actually need a coffee shop in the hotel. I've been weighing my options, but you've got something special going on there at Barry's. Any chance you'd be interested in opening a second location?"

Farrah covered her mouth. "Oh my gosh, Dad, that's an amazing opportunity."

Barry shook his head. "That's a big honor, Gage, but I'm going to have to turn it down."

My eyebrows drew together, confused by his immediate refusal. "You don't want to hear the offer first?" I knew it would be well worth his while.

Barry simply shook his head.

Farrah reached across the table, putting her hand atop her father's forearm. "Are you sure, Dad? That could be a great source of extra income for you and Mom."

Barry patted her hand. "You and Gage are still young, with lots of energy, but someday you'll understand where I'm coming from. The only thing you can't buy in this life is time, and I'm happy with the time I have to spend with Jenna and you and the kids. Taking on another project might make me more money, but what's it worth if I can't make it to Levi's games or hang out with the kids after school? I don't need a bigger house or more cash sitting in the bank. I have all I need right here."

The words hit me one after another. He hadn't meant them harshly, but I understood. The only thing I'd ever needed my time for was my business. How could I balance growing my business and serving my employees while also taking part in a life with Farrah? Would late evenings and weekends be enough?

I pushed the thought to the back of my mind. "If you want to connect me with your supplier, maybe we could do a 'proudly serves Barry's coffee' label like the chain that shall not be named."

Barry tapped his temple. "Now you're thinking, son."

Hearing someone call me son did strange things in my chest, and I took a deep breath, trying not to give away how much his kindness meant to me. "Barry's really is a special place, though. How did you set such a great company culture?"

"Lead by example, care about people, and you'll attract the right kind of team."

Farrah nodded. "The shop has always been a fun place to hang out. It used to be open until six at night instead of two in the afternoon, and I'd go there after school to do homework and hang out before I got old enough to work there. It was like a second home. Now Levi is working there too over the summer."

"That's a great legacy," I said. A family business like the one I'd always wanted.

The doorbell rang, and Farrah said, "That must be the pizza. Can you go tell Mom and Cora to come to the table?" She began walking toward the door. "Boys, turn that thing off and wash your hands."

Smiling, I got up from the table, walking back down the hallway toward the bedrooms. I could hear Cora and Jenna playing together farther down the hall. But on the way, I looked through the open bedroom doors.

The first room looked more mature, with darker bedding and furniture. The next one had an entire back wall basically papered in drawings. Andrew's. I smiled slightly. And on the left, I noticed a cozy room with twinkle lights along the ceiling. A white bed frame with soft pink bedding.

Farrah's space.

I smiled at it, and if she was with me right now, I'd

walk inside, take a closer look at the photos she had on her nightstand, along with the stack of books lying there. I wanted to know everything about her life here. But I needed to respect her privacy, so I continued to the back room.

Cora and Jenna sat on the floor, playing with dolls around a small table. Her bed was shaped like a little house with lights and flowers wrapped around the frame. On the door, I noticed a drawing in Andrew's style that said PRINCESS CORA.

I smiled at it before knocking on the open door. "Hate to interrupt you two, but pizza's here."

Cora immediately dropped her stuffed animal and jumped up, sprinting past me toward the table as she yelled, "PIZZA!"

Jenna and I chuckled at her as she whizzed by, leaving the two of us alone. I walked over to her, extending my hand to help her up.

She gripped it with both of her own. "I don't know why the floor seems so much lower than it used to."

I laughed. "Looks like you two had fun in here."

She glanced down at all the stuffed animals and dolls scattered on the floor. "It's a mess—that's how you know you had a good time."

I chuckled, walking with her back to the table, where everyone was sitting with paper towels for plates. It brought back memories of growing up on the days when Mom didn't want to do dishes, and I smiled at the thought.

There were good memories of my childhood. I found myself hoping that someday I could make good memories with my parents again.

"Can Gage sit by me?" Andrew asked.

Cora whined. "I wanted him to sit by me."

Farrah gave them an exasperated look. "You know he can sit by both of you, right? That is, if he wants to."

"Of course," I said. As they played musical chairs, I grabbed a couple slices of pepperoni, then sat between them.

The first bite of pizza had my mouth watering it was so good. "Where did you get this?" I asked, glancing toward the box.

"The gas station near here has the best pizza," Farrah said with a blush. "I know that doesn't make it sound appetizing, but..." She shrugged.

Jenna said, "You're probably used to eating high-dollar pizza, right, Gage?"

"I don't usually eat pizza," I admitted. My nutritionist worked with my chef service, so I mostly had my meals chosen for me unless I was eating out with a business contact or my siblings. "But this is as good as it gets." I took another bite.

Levi housed his first piece and was already working on a second. "Our coach says we should be eating healthier this summer so we don't derail our training."

Farrah said, "That's probably a good idea. I have some salad in the fridge if you want it."

He pushed back from the table and walked to the fridge. "It's half full—can I eat it in the bag?"

"Less dishes for me," Farrah said with a smile.

He came back to the table, holding the bag with ranch dressing drizzled inside.

"How's summer ball going?" I asked. I missed watching him play online.

Levi said, "It's good. We have a really good team."

"Will you be at shortstop again?" I asked.

He nodded, "I'm getting excited for our games to start."

"How far off is that?" I asked.

Levi shrugged. "First one's in a month, if you want to come."

I glanced toward Farrah, silently asking her permission, and she nodded slightly, a smile on her lips.

"I'd love to," I said. "I'll be there."

Levi smiled half a second. "Great."

Behind Cora's back, Jenna patted my shoulder, an impressed look on her face.

Levi groaned loudly. "Don't make it a big deal, okay?" he said before stuffing more lettuce in his mouth.

I chuckled. It might not have been a big deal for him, but it sure as hell meant the world to me.

52

FARRAH

Between managing the furniture installers and the linen shipments, I barely got a chance to sit down for most of the week. Gage and I fell into a routine of texting throughout the day and then calling each other once the kids went to bed.

I wanted to invite him to stay over, but my instincts, and maybe my fear too, told me to hold back. Everything seemed perfect, but he still hadn't spoken with his parents, and I needed to stick to my word. My standards. Because even though I wanted to get swept away by the excitement and big feelings of new love, I knew what it would turn into. I didn't just want a boyfriend for the moment; I wanted a life partner.

And my kids deserved someone who would follow through his word. If he at least talked to his parents, I would feel confident moving forward, letting him stay over and spend more time at the house. Even if they didn't patch things up, I'd know he'd put himself out there for me. For us.

Over the next few weeks, I still spent as much time with him as I could without taking too much time away from my kids. One day, he picked all of us up after work and took us on a private tour of the zoo. Another day, he rented a fun house, and watching the kids run into every mirrored surface made me laugh so hard I nearly peed my pants.

All those moments on top of flower deliveries to my house, the occasional lunch order to The Retreat so I'd have something good to eat on the long days of work... he made me feel more special than I'd ever felt before. And I tried to enjoy it without worrying if it all would end.

And I tried to remind myself that just because my marriage had ended didn't mean this new relationship would. I did my best to enjoy the moment, especially when Caleb and Melinda surprised me by offering to take the kids on a weekend trip to Lake Texoma. Melinda's family owned a cabin there, and they had tons of fun planned for the kids.

They picked the kids up on their way out of town on a Friday, and even though I wanted to rush to Gage's penthouse and surprise him, I took my time showering, shaving, and putting on my nicest lingerie under a wrap dress.

It wasn't a trench coat, which of course was the sexual fantasy, but June in Texas called for something lighter.

When I was all done up, I got in my car and drove to Gage's building. Even though it was almost nine, the sun was barely setting. He'd said he had a meeting late this evening with Jason Romero, but I had a code to get into his place, and I didn't mind waiting and surprising him.

I got out of my van in the parking garage, feeling a

delightful breeze under my dress as I walked toward the elevator. I didn't see his car, so waiting it was. Strutting in a pair of heels, I pressed in the code to take me up to his place.

When I walked into his condo, it was dark save for the dimming sky out the windows. Leaving the lights off, I went to his room, glancing around at the perfectly clean space and neatly made bed.

How had it been a month since I spent a week in this place, making some of my favorite memories with him? I couldn't wait to make more this weekend and make up for lost time.

I slipped out of my heels, letting my feet sink into his cushy rug and then went to his bed, lying back in the welcoming, soft pillows. I pulled up my phone, flipping through photos I'd taken of us at the zoo. There were so many fun ones, from Gage holding Andrew on his shoulders to Cora riding an elephant. Even Levi had smiled when they let us feed the giraffes and we saw their long tongues reach out and wrap around the romaine leaves.

When I heard the elevator ding, announcing someone had entered from the ground floor, I hurried off the bed, slipping back into my heels. Then I slowly untied the knot of my dress, putting my arms around my waist.

The elevator dinged again, the doors opening, and I called, "In here."

"Farrah?" Gage called, sounding surprised.

He walked to the bedroom door.

"Thought I would come and surprise you," I said, pulling my dress open and showing him everything underneath.

A heated look filled his eyes, and he scrubbed his hand over his chin. "Fuck, Farrah."

I grinned. "You like?"

"Like? I'm fucking obsessed." He crossed the room, gaze smoldering on me before he took my mouth with his own.

It was a desperate kiss, crushing with its intensity, its weight.

So different from the fun and playful kisses or slow and savory ones we'd shared in the past. This one carried a different type of need. One I couldn't identify.

But I loved the way he devoured me. Ripped the dress down my arms and tugged at my thong until it came apart, turning to threads in his hand.

His lips stayed on my body as he laid me back on the bed, already reaching for a condom in his nightstand drawer.

His rush made me worry, but I tried to brush it off and stay in the moment. Maybe it had been too long since we last touched this way, and there would be more time to slow down this weekend.

But I held on to his shoulders as he thrusted into me. Savored the feeling of every inch of his skin on mine. I'd missed this closeness with him, along with all the little touches. I hoped it would be sooner than later when we could spend more nights together. When I could feel his arm curl protectively around my middle. When we could savor kisses that turned into slow burn touches and then intimacy with fireworks that lit the skies of my life.

I wanted all of it with Gage. This man who fucked me and made love to me and made me feel like the sexiest woman alive either way.

Thinking of our future, of how I felt for him, mixed with the pounding rhythm of our sex, the slapping of skin, his harsh breath on my cheek, it tipped me over the edge. I cried out his name as I tightened around him, the sensations too good to deny.

And when we were done, he stayed silent, tossing the condom in the trash and putting on his underwear before sitting on the edge of the bed instead of sliding in under the covers with me.

My throat felt tight, because this wasn't the Gage I knew. There was no smile in his eyes. No kind words or adoration on his lips.

"Is everything okay?" I asked, sitting next to him, placing my hand over his beating heart and looking for some sign that if things weren't okay, then they would be eventually.

He shook his head slightly.

Dread filling my stomach. "What happened? I know the soap dish shipment fell through, if that's it, but I'll be able to find a replacement in time."

He kissed my forehead, silent for a long moment. "It's not about The Retreat."

"Then what?" I asked, feeling so much more naked than before. "Because you're scaring me."

He turned his gaze on me, blue eyes dark, and then looked away again without a word.

I almost felt dizzy with worry. Was this it? The part where he got what he wanted and then left? Was he giving up on making amends with his parents? Or did he just not want me anymore? *What?*

I wanted to voice all my fears aloud, but I stayed silent, watching him as he put on his stony exterior, the one that didn't let me see past the walls he erected around himself.

It was the old Gage. Not the one I knew.

Not the one I loved.

"My meeting with Jason didn't go as expected," he finally said.

Relief swept through me. There was an issue with his partnership. Not with us. I rubbed his back, but he seemed to tense even more. Letting my hand fall, I asked, "What happened?"

His eyes landed on mine, darker, emptier than ever before. "He said our...relationship is damaging to his campaign. He said if I wanted this partnership to go through, I needed to end our relationship, publicly."

My lips parted, but inside, I was screaming, flailing. Gage's partner wanted him to end things with me? Why?

Was my relationship with Gage really that detrimental to him becoming governor, or was it something else entirely?

"Wh-what are you going to do?" I asked, afraid to hear his answer. But I needed to know. And if I was being honest with myself, I knew it would always come down to this:

Would he choose his business?

Or would he choose me?

"I can't let this deal fall through," he said. "People are counting on me. The new jobs this project was going to bring to West Texas... do you know how many families there were praying for something like this? And now Jason wants to cancel it."

But what about our family? I wanted to ask. *What about the three children who love to spend time with you? What about me?*

But I couldn't ask those questions. Because Gage still hadn't spoken with his parents. It had been weeks since I'd asked him to, and still nothing. That should have been answer enough.

I got up, putting on my wrap dress to cover myself. "So that's it," I said, hating the quiver in my voice. "It's over."

He reached for my hands. "I don't want it to be. He said the only way we could prove to the public that our relationship wouldn't affect the business was if we got married." His eyes searched mine. "We could go to Vegas and do it this weekend, Farrah. We'd have to move in together because it would look worse to the press if we didn't, but I can stay in a separate room until you feel comfortable. Please, Farrah? It's the only way for us to be together in public. I'll do this in secret until the plant is built if I have to, but I really don't want to."

With each word, the acidic taste in the back of my throat grew even stronger. This was all *wrong*.

I pulled my hands away from his, pacing in his bedroom.

"What are you doing, Farrah?" He stood and walked around the bed to stop my pacing. "You don't want to break up either; I know you don't. Let's just get married. We both know that's where this was going anyway."

My lips parted as I shook my head in shock. In anger. "How dare you ask me to marry you."

His shoulders squared, his brows drawing together the only hint at his emotions. "You don't want to be with me?"

I stared at this man. This beautiful man standing in his boxers like a model fit to be carved into a statue. Only an hour ago, I would have said he was *exactly* what I wanted, but now I knew better.

"I was married for fourteen years to a man who stayed with me for a child he didn't plan on having." Angry tears stung my eyes. "The fact that you thought I would *ever* want you to marry me to keep a business deal..." I shook my head. "It's demeaning, and most of all, it's cruel."

"It's not only for the deal, Farrah. I love you. But I don't want to be with you in secret," he said. "I thought this would work for both of us, a way for us to stay together."

"It's not a way for us to stay together. It's a way for you to choose your business over us—over me and my family. Painting it any other way is only hurting us both."

"That's not what I'm doing, Farrah. I want to be with you."

"So you would have proposed to me this weekend if Jason hadn't said anything?"

Gage stayed silent.

I shook my head at him. "You don't understand. My dad turned down a deal with a literal billionaire because it would take away his time with his family. But you wouldn't stand up for me to a man who would judge a single mother?"

Gage opened his mouth to speak, but if I didn't get the words out now, I'd never be able to speak them. Never be able to walk away.

"When I left Caleb, I promised myself I would never settle ever again. If I accept your 'proposal', I'd be showing my daughter that marriage is a business transaction. I'd show my sons that women are pawns to be used

366   HELLO BILLIONAIRE

for financial or political gain. I'd show them that the men in their lives are there out of obligation rather than love and commitment. And the fact that you'd offer that only proves to me that you are not the man I thought you were."

I shook my head at him, getting my purse and walking to the elevator door. I jammed my finger on the button, praying I could get inside before the floodgates opened and I fell apart.

"Farrah, don't do this," Gage whispered. "I didn't want this."

I stepped inside and pushed the button for the parking garage. "No, but you chose it."

53

GAGE

TWELVE YEARS AGO

At Wednesday night dinner, I put the sale page for the land neighboring our family farm on the table in front of Dad. Even though I went to tech school in Dallas two hours away, I still came home Wednesday nights to spend time with my family. It was one of my favorite days of the week—a chance to see my siblings, all still in high school, eat a home-cooked meal instead of the ramen and PB&J sandwiches I lived on, a chance to be on the farm instead of in the city.

Dallas had so much to offer within its city limits, but Griffen Farms? It was the only place that had ever felt like home. And I hoped, with this plan, I'd be coming home soon. This time for good.

Dad finished chewing his steak, glancing over the paper. "I heard the Fosters were selling. Damn shame if you ask me. A family farm means something. You can't just give up on it when you hit tough times."

My hands were shaking with anticipation. With nerves. I'd gone over this plan at least a dozen times with my real estate mentor I worked for in Dallas. Since I started working for him a couple years ago, he'd taught me so much about growing real estate holdings, managing rental properties, and so much more. All while I helped him fix up the properties he owned and managed.

Tyler said, "Connor told me they're moving to the city as soon as it sells."

Dad swore under his breath. "That's just what those kids need. They get into enough trouble as it is."

Mom frowned. "They won't even finish the school year?"

"Not according to Connor," Tyler said.

Liv looked devastated. "Connor was supposed to take me to prom! I hope no one buys their place before then."

"I hope we do," I said.

All eyes turned on me, but even Rhett didn't seem amused. They all stared at me like I'd grown a second head.

Mom spoke first. "What do you mean, Gage?"

"I've been talking with Mr. Price and his banker, and they've taught me a lot about real estate and funding for new business ventures. The Fosters' farm is over a thousand acres. We could expand the feedlot to take in cattle from neighboring ranches, and we could use the extra ground to run more cattle. They even have some dryland farm ground we could use to grow extra feed to accommodate the increased herd size."

I realized I hadn't breathed that entire time and took a quick breath. "And with that many cattle and that much land, we could support at least two families, maybe three if we manage it properly. Nicole and I won't need much when we're first married. It'll give us time to grow the operation, settle in. And by the time Liv's done with school in a few years, we could purchase more land. Grow even bigger and make this family farm something real. Something that could sustain us across generations."

Liv had a small smile on her lips, and Tyler was nodding thoughtfully. But Mom was watching Dad, and so was I.

His lips were a straight line under his mustache, unimpressed. Uninspired. "Those are big dreams, Gage. But big dreams take big money."

"This banker I was talking to said we could easily get an equity loan to cover the cost of a down payment for the Fosters' land since our land's been paid off since before Grandpa passed it to you and Mom. And the Fosters already have a house built there, so it wouldn't cost any extra to keep me on full-time, aside from utilities and food."

Dad stayed silent for a second and then chuckled. "Send you to the city, and all of a sudden, you come back with these crazy ideas."

Everyone around us averted their eyes from me, and shame filled my chest. "It's not a crazy idea, Dad." I pulled out the manila folder with the business plan I'd pored over with Mr. Price. I knew my dad well enough to know he'd take at least a little convincing. "I worked up a business plan, and I think within two years, we'd be breaking even. Years four and five, we'd see greater returns than you've made in the last five years combined. Imagine what you and Mom could do with all that money, Dad. Maybe you could finally take Mom on that cruise she's been wanting to go on."

"We don't need more money," he snapped, ripping the folder, my plan, in half. "And we sure as shit don't gamble land that generations of Griffens have broken their backs over so that we could have it now. You know how great-grandpa Griffen bought this land?"

I nodded, exasperated with having heard the story a million times before. "He moved here from Missouri and worked for years to save up the money. Bought eighty acres at a time. Great-grandma didn't even get an engagement ring until she was on her deathbed. I know. But Dad, they took a risk; they invested their time and money and sweat into this farm because they believed in what it could be. Why are you *so* determined to keep it small when it could be so much more?"

Dad stood up from his chair, putting his hands on the table and glaring across it at me. "I don't want some twenty-year-old kid who's been hanging out with a money-hungry vulture telling me how I should run this business. I thought I'd raised you with morals, with respect for traditions, hell, some humility, but two years away and this is what happens? You think you know everything!"

"I know that you could be making more money than the pittance you're living on," I snapped.

Dad sneered. "You're just as greedy as he is."

His words cut deep, and I glared at the man who raised me, my chest heaving with anger. With shame. Especially with all my siblings and my mom watching, saying *nothing*. "Mr. Price is not greedy. He's given me a job, paid me more than what's fair, and he provides housing to dozens of families—"

"All while lining his pockets and thinking of number one."

"And who are you thinking about?" I demanded. "This is supposed to be a *family* farm, but how the hell am I supposed to come back here and raise a family on it when you're barely making enough to keep a roof over your head?"

His face was turning red. "You ungrateful little shit. Your mother and I busted our asses to give you a damn good life. You always had food. You always had a place to sleep at night. You traveled all over the fucking state to play baseball. Tell me what you wanted for, and I'll show you an entitled little brat."

I ground my teeth together, biting back venom. "What am I supposed to do, Dad? Work as a hired hand for some other farm the rest of my life, barely getting by? You know it doesn't have to be that way, Dad."

"The fact that you said that proves you're just as money hungry as he is. Always looking out for how things can get better for number one. And that greed? It has no place here."

I shook my head, fighting the tears pricking at my eyes and the anger pooling in my throat. "Then I guess there's no place for me here, is that it?"

Dad stayed silent, glaring at me across the table. "Not with this attitude."

There it was. The truth. He didn't want anything to do with me or my 'crazy dreams.' He didn't want me to try and make this place better. He didn't want *me*.

I stormed away from the patio table where we were

eating, and the sound of a chair scraping over cement echoed behind me.

"Gage," Mom called out.

But Dad snapped, "Let him go." Then he raised his voice so I was sure to hear him. "Have fun chasing your money. See how far that gets you."

"Fuck you," I bellowed back. I got in my truck and slammed it into gear, peeling away from my home.

Away from my family.

And my mom? She let me go.

My dad? He never called.

And me? I never stopped trying to prove him wrong.

But the problem was... even now, all these years later... I still worried he had been right.

54

MIA

On Monday morning, Farrah called my private cell. Her voice was raw as she said, "Hey, I'm not feeling well. I'm going to have to call in. I'm not sure how this works, since I haven't taken a day off since the big office move, but someone's going to need to let the furniture guys in and make sure they actually take their trash out today."

How was she focusing on work if she felt half as bad as she sounded? "What do you have?" I asked, leaning over my desk. "You sound like shit."

Gage walked past my desk, keeping his gaze straight ahead and going into his office.

"Loverboy just walked into work, by the way," I said. "Did he ask you to call me about this? He seems pretty hands on with The Retreat. Although we both know why," I teased.

She made a sniffling sound. "I figured you'd be handling the details anyway. Will you let him know? I'm just going to hole up today and hope I feel better."

"Sure thing. Do you want me to bring you something

after work? I can ask my mom to make her chicken soup."

"I'm good. Talk to you soon." Her voice broke on the last word, and then the line went silent.

I drew my eyebrows together, confused. Farrah never turned down chicken soup. Not when we lived together in college or even the couple years after, when we lived in the same town. She must have been feeling especially bad. Good thing her parents were around to help with her kids.

I got up, walking to Gage's office, and knocked on the clear glass door. Not looking up from his computer, he waved me in.

"Farrah sounds awful," I said, finally getting his attention. "I'm going to make sure the security guard at The Retreat knows to let in the furniture installer, but is there anything else you need me to do? Want me to see if Doctor Madigan can check on her?"

"You think she needs a doctor?" he asked, seeming taken aback.

"Don't tell me you're one of those tough-it-out kind of guys. There's nothing wrong with taking medicine when you're sick."

He shook his head sharply. "Tell him we'll double our regular rate. He can see her if necessary or do a video visit, and we'll cover the medication for whatever she's sick with. And make sure she gets meals and hydration around the clock."

I stared at him, confused. "You don't know what she has? Aren't you two constantly texting each other?"

"I'm busy today," he said curtly, and that was my sign to go. But now I noticed the dark circles under his eyes.

This partnership with Jason Romero was stressing him out like I'd never seen before. He and Jason had been in the office until well past eight o'clock Friday night, which meant I hadn't gotten home to my place until after nine.

Not that I saw much of my apartment, always going between work and checking in on my parents where they lived in assisted living. But still, I liked to see the place I paid out the nose for from time to time.

I returned to my desk and glanced back toward Gage's office, seeing him holding his phone to his ear, pacing back and forth in front of the window. He grimaced and then put his phone forcefully down on the table. His lips formed a string of swearwords.

Holy shit, that call must have been bad. I hadn't seen him wound this tightly in months. Maybe he was just really worried about Farrah.

I sat down at my desk again, running through my usual list of tasks and then having Gage's meal service deliver meals to Farrah's place on a regular schedule for the next few days. Then I added a bouquet of dandelions for good measure, from me and Gage.

But a couple hours into the workday, my personal phone rang again, and Farrah's mom's number came up on the screen.

"Hey, Jenna, everything okay with Farrah?" I hoped Farrah hadn't needed a hospital visit, but I'd never heard her that sick before either.

"I'm not sure," Jenna said, her voice full of worry. "I saw on the news that Gage and Farrah separated, and when I call Farrah's phone, she's not answering. I have the kids, and it's not like her to screen calls when I'm watching them, even if she's at work."

"Maybe she's in the shower or something?" I suggested, trying to ignore the worry forming in my chest. "I work with Gage, and he hasn't said a thing about a split. I'm sure it's just a silly rumor and PR will be on it before you know it."

She didn't quite sound convinced. "Can you check in on her again?"

"Sure thing. I'll text you when I know more."

We hung up, and I tried calling Farrah, but she didn't answer. Hopefully she was just sleeping off whatever bug she'd caught. But since I had the other half of the relationship here, I went to his office and knocked again.

He waved his hand, signaling me to come in. "Yes?"

I said, "I'm sure Tallie's on it already, but a rumor about you and Farrah splitting up is in the news. I just wanted to make sure you were on top of it since you've been so busy."

He let out a heavy sigh, running his hands over his face. "It's not a rumor, Mia."

I swear my heart stopped. "*What?*"

"We broke up Friday night. It wasn't working out."

My lips opened and closed as I remembered the last time I'd seen them together. They had looked so happy. Farrah hadn't been that in love since I met her. And Gage? He was actually smiling at people now. How could they go from that to being over in the span of a week?

"Did you cheat on her?" I demanded. Farrah hadn't even been this torn up when she found out she had HPV. But a second time of a man cheating on her? That would tear anyone up.

Gage glared at me. "Don't insult me, Mia."

"I'm sorry, but Farrah is the best person I know. So if something happened..."

"It's my fault, is that it?" he snapped.

I folded my arms over my chest, silence the only answer he needed.

But then I saw his shoulders sag, and his features soften. "She hasn't talked to you about it?"

I shook my head. "I really thought she was sick when she called this morning."

"She could be. She hasn't answered any of my calls or texts. But I suspect the real reason for her radio silence is that she wants nothing to do with me." He let out an angry grunt and pounded his fist on the table, the least controlled I've ever seen him.

I blinked, assaulted by all the emotions of the most stoic man I'd ever met. "Gage, what happened?"

"Romero said approval ratings haven't come back up since word spread about my involvement with Farrah, and it had been a month like we agreed on, so I had to make a choice. Marry her, break up, or date her in secret."

Shock had me bringing my hand to my mouth. I knew Jason Romero was a pig, but making Gage and Farrah break up was awful, even for a sleazy wannabe politician. "He really said that?"

Gage nodded. "I can't blame him because it makes business sense. If you're doing something that hurts the bottom line, change it. But it's Farrah."

I shook my head, disgusted. "I hate that asshole."

"I do too. But if he backs out, that's hundreds of jobs for hundreds of families, gone."

I could feel my heart breaking for him and Farrah. I

knew how much Gage cared for other people, but he loved Farrah too. "You broke up because you couldn't ask her to marry you."

"I did ask her." He loosened his tie, leaning back in his chair like a man defeated. "And it was a big fucking mistake."

I nodded, already understanding. Farrah needed a man who would choose her on his own terms. But Gage's hand had been played for him. "She walked away from you then?"

"Yes." He pressed the heels of his hands into his eyes. "And I can't get the image out of my fucking head."

"What are you going to do about it?" I asked.

His arms outstretched at his sides. "What the hell am I supposed to do? My hands are tied. It's a hundred families or me and Farrah. You can't think I should be that selfish."

I shook my head at him, not believing what I heard. "You're telling me a man who has spoken in front of congress, eaten dinner with the president, negotiated with the biggest sharks on Wall Street, and grew up riding wild bulls for whatever dumb ass reason—*that man* is giving up on the love of his life?" My lip curled in anger, in disappointment. "That's not the man I've worked with for the last three years. That's not Gage Griffen."

His angry blue eyes pierced mine, but I didn't look away. My friend's heart was on the line, and he was letting it break.

"Go to work, Ms. Baird," he ordered roughly.

"I don't think so. I'm taking a personal day, Mr. Griffen."

55

GAGE

With my assistant gone and my heart in tatters, I left the office. Because no matter how much I tortured myself in the gym, no matter the amount of scotch I poured over ice, no matter how many times I tried to bury myself in work, the image of Farrah disappearing behind the elevator doors was seared into my mind.

My personal torture.

The price I paid for choosing the good of hundreds over the good of a woman who truly mattered to me.

Because I couldn't choose her for myself. I couldn't focus on what would make me happy.

Not when I'd spent my entire life growing a business to serve other people. Not when I wanted so desperately for my dad to be wrong about me.

I felt a renewed sense of pain and rage all over again, like Dad and I were fighting that first day.

So I got into my car and began driving the path to Cottonwood Falls, needing to handle what I should have done all those years ago. What I should have done the second Farrah asked me.

And since nothing could distract me from that ache in my chest that was Farrah leaving, I sat with it. I stewed in it. I let it eat me from the inside out because I knew there would never be another like her. There would never be someone who wholly understood me and loved me without asking for anything in return. All she asked for was my dedication. My heart.

And it had cost me too fucking much to give.

My Tesla had never seen a dirt road before, but now I drove it down the gravel path to my family's home, driving under the metal arch that said GRIFFEN FARMS with a cow silhouette on either side.

Dust flew behind me as I sped toward the white farmhouse waiting at the end of the lane. A glance at my clock told me it was almost noon. Dad should be back for lunch any minute now if he wasn't there already.

A car and two pickups sat in the drive, and I figured one of them was his.

I let anger, hurt fuel me as I got out of my car, and marched to the front door, rapping the wood not covered by a massive wreath with lots of gingham ribbon and a large white G in the middle.

Footsteps sounded on the hardwood inside, and my mom opened the door, her lips pulling into an O at the disheveled sight of me. "Gage, what are you doing here? Come in."

I walked past her, saying, "Where's Dad?"

"At the table, why?"

"We need to talk," I replied, stepping through the living room. They still had the same couches, same layout from when I'd been there more than a decade ago. Some things didn't change. But I had.

When I made it to the kitchen, Dad was getting up from the table, asking, "Who is it?"

Then he laid eyes on me.

His jaw tensed as he took me in, reading me just like I was reading him.

"Well this is a surprise," he said. "Mom just made lunch. We have some extra if you want it."

What the hell was going on, and why was he offering me food? "That's not why I came." My anger was already fading, being replaced by pain. Guilt. Regret.

"Then why did you come?" he asked. There were new wrinkles around his eyes. More salt and pepper in his mustache than ever before. But there was also a kindness I'd forgotten existed since he'd caused me so much hurt all those years ago.

"My girlfriend and I just broke up," I said.

"The single mom?" he asked.

My eyebrows knitted together. "How did you know?"

He glanced toward my mom coming into the room, and I turned my head just in time to see her say, "We still keep up with you as much as we can... We miss you."

"We?" I demanded, looking at Dad.

He looked down, away.

Mom's voice came loudly, "Damn it, Jack, we've talked about this." When I looked at my mom, I saw angry tears in her eyes.

Dad gritted his teeth. "So what? I'm supposed to admit I was wrong, and it'll all go away? It's been *years* without a word, without a phone call. And when you looked at me in that diner, I could see it in your eyes. You hate me. You want nothing to do with me."

"You raised me and then you wrote me off the second I disagreed with you! What was I going to do? Beg my dad to love me?" I choked on my words, hating how weak I felt saying them. I was a billionaire, had a thriving company. Shouldn't I be past this by now?

He shook his head, his voice gruff. "Of course I love you. But when Easter came and you didn't show up, then Thanksgiving came and you didn't show up, and then Christmas... months turned into years turned into a whole damn decade. I thought you'd made your choice. You were done with me."

I shook my head. "You never called me either. Mom's the one who's been having Liv sneak me zucchini bread for years."

"Of course. She missed you," Dad said. "Hell, I missed you."

His words wrenched my already broken heart around in my chest. "Why haven't you called if you miss me?" I asked, not believing it.

"I tried to call you at your office a couple years ago, and your assistant told me I wasn't on the approved list." He shook his head. "I could have tried harder, but I figured you seemed to be doing well. Why would I mess that up for you?"

My heart was holding on to all the hurt, all the anger, but it was fading despite my efforts. "Why would you miss someone who, in your mind, only cares about money?"

Dad ran his fingers through mostly gray hair. The top half of his head was pale where he wore his hat. "We know that isn't true, Gage. Anonymous donor rebuilds the baseball field in Cottonwood Falls with state-of-the-art equipment? Another anonymous donor makes sure the school has brand new textbooks every three years? Not hard to guess who has that kind of money. And buying that schoolhouse for your brother and his wife?" At my surprised look, he nodded. "Tyler told us. Not to mention, your mom saves every press release about you— and they're all good. Donating to small-town farmers and ranchers. Investing in infrastructure abroad? You've done it all. You proved that you were the one guided by your heart, Gage Griffen, and I was the one guided by fear."

My legs felt weak, and I sat at the table. The same table where I'd done homework and eaten breakfast, lunch, and dinner for so many years. But I wasn't the same idealistic kid who used to sit here and dream about a life on the ranch with the girl I loved and a house full of babies.

I was a guy who'd given up on the love of my life to play hardball with a politician who cared more about his bottom line than doing the right thing.

"I'm not sure that's true," I said.

Mom sat next to me, laying a comforting hand on my arm that almost brought me to tears. "What happened with Farrah?" she asked. "We never met her, but you two looked so happy in all the photos."

I had to swallow down the painful ball of emotion in my throat to speak. "I fucked it up. You know she wanted me to come and make up with you guys when I told her about the fight? She said she wanted a whole family to be behind her and her kids."

Mom laid her hand over her heart. "She did?"

I nodded.

Dad cleared his throat. "When we saw that interview with you and her on the news, your mother told me in no short order it was time for me to put my pride behind me and make amends with you. The thought of me dying without ever knowing my grandkids. Without telling my son that I'm proud of him..." His voice broke up. Then he looked at me with murky hazel eyes. "I promise I won't make that mistake again. We're here for you, Gage, and whoever you choose to love."

"I love her, and it wasn't a choice," I said. Falling for Farrah was just as inevitable as a raindrop falling from the sky. "And I love her kids. I haven't known them very long at all, but it's this feeling like...I want to experience life through their eyes."

Mom and Dad exchanged a glance.

Dad said, "Gage, if I've learned anything while we've been apart, it's that hanging on to being 'right' is the worst thing you can do. I may have gotten to stand by my opinion, but I missed the chance to stand by my son."

Moisture pooled along my bottom lashes, and I wiped it aside. "This whole time, I've been waiting for you to reach out, Dad. My assistants never told me you tried to call and that's on me... But you could have gotten my number from my siblings too. I thought—" I had to clear my throat to speak. "I thought you hated me."

Dad shook his head, putting his hand on my back. "I never hated you. I was mad at you for showing my own shortcomings. There was a twenty-year-old kid with the guts, and the brains, to do what I couldn't. And after a while, when you didn't come by, I figured you were better off without your old man stomping on your dreams."

My voice broke. "I just wanted you to be proud of me."

He put his hands on both of my shoulders. "I've never been prouder of you than I am right now. You're twice the man I could ever hope to be."

56

FARRAH

Knocking sounded on the front door, but I ignored it. Whoever it was could call and leave a message like my mom had been doing all morning. Or come back later.

I was too busy trying to cry it out in my bed before I had to pick up my kids tonight. I didn't want them to see how devastated I was, even after I had the whole weekend to grieve. This breakup was tearing me apart even more than the divorce had.

Leaving Caleb had felt like an inevitability. Even before I found out about the cheating, I'd sensed him pulling away, becoming less invested in me. There were the forgotten birthdays, the months that passed without flowers or even a date.

So when I found out about the cheating, it was more about my loss of identity. Realizing all I'd given to a man who wouldn't remain faithful to me. Wondering which parts of me weren't good enough to earn fidelity.

And mourning the life I'd dreamed of having with my

kids. Grieving for my children, the loss of a cohesive family unit, a mom and a dad who were home at night.

But this heartbreak? It was different.

Because I'd let myself love Gage Griffen with every broken piece of me. I'd loved him despite every worry that love wasn't in my cards. Despite every fear that this relationship would end too, taking just another person away from me and my kids.

And yet... that love wasn't enough to keep him here. Because his first priority was his business and the people he served. And me and my kids? We were second place to another mistress.

He'd left us all. Because he'd met my kids, and I'd seen the way he looked at them. Like he would do anything for them. He never judged Andrew for his glow-in-the-dark fingernail polish, and he never tried to make Levi see him as more than a friend. And Cora... he'd treated her like the princess she wished she could be.

It was a loss for all of us, all over again.

The banging continued, louder this time, and I put a pillow over my head, trying to drown it out. Trying to drown out the thoughts of Gage too.

But then it got louder.

Seething with anger, I got up and went to the door, flinging it open, ready to tell whoever was there to go the eff away.

But Mia stood there, worry in her eyes, and before I could yell, she wrapped her arms around me in a hug.

I fell apart in her embrace, and she practically carried me inside to the couch, where I cried on her shoulder, saying incoherent things about Gage and heartbreak and the kids and anything else that crossed my mind. But mostly I cried as she smoothed her hand over my hair, saying, "I'm here" over and over and over again until the tears finally subsided.

My phone went off with yet another message, and I pulled it out of my pocket.

"Your mom said you aren't answering the phone!" Mia accused. "This would have been easier if you'd just texted me back."

"I still have to check that nothing is wrong with the kids." But the message on the screen made my heart sink.

Pascale: Photos are in your inbox.

Looking over my shoulder, Mia said, "Oh, Farrah, don't do that to yourself..."

But it was too late. I was already clicking through to my email, where his message was at the top. A link to an online gallery with all the pictures from the photo shoot.

The first one I saw had a fresh wave of tears spilling down my cheeks.

Gage and me in bath robes, mine slipped down one shoulder while he kissed it gently. Then Gage and me in bed, reading magazines side by side. Us jumping on the bed together. Running down the hallway in sock-clad feet.

And then the ones of our family together hit me even harder.

Cora and Gage sitting on the bed, a smorgasbord of room service spread around them. Gage and Levi giving each other a look while Andrew and Cora danced together. My mom reaching up and patting Gage's cheek while he smiled down at her.

Pascale hadn't just snapped stock photos for the sake of filling a frame.

He'd captured a love story.

And now that it was over, it only broke my heart more.

57

LEVI

I worked at the coffee shop with Grandpa all day, which meant my phone had to be in the employee cubbies under the counter. Gramps was a great boss, but a little old-fashioned—no phones allowed at work.

The days usually went by pretty fast, though, which was good because not texting Alyssa, even for eight hours, seemed like such a long time. After work, I always laid out on the couch and texted her til Mom and the younger two got home a few hours later.

But today when we finished cleaning up the shop and locking it up, Grandpa didn't take me to my house; he brought me back to his.

"Did you need to pick something up before we go to my house?" I asked him in his car. It was the same one he'd had since I was a kid—an Oldsmobile with leather seats. I could still see the dark gray gum stain Andrew left in the middle seat when he was four and promised he was big enough to have bubblegum in the car.

"I'm taking you to practice tonight," he said.

My eyebrows drew together. We'd gotten in late last night from Lake Texhoma, and I hadn't spoken much with Mom. She cried a little more than normal, saying it was because she'd missed us. I figured she'd want to hound me with questions before practice at least.

"Did she have to work late?" I asked.

Grandpa was quiet a second too long, and my stomach sank.

"Did she lose her job?"

"No, it's nothing like that."

"What is it?" I asked, trying not to get frustrated. I felt like I had a right to know.

But then my phone went off with a text, and I stared at the screen.

Alyssa: Dallas Deets said your mom and Gage broke up. :(Is she okay?

I looked from the phone to Grandpa. "Mom and Gage broke up?"

He cringed as he nodded. "I don't know too much about the how or why of it all but seems like she's taking it pretty hard."

My hand clenched around my phone. So that was it? Gage could go from taking us all to the zoo last weekend like we were one big happy family to getting rid of us all? How had he fooled everyone into thinking he cared for us when it was all going to end without so much as a word to any of us kids?

Andrew thought of Gage like he was a god, and Cora loved him too. They would be so broken up. And here was yet another guy in my life, promising to show up to my baseball games without any intention of following through.

By the time we got to Grandma and Gramps's house, I was seething mad. "I'm taking a walk," I said.

He studied me for a moment over the top of the car, then nodded. "Just remember the toothpaste rule."

"Yeah, I know. Can't put it back in the tube once it's out." I really didn't want a lecture right now. But luckily, that was enough for Grandpa. He lifted his hand in a wave as he walked to the house.

I turned and paced down the narrow sidewalk, the late June sun beating on my back, already making me sweat. It was so freaking hot and only pissing me off more. I jabbed my finger at my phone, dialing Gage's number. He'd given it to me a couple of weeks ago "in case I ever needed anything."

After a few rings, he picked up. "Levi, how are you—"

"I guess you're not coming to my baseball game anymore" were the first words out of my mouth. And in that moment, I realized just how tight that feeling in my chest was, just how close I was to tears. And I really hated to cry. Especially in public, even if everyone was inside their air-conditioned houses.

Gage was silent for a long moment as sweat beaded at the spot where my phone touched my cheek. "I'm sorry."

"That's it?" I demanded. "What the hell happened?"

"It's complicated."

I pulled my phone away from my face, glaring at it. "Adults always say things are complicated when they're not. Do you love my mom?"

"More than anything."

"Then it's simple, because I know she loves you. Stop being a jackass and make it right."

I clicked my phone off and walked back to the house, my anger subsiding and being replaced by a tiny spark of hope. If he loved her, there was still a chance.

58

GAGE

Sometimes it takes a fourteen-year-old kid to help you pull your head out of your ass. At least, it did for me. I wasn't going to be another guy in his life missing his baseball games. And the way Levi spoke? The way he fought for what he wanted? Who's to say he wouldn't go on to change the world in a big way with a little bit of guidance?

Maybe I'd been looking at this the wrong way. Maybe my love for Farrah... maybe it could change the world and create a ripple effect. One where I could feel good about the work I did and live the life I wanted to live. With Farrah by my side.

Maybe he was right.

It could really be that simple.

I CALLED Jason Romero in for another meeting the next day. Mia's smile was as fake as it got as she walked him to my office. As soon as his back was turned, she scowled at me. I still wasn't forgiven.

But if I had it my way, all would be righted soon. There were just some things I needed to handle first.

Jason Romero wore a sharp black suit with a white shirt and red tie. He clasped my hand and said, "Approval ratings are already up five percent, and we expect to see them climb even more this week."

"That's what I called you in about," I said. "Our partnership is dissolved, effective immediately."

He chuckled. "Good one, Griffen."

"I'm serious." I slid a manila envelope across the table. I'd called legal and PR after talking with Levi the night before and paid them handsomely to stay up preparing this for my meeting today. "This is a written document stating my separation from all dealings with Romero Corp, along with a press release we'll be issuing tonight."

Jason's face flooded with color as he flipped through the pages, stating in not-so-fine print that Griffen Industries would be investing in another company that would bring even more jobs to West Texas, without Romero Corp's involvement. They were, of course, welcome to continue with the plant, but we both knew he didn't have the capital for it to make a difference before elections.

Taking satisfaction in his reddening face, I said, "Thanks for coming in, but now it's time for you to leave."

His mouth opened and closed as he sputtered, "You can't do this. I have sway in that area, and I will ruin you. You'll be tied up in litigation so deep that you'll regret the day you ever chose that whore over our business deal."

I held up my phone, showing the recording of our conversation. "I'm sure your constituency would love to hear about your multiple attacks on a single mom of three."

His lips curled into a sneer.

"The investment you've made thus far in marketing is being wired to your bank account as we speak." I stood, using all my energy to keep from punching this jackass in the teeth like I should have three days ago. "Now get out of my building, or I'll have security throw you out on your ass like you deserve."

He snatched up the manila envelope, storming out of the office.

I followed him to my door, watching as he disappeared into the elevator, then I said, "Mia, will you get Shantel and bring her in, please?"

"Yes," she said, her voice slightly less cold.

I walked back to my space, looking out over the horizon for longer than I ever allowed myself to. The city was beautiful, sprawled out before me. I imagined how many hands it had taken to build the roads piling atop each other like strings of spaghetti. How many people had worked to construct the high rises and homes.

So many people working together to create something amazing.

I'd spent more than a decade of my life turned away from this window, focusing on my company.

Now, it was time to turn around and face the beauty I'd missed all these years.

The glass door opened, and I turned to see Shantel and Mia walking in the office together.

"Take a seat," I said, gesturing at the table where Jason had sat moments ago.

Mia and Shantel did as I asked, and Mia said, "If you're going to fire me, I'd prefer you do it quickly."

I smiled at this spunky woman. "You know this business's growth wouldn't have been possible without your dedication to your role over the last few years," I told her. "You have put in more hours than half the C-suite and know just as much about my job as I do."

She studied me closely. "Then why am I here with HR?"

I walked closer to the table, placing my hands on the glass top and looking directly at her. "Because I am stepping down as this company's CEO, and that means there's an open position with your name on it. If you want it."

Her jaw dropped, and she looked to Shantel for confirmation.

Shantel nodded, a smile on her lips.

"You're stepping down?" Mia asked.

I stood straight, looking back out the window. "This business has been my life for sixteen years. And I'm thankful for all I've been able to do and learn here. But growing something like this has come at a cost, and it's a price I'm not willing to pay anymore."

I faced them again. "If you decide to step into this role, Mia, it will take commitment, dedication, and you'll have pains as you grow with it. But it's also an opportunity to change our corner of the world as we know it. I know you're capable of it, but only if you want to be."

"I've never been in the C-Suite before," she said. "I've only ever been an assistant."

Shantel shook her head. "I started out as Gage's first employee, and I've always been stretched into a better version of myself with each promotion. Gage provides excellent training, and growing with this company has been a highlight of my life."

I nodded in agreement. I had full faith that Mia could do this. "You graduated summa cum laude from Upton University with a degree in Business Administration, and then earned your MBA while working overtime. You have the education, and you know this business better than anyone else."

"What will you do?" she asked.

"I'll train you, for the next six months, if you accept the position. And then I'll stay on as a consulting board member, but I won't be working long hours anymore."

Shantel passed Mia a manila envelope with details of the position, including her starting salary to be bumped up when she completed training.

She flipped the folder open and covered her mouth at the final page. "This is real?"

"As real as it gets," I replied. "If you need to sleep on it, I understand."

"I don't need to sleep on it," she said. "For the last three years, I've seen you put in more hours than anyone I've ever known. I've watched you make decisions that cost you money to better the lives of others. And I've seen you fall in love with the woman of your dreams and then give up everything for her." Her eyes filled with tears. "It would be my honor to take this position and follow the amazing example you've left."

She got up from the table, wrapping her arms around me, and said, "Go get your girl."

59

FARRAH

The day of Levi's first summer game, I put on my royal-blue Titans T-shirt that Andrew made for me one day at Mom's house, using puff paint to create the team's design. Cora had a matching shirt in her size, and I added a big blue bow to her ponytail. For someone who was quickly running out of vacation time because of the breakup, I probably should have stopped spending money and spent more time looking for another position.

But quitting was like giving up on Gage. Even though it had been a week since we'd broken up, and he still hadn't called, my stupid heart didn't want to let go.

I finished adjusting the bow in Cora's hair and said, "Perfect. Ready to go cheer on Levi?"

She nodded with a smile and linked her hand with mine as we walked out of the bathroom to the living room, where Andrew and Levi were already dressed and laying on their stomachs playing video games.

"Time to go, guys," I said.

They paused the game, getting up. As Levi grabbed

his gym bag, Andrew picked up a bundle of blue fabric from the couch.

"What's that?" I asked.

"I made a shirt for Gage. He said he was coming."

My heart broke all over again. "Honey, I don't think we'll be seeing him anymore."

"Why?" Andrew asked.

"Yeah, why?" Cora added.

I struggled to find words, but Levi's jaw was tight as he said, "They broke up."

Not wanting to wallow in it, I herded everyone toward the door, changing the subject. "Do we get to meet Alyssa today, Levi?"

"She'll be there," he said.

I glanced at him. "That's not a yes."

He smirked. "It's a maybe."

"I'll take it," I said, getting into the minivan. There was still a spot of black paint on the door where I'd dinged Gage's car, and I made a mental note to cover it up with white fingernail polish later. I didn't need to be reminded of him every second of the day.

But I was too broke to throw out all my underwear. Especially when I didn't have another job lined up. I might be able to skip panties, but the girls were not suited to going commando.

"Mom," Andrew said.

Buckling my seatbelt, I said, "Get in your seat, hon. We're going to be late."

"But look," he said.

Annoyed, I looked over my shoulder to see him holding up a yellow dandelion.

"Your favorite," he said.

My eyes stung as I took the flower. "Thank you, honey. That was sweet of you."

"You could put it in your hair," he said.

"That's a great idea." I tucked it behind my ear, threading it through my curls pulled into a ponytail, and then made sure all the kids were buckled in before pulling out of the driveway. Every so often, I caught sight of the dandelion in the rearview mirror. This was a sign. Today was going to be a good day. I could do this. I could move on from Gage Griffen and enjoy life with my children. My family.

We reached the ball fields and parked, getting out of the car. While Levi jogged to meet his team, I lathered the younger two and myself in sunscreen and then grabbed the mom bag to walk with them to the bleachers.

We found Mom and Dad in the second row from the front, and they greeted us with smiles and hugs.

Mom squeezed me a second longer than usual, saying, "You look good today, honey."

I managed a smile. "I'm trying."

She rubbed my back, and we sat down. "Is Caleb coming?"

"Not today," I said. "But he'll be here for the games tomorrow."

"It's good he's stepping up," she said.

I nodded, trying not to think about Caleb living his happily ever after with his new fiancée while my heart was broken for a man who loved his business more than me.

While the team warmed up, Cora and Drew went to get snacks from the concession stand, and Mom, Dad and I caught up. Dad had his eyes on a new grill that could also be used as a smoker, and Mom grumbled good naturedly she didn't want him turning their backyard into a renaissance festival with smoked turkey legs.

I laughed, wondering if someday I'd be having similar conversations with a spouse. A life partner. Or if I was destined to be alone.

The game started, a kid on Levi's team going up to home plate to bat.

"Hey," Mom said, "did you ever get those photos back? I was thinking it would be fun to hang one over the mantel."

"Oh, yeah, I forgot to show them to you," I said, getting out my phone and going to the folder, trying not to fall apart at the sight of Gage and me happy together.

"Oh my god, it's him," Mom said.

I nodded, fighting tears. "He looks good in the pictures, huh?"

"No, look."

I tracked her gaze, seeing Gage getting out of his car by the field. He began walking our way, followed by all of his siblings and two older people I didn't recognize. Were those...

I gasped, covering my mouth. *His parents.*

"GO, LEVI!" Gage yelled, and I turned my head to see Levi walking out of the dugout with his bat. With a grin, he lifted a hand in a wave, going up to the plate.

The rest of Gage's family cheered as they walked closer to the bleachers, standing by the chain link fence.

Tears spilled down my cheeks as I looked between them and my son. Gage's entire family was here, supporting Levi.

The first pitch, he swung and missed. But Gage

clapped his hands together. "You've got this. Keep that elbow up!"

Levi nodded, hitting his bat against the plate and squaring up again.

Cheers for him filled the air. From my family, from Gage's family, from a group of cute teenage girls in the front row.

The next pitch came in fast, but Levi swung faster, his bat cracking against the ball, making it sail through the air... and over the back fence.

"THAT'S HOW YOU DO IT!" Gage yelled, pumping his fist in the air. "BRING IT HOME!"

Grinning ear to ear, Levi dropped his bat, jogging the bases.

We stood, yelling for him as he rounded the plates, and when he came home, he jogged to the dugout, still smiling.

A hand nudged my back, and I realized it was Cora, shoving me toward Gage.

My legs were rubber as I walked to him where he stood flanked by his family. But he stepped forward to meet me, and even though we were surrounded by people, we entered our own bubble. Just him and me.

His eyes were soft on me, drinking me in like a thirsty man. And then he reached up, touching the dandelion at my ear, trailing his fingers down my cheek.

I shuddered against his touch. My entire being craved for it to mean more. "What are you doing here?"

He glanced at his family, and then he looked at me. "I promised I would be here. And my family wanted to support Levi."

My heart constricted. This was for Levi. Not for me. I

tried to keep my voice from breaking as I gave a shaky smile and said, "Levi's going to be so glad you made it."

"And what about you?" he asked, tilting his head.

"What do you mean?"

"I mean, I came for Levi today, but I'm staying for you, Farrah."

"But your business..."

He shook his head. "I stepped down as CEO and cancelled the partnership with Romero Corp. I'm with you, Farrah. If you'll have me. I mean, us." He gestured at the people behind him, trying to act like they weren't watching and listening in. "I worked things out with my parents, my siblings love you, we are all here for you and your kids to make one big family. We might not be perfect. We might hold on to our pride and say shitty things when we're angry or scared. We might make bad choices at first and have to learn from them, but we're here. I'm here. And I love you, Farrah. God, I love you and your kids more than I've loved anything in my life. So please, forgive me for being a dumbass and taking longer than I should have to realize that you are the most important thing to me. You, Farrah, come first."

From behind me, Andrew yelled, "GIVE HIM THE SHIRT, MOM."

I chuckled tearfully and turned, getting the shirt from Andrew, who stood with Cora at the edge of the bleachers. Then I held it up, Drew's puff paint design on full display.

LEVI'S #1 FAN with a baseball and a bat.

"Will you be a part of our team?" I asked. "Forever?"

Emotion filled Gage's eyes as he took the shirt, pulling

it over his head and smoothing it over the white tee he'd worn.

I'd seen this man in designer suits, walking around his house like an underwear model, fully naked in all his muscled glory, but with the wrinkled fabric pulled over his chest, I thought he'd never looked better.

"Of course I will," he said. "I love you, sunshine."

And I kissed him, hard, before uttering, "I love you too."

60

GAGE

THREE MONTHS LATER

I pulled Farrah's minivan up to The Hen House in Cottonwood Falls, turning down the sunshine playlist blaring through the radio. "We're here!"

"Finally!" Andrew moaned as Cora said, "YAY!"

Levi finished texting and shoved his phone into his pocket. "Is Rhett or Grandpa Jack going to let us ride horses after? Alyssa wants a picture."

"I'm not sure," I said. "We'll have to see how the party goes."

Farrah said, "If not, maybe we can get a picture of the horses on the way home."

I reached across the console, squeezing her thigh. "Great idea, babe."

She smiled over at me and then said, "Let's go inside

before we're late. Drew, can you grab the present for Jack and Diedre from the trunk?"

"Sure," he replied.

When we were all out of the car, Cora said, "Can you carry me inside, Gage?"

"You're almost six," Farrah said. "You can walk."

"Can and should are two different things," I teased, picking Cora up and holding her on my hip. "What's the point in working out if I can't carry kids around?"

Farrah shook her head at us, smiling, and then licked her thumb, rubbing a spot from Cora's cheek.

"Gross," she said, dodging her.

Levi laughed, holding Cora in place while Farrah cleaned the spot.

"Ha ha," Drew said, catching up with the gift bag.

Farrah grinned. "You're next."

"What happened to us growing up?" Drew groaned, squirming away from her glistening thumb.

"You're never too old for a good spit shine," Farrah said. "Isn't that right, Gage?"

"Right," I said.

Levi got on my other side and muttered, "Whipped."

"Coming from the guy wanting horse pictures," I teased back, walking up the front steps.

He rolled his eyes at me, despite the heat in his cheeks.

Even though Tyler and Henrietta had honored the history of the schoolhouse, keeping the brick façade and a lot of the antique touches, you never would have guessed this used to be a school. The front porch area looked like it was made to be a meeting space with the hanging porch swing and rocking chairs.

An older couple sat on the porch swing in the corner, and the guy said, "You've got a great family there."

"Thank you, sir," I said, in complete agreement. Farrah held the door open, letting us into the lobby space where people were already making their way to the meeting area that used to be the school's cafeteria.

Henrietta and Liv had decorated the room in red for Mom and Dad's fortieth anniversary party. It was supposed to be the year for rubies, and they'd gone all out with the theme.

Henrietta stood at the entrance, holding red bead necklaces. "It's some of my favorite people!" she said with a warm smile. "Would you like a 'ruby' necklace?"

Levi bowed his head for one, and then Andrew copied him. Even though they got on each other's nerves, Drew looked up to him so much. Cora tapped her chin thoughtfully. "Do princesses wear rubies? I thought they only wore diamonds."

"This princess can," I said to her. "Princesses make the rules."

"Good point," she replied, tipping her head down. Hen winked at me as she laid the beads over Cora's curls.

Farrah took a couple necklaces for me and her, and then we went to the party.

Cora squirmed out of my arms, and she and Drew ran up to my parents, wrapping them in a hug.

"Did you get us a gift?" Cora asked.

Blushing, Farrah said, "It's their anniversary, Cora. That's why we got them presents."

"Actually..." my mom said with a smile. She walked to a table a few feet away and held up toys. "We thought you could play with these out in the garden if you want. They expand in water, and there's a bucket and a hose you can use if it's okay with your mom."

I grinned at my parents. In the last three months, we'd overcome a lot of awkwardness because they instantly loved the kids. Mom was constantly getting them toys to play with, and Dad loved having new people to drive around the farm. He was even building a treehouse out behind the house for the kids to play in when we visited.

"That's fine," Farrah said. "Thank you."

As soon as the three went outside, I said, "They're definitely riding home soaked, aren't they."

"Yep," she said.

Mom laughed at us, stretching her arms out for a hug. "Having you two here is the best present. Really—" Her voice broke with tears. "I have my son back. And now we get you and your kids? Farrah, it's the biggest gift I could think of."

From behind us, Liv said, "Good thing Gage pulled his head out of his a—"

"Language," Mom laughed.

Farrah shook her head. "Some things never change, huh?"

Dad smiled, his eyes shining too. "Not if you're lucky."

Other guests came to congratulate my parents, and Farrah and I mingled with the people there, hung out with my siblings, and ate the best barbecue I'd had in years. And when the party was over, the kids were so soaked that Tyler gave them extra clothes to wear. His shirts were so big on Cora and Andrew they basically fit like dresses, but Levi filled it out alright.

We drove down the dirt road toward Griffen Farms,

but instead of stopping by the barn to see the horses, we kept driving.

"What are we doing?" Farrah asked. "I thought we were seeing the horses?"

"I wanted to show you something," I said. "Levi, you get the gate?"

He nodded, getting out of the back seat and opening the gate to the pasture.

"Are you sure my van can make it out here?" Farrah asked. "We've only ever taken your family's trucks off the roads."

I chuckled. "I've seen minivans out here before. This path is pretty smooth."

When Levi had the gate open, we drove on the dirt trail toward one of my favorite spots on the farm. Even though I didn't want to own and manage a ranch anymore, this place would always have a special part of my heart. Even more so depending on how today went.

We crested a hill, and up ahead I spotted it. The same windmill from our sibling tattoo. It was one of the first things I showed Farrah when I brought her and the kids over the first time.

Farrah reached over and put her hand on my thigh. "Such a beautiful view. I can see why this place means so much to you."

It was pretty here—you could see forever, and with the green grass and black cattle dotting the hillside, it seemed like paradise. I rolled down the windows. "Smell that fresh country air."

"Smells like cow poop," Levi teased.

"Hey now," I said with a smirk. "Okay, maybe a little bit."

I pulled up alongside the windmill, where its pump spilled water into the tank, and turned off the car. We all got out, and Farrah walked to the tank, gazing into the water for cattle to drink.

When she turned back to me, I was on one knee, her kids on either side of me.

She covered her mouth with her hands and shook her head. "Gage, are you..."

"The ring?" I asked Levi.

He placed the velvet box in my hand.

"The flowers?" I asked Cora.

She retrieved the bouquet of dandelions I'd asked her to pick at The Hen House from behind her back.

"The drawing?" I asked Drew.

He pulled a wrinkled paper from under his oversized shirt.

I held up the drawing and flowers, waiting for her to read the words I'd asked Andrew to draw once I got all the kids' permission.

Will you marry me?

Tears filled Farrah's eyes as she looked between me and the kids. "You three were in on this?" she asked them.

Levi put his hand on my shoulder. "He asked us permission, Mom, and we all want Gage to be in our family."

Cora nodded. "We love him, Mom."

"And we know you do too," Andrew added.

"So say yes?" I asked. "Because I want this to be my family for the rest of my life."

Farrah carefully set her flowers and drawing on the ground and knelt in front of me, taking my face in her hands. "You sealed your place with us long before you asked. I love you, Gage Griffen, and I'd love to be your wife."

Happy tears formed in my eyes, and I slid the ring over Farrah's finger as her children cheered for us like we'd just scored the biggest home run of all.

FARRAH

I never thought I'd get a tattoo, but here I was in a tattoo parlor with my best friend and soon-to-be sisters-in-law, ready to go under the needle. I hadn't decided what I would get Gage for a wedding present, and with the big day tomorrow, we were running out of time.

When I confided my problem to Mia, she said, "What more could you give him than forever?"

That's when I knew that getting this symbol, permanently on me, would mean more to him than anything else I could think of. It had been his siblings' way of reassuring him that they'd always be there for him.

And now? It would be my sign that I would too.

Since there wasn't a ton of room in the tattoo shop, Liv and Mia sat in the front waiting area, and Hen sat beside me, her own windmill tattoo on her wrist.

The tattoo artist, a guy named Henry with more ink than bare skin, asked if I was ready.

I nodded. "Go ahead."

The needle sliced into my skin, hurting like hell. "Oh my gosh, that's worse than I thought it would be," I said, trying to stay still.

He didn't say much, just kept tracing the design.

To distract myself from the pain, I asked Hen, "What's it been like? Being a Griffen?" I planned to change my last name after the wedding. Even though I'd have a different name than my kids, it would be okay because we still shared what mattered most—our love for each other.

She smiled warmly at me, her grin so contagious. "It feels like when you've had a long day of work and you come home."

I smiled back, despite the tattoo pain, because I knew exactly what she meant. Gage and I may have had a rough start, but he'd been my safe harbor, even before we started dating. "I'm excited I get two new sisters."

She squeezed my free hand. "Me too."

The pain in my wrist stopped, and Henry said, "All done. What do you think?"

I stared at the stark black mark on my wrist, the perfect windmill matching all of the Griffens'. "I *love* it."

It reminded me of the ink on Gage's arm, the place we'd gotten engaged and promised forever, the place where my kids romped around the tank, happy and care-free, despite all we'd gone through in the last year.

And in that moment, I knew I wouldn't trade my story for anything. All the pain of being cheated on, of having to start over at thirty-four with three kids counting on me. I'd never give it up. Because even if this family didn't come about in the "ideal" way, it brought me four of my favorite people, who I knew would be there for me always.

It was perfect. And it was mine.

EPILOGUE
LIV

Acoustic guitar music played through the lobby of The Retreat, where guests filled two rows of white folding chairs. There were only about twenty people here, and when everyone on the guest list had arrived, Jenna came up to me and said, "I think this is it."

I nodded. "I'll go get the guys."

"Sounds good," she said, and I went to the elevator, riding up to the suite where Gage was getting ready with Andrew, Levi, Rhett, Tyler, and my dad. "It's time to go out."

Gage nodded, smiling as he did. Ever since he and Farrah got together for good six months ago, he'd been happier than I'd ever seen him. He worked less, hung out at the farm with our family now, and had come to Wednesday night dinner at least once a month, sometimes more.

Not to mention, he bought the house Farrah and the kids lived in. It was now theirs to share and make a million memories in, together.

Dad clapped his back. "Ready, son?"

"I am," Gage agreed. "I know the speeches are supposed to come after the wedding, but I just had to say how grateful I am to have you here. All of you. I know this isn't the way you might have imagined me building a family but—"

"It's perfect," Rhett finished with a smile. "You hit the jackpot, Gage. And you're already a billionaire. So unfair."

We chuckled, and I wiped at my eyes tearfully. Up until a year ago, I hadn't known if my family would ever make amends, and having us all here together... it meant the world.

Gage bent down on one knee and called Levi and Drew over. The boys sobered, each taking one of his outstretched hands.

"I fell in love with your mother, but I want you to know that you and your sister? You're just as important to me." His voice broke. "You, your mom, you're all my happily ever after."

Now I was sobbing, and even Rhett sniffled as the boys hugged my brother.

Tyler patted their backs and said, "We're lucky to be your family."

"Agreed," Dad said.

Tyler wiped at his eyes, saying, "Why don't you go tell Farrah and the girls it's time?"

"Sounds good," I said, trying to compose myself.

"Wait," Gage said. He reached onto the TV table, getting a red velvet box. "Can you give this to Cora?" Then he got a bigger gift and said, "This one's for Farrah."

I nodded, wiping at my eyes as I went to the stairs, walking down a flight to the suite where Farrah, Cora, Henrietta, and Mia were getting ready.

Farrah looked absolutely stunning in a blush-colored dress that hugged her curves and flared at the waist. Mia and Cora's dresses matched my own, one-shouldered gowns in a darker shade of pink.

"Is everyone ready?" Farrah asked me.

I nodded. "Except Gage asked me to give this to Miss Cora."

Cora's eyes lit up. "A present?"

I nodded.

She took the velvet box and opened it up, revealing a stunning silver tiara. "What does the note say?" she asked.

Farrah picked it up, reading his words. "Every princess needs a crown. Love, Gage."

And now I was crying again.

Farrah's eyes shone with emotion as she lifted the tiara from the box and placed it over Cora's curls while Pascale snapped photos in the background.

"Perfect," Farrah said, hugging her daughter tight.

I held out the other gift Gage gave me. "This one's for you, Farrah."

She took it, peeling back the silver paper and then stared at the frame, her hand covering her mouth.

"Is it a picture from that photoshoot?" I asked.

Farrah shook her head, smiling, and turned the frame to show me a scrap of paper with a phone number on it. She held up the card stock tapped to the back of the frame and read,

"I've kept this since the day you walked in my office. I knew you were special then, and I love you more than ever now. And I wanted

to frame it, because even if a relationship starts out with a few dings, it can turn into something beautiful."

Mia and I exchanged glances, and Mia wiped at her eyes. "Am I going to be crying all day?" she asked. "I'm supposed to be a big bad CEO on Monday!"

"I know I am," I replied. "Thank God for waterproof mascara."

Farrah wiped at her eyes, saying, "I hope they're happy tears. You know, I've always been an only child, and today feels like I'm not just getting a husband; I'm gaining an entire family."

Henrietta and I went to hug her, and Hen said, "Joining this family has been the biggest blessing in my life. I know it will be for you too."

"And I'm happy to get another sister," I said. "If Rhett ever gets married, we'll outnumber the boys one day."

"Girl power!" Cora said, pumping her little fist in the air.

We laughed and then fixed our makeup so we could go downstairs.

And Mia was right. I cried through the entire ceremony. Farrah and Gage wrote their own vows and had everyone there sobbing with how heartfelt they were. Gage even wrote vows specifically for each child, promising to be there for them always and to love them as his own.

Even though we were a small crowd, we had a reception, dancing to music played by a DJ who took more requests than chose songs on his own. The kids picked classics like "Crazy Frog" and "Barbie Girl." And at the end, there was a bouquet toss.

Mia, Cora, and I were the only ones standing to catch it when Farrah threw the bouquet over her head.

The flowers sailed through the air and landed directly in my hands.

Farrah turned, grinning at me, and said, "Your turn."

WANT to read Liv's happily ever after? Dive into *Hello Doctor* today. You can also save on the series when you get the bundle from my site!

Find out where Gage, Farrah, and the rest of their crew are nine years from now in *Take Me Out*, a special free bonus short story!

Get the free bonus story today!

Start reading Hello Doctor today!

Save on the series bundle!

ALSO BY KELSIE HOSS

The Hello Series

Hello Single Dad

Hello Fake Boyfriend

Hello Temptation

Hello Billionaire

Hello Doctor

Hello Heartbreaker

Hello Tease

AUTHOR'S NOTE

Nothing has put me on a roller coaster ride like being a mom. All of a sudden, you have a life entrusted in your hands and everything you do doesn't just affect you—it affects them too. Your time is no longer your own, because their needs have to be met. Your body and mind take the toll of sleepless nights, busy mornings, long days and worry filled moments. There are countless "shoulds" coming at you from every direction—your parents, books, social media posts, daycare providers, teachers, and more. And the person you used to be—the one who could roll out of bed at eight-thirty and get to work at nine is...gone. You're no longer defined as your name, but as someone's mom.

And I think that's one reason I was nervous to write a single mom romance. Because children aren't plot points for a story, they're full people with needs and wants and wishes. And the parents? Their child is just as much a part of them as their arms or legs.

And divorce? It's not that simple. Especially not with

kids. Not only are you losing a person who promised you forever, you're losing all these hopes and dreams you had for your family's future. You're losing out on time with the kids and shared memories. Even though I'm still married to my first husband, I'd be lying if I said it's been all smooth sailing. There have been times we wanted to throw in the towel, and all those worries about the kids flooded my mind.

I poured all that worry, fear, but also love of my children into this story. I really hope that shined through. Because even though having kids has been a roller coaster ride that's changed everything, I love them with all I have. They are three of the kindest, most creative and fun people I know. And even though I regularly worry that I'll end up in their memoirs (not in a good way) I hope they know how hard I've tried to do what's best for them.

Because really, that's all we can do, as parents. We do the best we can with the information and ability we have. I want to think I'm raising children who will know how to stand up for themselves and love others wholly. I hope they'll know how to pick a partner who meets them at their level and challenges them to be better. I hope their kids will be healthy and whole. I hope they won't have to deal with shitty bosses or backstabbing coworkers.

But the truth is... life is messy.

I've come to realize that I'm not raising the "ideal adult"... I'm raising people who will face challenges just like I do, and they're going to have to muddle through and learn to heal and come out of it stronger than ever.

If you're a parent, I hope you know that you're not alone. It's okay to be scared and worried and hopeful and happy all at once. If you're not a parent yet, I hope you enjoyed this glimpse at our life, both in the story and this author's note. It may not be pretty, but it's ours.

And if you're on the outs with your parents, if your parents couldn't be the people you deserved to have as a child, I hope you know that you deserved better, and that what they couldn't give you doesn't define you.

Only you can do that.

ACKNOWLEDGMENTS

Writing this book has been a whirlwind! And I have sooo many people to be grateful for.

Of course my children, for always bringing me a dandelion or a rock or a picture and making my whole day.

My husband, for supporting me always. Figuring out a balance between our career aspirations and caring for children has been challenging, but I love that he never gives up.

My team, Sally and Annie. I love you both with all I have. Working with you is one of the highlights of my life. Thank you for being on this team and helping me spread stories to the world.

My editor, Tricia Harden. Fabulous incarnate. I love working with you on these stories and being your friend.

My cover designer, Najla Qamber, and her team at Qamber Designs. I love working with them and adore the work I get to put on the covers of my books!

My narrators, Luke Welland, Allyson Voller, and Keegan Vaillancourt, thank you for bringing this story to life in audio!

The lovely people in Hoss's Hussies. I'm so glad we have a place to hang out, have fun, and talk books! Thank you for all the encouragement and fun we have!

I also have to give a special shout out to Ana Huang, who will probably never read this, but who inspired me immensely with her talk at Skye Warren's Romance Author Mastermind, and Theodora Taylor who wrote an excellent book for authors called 7 Figure Fiction.

Finally, thank you sweet reader, who made it all the way to the end of this story! It means the world that you not only cared to read my words but wanted to learn about me and the production of this book as well. I truly appreciate you more than you'll ever know.

JOIN THE PARTY

Want to talk about Hello Billionaire with Kelsie and other readers? Join Hoss's Hussies today!

Join here: https://www.facebook.com/groups/hossshussies

ABOUT THE AUTHOR

Kelsie Hoss writes sexy romantic comedies with plus size leads. Her favorite dessert is ice cream, her favorite food is chocolate chip pancakes, and... now she's hungry.

You can find her enjoying one of the aforementioned treats, soaking up some sunshine like an emotional house plant, or loving on her three sweet boys.

You can learn more (and even grab some special merch) at kelsiehoss.com.

facebook.com/authorkelsiehoss

instagram.com/kelsiehoss

Printed in Great Britain
by Amazon